CATALOOCHEE

RANDOM HOUSE NEW YORK

For John —

happy birthday!

Aug '07

CATALOOCHEE

A Novel

WAYNE CALDWELL

Published in the United States by Random House,
an imprint of The Random House Publishing Group,
a division of Random House, Inc., New York.

RANDOM HOUSE and colophon are registered
trademarks of Random House, Inc.

Portions of Chapter 8, "Plow New Ground," appeared in "The Burning Tree,"
published in *Now & Then* (summer 2001). Reprinted by permission of
Now & Then magazine and the Center for Appalachian Studies
and Services, East Tennessee State University.

Portions of Chapter 21, "No More Power," appeared in "The Pact,"
published in *Carolina Alumni Review* (July/August 1999).

Portions of Chapter 22, "Hangover," were published in a story of
the same name by *The Village Rambler* (May/June 2004).

ISBN 978-1-4000-6343-7

LIBRARY OF CONGRESS CATALOGING-IN-PUBLICATION DATA

Caldwell, Wayne
Cataloochee: a novel / Wayne Caldwell.
p. cm.
ISBN-13: 978-1-4000-6343-7
ISBN-10: 1-4000-6343-4
1. Cataloochee (N.C.)—Fiction. 2. Appalachian Region—Fiction. 3. Domestic fiction.
I. Title.
PS3603.A438C38 2007   813'.6—dc22   2006049229

Printed in the United States of America on acid-free paper

www.atrandom.com

2 4 6 8 9 7 5 3 1

FIRST EDITION

Family tree by Jo Anne Metsch
Book design by Dana Leigh Blanchette

FOR MARY

Goe little booke: thy selfe present,
As child whose parent is unkent.

—Edmund Spenser

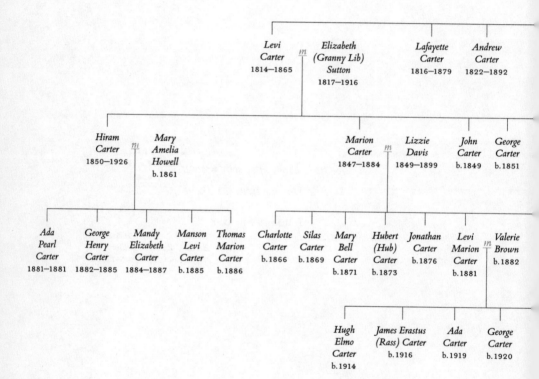

Descendants of James

(Old Jimmie) Carter

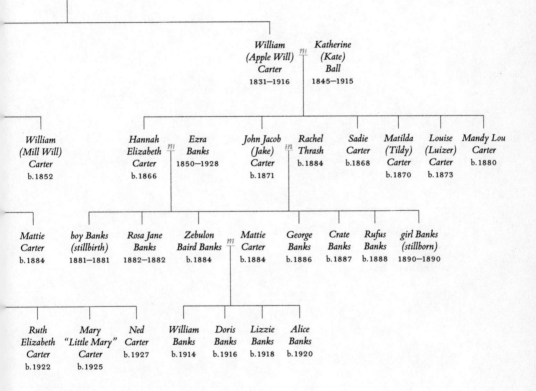

James (Old Jimmie) Carter

William (Apple Will) Carter *m* Katherine (Kate) Ball
1831–1916 / 1845–1915

William (Mill Will) Carter
b. 1852

Hannah Elizabeth Carter *m* Ezra Banks
b. 1866 / 1850–1928

John Jacob (Jake) Carter *m* Rachel Thrash
b. 1871 / b. 1884

Sadie Carter
b. 1868

Matilda (Tildy) Carter
b. 1870

Louise (Luizer) Carter
b. 1873

Mandy Lou Carter
b. 1880

Mattie Carter
b. 1884

boy Banks (stillbirth)
1881–1881

Rosa Jane Banks
1882–1882

Zebulon Baird Banks *m* Mattie Carter
b. 1884 / b. 1884

George Banks
b. 1886

Crate Banks
b. 1887

Rufus Banks
b. 1888

girl Banks (stillborn)
1890–1890

Ruth Elizabeth Carter
b. 1922

Mary "Little Mary" Carter
b. 1925

Ned Carter
b. 1927

William Banks
b. 1914

Doris Banks
b. 1916

Lizzie Banks
b. 1918

Alice Banks
b. 1920

Prologue

Jake Carter was far from dark-minded, but had inherited a streak of what his mother called "worriment," along with her conviction that while a body ought not hunt for trouble, nonetheless he should be watchful, for woe walks up and down in the world. It was 1928, the first day of October, the time of year yellow jackets turn ill. Nearly ready for winter—apples and beef cattle sold, firewood stacked in the dry—yet weather too warm to kill hogs. The in-between, a time when man thinks he deserves some rest, but woman knows none awaits.

At breakfast his wife, Rachel, pointed him to chores for which he had little relish. But, urged on by her, and two cups of bitter coffee that spurred a hasty trip to the outhouse, he produced bushel baskets, shovel, and rake from the barnside shed and made for the kitchen garden.

He spent most of the day there, harvesting tomatoes and peppers against imminent killing frost, turning rich earth, dropping writhing nightcrawlers into a Mason jar for fish bait, and sowing everything save the greens patch in winter rye, to be spaded under come spring.

Cataloochee consisted of two settlements, Nellie in Big Cataloochee Valley, and Ola, in Little Cataloochee, separated by four-thousand-foot Noland Mountain, ringed in all directions by mountains with such names as Sterling and Spruce and Balsam and Hemphill, many over six thousand feet. Jake's farm perched close to Davidson Gap in Little Cataloochee, which afforded a view of the ridgetops to the south and east and, when leaves fell, the church steeple a mile down the road.

Although trees had yet to shed in earnest, he eyeballed the roof, comb to valley, for accumulated dry leaves, perfect tinder for a house fire. Spying a small collection of sourwood leaves over the front room, he went to the shed for his ladder, fashioned years ago from two straight locust limbs for uprights and leftover chestnut for rungs, the knots on which were worn smooth as old bronze.

Then he figured he might as well fix the shed roof while he was there. A piece of misshapen metal had sprung from its moorings in a storm, and he hadn't gotten around to fastening it back. He pocketed nails and hung a claw hammer in the loop on the leg of his overalls, grabbed the ladder like a man might take a child by the shoulders to get its attention, and worked the base into the ground. Up three rungs, he laid hammer on roof and leaned toward the wayward metal, which curled toward the sun.

As he pulled, he smelled rain in the southern breeze. The galvanized steel popped and cracked, and he needed to rise one more rung to reach high enough to pull it flush with the roof, tuck it underneath its neighboring sheet of metal, and nail them fast. But as he stepped up a gunshot cracked in the autumn air—which nearly cost him his footing.

Steadying himself, Jake took off his glasses as if that would help him hear better. The fire came from either his nephew Zeb's place, which joined him a half mile down the mountain on the northeast, or Ezra

Banks's farm, which joined him on the southeast. Four o'clock by the sun. He put his glasses back on.

Ezra Banks was Jake's brother-in-law, married forty-eight years to his sister Hannah. Their oldest son, Zeb, was a quiet man whose lot in life was to live within sight of his father and near his three brothers, none of whom got along. Last night, in fact, Jake had heard Ezra and Zeb return from Big Cataloochee, arguing like a pair of sore-tailed cats.

After a minute another shot carried up the hollow. Grabbing his hammer, he moved the ladder enough to make it list to the right, then rock from side to side until he steadied it. He was about to descend when he heard four more reports. He raised fingers to count. Six shots—one, then silence about the space of a minute, then another, then four in slow but steady succession. These final four came from the same weapon. The fire seemed deliberately paced, like a man on the midway carefully trying to win a Kewpie doll for his lady.

The rung hurt his foot soles so he shifted them on the ladder. Only noises of birds and breeze now. He pushed the errant piece of sheet metal under its neighbor and nailed both to the sheathing.

No one ought to be shooting down there, at least not in such a pattern. Killing a varmint took one shot, two or three at most for a bear. Folks shot into the air Christmas Day but it was only October. Someone could have been sighting in a rifle, but Ezra was too chinchy to buy a new one and Zeb was no hunter. "Damn," he said, "I reckon me and Lilly ought to head down that way."

As he saddled the mule he figured the .38 owlhead pistol Ezra kept in his desk drawer likely made the first two shots, but the others were from something else, a rifle maybe, no cannon like Ezra's ancient .52 Sharps, but bigger than a .22. Or perhaps the breeze twisted and he'd heard six shots from the same weapon. Uneasy business, either way. "Hope ain't nobody hurt," he prayed, "but if somebody got shot, Lord, let it be Ezra. And, Lord Jesus, if it is Ezra, let him be killed dead. A bedridden Ezra Banks would be cause for the whole of Little Cataloochee to up and move. Don't reckon even Sis would put up with that."

CATALOOCHEE

1

TOO WORN OUT TO CRY

Ezra Banks sprang from a line of men pretty good at hunting and fishing and gambling and drinking. But at farming they piddled. Tenants. Ezra, third son in a brood of seven, knew early he didn't want to sharecrop. His father farmed ten or twelve hardscrabble acres near Spring Creek in Madison County, North Carolina. The land belonged to Bingham Wright, brother to Jonathan Wright next county over, in Cataloochee. Ezra's father, a bit too old to serve in the Confederate Army, had shown up just after the war started and leased Wright's poorest section. Some pasture was so steep a fellow needed two breeds of cattle, one with short right legs to stand in one direction and pick the thistle-ridden grass, the other with short left legs to pick going the opposite way. On level ground they could lean against each other to sleep.

In 1864 Ezra looked older than fourteen, lanky, a bit of beard already and a badly bent nose. His father had broken it three years before when they moved to the Wright place. The old man was trying to fix a fence gate. He banged his thumb with the claw hammer and splintered its handle when he flung it at the barn in a rage. He ran to the back porch and yanked a piece from the middle of his wife's stove-wood stack and started to whittle a new handle. As he smoothed it with his rusty hawksbill, the stack dissolved around the missing stick and fell off the porch. He yelled, "Get out here, woman, and pick up yer goddamn firewood before it rains on it."

Ezra, a boy given to moodiness, had been enlisted to help but had only dragged three tulipwood laps to the stile. He stood ten feet from his father, hands in his pockets, watching him like a cat. The old man held a crosspiece in one hand and a hammer in the other and realized he needed three arms to attach it to the gate. He glared at his son. "You think you're winder decoration? Hold this damn thing for me. Right there." Ezra hastened to the other end of the board. His father struck his last tenpenny nail sidelong, pinging it off the hammer end and scattering a couple of speckled banty hens at the barn entrance. He fumbled in his overalls for another nail. "Don't jist stand there like a sumbitching wooden Indian, boy, fetch me some nails."

When Ezra said, "Go get them yourself," the old man backhanded the claw hammer with no hesitation. Had Ezra not been quick he would have been dead. The jagged, rusty claw missed his nose but the hammer head's top hit home, spinning him into the dirt. "That'll learn ye to sass me, boy. Now get yer worthless ass up and fetch me them whorehopping nails fore I light into you again."

Ezra got up slowly, running the back of his hand as close to his nose as pain allowed, making up his mind to leave.

On a cold November Saturday just after his fourteenth birthday, Ezra saddled the horse, a gaunt, swaybacked strawberry roan, as his father's drunken snores shook the back of the house. He tied his stuff—

a piece of a shovel, a clasp knife, a wooden spoon, two shirts and a pair of overalls—in a bedroll back of the ratty saddle. His mother trudged to the barn to give him a pone of corn bread and a leather pouch his old man had hidden behind a hearthstone. He felt coins inside. "Son, will I ever see you again?"

He faced a woman too worn out to cry. He hugged his mother awkwardly, put on his hat, and said nothing. It would be bad for her when the old bastard finally woke to find neither horse nor saddle. Heading down the mountain he stopped and looked back. No help for it but to forge on.

The journey spurred his imagination. He rode through the valley and determined one day to own a farm like Bingham Wright's. Acre upon acre of bottomland sprouted corn and oats and anything else a man cared to plant. The valley floor narrowed and the road snaked up the mountain toward Trust, a settlement that seemed glued to the mountainside like an outsized doll village.

His mother's cousin Fred Owenby kept the general store, and sometimes when things got bad at home Ezra and his brothers and sisters had stayed with him. Owenby had taught him many things, including how to graft one variety of apple to another. He told Ezra to hold his head up, that he needed neither to emulate nor to cower before his father. Owenby made everything a contest, whether hunting supper or picking apples. Ezra didn't stop as he rode by the store but thought one day he would even beat Owenby at growing apples.

By dinnertime, as he rested the horse at Doggett Gap, he looked at the Little Sandy Valley. It spoke of field crops but the southeast face of Doggett Mountain looked ideal for orchards. Hard to clear, by God, he thought, but once a man gets shed of tulip trees and laurel hells, keeping an orchard's easier than growing tobacco. Besides, the steeper the land, the cheaper the price.

By evening he had forded the French Broad west of Asheville, at that point a lazy river of not a quarter mile's breadth, determined to join the Confederates. He was no patriot nor did he know anybody rich enough to own other men and women, but adventure appealed to him. He rode carefully, hiding from men riding together, for as the war wound down, the Home Guard had taken to shooting outliers instead of rounding them up for bounty, and he had heard of the Guard killing civilians.

Asheville was a city of about eleven hundred souls. He rode up the western hill from the river to Public Square and asked where to leave his horse for the night. A man with one eye pointed him to the liveries. He rode the block west to Water Street, which descended quickly to a series of squat wooden buildings smelling of hay and horse manure. The sign dangling by one chain told of cheapest so he left the horse there. The greasy proprietor gave him a wooden token with which to reclaim the animal. Ezra shoved it into his right boot and walked back to the Square. He felt easier when the token worked under his instep.

Ezra had never seen so many people in one place before, even at the county fair he once sneaked off to. People promenaded the plank Saturday-night sidewalks on Main and Patton. Nine or ten saloons bursting with cheap whiskey and loud music, and several hotels, some more refined than others, opened to the street. Through one doorway Ezra saw a slick-haired man in a monkey suit, playing what Ezra knew to be a fiddle, but a body could never square-dance to such music. He walked up and down, to and fro, eyeing people, feeling the token in his boot, wondering what it cost to enter such places. By midnight he found a watering hole on Eagle Street, where he purchased some foul fluid the barkeeper called whiskey, and the favors of a plain young woman. He was rough with her at first but after she slapped him he learned quickly.

Sunday morning he prowled the mud streets, peering into shop-fronts. He smelled coal smoke, bacon frying, horse manure. From the end of North Main clear to the end of South Main he watched folks emerge from hotels, some hungover and slow, others dressed for church. He turned back up the hill toward the Square, and saw people heading for the courthouse, a three-story brick building on a small rise east of the Square. Ezra in farm clothes and denim overcoat trailed decently dressed people carrying books and speaking quietly. He followed them up the steps into the central of three arched doorways and into a high-ceilinged room. A black-suited old man, smelling of shaving soap and cedar, greeted him icily. Ezra sat on the back bench.

It was clearly a courtroom but in front of the bench a hand-lettered sign proclaimed, "Welcome to the Asheville Baptist Church William Boland Standing To God Be the Glory." He wondered what kind of church didn't have its own building. A bearded man in a dark broadcloth suit smiled thinly at the assembly. Ezra figured him for Boland. Behind the preacher four fat women wearing faded lapel jewelry and two ancient men in yellowed shirts frowned in splint-bottomed chairs, hymnbooks in laps. They made a bare choir, ruined by war. A pasty-faced woman began to beat a poor rhythm on a piano off to the right. Ezra didn't recognize the tune, but he wasn't much of a churchgoer and she wasn't much of a musician.

When the piano lady finished, maybe thirty-five souls faced the preacher and watched the choir watch them. The men were few and old save one, a youth with an outsized head and a vacant stare. They made no effort to seat men on one side and women on the other, in the Baptist way. It would have looked lopsided, like a vineyard trimmed by an idiot.

Boland stood and opened a large Bible. He welcomed the flock, sipped from a glass, and began to read in a mournful tone: " 'And he spake a parable unto them, saying, The ground of a certain rich man brought forth plentifully: And he thought within himself, saying, What shall I do, because I have no room where to bestow my fruits? And he said, This I will do: I will pull down my barns, and build greater: and there I will bestow all my fruits and my goods. And I will say to my soul, Soul, thou hast much goods laid up for many years: take thine ease, eat, drink, and be merry. But God said unto him, Thou fool, this night thy soul shall be required of thee: then whose shall these things be, which thou hast provided? So is he that layeth up treasure for himself, and is not rich toward God.'

"The Gospel of Luke, chapter twelve, verses sixteen through twenty-two. Praise God for his holy Word." Why in the world, Ezra wondered, does this bunch on the front side of winter have any truck with some fellow and his barns? They stood for a hymn. Ezra kept his seat, squirming to get comfortable. He felt the beginning of a headache stomp like troops marching to the doleful tune the congregation droned.

Boland began his sermon by declaring that the rich man stood for the Yankee government. Soon God would turn the tide and require the souls of the Federals. He warmed to his topic, wandering into Paul's letters, quoting texts in First Peter and Ephesians about servants obeying masters. Ezra didn't know about slaves and masters, but believed all he needed to obey was the army, if he could figure out where to join. The rising headache, not helped by the sermon, provoked him to leave. A crude poster in the lobby showed a soldier pointing to a recruiting office, closed until tomorrow morning.

Dinner was a cup of hot water and chicory the counterman called coffee, and a plate of beans with chewy fatback. Ezra recovered the token from his boot, retrieved his horse, and rode east to the top of the mountain, where a battery of light artillery defended the town. Leaves were down, so he had no trouble seeing the western encampment on Battery Hill. A cold wind whipsawed the mountain, and clouds gathered like cotton wool around Mount Pisgah some fifteen miles southwest.

Back in town he spent money on a dingy room, and the next morning walked to the courthouse and enlisted. The recruiter saw an able-bodied man with a horse he said was his, so did not examine him closely as to age. Ezra rode thirty-odd miles north to Mars Hill, where he spent a week at military drill with a wooden weapon. They gave him a dingy gray uniform and a forage cap with a ripped crown but Ezra wore it proudly. Then they gave him a rust-pocked Fayetteville rifle and hurried him back to Asheville to wait. They policed the courthouse square of a day and at night slipped from camp to follow what few slatternly women wanted to be chased. When orders arrived two months later, he and twenty-five other men deployed west, in the early spring, into Haywood County.

He got his first look at Cataloochee when his company marched to Mount Sterling. Laid out before him were Big Cataloochee and Little

Cataloochee, bisected by Noland Mountain. High mountains covered in balsam and spruce encircled lush valleys that held tiny patches of farmland. Huge chestnuts promised abundant wildlife and clear creeks. It would make good orchard land. He determined one day to return.

They were sent to block George Kirk's raiders, rumored to be heading in from Tennessee. Colonel Kirk was a hero or a turncoat, depending on who told it. He had enlisted in the Confederate Army, then turned Federal when the prevailing side became evident. He attracted vicious men as easily as Jesus made disciples. Ezra heard campfire stories about Kirk and thought he wouldn't mind riding with him. Men like that knew how to profit from war.

Ezra's company did not stop Kirk nor slow him down appreciably, but Ezra wasn't captured and even managed to kill a Bluecoat, a boy his own age who wandered into the woods to relieve himself, britches down behind a scarlet oak. Ezra didn't hesitate to put a rifle ball between his eyes. Ezra's legs thrilled same as if he'd killed a turkey.

That was the first of April. Lee surrendered on the ninth, but word traveled slowly to North Carolina. On the twenty-sixth, Johnston surrendered to Sherman at Durham but no one in Haywood County knew it. Brown's Yankees burned the Asheville armory the same day and Ezra's company fired some of the last shots of the war at them as they came into Haywood on May 6. Then it was over.

Ezra rode thirty miles east to Asheville to muster out. He had killed a person and seen some danger. Now he wanted money. The livery he'd used before, sign still dangling, hired him, then fired him for drinking and fighting and laying out of work. He held a series of odd jobs, but after several saloon fights he figured sober country living would keep him out of trouble.

From Asheville he forded the French Broad at Long Shoals and wandered south. He signed on with an orchard keeper near Edneyville who would brook no liquor. First wages were bed, board, and training. He learned quickly, built on what Owenby had taught him, and soon all the work fell to him while the keeper laid about and slept. A year later the old man died of a stroke and Ezra became the keeper.

No one knew where Ezra got the stake to buy the farm outright from the owner. There was talk of a poker game. But by 1877, Ezra owned two barns, horses, an outsized apple house and orchards, a fairly prosperous farm worked mostly by tenants. He kept to himself except Sundays, when he rode a buggy to the Baptist church. He courted no women. He was tight with a nickel and lent money on strict terms to his sharecroppers. He made their children split firewood for him, promised them a little something, then neglected to pay.

He had never forgotten his first view of Cataloochee, and meant someday to live there. One of his wartime compatriots, a Haywood County Sutton, showed up at Ezra's farm every spring to tell a year's worth of stories and try to learn something about Ezra to tell the next place he lit. In 1879 Sutton told of Jonathan Wright, who farmed the last place on Big Cataloochee Creek, just under Big Fork Ridge. Wright had a pretty, marriageable daughter and a lot of land. Sutton also told of Will Carter, the largest landowner on Little Cataloochee Creek, also with plenty of land and a daughter of about fifteen. He depicted Will as fond of both politics and whiskey, but he didn't blame him for the latter, having to live with a wife, five daughters, and a sickly boy.

Early in 1880 a peach and pecan farmer north of Spartanburg named Dodd, tired of the hot summers down there, offered to buy Ezra's farm, and Ezra figured cash money would go a long way with either Cataloochan. He wrote letters to Jonathan Wright and Will Carter in January and both replied for him to come talk. So Ezra turned his face toward Cataloochee.

2

~~~~~~~~ ❧ ~~~~~~~~

The Enormous Iron Beast

Silas Wright and Hiram Carter rode like old men, creaky as their saddles though neither was yet twenty-three. A knowing observer would peg them for men used to working horses but seldom riding for pleasure. Mule and wagon better suited them for such distances as Cataloochee to Waynesville, some thirty miles as the crow flies, a trip they made every six months.

The Haywood County township, Cataloochee, bordered Tennessee on the northeast, the eastern Cherokees on the southwest, and was called "the back of beyond" even in Haywood County. In Waynesville, the county seat, folks fancied themselves too sophisticated ever to have been connected to such a backwater. One county east, in Asheville, residents regarded Waynesville as an outpost only to be visited on a mis-

sion of mercy or to uproot some dug-in criminal. Folks downstate in
Raleigh smugly claimed to have no truck with the mountains. Such
was society in Reconstruction North Carolina.

Silas and Hiram had been born late in 1850, so were too young to
seek what adventures might have befallen them had they enlisted in the
Civil War. Their fathers were too old for the army, so the boys spent the
war farming with them. In 1861 Silas's father had moved the Wrights
from Spring Creek to the final section of flat land in Cataloochee, two
miles past Hiram's father's farm, just before the road turned into a trail to
the top of Spruce Mountain.

Silas was eleven when they moved. His father, Jonathan, and his
mother, Velma, had packed a beat-up wagon, then hitched a mule to the
front and tied a milk cow to the rear. They roped the chickens' legs together and laid them complaining in the back. The journey wasn't fifty
miles but took the better part of two weeks. Up and down mountain-
sides they walked and rode, teetering on primitive roads, prying boulders, dodging rattlesnakes.

At Rush Fork Gap, Silas could have looked west three ridges and
said, "So that's where we're going. Seven miles as the crow flies. More
like thirty by road." But the right-hand wheels suddenly chunked in a
rut as mule sawed left and wagon went right, sending boxes and bags,
chickens and children overboard. If the wagon had turned over completely the whole kit and bilin' would have plunged five hundred feet
down the mountain. That afternoon they searched through poison oak
and catbriers for his mother's wooden butter print. His father kept saying he'd carve her another when they got to Cataloochee. She would
not budge. After an eternity they found it and she said they could go on.

One ridge west they'd have been too high for poison oak but at Rush
Fork it was abundant and potent. Silas's eyes swelled shut two days later
and he feared he might lose his right arm, pocked with weepy blisters.
After he recovered he made two vows: he would never again let himself
get poison oak, nor would he ever move.

Both young men were fascinated by the great trains of the East. They
talked about a locomotive's strength but disagreed whether a train could

outrun a good horse. Silas said nothing able to pull such loads could possibly go fast, as elephants are not noted for swiftness. Hiram, thinking of large jungle cats, bet a nickel it could. Hiram's mother, Lib, and Silas's father, Jonathan, regarded the argument as pointless, but gave them leave after the first hay crop to ride to Old Fort, terminus of the Western North Carolina Railroad.

The first day they climbed the old switchback road, ascending twenty-five hundred feet to Cove Creek Gap, then down to Cove Creek itself, and up Jonathan's Creek to Dellwood. By dark they made the Shook place at Clyde, where the asthmatic old Francis Asbury, proclaimed bishop of the American Methodists by John Wesley, had preached more than sixty years before, and where camp meetings were held until the war stopped such religious extravagance. The Shooks were happy to lodge honest vagabonds, so the boys spent the night in the barn loft, resting but excited, wakeful.

When crickets hushed and the sky grayed, they gave up on sleep, descended, saddled their horses, and made for Buncombe. By sunup they were nearly to Turnpike. Closer to Asheville they met no drovers but steady traffic, single riders and teamsters, some hauling firewood pulled by oxen with backbones jagged as the saws that cut their burdens. They passed frame houses, some with banks of yellow and purple irises beside inviting porches, others facing away from the road like misanthropes.

Clouds of pigeons occasionally obscured the sun but neither young man paid much attention. Atop the next hill sat a town five times Waynesville's size and twice as ugly, Hiram thought. Two-story brick structures lorded it over rickety wooden buildings facing streets clotted with mud. An east-west road met a north-south thoroughfare at the public square but otherwise roads ran in directions that led Silas to think they were laid out by a drunken man on a mule. In a half hour they surveyed the sights: courthouse, the cemetery beside the Presbyterian church, several liveries down Water Street, and stores and hotels on North and South Main. Well-dressed pedestrians stared at them disdainfully but toward the end of South Main they hailed an ancient man with a gray waist-length beard for directions east. He scratched an armpit and told them to keep south to the Swannanoa River, then follow it east to Black Mountain, then over the ridge. He'd heard talk of a train down that way.

Ten miles east they passed Alexander's Inn, a rambling structure blessed with a deep and wide porch full of rockers and hanging flower baskets. They made camp a mile distant along the river, then caught a few fish but threw them back, for Hiram mistrusted eating creatures choosing to inhabit murky water.

Sunset was red and long-lived. Silas inhaled the aroma of frying pork. "You know, back in Catalooch, with them high mountains, the sun sets between three and four. This broad valley lets daylight stay longer."

Hiram poked the curling pork with his knife. "Yep, a man could get used to such a sunset. But, all in all, I can't say I care for this country. I'm trepidatious to bed down here, there ain't nothing to hide behind. If it wasn't for getting my nickel, I'd think about going back home."

Silas sighed. "It's *my* nickel, neighbor. But I'm with you. This here country is too you might say changeful to suit me. All them people running around back yonder in Asheville. I don't know where they all come from, and I bet half of them don't know where they're going. I'm glad I live where things are quiet."

After supper they laid out bedrolls, smoked, and listened to night sounds, frogs both large and tiny, zinging small insects, a lead gander honking to his fellows, saying, See, here is water. Some unseen thing knocked in no discernible pattern against a rock in the river. Hundreds of dragonflies swarmed the hull of a dead birch leaning over the river, then disappeared after a bat devoured one of their comrades. In a while the men slept soundly, rocked by the rhythm of the river.

They woke to the creak of departing geese and watched a lone heron, thin to disappearing when it faced them, stab prey in the shallows. Whitetail deer faded into the woods across the river. The young men's breakfast was cold and hurried, for they meant on this third day to see a train.

They headed out of Buncombe County toward the gaps at Coleman and Graphite in bright sunshine, fanning insects from their faces. Along the roadside grew yellow sundrops and five-pointed red flowers with ends that appeared pinked with shears. Hiram was glad the clean bright glint of a blacksnake did not spook his mount. They rested at the gap, then twisted down the mountain into McDowell County.

Halfway down they met gangs of men. Some were white, grading roadbed with mules and drag pans. Others were black, wearing striped uniforms and slouch hats, chained together, pitting picks and shovels against the mountain, overseen by grim white men with shotguns. Hiram and Silas passed them in silence, not knowing if it were proper to acknowledge such men with a nod.

Farther down they passed a hand-lettered sign:

Mr Wm Thompson & Wife
General M^{dse} & Board
Tourists Welcome

The new sign was driven into the ground some hundred yards before an old store building. Beside it was a frequently visited spring. The boys stopped to water their horses. Thompson, who with his wife had moved to North Carolina from Wyoming, greeted them. "Boys," he said, "what do you think? I'm going to make a geyser out of this spring here. It won't beat those in the new national parks in the West, but it'll do for here."

"What good's a geyser?" asked Hiram.

"Why, son, it'll attract tourists like nothing else."

"What's a tourist, sir?"

"Somebody that tours the country, son, somebody who comes in and leaves money with them that's smart enough to get it."

Silas and Hiram thanked him and headed down the mountain without conveying their doubts about his enterprise or buying sweet milk or pie from Mrs. Thompson.

They wound downward until the road flattened near the Catawba River and the settlement called Old Fort. A station newly hewn from chestnut and oak had not yet benefited from paint. Beside it parallel steel ribbons lay spiked on logs perpendicular to rails laddering eastward.

Hiram and Silas hitched their horses. They saw a town small enough to fit in the Cataloochee valley, even if here the post office was separate from the general store.

On the plank sidewalk beside the station sat a bench holding up the backsides of a trio of whittling men. Silas caught the eye of one, about sixty, wearing flannel despite the warm weather. "Howdy, mister. I'm Silas Wright. This here's Hiram Carter. When you reckon the train'll get here?"

The man shrugged and poked his neighbor's ribs. "I'm Tom Peek, son. Train's been by not long ago."

"How can you tell?"

"Can't you see its tracks?"

The men chuckled, then slapped knees and wheezed with laughter. A red-faced Hiram grinned, took off his hat, and mopped his brow. "That's a good one, Mr. Peek. Now then. We came from Catalooch to see this train. Will it come again today?"

Peek looked them over. "Where'd you say you hail from?"

"Catalooch. In Haywood, forty mile west of Asheville. Prettiest country you ever seen. Not near as hot as here."

"I wondered where such wild-looking critters as you might come from." He opened a pocket watch with his thumb. "The train'll be here at four thirty-eight. Five minutes."

"Thank you, Mr. Peek. Mind if I take a look at that?" asked Silas.

"My watch? Don't you have timepieces in—what'd you call it? Catty-loose?"

"Catalooch. No, sir. There's a case clock at the post office but nobody's got a pocket clock." The man opened and gave the watch to Silas. An Elgin with regular hands plus a small dial with an arrow to mark seconds, it had appreciable heft.

Silas handed it to Hiram. "It's pretty," he said. "Sounds nice, too." He handed it back to Peek. "But I wouldn't have much use for it."

"Truth to tell, son, I never needed one till the train came. Now I don't hardly know it's dinnertime without it. You fellows might want to move them horses before the train shows up."

They led their mounts to the edge of town and tied them to saplings. Soon they heard a distant metallic rumble. After the train pulled the grade east of town and chuffed by the Padgett place, they saw a pillar of smoke pulsating toward town amid a growing roar.

When the locomotive started to brake for the station Silas and Hiram gentled the horses best they could. Dirty woodsmoke and sparks flew from a beveled smokestack big as the Cataloochee grist mill's forebay. A Cyclopean lantern hung on the locomotive's face, and behind the smokestack two humps bristled in front of a cagelike box in which a man peered forward through smoky chaos. The enormous iron beast stormed and clanked and whistled as wheels shrilled on the tracks.

They gawked at the train, bound back for Morganton by dark, taking on water and wood. A few tired passengers with bags emerged, dusting their clothing. Two black men unloaded crates of vegetables and a sack of mail. More swarmed over the locomotive like ants holding oil cans.

As it whistled again Hiram and Silas mounted and steadied their horses. Past the town the track looped to head the train east and as the machine turned, the boys began to race with it. The locomotive gained speed as it neared the station. Silas and Hiram kept up with it for a quarter of a mile past the structure but the monster quickly pulled away as they slowed their winded mounts.

"You owe me a nickel," said Hiram. "I told you they don't call it an iron horse for nothing."

"You'll get it, friend. I just need a blow. That thing is amazing."

"Double or nothing I can beat you back to town."

Silas patted his horse. "Better give them a breather, too. We can race up the mountain in the morning if you want."

As they neared the station Peek motioned to them. "Did you boys really think to outrun a train?"

"We just wanted to see how fast it would go," said Hiram.

"Son, you got a lot of catching up to do. One of these days a man will be able to go from Carolina to California without putting a foot on the ground. It's progress."

Hiram smiled. "You think that thing will really go up the mountain?"

"You bet. If they get it to Asheville, they can put it into Catty Loose, too."

"They do that, we'd have to move to Montana for peace and quiet," said Silas. "How do you put up with the racket? I think it'd make me sick."

"You know what it sounds like to me? It sounds like money. A man can live with that easy enough. You boys got anything against money?"

"How come you think that sounds like money?" asked Silas.

Peek looked at him like he might be from some strange planet. "Look around you, boy. Twenty years ago there wasn't none of this. This place wasn't even a place, it was just nowhere. Now we got a hotel and everything. Trains bring money, son. You'll see. You boys heading east?"

"No, sir," said Hiram, "we're heading home tomorrow."

"I got shelter for horses if you want to stay tonight with me and the old woman. We'll open a keg of nails and bite their heads off." Peek peered at his watch.

"You sure we wouldn't be in the way?" asked Hiram.

"Lord, son, it ain't but me and her now. We'd be proud to feed some young folks for a change. Might teach you a little about this modern world, too. We're down this road, turn in at the gate with the upside-down horseshoe. I'll be along directly."

3

A DECENT ENOUGH ROSEBUD

Like most of his kin, Hiram Carter liked to dwell on family history. If he didn't know a detail he'd make it up. Countless times he told how the Carters came to Cataloochee.

The telling varied somewhat, but always began with his grandfather, called "Old Jimmie" Carter because in his thirties his hair turned solid white. Two years before President Jackson ran the Cherokees off to Oklahoma, in 1836, Old Jimmie and his sons—Levi, Hiram's father; and Levi's brothers, William, Lafayette, whom they called Uncle Fate, and Andy—stood at Cove Creek Gap, peering into Cataloochee like Moses looking at the Promised Land, except they got to go in. They had come from Spring Creek, then in Buncombe County, which Old Jimmie said was getting too populous for him. "It's getting so people live right on top of you," he'd say. "It ain't natural."

So he bought a hundred acres from Colonel Love the land speculator in a region the Cherokees called "Gadalutsi," which meant something like "standing in rows." By the time Love got through with the name, all any white person knew to call it was Cataloochee, and in another generation most had shortened that to Catalooch. When the Carters spied out the land, they found nobody there, so they cleared the footpath Love had the brass to call a turnpike enough to drag a mule-drawn sled without it skittering off the mountainside. They went back to Buncombe, loaded up their families, piled sleds high with cookpots and chicken coops, tethered milk cows behind, and journeyed four days to Jonathan's Creek. Then they held on for dear life up seven miles of corkscrew road from Cove Creek, and then the same from the gap down into Big Cataloochee.

It was mostly wilderness then, trout the size of handsaws, poplars big as silos, poison oak vines thick as a man's leg. They built a cabin by the creek, and at night the big cats they called painters screamed at them, some nights from the roof peak, sounding for the world like women being beaten. Old Jimmie hurt his back badly and moved back to Buncombe after the first winter. But Hiram's father, Levi, took root, and he and his wife, Lib, made a good farm. Next year a family of Howells settled down the creek from them, and they all built a Methodist church.

Hiram's uncle Will, much like his father, said, "Brothers, I'm going over the mountain where it ain't this crowded." He settled in Little Cataloochee among a nest of Davises, all Baptists. They were not hardshells, so Will joined them. "The only difference in Methodists and Baptists is water, and I don't reckon that's worth fighting about," he said.

In 1861, six families lived on Big Cataloochee and four on Little Cataloochee. Both settlements had a store and post office combined, and a grain mill, and there was even a sawmill beside Cataloochee Creek. Normal life was shattered that year when all the men went to fight on one side or the other, except those too old like Hiram's father, Levi.

Hiram was fourteen the spring of 1865. Levi and Lib, and Hiram's four younger brothers, didn't have much to eat that year besides turnips and honey and fish and what game they could shoot, and had run slap out of salt. Lib dug dirt out back where she had tossed dishwater for years, and boiled it down in an iron kettle, over and over, till something crusted in the pot a man could call salt if he didn't look at it too closely nor taste it too tightly.

When Colonel George Kirk scattered Ezra's company and came through Cataloochee, Hiram and Levi hightailed it toward the mountain but the Yankees ran them down, marched them to Old Man Bennett's place, and tied them up in the barn.

The soldiers found Bennett's whiskey. Hiram worked himself loose and untied his father and Bennett while the Yankees drank and shouted and knocked over a coal oil lantern. Hiram stuck his nose out of the barn to see the house crackling and roaring.

Hiram and Levi dove into the ivy while Old Man Bennett stood in his yard and cursed what he called the heathen bastards. Kirk's men beat Bennett and caught Levi when he tripped over a root, but Hiram hid until the company moved on.

Lib and Hiram heard no word from Levi until the next October. Hiram was helping pickle kraut when a hoot chorused from the edge of the woods. Hiram wondered what an owl was doing out at ten in the morning, then remembered Levi's hunting signal. Levi sidled out of the woods. He was so thin Lib nearly killed him with her hugs.

They had no fatted calf but Hiram shot a couple of squirrels. Levi had always said he would raise out of his coffin for Lib's squirrel stew, but he only sipped at a spoonful. He had spent nearly a year on the run, sleeping in barns if he were lucky, stealing from people's gardens, hiding from a war he didn't know was over. Once home, he stayed in bed, and died before the first snow.

After that, Lib kept up the motions of life until the last child was out of school, then looked at Hiram and said, "I'm through working, son." Hiram laughed, but she meant it. That was the spring of 1879. She was sixty-two, and would live to be nearly a hundred. The rest of her days she wouldn't hardly strike a lick at a snake. She sat on the porch or in the chimney corner and dipped snuff. Except for a rare fit of loquacity, she was silent. Hiram allowed she was saving up talk for Levi, and when she got to heaven she'd give him an earful for dying on her like he did.

Hiram said he had no time for courting, but that spring he was haul-ing produce from Cataloochee to Waynesville when he spied a young woman perched on the low rock wall by the Baptist church in Cove Creek. She wore a red dress and bonnet. When he stopped to water his mules at the creek he spoke to her, and when she took off her bonnet the red streaks in her black hair nearly took his breath. She was eighteen and he was nearly thirty but he asked if he could visit her family. Her name was Mary Howell. They were married four months later, and set up housekeeping with Lib on Cataloochee Creek.

The late February morning in 1880 when Ezra Banks rode into Cat-aloochee, Hiram had just put his mule in the stall after busting out a to-bacco bed. Last fall he'd manured and planted the bed in rye, which this morning his plow had turned under to fertilize the seedling tobacco. The work wasn't all that difficult—the bed was on a flat next to the creek—but it was the first plowing of the season, and he had raised a sweat. He was headed out of the barn, pulling up his sleeves—he took poison oak easily and always wore long-sleeved shirts—when over the noise of the creek he heard an unfamiliar horse trotting from the direc-tion of the schoolhouse.

A large bay mare headed dead for him. She was of better blood than any horse in the valley except Jonathan Wright's black and Hiram's own roan. The horse looked almost arrogant, like she might run over him if he didn't step back.

Astride this beast sat a man of middling height, clad in black except for a boiled white shirt and a piece of orange feather in his hatband. A black four-in-hand tie swung with the rhythm of his mount, and he wore a Sunday hat, wide-brimmed, high-crowned, although it was only Tuesday. The man's black mustache lay under a prominent and crooked nose that cast a shadow on his face.

He saw Hiram and pulled on the reins. The mare lifted her neck and stopped just short of Hiram, who wiped his brow with a yellowed handkerchief. Hiram looked up at the stranger, who glanced at him and then surveyed the valley floor.

"Howdy, stranger. Hiram Carter's the name." He held his right hand up to the man on the horse.

For a minute the man said nothing nor did he look at Hiram's proffered hand. He took in the barn and the house and the old smokehouse and the sycamore beside the creek and then Hiram, who by then had given up and returned hand to pocket. The man sniffed like he wasn't quite over a cold. "Howdy yourself, Hiram Carter. I'm Ezra Banks. You work on this here place?"

"Well, sir, such as it is, it's my farm," Hiram said. "I don't recollect that name hereabouts. Where do you hail from?"

"South Carolina by way of Buncombe." Ezra turned to gaze at the upper end of the valley. He made no move to dismount. He looked about Hiram's age, and carried saddlebags and a rifle behind.

"How much farther to the Wright place?" he asked sternly.

Hiram shifted on the balls of his feet. "Maybe a mile up the creek, on the left. Heck, it's the *only* house up that far. You can't miss it."

Ezra shifted the reins to his right hand and nudged the mare with his heels. Heading up the road, she broke into a trot.

Hiram shook his head and spat in the dust. "I never," he said to himself. "Miserable rascal wouldn't even shake my hand. Even poor folks can afford manners."

Heading to the house for dinner, he stopped to kneel at a patch of crocuses beside the springhouse, two colors, yellow and white, with yellow-orange centers. He gingerly picked a white one for Mary. She was a fool for flowers, whether a violet or a sprig of galax or a strawberry bloom. The crocus disintegrated, but he decided petals would do. At the front porch he cupped them in his hand.

"Mary, oh Mary, how's my best gal today?" he sang from the porch.

"Hiram, is that you?" she called from the back porch. "I'll be there in a minute." He smelled the cookstove's bouquet—soup beans, ham hocks, cornbread. He went to the pantry for her glass dish in which to display the petals.

She came from the porch, apron flying, "Lord have mercy, I'm about to burn the bread." She rushed to the cookstove while he poured spring-water in the dish and set dish and petals on the table. She turned from the stove and beamed.

"Hiram Carter, you are a perfect dear," she said, and went to embrace him. He enjoyed her kiss and hug for a moment. "You smell like a mule," she said. "Now get your mama, if she'll come. It's time for dinner."

In the front room Hiram asked Lib if she would take a meal with them but she only stared at the fire. He patted her bony shoulder. "Mary'll bring you a little something directly."

The table, which old Levi had made years before from a chestnut log, held dishes of ham hocks in their own juice, pintos, a pone of corn bread, a bowl of applesauce, and another of kraut.

They sat at the table, held hands, and bowed their heads. "Lord," he said, eyes not quite closed, "we've made it to dinner again, for which we thank you. Now bless these pretty hands that cooked this fine dinner. Amen."

He sliced a hunk of cornbread in two, doused it with liquor from the pork, crowded meat and beans onto the rest of his plate, and forked a big helping into his mouth. "Lord have mercy, this sure is good."

"Hiram, I can't make out a word of that. How many times do I have to tell you . . ."

He swallowed. "Sorry, but I do love good cooking, almost as much as the one that fixed it."

They ate for a few minutes in silence, when Hiram remembered the stranger. "Mary, I just met a man that didn't set right with me. He come from toward the schoolhouse on a bay mare that just about run me down. Fellow about my age, all in black, toting a rifle. You heard any-thing about him?" He spooned applesauce onto his plate.

"They say somebody was coming to see Mr. Wright about some kind of business." Mary was still hungry, but only nibbled at a piece of corn bread. Women in her family tended to heaviness. "I heard he wasn't from around here. What do you mean, he didn't set right with you?"

"I don't know," he said, sopping up the last of his applesauce and cornbread and hog gravy, "he appeared kind of standoffish. Wouldn't shake my hand."

"Well, he don't have to live with us, so I reckon we will be fine." She began to clear the table. "I wonder how he'll get along with Jonathan Wright. He ain't a body to put up with trouble."

Hiram laughed. "You're right about that. That's why he built so far up the creek, to get away from people. By the way, I appreciate the dinner."

She grinned. "You're welcome, Hiram Carter. And that's a pretty flower, even if you tore it up getting it here."

"Well, I couldn't help it. Them things is kind of tender. Like you."

"When you get back this evening you might get a surprise."

"If I didn't go back out, could I get it now?" He reached for her and jerked her apron string untied.

"Get out and go back to work, Hiram Carter," she said, blushing. She picked up the apron. "Surprises come in their own good time. Besides, I'm going to Henry and Callie's this afternoon. Take the new neighbors a basket of rhubarb."

He stood and put on his hat. "All right. That surprise'll keep me working all afternoon—at something or another, if it ain't but thinking about you."

Hiram had built a new smokehouse behind the barn. Levi's old smokehouse had become Hiram's woodworking shop, walls lined with tools and shelves filled with jars of pegs and glue and pumice. He opened the door and smelled fresh-planed pine and cherry alongside the faraway odor of cured hams. A carpenter's apron hung on a nail on the back of the door, and he tied it behind him. A cherry box tall as a coffin but narrower leaned against the east wall. He lit a laid fire in the cast-iron stove at the east wall and put a pan of water on to simmer.

Across two sawhorses lay three clamped wild-cherry boards. He removed the clamps and ran his fingers over the smooth wood. The lower part of the panel was routed for a pane of glass. He scooted the box to the middle of the room and held the panel to it. Finished, hinged, and glassed, it would be a perfect door for the long clock he was making for Mary's nineteenth birthday.

To adorn it he had in mind a trellis with a dozen roses. The trellis was easy. Thin walnut strips would fit the cherry front perfectly. The roses made him scratch his head. He had carved some out of walnut, but they looked more like butter beans than rosebuds.

He studied a piece of spruce, turning toward the window for more light, and looked up and beheld the field, full of robins. Several hundred stood in perfectly random order, poking in the grass, jumping a few feet, crying and thrusting their beaks again until they found food. He took his glue pot off the shelf and stuck it in the pan of boiling water.

The flock of robins made him think of the journey he and Silas Wright had made to see the train. They had seen flocks of hundreds of robins in the fields, and passenger pigeons by the thousands clouding the sky.

In 1880, seven years later, the track extended to Asheville, and there was word that the train would come all the way to Waynesville, only about twenty-five miles from Cataloochee, in a year or two. Hiram shook his head. "I know what Silas'd say. Won't bring a thing we need to Haywood County. Tourists and racket, mostly, and ever flimflam man with the price of a train ticket," he muttered, stirring his glue. "Still, like that man said, it brings money."

He tried the spruce with his knife, and after fifteen minutes had shaped a decent enough rosebud, at least looking less like a legume than his walnut efforts. "Two'll serve good as a dozen." He finished them and glued the trellis to the cherry front. His creation wasn't bad. The multi-colored walnut grain highlighted the dark cherrywood front panel, and the spruce roses would be light enough to show up like real flowers. He glued the rosebuds after he installed the face and works, then assembled the cabinet and finished it with a coat of beeswax. The face showed lunar phases in shades of dull brass against a polished background. The weights were said to be cones of a pine but Hiram thought they more closely resembled she-balsams.

Only trouble was, with the works in, it was too heavy to carry by himself. "Dad-jim it. You'd think a man thirty year old would have better sense than to make something he couldn't carry."

The seed store in Waynesville had just the ticket, a fancy hand truck, but he'd have to make do with a mule and wagon. To a chorus of cawing crows he sawed the wagon back and forth to get even with the porch edge. Spreading a horse blanket in the bed, he went inside to remove the weights. Twine tied around the clock frame kept the door from flying open. He walked it, tilting it first to one side then the other, and the clinking chimes made him think of a dance. On the porch he faced the back of the cabinet to the wagon, then eased it down and pushed it completely into the bed. Mule and wagon with the supine clock reminded him of a catafalque. "Get them thoughts out of your head, Hiram. This is Mary's birthday, it ain't no bad luck."

He brought the wagon to the cabin and reversed the process. Inside he walked the clock to the back wall. "Someday," he said, "I'll build her a big house around you." He hung the weights, started it, and, noticing the angle of sun and shadow, set the time.

His mother paid little attention at first but when the clock got going she stared at it like it might bite her. "H'arm, that infernal thing'll keep us up all night." She fumbled in her apron pocket for snuff to load her birch-twig toothbrush.

"Mama, you'll get used to it. In a day or two it'll put you to sleep. What do you think?"

"No sense tempting fate."

"What do you mean?"

"That thing ever stops running hit means death's a-coming, as sure's a bird pecking at the window."

"Mama, I wouldn't make Mary nothing that'd cause trouble."

He picked up the blanket and returned to the porch. Mary still was not in evidence, so he put up the mule and wagon and straightened the shop. Outside he saw her ambling down the road, a basket under her arm. When she got to the edge of the yard Hiram whistled at her like they were courting. He saw her dimples deepen when she smiled.

She trotted up the steps and kissed him. "Hiram Carter, what are you up to?" She giggled, bumped off his hat, and tousled his thinning hair.

"Not a thing in the world." He hugged her shoulders. "What's in the basket?"

"Callie give us some blackberry jelly."

"You all right, honey?"

"Course I am. Why?"

"You looked a trifle worried."

"I guess I was thinking about Callie. She's kinder quare. I never was around anybody quite like her."

"What do you mean?"

"Well, everything she talks about's connected one way or the other with the Bible. She'll be telling about the weather and all of a sudden she'll go on about the Revelations. Then she'll start in about seeing all these robins we've been having lately, and next thing you know she's quoting 'ere a sparrow that falls' and that gets her going about that king turning into a bird in Daniel. It's hard to keep up with."

The clock chimed Westminster and four measured bongs.

"What in the world?"

He squeezed her arm. "Happy birthday, honey." He followed her quickly into the house.

"Hiram, we can't afford nothing like that. You tell me right now where you got it."

"Honey, I built the cabinet myself, and I traded hams for the works."

"I never seen nothing that pretty. And you *made* it. Two little sweet peas, one for each of us. That's so darling."

"Honey, them's roses."

Mary ran her hand over the trellis. "Why, of course they are. Mama Carter, what do you think?"

She shifted her birch twig from one side to the other. "Sure does make racket."

Mary touched her mother-in-law's shoulder. "Honey, you'll get used to it. Soon you'll think it's music."

The old woman grunted.

Mary skipped back and rubbed each side of the cabinet. "It's so smooth. Who learned you to do this?"

"My daddy. I could use a drawknife and plane when I was a young'un. I wish he could see how big a fuss you're making."

"Hiram, I believe he's looking at us right now. And he's proud of his son."

When it chimed the quarter hour Mary clasped her hands in delight. "Hiram, you shouldn't have. It's only my birthday and that ain't nothing much."

"Honey, you hush. I love you more than I can count. Besides, we'll pass it to our young'uns and they'll pass it to theirs. That cherrywood'll mellow out good and red. It'll get prettier as it gets older. Like you. When we build us a new house we'll move it into the hall and you can be proud of it all your life." He lowered his voice and put his arm around her, hand touching the edge of her breast. "You can thank me tonight— you remember? That surprise?"

She looked at Hiram's mother and nodded. "I might just do that. Lordy, look at the time. I got to get supper on." She shed her shawl and headed to the kitchen, a grin covering her face.

He went outside and heard hoofbeats from up the creek. In a moment he saw Ezra Banks riding out of the valley, looking neither to the right nor the left. Ezra never acknowledged him nor did Hiram raise his hand. He would ask Silas if Jonathan ran him off.

1

A WOUNDED BIRD

Silas Wright's father, Jonathan, had been wary of Ezra Banks but enjoyed a sip of bonded whiskey from a bottle Ezra pulled from his saddlebag. By noon half the contents were gone and they had talked of Ezra buying fifty acres, what they called "the upper place," and working apples on that farm and Jonathan's. Wright was even receptive to Ezra courting his daughter, June, although at fifteen she showed no interest in a man twice her age.

Silas had been plowing when Ezra first showed up. Ezra, washing his hands before dinner, saw Silas corner his father and lead him in earnest conversation toward the barn. Ezra had made progress with Jonathan but this was inauspicious. Ezra knew he needed to charm the women at dinner, but his small talk clanged on the table like horseshoes. When he asked June to accompany him on a walk afterward, her mother snapped at him like a mud turtle, and the message from Silas's stern face was plain—get moving.

After dinner Ezra, who hadn't drunk whiskey in years, gave Jonathan the rest of the bottle and got directions into Little Cataloochee.

"If it's any of my business, Mr. Banks, who are you going to see over yonder?"

"I mean to visit with Will Carter."

Jonathan laughed and looked at the bottle. "You give him whiskey this good, he'll likely give you his farm, all his girls, and that sickly boy, ever one."

Ezra mounted his horse, tipped his hat brim, and headed back down the creek. He'd come in by the main road, but Wright told him of a shorter way, what they called the "dug road," built by the Carter family before the war. About a half mile past Hiram's he turned left up Indian Creek, rode past the mill not quite a mile, where a narrow trail turned left and headed straight up the mountain beside Davidson Branch. Ezra glared up the mountain, quirted his horse, and started up.

The road was fairly well kept but was steep at the top and barely wide enough for one rider and mount. The Carters had dug the road thinking it would be easier than taking the long way to Little Cataloochee but its steepness scared off most folks.

At the top Ezra found a deserted shelter, the remains of a camp used by men to check the summer pastures. After feeding and watering his horse he kicked detritus on the shelter floor, skullbones of rodents, snakeskins, pebbles, scat, cones, leaves, remnants of long-dead creatures and their pursuers. As he spread his bedroll he spied a yellow flash beside the front door. "By God," he said, and knelt by the threshold, brushing a hairy section of as yet leafless poison oak vine.

He turned his head every direction to recapture the flash but the dwindling light was not accommodating. "Damn it, it's bound to be here," he said, lighting a pine knot, the rich resin popping and hissing.

In its light every fleck of mica looked like a bright coin. He dug around the entrance with his knife but found nothing. "Damn it all, I could have sworn it was gold." He lay down for sleep against tomorrow's visit but when it finally came it was lean and fitful.

Will Carter was thirty, just married, when the war broke out. When he returned from fighting he took to making children. His wife, Kate, formerly a Ball from Crestmont, prayed for a girl, and when 1866 gave her one she named her Hannah Elizabeth. After two more girls they had a son, Jake. But two girls later Will decided he would rather make whiskey than young'uns if all he was going to get was girls and one puny boy. Jake had scarlet fever when he was little, but survived. Kate, in Will's view, spoiled him something awful.

Hannah was dark of hair and light of complexion like her mother, with a dimple in her chin. She developed a knack for solitaire, and she and Jake would play double sol for hours on snowy days. When Miss Crawford, the schoolteacher, loaned her a volume of poetry, she devoured it quickly, then savored it again, like hard candy she wanted never to melt away. Her favorite was Keats, who died so young, but she memorized Shakespeare and Hood with equal fervor. When her mother got an almanac Hannah pored over it like it was a rare gospel. Hannah went to Ola—Little Cataloochee's post office was named for the postmaster's daughter, Ola Davis—every day she could to see if there were any news of the outside world.

The morning Hannah had handed her father Ezra's letter—exactly the same he'd sent Jonathan Wright except for the names—Will had set up his grindstone to sharpen tools for spring. He took the letter and turned over a wooden bucket to sit on. The postmark said Edneyville. "Where in tarnation you reckon that is? And who's it from?"

"Papa, I don't know. It isn't polite to read other people's mail."

"Well, I figured you'd have read, and maybe even answered, it by now." He chuckled.

"I'll read it to you if you want me to."

"Sure, gal. I'll just set here and listen."

She unfolded a sheet of deckle-edged paper, yellow on the left like it had been in the sun awhile. "It's from a Mister Ezra Banks, Papa. You know him?"

"Don't think I ever heard that name before. What's he got to say?"

She took a breath like she was about to recite in school. " 'Deer Mister Will Carter, it gives me grate plasure to inquire whether I might come to see you to the purpose of reechin a bidness agrement. I have a farm with sizable orchard bidness and am lookin for land in Cataloochee to pursue same. I have it to understand you might be intrested in a partner in yer interprises. I culd come to Cataloochee wether permits the end of the month. Plese let me kno by return post. I fought with Capt. Howel up clost to yer farm in the War. Hope that comends me to you, I am yours in full, Ezra Banks.' "

She looked at her father. "He sure can't spell much good."

"Likely he didn't get much schooling, sugar. Robert Howell's unit was barrel scrapings, you might say. Anybody with him was too old to fight in the regular army or so young they got in at the tail end of the war. I'd say Mr. Banks was one of the young ones, else he'd be a sight older'n me and would have no use for farming."

"Papa, are you going to let him come?"

"Sugar, I'm studying it. A man don't get such a letter ever day."

The next day he asked Hannah to write to Ezra and invite him to visit. She posted the letter at the Ola post office on Friday, and they got a reply the next Thursday saying Ezra would arrive Tuesday. Kate cleaned house two solid days, even taking vinegar and water to the windowpanes. Will stayed at the barn more than usual. "Fellow wasn't careful," he told Hannah, "he'd get scoured and dusted and maybe even polished if he stayed in the house too long."

Tuesday morning the young'uns were home because Miss Crawford was sick. Hannah was sweeping the little yard when a horse and rider swung around the turn and headed toward the house.

He rode straight and tall, like Hannah's image of a dashing Confederate officer. As he approached she made out his mustache and the leftward slant of his nose. She put the broom beside the porch and wondered what lay behind those steely eyes.

As Ezra dismounted, Will walked from the barn and Kate came onto the porch wearing her special company apron, a dazzling white she'd never wear in the kitchen. Ezra tipped his hat brim. "Morning, folks. Name's Ezra Banks. I take this to be the Carter family."

Will stuck out his hand. "Will Carter. Some folks call me Apple Will. Pleased to make your acquaintance, Mr. Banks."

Ezra studied the hand, then gripped it. Will, smelling of whiskey and hay dust, pulled a plug of tobacco from his overalls and offered it.

"Don't chew," Ezra said. "You go ahead."

The other girls joined Hannah and Kate on the porch. "Mr. Banks, these here are my womenfolks. My wife, Kate, yonder, she's the oldest one." He chuckled. "That'n next to her's our oldest gal, Hannah. Them other'ns is Sadie and Tildy and Luizer and that least one playing peeka-boo is Mandy Lou. The boy in the door frame's Jake."

Ezra doffed his hat and bowed formally. "Pleased to see you all this morning." Her sisters giggled as he looked Hannah over slowly. "Espe-cially you, Miss Hannah." She blushed, and shooed her sisters back in the house like bobwhites.

"You gals get to your chores. Me and Mr. Banks got talking to do," said Will. Once Kate went inside with Jake, Ezra reached into his near saddlebag for a fresh bottle of bonded whiskey.

Will shook the bottle and held it to the light. "Mr. Banks, this here's pretty liquor. I sure thank you. Would you have a sup?"

"No, thanks. Don't touch it myself except when I got a cold."

Will sniffed it like it was fine perfume, then took a swig. He corked it and grinned. "Best I ever had, lessen it was that batch my brother Andy made up Indian Creek one time. Never did make a run that good again. I reckon a possum fell in it." He cackled and led Ezra to the barn, where he nestled it in an unused stall behind some hay. "Now let me walk you around the place."

Before dinner they had seen fields and orchards and the rock apple house tucked into the side of the hill. Some of the farm was as steep as Ezra's daddy's old place, but most was ideal orchard land, well watered, rising and falling like ocean waves. After their tour they sat on a rock wall while Will talked and Ezra nodded and grunted and even grinned at Will's cornpone jokes. "What you going to do with this land?" Ezra asked, picking up a stick and turning it over in his palm.

"I reckon I'll farm it till I die."

"What then?"

"Won't much care then, will I?"

Ezra tossed the stick toward a banty hen, which clucked and pecked at it. "I mean, you ain't got but the one boy to help you, nor work it when you're gone. Not that I'm wishing it, mind you, just talking facts."

Will looked at Ezra. "No hard feelings, sir. I knowed what you was talking about. Jake's right puny but they say he'll grow out of it. Besides, one of these days I'll have me a son-in-law. Hannah's nigh about fifteen and Sadie's just two years behind."

"Would I fit that bill, Mr. Carter?"

Will stood, turned toward Ezra, and crossed his arms. "Mr. Banks, are you wanting to court my Hannah?"

Ezra looked up. "Let me put it this way. I'm interested in buying part of your place, and if a wife came with the deal I wouldn't throw her out."

"But I don't know nothing about you, Banks, except you say you fought in the war."

Ezra looked at the treeline. "Ain't nothing I ain't told already. I left home when I's nearly fifteen and ain't been back. First time I saw this country I vowed I'd live here someday. I been farming in Henderson County. I'm what you call land poor, but a man wants to buy me out over there, so I could pay cash money for a section of yours fair and square. My place in Edneyville's too damn close to that road into South Carolina and they's no good comes of living next to a highway. A man gets a place in here, ain't nothing going to bother him. Not roads, not even government."

"Been married before?"

"Ain't had time."

"Been in trouble with the law?"

"I mind my own bidness and other folks mind theirs." He spat in the yard.

"Well, Banks, if Hannah'll have you I reckon we could work a deal. That upper place yonder's a good forty acres and I'm getting to the age where I ain't going to clear it myself. It'd make a fine dowry."

"I'd pay you, Mr. Carter. I ain't beholden to nobody and I don't aim to start now."

"Suit yourself," said Will. "Say we have a little sup before dinner? Whet your appetite?"

With that they went to the barn till Hannah called them to dinner. Watching them shake hands, something caught in her throat. She felt like a wounded bird.

They were married in April in Will and Kate's front room by the Baptist preacher. Ezra looked proud in his black broadcloth suit, and said his vows in a strong voice. Hannah kept eyes either on the preacher or the floor and her family had trouble hearing her. The preacher declared them wed and they moved into the old cabin, Will and Kate's first home, down the hill from Will's new frame house.

Ezra had sold his Edneyville farm in March and had spent the rest of the month hauling young trees by the wagonload and tools and other possessions the sixty-odd miles between Henderson and Haywood. Immediately after they got married he started clearing his new land and planting. In his spare time he grafted hardy varieties onto Will's orchard, sometimes five or six on one tree. Will vowed it wouldn't work, and that first season only let him graft in a small corner. Ezra imagined new apple houses to handle the crops. A new barn, too, for that matter.

While Ezra worked, Hannah had the house to herself, which mostly suited her. Being married, in fact, relieved her of the ruckus and responsibility of her brother and sisters, and Ezra was not hard to be around. He brought her odd presents, like a pile of red feathers left over from some critter's dinner, or arrowheads, of which three made from quartz were lined up in her kitchen window. Every time Ezra left for Edneyville he returned with newspapers and some object from the outside world, once a saltcellar shaped like a beehive, another time a gold-colored thimble, with which she pieced quilts until it turned her fingertip green.

She enjoyed reading the newspapers, which she passed on to her father, who delighted to read about politics. They were full of stories about modern life in cities with telephones and electric lights. When she spoke of such to Ezra he listened halfheartedly as though none of that would ever have to do with them. Not even news of Kansas going dry early in 1881 got much of a rise out of him.

She hadn't noticed Ezra's broodiness until after they moved into her parents' old cabin. Perfectly civil and loquacious one minute, he might suddenly stare into some unknown space as if counting bushels of unseen apples. If she asked him about it he'd snap at her and go back into his thoughts like a dog circling for a nap. She put it down to his working so hard.

The old cabin had an ancient, damperless cookstove. Hannah knew the exact angle to set the damper on the stove where she grew up, but the first time she baked biscuits in the old stove they featured undersides burned black but doughy middles. Ezra sniffed one and broke it in two. "Hannah, I reckon you just got to get used to that old stove," he said. After Ezra left she begged biscuits from Kate and brought them to Ezra in the orchard.

After a week or two she had corn bread down pat. The next Sunday she ventured to make biscuits, which this time were light brown on top, but she could have thrown them at the barn to the barn's detriment. She was about to toss them to the chickens when Ezra came into the kitchen corner.

"Breakfast ready?" He plunked himself into a chair. "I could eat a wampus cat."

"Ezra, these here biscuits ain't no good. I'm sorry." She poured coffee and set a plate of ham and gravy in front of him. "You'll just have to make do with cornbread until I get this right."

"The hell you say, woman. I can't put gravy on corn bread." He stood. "Let me see them biscuits."

"Ezra, they ain't no good, I told you. I'm sorry as I can be but I can't do miracles." She stood between him and the stove, and the smell of hot cast iron and ham made her shudder.

Ezra came around the table and drew his arm back. Like a cat, she moved quickly but not before his back-turned hand grazed her shoulder. A straight blow would have knocked her down.

Rubbing the stinging hurt she stared him in the eye. "Ezra Banks, you listen to me." He gazed away from her. "Are you listening? I need to know because I ain't saying this but once. You *listening* to me?" She grabbed his shirt sleeve. "You even *look* like you're about to hit me again and I'll be out of here quicker'n two shakes of a sheep's tail. I won't put up with such an outrage."

"Hannah, I—"

"I don't want to hear nothing except 'Yes, you heard me.' "

She watched his mouth move from a scowl to a smile. "Yes, Hannah, I heard you." He took her hand. "I don't know what come over me. I won't do it again."

"You remember that promise. And you remember mine. I ain't getting hit by nobody. If I was to tell Papa what you just done he'd come up here and kill you. Now set down and eat. We'll be late for church if we don't hurry."

After dinner with her family—Ezra ate four biscuits—the women cleaned the kitchen and came out to the porch. While Ezra and Will and Jake inspected the orchards, Hannah asked Kate if they could take a walk without her sisters. Kate shooed them into the house. "We got women talk to do. You young'uns lay down for a nap."

Kate studied her daughter's profile as they walked toward the road. Lilies poked through at the edge of the path. "What is it, Hannah Elizabeth?"

"Mama, I don't know."

"Is he drinking?"

"No, it ain't that."

"Is he tomcatting on you?"

"No, Mama." She looked at a bluebird on a branch, beak filled with bits of straw. Mayflies bobbed in the sunshine in front of the murmuring creek.

"Well, child, what's wrong?"

"It's my biscuits. They're hard enough to shoe a horse with."

"Lord, child, is that all?"

"Well, this morning I told him I was sorry, but . . ." She caught a sob in her throat.

Kate stopped. "Child, did he raise his hand against you?" She pulled Hannah toward her, cupping her daughter's chin in her hand.

"It wasn't much, Mama. I ducked and he just touched me on the shoulder. He says he won't do it again. But . . . You ain't going to tell Papa, are you?"

Kate studied her. "Child, if I did he'd run over and shoot him. Your daddy's always said a man who'd hit a woman's lower'n a snake's belly."

"No, Mama, don't tell him. Promise me." Hannah picked at a string on her sleeve. "I told him never swing at me again. He's good to me, except when he gets broody. He says we're going to make a lot of money off our apples when everything gets fixed right and he wants to build us a great big new house next to the orchard."

Kate smiled wanly. "Men sure can sound grand. Your daddy used to say we was going to get rich, too, but then that war come along and it's took us till now to get back on our feet." She looked toward the house. "Now then, we're not going to let on about this. But promise me faithfully if he ever again makes to hurt you you'll come back to us—quick."

"Yes, Mama."

Strolling back they felt a breeze from the south that turned maple leaves silver-backed in the sun. "Going to get some rain, child, that'll work into a shower pretty soon." Kate nodded toward the front porch. "Now I want you to look at that."

Jake's spindly legs dangled from the front porch, and on one side of him sat Will in his Sunday overalls. Ezra in his black broadcloth suit rested on the other. Will whittled while Ezra peered catlike from under his hat brim. Beneath the porch slept three pot-likker hounds of a breed not quite Walker and not quite Plott, noses shoved into the sunshine. Kate chortled. "If you could paint a picture of that, you could call it *Waiting for the Mischief to Come,* or some such. You'd make a killing."

Jake jumped down and ran to them. "Mama, Papa's making me a boat and we're going to float it in the creek. You want to come see?"

"Son, I'd love to," said Kate. "Hannah, what do you say to that?"

"If we're still here. Ezra likes his Sunday nap."

"Well, child, he may like his nap, but I've heard him working on Sunday, too, and that don't set right with me. You know what the Bible says."

"Does that mean Papa's sinning by working on that stick?" Jake asked.

Hannah put her hand on Jake's shoulder. "Of course not, silly. He isn't working, he's making something special for you."

Ezra stretched and said they needed to go, for it was his naptime. After he and Hannah left, Kate sat by Will on the porch.

"Well," said Will, "I bet in a while we can get a good nap listening to rain on the roof." He brushed out his lap and eyed the piece of wood. "Jake, I don't know if I'll get this done before dark. Might have to take me a nap in a minute."

"Papa, if you show me how, I can carve on it until you get up."

"You'll do no such thing," said Kate. "I don't want you cutting your fingers off."

"Oh, Kate, let him be a boy for a change. He can handle a knife."

"If you want his blood on your head, that's fine. I wouldn't let him if it was up to me. Son, you be careful." She rose and went inside while Will handed Jake his knife. "I'll be out in a hour or so. Do like your mama said and don't cut your tallywhacker off." He patted Jake's head like he would a favorite dog, stretched, scratched his belly, and looked over the south ridge, where clouds blackened. After he went inside it poured for twenty minutes. A half hour later the chink of a go-devil and wedge from Hannah and Ezra's place woke Kate. Her son-in-law was working firewood on Sunday.

5

A Man Makes His Own Luck

In Little Cataloochee, Will Carter kept up with politics and told everyone how to vote. His new son-in-law, Ezra, cared nothing for such matters but had money left over from buying part of Will's property. When folks discovered that fact, those who needed cash came to borrow. Ezra had no ear for their troubles but asked them how much they needed and drew up a paper for their mark. He normally had half a dozen current notes. One morning Ezra visited George McGee to collect a note McGee had fallen behind on. Instead of money he came away with an old Colt's pistol and the promise of a yearling calf to be brought later that day.

At the post office he had a letter from an apple broker. A man slouched out of the shadow on the north wall. "Well, Mr. Banks, how in the world are you?"

Ezra turned to see Judson Cook, who never asked Ezra for a loan but always offered him some disadvantageous trade. Ezra had shoved the pistol in his belt and forgotten about it.

"Damn, Banks," said Jud, "you expecting Jesse James?"

"No, I ain't expecting trouble."

"You might ought to," said Jud, leaning against the door frame, sunlight haloing him. "If that's the pistol I think it is, it ain't nothing but bad luck. That the Colt's used to belong to my cousin George, ain't it?"

"It might be."

"You trading on it today?"

Ezra glared and shook his head.

"Win it at cards?" He moved out of the doorway to make room for Naomi Coggins, just arrived for her mail.

Ezra nodded to her and looked at Jud again. "You ain't told me about this bad luck yet."

Jud took off his floppy hat and smoothed his stringy hair. "Well, you know George ain't the first one had that gun. It used to belong to his wife's uncle Taint. He found it after one of them battles. You never knowed old Taint Wright, but he was real bad to drink. One evening he'd had more'n usual and something woke him up. He looked straight down the bed and seen something moving. I reckon he thought them Davis boys he was feuding with was in the house. He took that Colt's and shot his fool big toe clean off, he did. Blowed a hole in the wall you could throw a varmint through. Ain't that right, Miz Coggins?"

She looked at the men like they were a pair of jaybirds pestering her cats. "I wouldn't know," she said, picking up her mail and breezing out the door.

"Anyhow, he rubbed some chimney soot on that stump of a toe, tied a rag over it, and went back to bed. He give that pistol to George the very next week."

Ezra looked at Jud. "So how does that make this a bad luck gun?"

Jud grinned. "Well, Mr. Banks, I could have swore a man rich enough to ride in a buggy could figure that out. Old Taint done shot off his big toe, and before that some soldier died a-holding it, and if that ain't enough, then looky what happened to Cousin George after he got it. In sight of two year he's lost his wife and two good bear dogs. Used to have a tad saved up, but if he's paying you with that there pistol, I'd say he's got hard times all the way around."

Ezra's finger traced the length of his nose. "Way I figure it, a man makes his own luck, Mr. Cook."

"So you ain't afeared to own it?"

Ezra pulled his jacket back. "No, Mr. Cook, I ain't."

While Ezra was out, Hannah had visited her mother. They talked of weather and church, and Hannah at last mentioned that lately she had felt strange. Kate listened to Hannah's symptoms, then put her hand on her daughter's forehead.

"Mama, do you think I'm sick?"

"Child, you might be in a family way." Hannah stood at the mantel and turned sideways like a squirrel, staring at her mother. She dropped into the rocker.

"Are you sure?" Hannah said, her voice halfway between fright and excitement.

"Law, child, the only thing I'm sure about is crows is black and Jesus loves us. But from what you say, it's likely."

Hannah picked at her apron hem and bit her lower lip. She looked at her mother, hesitation all over her face.

"Now, sweetheart, you'll be fine," said Kate. "Carter women is good at birthing babies. You're a little young, but you're strong. You got to eat good. I got some fresh turnip greens that'll put some iron in your blood." She walked over and put her hand on Hannah's shoulder. "My baby, having a baby of her own."

"Mama, I'm scared."

"Child, ain't nothing to be scared of. God made us to have young'uns. I just wish He hadn't give us pain to go with it, like it says in the Bible." Kate cocked her head and grinned. "It's kind of like shitting a watermelon but afterward it's so nice."

Hannah couldn't remember her mother saying such a word even in anger. Both women laughed, then cried, then laughed again. Kate sent Hannah home with a poke of greens and a mother's hug.

Home from the post office, Ezra hung his coat on a kitchen chair. He laid the pistol on the table, found one of Hannah's damp dishrags, and cleaned the walnut grips. He sat and studied the weapon.

It looked like an Army Colt's missing most of its trigger guard. What was left of the guard looked to be brass. It was .44 caliber, not much of a wound going in but a cantaloupe-sized hole at exit. The end of the barrel wasn't perfectly round but he thought a rat-tail file would fix that.

He removed the barrel assembly and cylinder. The weapon hadn't been fired in a while but the rifling was so dirty he went into the back room for a bottle of oil and a rag. He found a stick of about .44 caliber and oiled the rag and pushed it through, enjoying the bright smell of gun oil. When he put it back together the loading lever clicked but not absolutely. He broke it down again, relatched it, and wiggled the barrel. A thirty-secondth's play at the latch. He pointed the pistol at the kitchen window and pulled the hammer with his thumb. It clicked once, then twice. It felt heavy, too much so. He released the hammer, then turned the gun to his face and cocked it. The cylinder didn't quite match up with the barrel. He frowned and released the hammer. A lead-spitter.

Ezra put up his gun oil and was about to pick up the pistol when Hannah, carrying the turnip greens, opened the back door. The rustle of the sack as she laid it beside the woodstove reminded Ezra of paper money.

"I see you got back," she said, and turned to him. Her eyes rounded when she saw the pistol and her dishrag. "Ezra Banks, what in the world is that thing doing in my house?"

"It's my house, too." He put the pistol in his belt. "I traded George McGee out of it. He's supposed to bring over a calf and we'll be square. You got something against pistols?"

"I don't mind a shotgun and I don't mind that deer gun neither. I like a mess of venison as good as anybody. But all that thing's good for is killing a man and I'd just as soon throw it in the creek as look at it."

Ezra frowned. "Hannah, I thought maybe you might want to learn to shoot it, for when I'm gone to Newport, you know, for pertection."

She snorted. "I can take care of myself. Besides, who in the world would hurt me?"

He pulled out a chair and sat it backward. "Hannah, there's two kinds, them that got and them that don't. I'm a fellow that's got. Them that don't, well, they want what them that's got's got. You understand?"

She untied her apron, folded it, and laid it over the back of his chair. "Here's what I understand. My uncle Fred had one of them things. Heard something ratting around the house one night and first thing he knew he'd killed his oldest boy. Thought he was trying to break in the house, when all he was doing was sleepwalking. I want it gone. Now. And you done rurint my good dishrag."

"Hannah, all you got to do is wash it good."

"You ever did any washing around here you'd know it ain't that easy." She waved the dishrag at him. As Ezra picked up the pistol she stretched the dishrag across her chest like a shield. "Lord, Ezra, just get that thing out of here."

"Woman, the damn thing ain't loaded. I ain't got ammunition." He looked at her, then the pistol. "I'll lock it up." From the cupboard he brought a poplar box. A metal hasp dangled from the lid and meshed with a fence steeple underneath. A small padlock kept it closed.

Ezra fished in his trouser pocket for the key. In the box lay papers tied with twine and a black leather pouch with a drawstring. He put the gun on top of the papers, closed and locked the box, and put it back in the cupboard. He patted Hannah's shoulder, then went out the back door toward the barn. She watched him disappear, then started washing greens.

By the time she saw George McGee with a plowline pulling a roan calf into their lot like a sled, Hannah wondered if she had been too hard on Ezra. She had been out of sorts lately and felt rocky in the mornings more often than not.

She smelled greens and fatback boiling and looked out the kitchen window. Ezra and George had wrestled the calf into the pen and stood, each with one boot on the lower rail, talking and pointing.

Before she started the rest of their supper she went to the front porch for a breath of air. The sun was behind the house so she went back inside for a shawl. Promise of a cool night. Outside, she looked to the ridgetop, still washed in light. It reminded her of the way light came into church sometimes, brushing the pulpit with gold. "Lord," she said softly, "if you give me a boy, I'll do my best to make him a preacher."

Sitting on the stoop, she couldn't think of a preacher at all in her family, and surely not one in Ezra's. A man of God out in the world, maybe he could preach at our church when he comes home, she thought. She would name him Samuel after Hannah's son in the Bible and William after her father. Samuel William Banks. She watched the sun set behind the ridgetop.

In the kitchen the musty smell of greens filled the little room as she tied her apron behind her. Ezra came in like he had beaten someone at poker. He'd even kept McGee's plowline. "George and me are square." He sniffed the air. "Greens smell mighty good."

"I don't know if they'll cook down before suppertime," she said. "We'll have taters and corn bread and beans if they don't."

"That'd be fine. I can eat most anything. Hope I didn't make you too mad about that gun."

"Well, I still don't want it here, but long's it's in that box it'll be all right." She put her hand on his sleeve. "Ezra, I got something to tell you."

"What's that?"

"Mama thinks I'm in a family way."

His eyes brightened like pennies. "You really mean that?"

She nodded.

"Hannah, that's mighty fine news. I hope it's a boy. For a fact I do. Zebulon Baird Banks. How's that for a name? I been turning it over in my mind ever since the war." He hugged her and turned her around in a little dance.

She bit her lower lip.

"Don't you like the sound of it? You remember our governor during the war? Zeb Vance is the only one a soldier could name a son after. He kept us North Carolina soldiers in food when Tennessee's didn't have none. I couldn't hardly name a first son nothing else."

"I'd thought to name him Samuel William."

He let her go and sat at the table like he was mustering troops in his head for a fight. "You don't know my old man's name. Samuel. I wouldn't name a damn goat after him. And the William's after your daddy, I bet—he's a good man but he's too fond of his liquor. In fact, he's about as bad a drunk as my old man was except he don't get mean with it. No, my boy'll be named for a great man. That's all there is to it."

Ezra went to the front porch to look at the mountaintop and scratch himself proudly. Hannah stirred up corn bread and hoped her firstborn would be a girl.

6

A MIGHTY LUCKY MAN

In the spring of 1884, Lizzie, the wife of Hiram's brother Marion, packed a cloth bag and left her eldest daughter, Charlotte, in charge of the young'uns. After Granny Lib took to her rocker, Lizzie had birthed most of the babies in Big Cataloochee, and Hiram's wife, Mary, was due any day.

Lizzie walked down the steps and halfway to the road, then turned to wave at Charlotte, who held her little sister Mattie in her arms and her little brother Levi Marion's hand by the front door. Levi Marion, three come August, stomped and turned his face into his sister's dress. "Son, you got to be my little man while I'm gone," Lizzie hollered. "Won't be but a few days." She waited for Levi to finish his pout, but it wasn't to be. She waved again and ambled to the road.

Lizzie and Marion lived on what Old Levi's children called the upper place, fifty acres joining Levi's brother Andy's farm on the northeast. Hiram lived in the home place, on the south side of what they called the big field, halfway between the schoolhouse to the east and Jonathan and Silas Wright's place to the west.

A quarter mile down the road at Uncle Andy's corner she passed the big chestnut, alive with a maelstrom of squirrels. If Marion were here they'd have a stewpot full tonight. When she turned back to her journey, she spied Hiram and Mary's place across the field.

She and Marion had married there in 1865, not long after Old Levi came home from the war and died, nearly twenty years ago. On their wedding day Marion wore Levi's suit and Uncle Andy led them in their vows. Uncle Andy was rail thin, with hair the color of windowpane frost. He was handy with a fiddle, and Uncle Fate played a mouth harp, and somebody she didn't remember played the washboard. They didn't have a banjo because the Pangle boy got killed toward the end of the war. He wasn't right in the head but could coax marvelous sounds from a banjo. Everybody had a good time, drinking cider and what whiskey the men could sneak a tope from. They fried chickens and Granny Carter roasted a groundhog. Nobody now would eat a groundhog, but back then folks ate what they found. Prepared and cooked properly, groundhog tasted like a big squirrel.

Lizzie rejoiced in her seven children, but all the young'uns to keep up with, plus canning and preserving and cooking and washing and mending, made time fly, and kept a body tired. She had seen in the newspaper where some folks got what they called vacations. She determined this week would be hers.

Uncle Andy's cabin sat just past the orchard. As his family had grown, he had added a back wing and an upper story. Even the outbuildings sprouted sheds like fungus on the side of a dead tree. Lizzie passed the apple trees, just coming into white bloom, pink centers moving in the breeze. Years ago Aunt Charlotte—Lizzie had named her eldest daughter for her—had set out a juniper at the corner of the yard, and Lizzie stopped to smell its sharp aroma. Something moved inside,

not jerky like nesting birds. She pulled needles back slowly to see a slender black and white snake stare at her.

The pattern on its back looked like a chain and the white on its sides
made her think of bandages. Marion was quick to kill rattlers and copperheads but always liked to see this kind around the barn. Black tongue
flicking, it began almost imperceptibly to move, head raised to catch the
next branch. She turned to the road, swinging her bag.

It was maybe a quarter mile down to Hiram and Mary's place, and
she enjoyed dandelions yellow on the roadside and little blue butterflies—Marion called them flutterbys—on horse manure in the road. She
often wondered why something that pretty liked to sit on nastiness. A
patch of creesey greens on the left told her she was inside Mary's bound-
aries. Closer to the house a rhubarb patch reddened in a ditch and jon-
quils bloomed. She spooked Mary's leghorns and banties as she came
into the yard. A potted fern took the sunshine in one porch corner and
she stopped to remove dead fronds. She scattered the dry leaves and
knocked.

"Latchstring's outside," came Mary's voice. Lizzie opened the door.
Mary greeted her with the best hug she could give, big as she was.
"Mighty kind of you to come, Lizzie. Have a seat and rest awhile."

Lizzie listened to the clock tick and greeted Granny Lib. The old
woman paid her no mind. "You might have to go over there," said
Mary. "It's hard to reach her most days." Lizzie walked over to Granny
Lib and touched her arm, but the old woman didn't stop rocking nor
look up. She did put her gnarled hand atop Lizzie's. "It's Lizzie, Granny
Lib. Marion's wife. I've come for advice about birthing Mary's new
young'un." Granny Lib nodded and laid her hand back in her lap.

"How's that little George Henry?" Lizzie asked Mary.

"He's fine. I sent him over to Henry and Callie's—the neighbors up
to Deadfall—for a few days. The boy's walking now, into everything.
Callie's going to have to step lively."

"Seems like just yesterday we was here having him. I was thinking
about the day Marion and me got married here in the yard, and that's
been nearly twenty years. Now my own Charlotte's just got married."

Lizzie saw tears pool in Mary's eyes and knelt next to her chair. "Lord, Mary, I'm sorry. I didn't mean to make you sorrow."

Mary bit her lip. "It's all right, Lizzie, I can't help it sometimes. I'd hoped my Ada Pearl would have grown up, too. Don't seem like I can ever get her off my mind." Mary's first had been a stillborn girl they buried under a lilac bush beside the back door. Hiram had said there would be plenty more and ceased to refer to his daughter but Mary kept her grief like a flower pressed in a Bible.

"I know. She was such a pretty baby, prettiest one I ever seen. Where's Hiram?"

Mary let Lizzie's hand go and wiped her face. "Gone to South Carolina hauling something or another. I told him if he come back and I still ain't had this young'un, he could just turn around and go back again."

They both smiled. When George Henry was born, Hiram had taken a great deal of the credit, but mostly got in the way. Lizzie stood, knees popping.

"Them's pretty flowers on the mantel. Hiram pick them for you?"

"Yes, he's always brought me flowers."

Lizzie nodded. Marion worked so hard most nights he'd be too tuckered out to recognize a flower, much less pick it for her.

The clock struck the quarter hour. Lizzie ran her hand up and down its side. "I've said it before, Mary, if you ever take a notion to get shed of this, I'll take it off your hands. It's beautiful the way this cherry has mellowed, turned just as red as can be."

"Hiram says he's going to build us a big house to put it in. Said he always figured it for a hall clock. The other night he drawed out a plan with four rooms downstairs and a hall down the middle. Said we'll fill it up with young'uns."

Mary was twenty-three. "Well, I hope so, child. George Henry's a fine start, and we'll add your new one soon. Marion gets our new ground broke, he's going to fix up that old cabin down there, but I don't reckon it'll ever be all that big."

Lizzie put her bag by the steps up to the loft, then went to the back room and clattered at the cookstove. "What are you doing in there?" Mary asked.

"Making coffee. I'll pour you some. It might help."

Mary's labor started about dark. About four that morning, after considerable groaning from Mary and encouragement from Lizzie, a little girl came squalling into the world, black-haired, hungry. Lizzie cleaned her, cut the cord, wrapped her in a blanket, and handed her to her tired sister-in-law. Coming out of the back room Lizzie found Granny Lib still in her rocker. She had poked up the fire, and a piece of poplar hissed and crackled. Granny turned toward Lizzie and cocked her head like a bird.

"What is it?"

"A little girl. Head of black hair and a good set of lungs."

"Got a name?"

"Mandy Elizabeth. The Elizabeth's after you and Mandy's after her other grandmother."

"Hit's good to have a namesake when you ain't too long for this world." She turned to Lizzie, recognition in her eyes. "Child, how's Marion a-doing? I ain't seed him in ages."

"He's fine, Granny. He was here Sunday, don't you remember?"

She shook her head slowly.

"Well, he sat yonder in that chair. I had to poke him awake, remember? Poor thing works so hard all week clearing new ground, I don't get to see him much."

Granny nodded. "Child, he's got his papa's blue eyes." She straightened and grabbed Lizzie's hand.

"What is it, Granny Lib?"

"There was times I'd go weeks and not see Levi except at supper. He'd be out before I got up, fooling with the livestock or stringing fence. Nights he'd eat and fall in the bed with his clothes on." Mandy Elizabeth squalled from the back room, and the two women stopped until Mary eased the baby back to her breast. "That ain't no way to be married. Lord knows how we got all them children with him a-working like that. You keep up with Marion. I got a feeling."

Granny Lib was known as a woman with second sight. Lizzie shuddered. "Granny, don't talk like that. Not with a new grand-young'un in the house."

Mandy Elizabeth was born Tuesday morning, and Callie brought George Henry back home Thursday, and would stay with Mary until she got on her feet. Lizzie took her bag to the porch, ready to head home on a bright, clear morning. Spring had moved ahead without her, and she itched to see Marion. He was likely working the new ground, so at the road she turned left toward the church. Birds sang and butterflies flitted drunkenly.

She crossed the footbridge where Indian Creek poured into Cataloochee Creek and walked by the clapboard church, its face hidden in morning shadows. Another quarter mile brought her to the Nellie post office, the road following the murmur of the creek, winding by moss-covered rocks and splashing sunlight.

Past the settlement at Nellie she came to a two-acre clearing on the left-hand side of the creek, the only level place on their new property. Crossing the creek, she started up the trail into the woods where Marion and the mule came daily. The ground steepened quickly and she pulled her skirts up as she climbed, careful not to brush against poison oak just leafing. She heard Marion's ax and smelled coal oil smoke swirling off a dead black gum that reached to eighty feet. He had girdled it the season before and now set it afire every morning, hoping it would soon be consumed. Keeping her eyes on the ground, she climbed toward Marion, thinking it was about time for snakes underfoot.

Halfway up the hill she saw Marion kerchunk his ax into a sourwood not quite big enough for lumber. She leaned against a maple and folded her arms across her chest. Smooth motion, ax head doing most of the work. Marion seemed in no hurry, measured chops scattering large chips into the air. She didn't hear the tree begin to crack, but knew it had when he stroked the ax and stepped back. The tree swayed slightly earthward, then stopped. Eyeballing it again, he swung once more. Wood cracked as the tree fell to ground. Marion leaned the ax against his leg and tamped his pipe with his thumb. He was fishing for a match when Lizzie came up behind him. "Hey, honey," she said.

He jumped and turned at the same time. "Woman, don't spook me like that," he said, red-faced, jaw dropped. "What's wrong?"

She thought his blue eyes might burn a hole in her. "Why, honey, not a thing. I wanted to see you, that's all. Mary's got a fine daughter, Mandy Elizabeth."

"Just come to see me? That's all?"

She put out her hands and he took them. The sides of his fingers felt rough as tree bark. "That's all. I been missing you." She smiled, her head cocked sideways.

"Well, you seen me." He relit his pipe. "Now what?"

She shrugged. "It's up to you, honey. I got all morning."

Smoke seemed to pour out of him. "I ain't, woman. I got to get this ground cleared and broke." He ran his hand up and down the ax handle.

"Marion Carter, you can take time to talk to me, can't you?"

He took it not to be a question, leaned the ax against a tree, and patted the wagon bed like there was a feather pillow for her.

He had cleared enough to the southeast so they could see the ridgetop across the creek, full of crows calling over the dim noise of the water. "Look at all them birds, Marion. You ever wonder if they marry and have families?"

"Well, I don't rightly know. I've seen doves mourning for a dead wife but I never seen a crow do much besides thieve corn and make racket. Mama used to tell how Papa cotched a screech owl and tied it to a pole and when the crows come to devil it, he shot them. She never said nothing about their wives. I expect they're laughing about how bad you spooked me."

"I didn't mean to, but when you get lost in your work you wouldn't know if General Sherman was about to set you on fire."

"I get caught up in my work, it's a fact. You know I love results. Remember when we had to do sums in school? I didn't see no sense in doing them over and over with nothing to come of it. If I was going to do numbers I wanted to make something out of them, not just line them up to get erased."

"In school and you'd be the only one staring out the window. Always wondered what you was looking for."

"You was two grades behind me. What was you doing spying on me?"

"Marion Carter, when I was in fifth grade I knew I was going to marry you."

"You didn't."

"Yes, I did. You had the prettiest blue eyes and I thought you was the best-looking thing." She craned around. "You still are." She kissed his forehead.

"Honey, that was near about thirty year ago."

"You ain't changed much except you look wiser."

She felt girlish as she stepped off the wagon and waltzed to a silent rhythm. Suddenly she reached for him and they danced slowly in the bright sunshine amid the stench of the burning black gum and the sweet smell of cut sourwood. A kingfisher keened toward the creek.

She stopped as quickly as she had started and hugged him harder than she had in years.

"Honey, what's got into you?"

"Marion, I don't know. Maybe I missed you while I was at Mary's." She smiled at first but soon sobbed. "Just hold me."

Arms around her, he watched crows on the ridgetop moving one by one, then seven by seven, heading across the mountain in western procession. He looked toward the road and, seeing no one, put his right hand on her breast.

She knocked his arm hard. "Marion Carter, it's broad daylight. What in the world are you doing?" But she grinned through her tears. "You'd think we was just married."

"You remember Uncle Andy fiddling on our wedding day?"

"Why, Marion, I was just thinking about him on the way to Hiram and Mary's. I'd give anything to hear Uncle Andy play 'Black Velvet Waltz' again."

"Was that what you was dancing to?"

"I reckon so, yes, I think it was."

"You know what he told me that afternoon?" He put his hat on. "He looked at me, you know that look he'd get when he wanted us young'uns to listen real good, and he said, 'Marion, you're getting as good a girl as ever come out of this here valley.' " Marion paused and fished in his pocket for his pipe. "Then he said, just as slow and serious, 'She might make you into something if she gets half a chance.' You reckon he was right?" He struck a match.

"Marion Carter, you was something when I first seen you and you still are. I loved you in fifth grade and that's just got deeper over the years."

He could not have looked happier if she had given him a twenty-dollar gold piece. She blushed like a schoolgirl. "Honey, I love you, too," he said. "And that's the honest truth. I'm a mighty lucky man."

"Marion, I'll remember this morning a long time."

She walked a few paces toward the road. As she turned to blow him a kiss, he stood framed by sunlight in the clearing, ax in his hand.

7

A MAN TO MAKE HIS FATHER PROUD

Cool rain fell the morning Zebulon Baird Banks was born in 1884. Hannah had labored through the night, tended by Kate, who banished Ezra to a pallet on the porch. Dawn discovered his blue pipe smoke curling into the mist. He had stuck his head in the back door but no food waited in the cookstove's warmer. He meant to go to the new house and work, and maybe later someone would fix his dinner.

Ezra and Hannah's marriage was four years old, childless, although not from lack of trying. Their first had been a finely featured boy, stillborn, that Ezra refused to spend the name Zebulon Baird Banks on. Another, a girl Hannah named Rosa Jane, with the blackest hair anyone could remember, died at three months. Hannah had prayed fervently over the child with which she now labored.

She travailed in their old place, built in 1855 by her father, into which she and Ezra had moved when they first married. It was maybe thirty feet wide and twenty-five feet deep, one room divided by an imaginary hall anchored by front and back doors, chestnut logs gray as the early June morning. Ezra knocked out his pipe, got his toolbox, and headed up the hundred-odd-yard path to their new house.

He had been working on it for nearly two years, replicating the two-story frame house with a wide porch he'd lived in before he came to Cataloochee. Behind the porch was a large sitting room and behind that a generous kitchen, to be Hannah's territory. The front room on the left Ezra called his office, for which he had contracted with Hiram Carter to make a desk. Behind the office was a bedroom. Upstairs there was a large bedroom over the right-hand side and two smaller ones on the left.

The new-laid chimney on the left filled the space between the lower windows, narrowing as it traveled through a notch in the roof. Ezra and Will had laid it themselves. When they finished Will lit a piece of rich pine and held it in the flue opening. Smoke scrambled up the flue as if some hobgoblin chased it. Will grinned at his son-in-law. "That flue'll draw the dress tail off a woman."

Today Ezra meant to hang doors. He set the toolbox on the porch, then wiped the handsaws and chisels, eyeballing their edges. He turned the brace he had borrowed from Will slowly, listening to the gears mesh. He wiped the bits, then the claw hammer. Under the bits and claw hammer all was dry, down to the bent nails and rusty bolts in the bottom.

The front door lay on two sawhorses in the front room. Ezra had worked a day making tongue-and-groove joints in three two-by-ten chestnut planks, and gluing and clamping them. For good measure he'd screwed two rails onto the interior surface. Yesterday he had chiseled for the hinge butts both on door and frame.

He carried two spare sawhorses to the yard. Rain had turned to a hovering mist, and it wouldn't be long before sunshine. He briefly re-gretted building the door out of chestnut. To lift it off the sawhorses was all he could do by himself. He leaned it onto some gunnysacks and scooted it against the porch column, then moved the yard sawhorses closer and slowly tilted the door onto them.

Inside he got his ruler and pencil and a small box holding galvanized hinges and a lock bought in Waynesville. Ezra rattled the box with satisfaction. Unfolding the paper template packed with the lock, he put it on the door and marked the spindle hole. He fitted a three-quarter-inch bit into the brace, tightened the chuck, and started two pilot holes. A voice startled him.

Hannah's brother, Jake, often helped Ezra, sweeping and carrying lumber and making himself handy. Hannah had encouraged Ezra to be kind to Jake, who at first was scared of his brother-in-law. "Morning, Mr. Ezra," he chirped.

Ezra peered at Jake, who was twelve or thirteen, Ezra never could remember. Kate Carter had, according to everyone, spoiled her son, known to be averse to hard work unless it involved food, and then not the picking of it, but the stringing or breaking of it, preferably in the shade. At the house site Ezra tried to keep him working instead of talking, but it was a battle.

The boy wore overalls with the right gallus twisted and a black patch on the left knee, one leg rolled a bit higher than the other. Jake's face was almost round as the hand-me-down wire spectacles that curled behind his ears. In a certain light he reminded folks of an owl. "You come to help an old man today?"

"You ain't old, Mr. Ezra. What're you fixing to do?"

"I'm about to bore a hole in this door."

"What for?"

"Starting the morning with one damn question after another, eh? Well, I'll show you." Ezra pointed to the box. "See that? It goes on the door."

"What is it?" Jake took off his glasses and examined a metal piece about four inches square.

"See? It goes here like this, and then you put this part on the jamb yonder and when they come together you can"—he pulled a key out of his pocket—"use this to lock it up."

Jake screwed up his forehead. "Why do you need to lock your door?"

"So nobody can steal." Ezra laid the parts on the porch, and hefted the brace and bit.

"Papa says anybody wants something of his'n bad enough to steal it, they might need it more than he does."

"Sounds like something Will would say—Jake, let me tell you something. I been out of this valley, where they's people wouldn't think a thing about breaking in a man's house." Ezra scowled. "Son, the whole damn country's full of Yankee carpetbaggers scuttling off these trains like buzzards with luggage. It ain't but a jump from Asheville to Catalooch anymore. See, once Yankees see these mountains they'll want them for themselves, mark my words. Their lumber companies are already in here buying up timber, I hear. These locks are insurance, or at least a stumbling block, to slow them down enough to let me get a gun and take care of my bidness."

"You'd shoot a fellow, Mr. Ezra?"

"In a trice, if they threatened me. Or your sister."

Jake brightened. "You reckon Hannah's going to make me an uncle today?"

"Son, I don't know. I'll sure be glad when she's on her feet. I ain't been eating too regular lately." He looked around. "Kate didn't leave you no dinner, did she?"

When Jake shook his head Ezra returned to the door. "Here, what say we put this lock on? Hold this door steady so I can drill a straight hole."

Ezra contemplated the scribing on the door's edge and Jake went to the other side. He put his hands on the door, palms down and pointed out. "Like this?"

"Fine, boy. Just don't let it move." Ezra set the screw point into his pilot hole, straightened the brace, and began to turn. A shaving curled like smoke. Jake put his whole weight on the door, puffed his cheeks, and held his breath while Ezra bored. After the bit broke through Ezra backed it out and smoothed the edges with a rat-tail file. Jake started kicking pebbles.

"Get back here, boy. We got to drill another one."

Jake shrugged. "What for?"

"You got a top hole for the doorknob and a bottom for the keyhole. How else you going to get in if it's locked?"

"Why, Sis'll let you in."

"What if she ain't there, Mr. Smarty?"

"Then your boy can do it."

"I ain't got no boy yet. Just hold the damn door down." He drilled, cleaned, and smoothed the second hole. "Now fetch me that square thing." Ezra got his hammer and nail and Jake brought the lock. After making three pilot holes, they screwed the box onto the door. "You reckon me and you could turn this thing over?"

"Sure."

"OK, let's scoot the door toward the edge of the sawhorse, then you get your hands under that edge and make sure it don't go down. I'll push the other edge up and we'll flip it. That's when we'll swap ends—you run to the other side and catch this'n as it flips towards you. We'll set it down real gentle."

After they turned it Ezra fastened the round plate on the outside of the door. Then he looked for the escutcheon. "Here, help me find this damn keyhole cover." Ezra liked to brag that he could see a flea on a gnat's ass from a hundred yards but it was Jake who found the plate—under the box it had come in. Ezra gave him a grudging smile and screwed it on, then slipped the exterior knob onto the square spindle and tightened the set screw. He put the spindle through the hole in the lock and installed the interior knob. When he turned the knob the latch moved in and out. The smaller knob turned the deadbolt with a satisfying click. Ezra looked proud as a jaybird. "Works like a charm."

"How's that going to keep a body out?"

"It ain't finished, boy. Keep your shirt on."

They put the hinge butts on, reversed their routine to get the door on the porch, walked the door to the opening, and hung it. Ezra swung it, satisfied it was plumb. He mounted the strike plate on the inside jamb. All came together perfectly. He locked it with the metal catch and tried the key. "Now you see how I'm going to get in my new house?"

"What if you lose your key?"

"Son, you ask too many questions. Besides, I never lost nothing in my life. I'm a man that keeps up with his things."

They worked in silence for several minutes, until Jake cleared his throat. Then he coughed. "You ain't sick, are you?" Ezra asked.

"No, sir, I was just wondering if I could get that nickel, remember, for working last week."

Ezra took off his hat. "Well, if you ain't the beat. Friday's payday around here. If a man don't show up on payday I figure he ain't hungry enough to get paid." Ezra pocketed the key.

"I had chores for Papa till dark. Then Mama said I didn't need to be running around of a night."

Ezra's stomach growled. "So you think I orta give you that nickel even though you didn't show up Friday?"

"Yes, sir." Jake looked at the floor.

"I can't do bidness with a man who won't look me in the eye." Ezra reached deeply in his pocket for a leather pouch. Loosening the string, he shook a single nickel into Jake's palm. "Be sure Friday you show up, you hear?"

"Yes, sir, Lord willing and Papa don't have me doing something else, I'll be here."

"Good." Ezra eyed the boy. "Tell you what. Let's you and me go to the house and see if Hannah's had that young'un. If she has, Kate'll fix us some dinner."

Jake leaped into the yard and started running toward Ezra's cabin.

"Wait a damn minute." Ezra caught up with him, and complained of his belly all the way back. In the yard they heard a baby squall. Jake stopped still as a stone. "I'm an uncle," he said.

Ezra stepped on the porch. "Stay here, boy. I'll see to things and you can look at him—God, I hope it's a him—in a minute."

Jake slouched on the porch until Ezra emerged with a squalling baby swaddled in a quilt. Beaming, Ezra stepped into the yard. "John Jacob Carter, meet Mr. Zebulon Baird Banks. He's a man to make his father proud."

Zebulon Baird Banks was not happy to be away from his mother, but Ezra strutted around the yard, showing him the barn and the outhouse and the corn crib. He nuzzled his son's cheek with his stubbly face, which made Zeb scream louder and turn a deeper shade of red. Kate appeared, shaking a finger.

"Ezra Banks, bring that young'un back before he pops a mainspring, or you won't get no dinner a-tall, you hear?"

Ezra gave Zeb to his grandmother, who stroked the baby's cheek with her fingertip and took him back inside.

Ezra looked at Jake. "Did you ever see such a head of hair? He'll be a fine-looking man, that boy will. Looks like he's got his mother's chin. A fine set of lungs, too—did you hear him squall?"

"When can I play with him?"

"Right now all he wants is his mama's tit. But we'll learn him things, won't we?"

"You bet. Before long he'll be helping us on the new house. I bet he'll help us build everything else, too."

"Damn, son, we'll have that house built before he can help on it, or I'll be crazy by then. But we'll have something for him to help with. I'm about to need a barn."

8

PLOW NEW GROUND

Anyone watching Henry Sutton plow would have said he was in deep conversation with his mule Sal's backside. Henry had found himself standing asleep behind her more than once, so now he kept up a dialogue not so much with her as with himself as they worked. He stopped and wiped his forehead as Sal flicked her ears and snorted. He said, "Get up, old gal," and she slowly responded.

"Used to think," he said, "when I was growing up on Hemphill I'd not leave it for nothing. Mama said where you was born was where God wanted you. She was a fool for trout. Claimed she could tell what creek they come from by how they tasted. She was uncommon fond of Cataloochee trout, said they tasted cleaner'n any others. Pop knew Cataloooch pretty well, he worked for the Carters on Big Catalooch ever now and then, putting up hay and building fence. When it was raining he'd wear his big old slicker, he'd line them pockets with leaves and fill them with fish and bring them home to Mama.

"One night Pop and I headed up to Hemphill Bald and down Cataloochee Mountain. It was a big old strawberry moon, leastways that's what Mama called it, but we knew an Indian woman called it the corn moon or something, let's see, it was green corn in June and ripe corn in July, anyhow it was June, moon busting bright so we didn't have no trouble getting down the mountain, we was in the creek by daylight. Up in the morning we'd fished that hole in front of the church and was on our way down the road looking for another when Cumi Bennett and her two oldest girls, Callie and Bess, come from down at Nellie. Miz Bennett nodded to Pop but paid me no mind. Callie, she smiled at me and that was all she wrote. Lit me up like a firecracker. After while Pop ast me if I was tired of fishing and I said I reckon and he said did it have to do with that gal and I didn't say nothing. He said she's a pippin all right.

"I come back quick as I could and asked if I could court her. Took two year fore she'd agree to marry. One evening after church, lessee, that was 1878 'cause I was nineteen then, I give her some roses and ast are you going to marry me, and she said she would if she could stay in Cataloochee. Said to her it was the Garden of Eden. How can a man argue with that? And that's how come I'm plowing in Cataloochee instead of Hemphill. It's the beatenest thing, don't know if it's happenchance, or God's will like preachers say—what in tarnation is that school bell going off for?"

Stopping Old Sal, he stared toward the schoolhouse. The bell stopped for a quarter of a minute, then rang again ten times, the sound hanging in the air like a man could touch it. It wasn't a fire; at least there was no more smoke than cookfires and burning trees would account for. Two o'clock on Friday afternoon, he thought, that fool bell shouldn't have been ringing.

He dropped the reins, patted Sal and told her to stay put, and started toward the house. Callie stood on the porch shading her eyes. As Henry got to the road Silas Wright came tearing from up the creek on his big black mare. Silas, Henry's up-creek neighbor and a man given to no foolishness, stopped and asked Henry did he want a ride. Henry got up behind Silas and they tore off down the road. Henry waved at Callie and held on for dear life.

They met people both running and riding, from all around the midsection of the valley. Close to the creek, they rode in deep shade from the trees on the left and the mountain on the right. Henry thought he saw the white flash of a doe's tail across the creek. At the schoolhouse patch a crowd of children and women milled about.

Henry scooted off the mare and found the schoolteacher. "Miss Valerie, what in the world is going on?" After he spoke he remembered to take off his hat. She was only eighteen, a mess of freckles dotting her face, red hair fiery in the sunshine. What little hair Henry had went six ways from Sunday.

Her expression said he ought to put his hat back on. "There's trouble at Lucky Bottom, Mr. Sutton. I'm keeping the pupils until it's safe for them to go home."

"Much obliged," Henry said.

"Let's head back thataway," Silas hollered. Henry hauled himself back on the horse and Silas sawed the reins. About a quarter of a mile from the church someone had broken a hole in Marion Carter's new worm fence, laid a couple of months ago from rails split in the dark of the moon. Marion would sure get put out over that hole, Henry thought, for he was a man who liked things right, planted by the signs, even started tanning the leather for his new work boots when the moon was just right.

That morning Marion had eyeballed the huge black gum Lizzie had seen when she'd visited him at the new ground. The trunk was four feet in diameter and rose fifty feet before there was a limb. Then it bifurcated, looking like a Pentecostal preacher straining an altar call among perfect heathens.

It was the custom to cut smaller trees and grub the stumps, but large trees required girdling one season and burning the next, over and over, until they were gone. Marion slung coal oil high on the trunk and lit it with a kitchen match. Fire leaped up the trunk lizard-like, spiraling fast. A hawk watched atop the left-hand limb, lifted, circled once, and flew toward Noland Mountain.

The trees were mostly gone, and Marion's immediate task was to bust out a half acre for sweet potatoes. Every couple of feet plow points caught roots of bygone plants and he halted the mule, backed the plow, and grubbed them out. He found a black arrowhead and put it in his overalls pocket for Lizzie.

At noon he ate dinner in the shade of a poplar opposite the black gum. Lizzie had packed a piece of pork roast, some corn bread, half a baked sweet potato, and a few dilly beans. For dessert he bit into a fried apple pie, fruit squishing onto his bare cheek. As he wiped his face with his shirtsleeve, a flake of crust fell into his lap. Marion finished the pie and washed it down with some sweet milk. He looked toward the flat, where he'd laid out foundation logs for a new house, then put hat over eyes for a short nap. He liked a full belly almost as much as he liked work with results to it.

When he awoke the tree was still burning. Wind came from down the valley and boiling coils of smoke trailed west from the upper limbs. He and the mule got back to work. The last thing was, after a while, an odd crack, like thunder, overhead.

As Henry and Silas dismounted, several men wrestled with an outsized smoking limb that had fallen just behind the mule, now standing thirty yards away. The limb was big around as a man at the base and arched upward about twenty feet. Under it Henry saw spindly legs askew, feet shod in Marion's new boots, toes downward. Henry cried, "No!" and ran to help the struggling men.

Turning the limb enough to see if the man under it might still be alive, they found Marion Carter, impaled by the remnant of a smaller limb that poked out his belly on the other side. Blood oozed from his mouth and nose.

When they wrestled the limb to an angle they could manage, Henry and Silas managed to pull Marion off it. Absently, Henry put the hat back on Marion's head, then he and Silas laid him in the wagon bed. It was all Henry could do to keep from vomiting.

One of Marion's eyes skewed far right and the other looked straight ahead. A pink pump knot shone on his forehead and charcoal streaked his face like Indian paint. A man brought a bucket of water, and they wiped Marion's face clean with their shirttails. "I sure hate for Lizzie to have to see this," Henry said. Over and over he said, "God, why?"

"Somebody go tell Lizzie," Silas said. "Get some women to help. We'll hitch the mule and bring him on directly." Folks ran toward Lizzie's house, dreading to face a woman who did not yet know she was a widow.

As a black clot of blood seeped over the wagon bed, Silas unhitched Marion's overalls and unbuttoned his shirt. The limb had gone all the way through Marion just above the navel. Seeping from that hole were what Henry figured to be intestines. They cleaned his front off best they could and Silas rebuttoned the shirt. Henry tucked it in and rehitched the overalls. Marion's tobacco and pocketknife were in the bib along with a dirt-covered arrowhead. His side pockets held a buckeye worn black and slick, a handkerchief, and a clip with a two-dollar bill. Henry put these in his pocket for Lizzie.

Silas hitched the mule to the wagon while Henry found Marion's coal oilcan, lantern, and dinner bucket. Henry's mind raced. Marion wasn't but thirty-six or -seven, he thought, about to build a new house, start a new farm. God, it ain't fair. It just ain't fair. Still, there's one thing—he never knew what hit him. A man could be in worse shape. Henry flicked the reins and started back to the house with his burden, not urging the mule to hurry. Silas tore home to get his wife, Rhetta.

Henry took his time. Approaching Hiram and Mary's place he saw Mary, having heard the bell, standing on the porch holding Mandy Elizabeth. As the grim procession neared she motioned to Henry, and sat heavily in a rocker, baby in lap. Henry braked the wagon, removed his hat, and trudged to tell what had happened to her brother-in-law. "He never knew what hit him," he said, trying the line aloud.

Mary took a deep breath. "Lord, Henry Sutton, that ain't no consolation to Lizzie, least not yet. Go on with him. Hiram's due back from Waynesville any time. Go, before George Henry wakes from his nap. Soon's Hiram gets here we'll come on."

"Yes'm. I sure hate it."

"We all do, Henry Sutton. We all do."

At Marion's place Rhetta and Callie sat inside with Lizzie, whose wailing rattled the bare front yard. Folks on the front porch motioned Henry to pull the wagon around back.

The women had covered the table on the back porch with oilcloth, and Henry and Silas laid Marion there. After Henry put the mule in the barn he and Silas, with mattock and shovels, headed across the field and up the hill to the cemetery on a path so steep they used their tools for purchase. They dug a grave beside Old Levi, Marion's father, leaving a space for Granny Lib. When they returned, the women had made Marion into a presentable corpse lying in a casket on a backless bench in the front room.

Henry removed his hat and went inside, Silas following. Lizzie was upstairs, with Callie, the women said, praying. Henry bent to Marion, who might have been asleep, except for the knot on his forehead. He touched Marion's cold hand and tears started from his eyes. He laid Marion's things on the table.

Outside, he blew his nose and looked across the field. Toward Lucky Bottom smoke trailed in the fading daylight. "Silas, you can see that widow maker burning down there, you know it?" Silas nodded and spat, careful not to hit the flowers. "What kind of luck is it when a man's minding his own business and a dad-gum tree falls on him?"

Silas stretched to his full height, then sat on the step. "I don't reckon I know. What I do know is a good man is laying dead in there. They'll set up with him tonight and we'll carry him to his grave tomorrow. And we won't never see him again till we get to heaven ourselves."

"You reckon he had an idea he was about to die, Silas?"

"Don't know, Henry. Seems a man's always just a cat hair away from dying around here, whether it's a tree falling on him or snakebite or his horse spooking and throwing him off and busting his head open. Or the old devil getting him drunk and making him crazy, like when Uncle Lige Howell got tiddly, remember? He thought that old she-bear was an Indian and tried to run her off with a hoe. This place is pretty, and I love it, but by God it can be deadly. Marion yonder's proof of that."

Henry squinted. "My brother died of the bloody gravel when he was ten or eleven, and howled like a painter for days. At least Marion don't have to look forward to that."

"Yep, I hope when my time comes it's like Marion, sudden-like . . . how you reckon them women got him looking so good?"

"I don't know. He made a right good corpse."

They sat and watched the light fade. Soon they saw moths, and smelled the food neighbors had brought, and heard crickets start. Callie and Rhetta found them silent and watchful and told them to come in for some fried chicken.

After supper Silas and Henry rode Silas's horse back up the creek, leaving Rhetta and Callie to sit with Marion. Silas stopped the horse at Henry's, where they listened to the horse's breath and the creek's murmur. Henry dismounted and looked up to the zenith. "Look at them mare's tails moving from the southwest. Might rain tomorrow."

A screech owl hollered close to the house. "That'll tell you about rain coming," said Silas. "I'm glad I live a mile up the creek. You get to listen to him tonight."

Henry waved and Silas rode on up the creek. "Never did believe that foolishness about a screech howl," Henry muttered. "I've heard them holler in dog days, when it wouldn't rain for weeks."

If Marion had died the Saturday before, the Methodist preacher would have helped bury him, but he'd not be back to Cataloochee for a month. They might have found the Baptist preacher, but Marion would have climbed out of his coffin if he knew a Baptist might bury him. Silas and Hiram had been close friends since they were children, so Hiram and Lizzie asked him to say some words over Marion.

Silas put up the horse and heard the cow's discomforted lowing.

Daisy got milked by lantern light. When Silas got back he lit lamps in the front room and kitchen, then built a fire in the cookstove. He threw out the stale coffee, but decided to reuse that morning's grounds.

In the front room he found their Bible and sat in his chair, next to Rhetta's before the fireplace. The perking pot called him to pour coffee yet too hot to sip. He poured some whiskey in the coffee, then looked at the jug. What the hell, he thought, Rhetta ain't here, and took a deep drink.

Rhetta was Granny Lib's niece, the daughter of Lib's sister and her husband, a Morgan from Buncombe. Rhetta Morgan's eyes were the color of green bottle glass. Silas had taken an immediate shine to her, even though Rhetta's mother was square-shaped, and his father had told him never to court a daughter whose mother was broad-beamed.

It wasn't that Rhetta was a hardshell or a teetotaler. She'd made it clear to Silas before they married that she didn't mind him drinking as long as he didn't get drunk and didn't keep it out in the open.

He found some Scriptures he thought might fit, then went to the front porch. The breeze had died. Crickets chirped over the racket of the creek. Too late for peepers, too early for katydids. He lit his pipe and when he finished his coffee he poured the cup half full of whiskey. "I need to think, and I need to sleep. This'll help both." He went back to the front room and sat down.

About two that morning he started, suddenly awake, Bible in his lap. A screech owl hollered across the creek. "Damned thing followed me home. Jesus. I need to get to bed." He removed his boots, blew out the lamps, and got in bed, clothes and all.

Silas rode through the gray morning toward Marion's place, where he found all manner of animals and buggies and wagons. Silas tied his horse in the barn lot and walked toward the porch, where Henry in his Sunday overalls met him.

"Morning. You don't look too pert."

"That fool owl followed me home, so I could have slept better. But I'll do. I reckon I got to."

Hiram came out, letting the door creak slowly shut. As they shook hands, Silas tried to avoid staring at Hiram's red-streaked eyes. "Friend, I've been better. It hurts like hell to lose a brother. I'm beholden to you for your words today. Lizzie wants to see you."

Silas hugged Marion's daughter Charlotte and shook hands with her brand-new husband. In the front room, dark except where Marion's white pine casket lay on a bench under the north window, Silas nodded to Rhetta and Callie, who sat in straight chairs on either end. The mantel clock was stopped at a quarter to three, about the time Marion died, and the mirror had been draped with a black cloth. Lizzie stood, arms folded, before the fireplace, her three-year-old, Levi Marion, beside her.

Silas, hat in hand, went to Lizzie, who gave herself to be hugged. "We done lost a fine man. Anything Rhetta and me can do, just holler." He tousled young Levi's hair, and the boy buried his face in his mother's black dress.

"We'll get by with God's help," she said. "Thank you for what you're going to say."

"I didn't bring a Bible. I figured to use Marion's if you wouldn't care."

She nodded and pointed to the table. Silas figured the last hand to touch it had been Marion's, when he had read to his family just before bedtime two nights ago. He picked it up and headed to the porch, rubbing its stiff cover with his thumb. Lizzie walked to Marion's coffin, where Rhetta and Callie silently flanked her.

Meanwhile, Hiram gathered the immediate family into the front room. The children were quiet, except for little Zeb Banks, who fussed in Hannah's arms. Ezra, who had never met Marion, had not bothered to journey over the mountain.

Hiram came to the porch. "It's time," he said quietly. Silas nodded and made his way past a whole raft of cousins and neighbors.

Lizzie sat beside Marion's head, holding her least one, Mattie, in her lap. Eight months old, she wore a white dress and crocheted booties. Young Levi beside her stared at his father's darkening face and held her arm. Charlotte and her new husband stood behind Lizzie. Arranged around them were Silas's namesake, fifteen and sullen-looking; Mary Bell, thirteen but nearly tall as Silas; Hub, eleven and the spitting image of his mother; and Jonathan, an eight-year-old worrying with his right shoe like his foot hurt. The rest of the room held Marion and Lizzie's brothers and sisters. Propinquity dictated who stood in the kitchen and on the porches and in the yard. Even dogs seemed to sit in ranks.

Silas opened the outsized clothbound Bible, the only book this family owned, and cleared his throat. In the silence he heard random raindrops hitting the roof. "You all help me now," he started. "The Twenty-third Psalm." He read the ancient poem haltingly at first but soon was buoyed by the rhythm of the rest of the voices. "The Lord is my shepherd; I shall not want," they began. "He maketh me to lie down in green pastures: he leadeth me beside the still waters." The rhythm of the creek was counterpoint to their recitation. When they finished the part about the cup running over, they took a collective breath and with conviction finished: "Surely goodness and mercy shall follow me all the days of my life: and I will dwell in the house of the Lord forever. Amen." Lizzie rocked back and forth in her chair.

"Yesterday," he said, "this good man went to plow new ground. He hadn't no idea he'd be laying here like this today. A man with a good wife and sturdy family. A man, like the rest of us, trying his best to keep food on the table and a roof over their heads. He was starting to build a new house. A man who'd no more think of cheating anybody than try to fly. I never knowed Marion Carter to do nothing low-down, unless you count that time he busted me back of the head with a rock when we was eleven or twelve. Of course, truth be known, I asked for it."

Some in the crowd laughed and others blew in their handkerchiefs. Children unused to shoes on a weekday shuffled their feet.

"I tried to think about what comfort there is in this book in this time of woe. For a fact Marion was a baptized Christian and is now talking with Jesus. It's all right with his soul, no matter how it is with us. But I kept coming back to a couple of things."

He thumbed backward from Psalms. "This is from the Book of Job. Says here, 'Although affliction cometh not forth of the dust, neither doth trouble spring out of the ground; yet man is born unto trouble, as the sparks fly upward.' The fifth chapter, verses six and seven.

"And this here is from Ecclesiastes. 'To every thing there is a season, and a time to every purpose under heaven.' " When he finished that passage he turned ahead. "This here's in the same book. 'For man also knoweth not his time: as the fishes that are taken in an evil net, and as the birds that are caught in the snare; so are the sons of men snared in an evil time, when it falleth suddenly upon them.' "

He laid the Bible on the mantel. "Folks, I ain't no preacher and I ain't had much schooling. But I see Marion yonder and it don't seem right that today we'll put him in the ground he was plowing just yesterday. We've all knowed men that weren't worth a plugged nickel and died of old age, smiling in their sleep. Here we got a good young man tore from his family, untimely-like. All I can say is God's got a plan and this book says we are part of it. Some of us was born in Catalooch, like Marion. Some of us wandered in here, like Henry Sutton, and married into it. But all of us is part of that plan. And when we get to heaven we can ask him why. Right now all we got is what we remember about Marion Carter, and we got to keep them memories alive. He was a good man and I ain't going to forget him. And, Lizzie, we'll finish that new house down there for you and the young'uns, you can be sure of that."

Silas looked at his hands. "I reckon we ought to pray." Lizzie cried out once, then clasped Mattie to her chest. Many heads bowed, while others stared at Marion and Lizzie. "Heavenly Father," Silas started, "look down on your poor people in this here place. We'd sure love some comfort. We put ourselves in your hands and commit this good man into your ground. Bless this widow and these young'uns. Keep us from sinning. For Jesus' sake, amen." Others joined his "amen" and feet shuffled. Thunder growled outside.

Rhetta and Callie took Lizzie's arm and helped her stand; she leaned over Marion with little Mattie, who reached for her father's face. Lizzie guided her hand, smoothing Marion's hair. She started to sob, then caught a last ounce of composure, letting Rhetta and Callie lead her and the children upstairs.

Marion's brother John fitted the lid over Marion. He plucked a screwdriver and six screws from his inside pocket and meticulously tightened them before he and Hiram gripped the head of the casket and Silas and Henry the foot. They carried it outside, where nephews waited with Marion's mule hitched to a sled with sourwood runners, and tied the coffin to the sled. Lightning and thunder were nearly instantaneous. A raindrop splatted the lid. "Boys, get your uncle up there before it comes a gullywasher," said John.

Henry and Silas watched the procession of nephews, four on each side of the mule and sled. "Boys, it's bad luck to watch something out of sight," Hiram said. "Let's get inside before we get drownded."

"I always heard that happy is the corpse the rain falls on," Henry said, as they headed for the porch.

Hiram turned to Henry. "Least Marion ain't worrying about rain now. Or how to feed a family."

John and Hiram brought the bench that had been Marion's bier to the front porch, where Charlotte appeared with her least sister, Mattie, wide-eyed and curious. Hannah Banks came out with her Zeb, only six weeks old, some seven months Mattie's junior.

Henry fingered his chin. "You know, it wouldn't surprise me if them babies didn't get married and raise their own family some day."

Silas thought a moment. "Well, that Zeb Banks is half Carter hisself. Hannah's daddy, Will, is a brother to Marion's daddy, Levi. That makes them young'uns second cousins, don't it?"

Hiram pondered. "I think that makes them first cousins oncet removed, but that could be same as a second cousin. I heard of such marrying before."

The nephews returned to the porch just as another crash of thunder shook the house and the heavens opened. Inside, everyone ate like thrashers. Silas and Henry brought plates to the bench and listened to rain cascading down the shake roof. They finished together but went for more one by one, so they wouldn't lose their seats. Henry stopped after his second plate. "I'm eating like this's my last meal. I ought to quit."

"Go ahead," Silas said. "Marion might've eat heartier yesterday had he knowed what was about to happen to him." He looked down the valley. "At least that old widow maker ain't burning no more."

9

You're Both of Them

Hiram Carter had to admit it was a pretty desk. He walked around it in the afternoon sun, admiring its finish, workmanship, and heft. It would take two stout folks to maneuver it into a room, and three would be even better. He had built it mostly from wild cherry and walnut, and made it to sit out in a room so a man would be proud to see all sides.

It was the nicest piece Hiram had ever built, and it galled him that he had made it for a man as ornery as Ezra Banks. Ezra had ridden over Noland Mountain to Hiram's farm back in the winter and told Hiram he was building a new house with an office, and he wanted a desk with three drawers, one of them to lock. He had sketched it on a piece of brown paper.

"Banks, that's six foot wide. That'd take from now to harvest," Hiram said. "You could get one in Asheville a whole lot quicker."

Ezra ran his finger up the side of his crooked nose. "But it'd have something wrong with it, sure as there's a Kingdom. You're known as a man who don't let nothing out unless it's right."

"Maybe so, but it'll cost you ten dollars. Plus fifty cents haul bill. That's ten-fifty cash money, and I need half down to start."

"I can get one in Asheville for five."

"I thought you said it'd have something wrong with it."

"I did. And it would. That's why I'm asking you to build me a five-dollar desk that don't. You ought to be neighborly enough not to charge me twice that." Ezra's lips twisted into a corner but it wasn't a smile. "And you ought to be glad I'm not asking for a kinfolk discount, seeing as how I'm married to your cousin. I pay what things is worth."

Hiram saw Ezra meant to have the desk no matter what, so he finally agreed to Ezra's price, cursing both Ezra and himself repeatedly while he built it. But, he had to admit, it had helped keep his mind off his brother Marion's death in the spring, and nine months' work made the desk shine like something a man might see in a window at Morris Rich's Atlanta store. The drawers fit precisely and the lock worked slick as soapstone. All it needed was another coat of oil, and a couple of blankets to pad it for its journey over the mountain into Little Cataloochee.

Normally such a large piece would have its legs pegged after going into the room it would live in, to assure it could get into tight places without being marred. But Hiram had already pegged and glued the legs into the apron because Ezra had assured him there would be plenty of help to unload. He oiled it, wiped the excess oil with a chamois cloth, then wrapped the top in old woolen blankets. After tying the blankets with twine, he backed the wagon to the porch and wormed the desk in. He tied it to the cattle sides and shook it to see if it would move. It did not.

On his way to the house he found a white clover bloom for Mary, whom he found squatting by Granny Lib's rocker, trying to get her to talk. The last time she had uttered a word was to Lizzie, the spring before Marion was killed. Hiram gave Mary the sprig of clover. "Mama

Carter, look what Hiram brought in." She twisted the stem between her fingers and the spinning flower held the old woman's attention. She extended her knobby hand and Mary put it between her thumb and forefinger.

Mary stood. "Thanks, honey. It'll be a comfort to her. You ready to travel over yonder in the morning?"

He sighed and stretched. "I reckon. You know, if I could buy that rascal for what he's worth and sell him for what he thinks he's worth, we could build a new house and fill a closet with store-bought dresses for you to boot."

"Hiram, I know you don't like him. Nobody much does, except Hannah, and I suspicion she's as wary of him as she is in love. But you and him got business, so you might as well quit complaining—and bring my blankets back, too."

The dug road was the closer way over into Little Cataloochee but its width would not accommodate a wagon. So Hiram set out early in the morning, beside the creek, and up past the Bennett place, where the Yankees had tied him up in the barn with his father, Levi, nearly twenty years before. Sometimes he had nightmares about that night, but in dreams the fire was too huge and noisy to have happened to such a house as he saw this morning.

Halfway to the gap the road down into Little Cataloochee turned left and flattened beside Little Cataloochee Creek, the only level spot before the Carter and Banks places, after which the road wound up the mountain in a series of switchbacks. It was late afternoon when Hiram finally got to Will and Kate's place, where he planned to spend the night.

Hiram was uncommonly fond of Will's apple brandy, and both men were feeling right by the time Kate hollered at them to come for supper.

Will sat at the head of the table and Hiram took Kate's place at the foot, and around it sat Kate and their five children, who had been told to put on their company manners. They had so few visitors the youngest didn't know what that meant. Sadie was the oldest left at home, nearly seventeen, the spitting image of her mother. Normally serious, she could not help but laugh at Hiram's tales of his trips to South Carolina, including one about getting caught in a four-day deluge with a wagonload of peaches in Inman. Before he could get them up the mountain, half of them had rotted, so he ended up trading them to a hog farmer for a hound dog. Jake, Will's only son, hardly took his eyes off Hiram, as though he hailed from some exotic land. After dinner Will and Hiram retired to the porch for a smoke, Jake following closely.

"Don't know what to think about politics this year," said Will. "I'd have thought President Arthur'd been as bad a one as we've had, stepping in when Mr. Garfield got shot down, but derned if he ain't turned out a good man."

"That's right," said Hiram. "You think he'll get the nomination this fall?"

"Well, I hope so. Not that I love a dad-jim Republican, mind you, but he's turned out a good man and so is Grover Cleveland, so either way we'll be all right." Will chuckled. "So you've got a desk for my son-in-law," said Will. "My back's out or I'd help you in the morning. Jake here'll have to do, I reckon. You know, I never thought I'd have a son-in-law fancy enough to own a desk, much less have one—how do you say it—permissioned?"

"Ordered," said Hiram, "that's what I'd call it."

"Don't much like him, do you?"

"No, Will, I got to say I don't."

Will looked at Jake. "Come here, boy, we ain't saying nothing you oughtn't hear." Will tousled Jake's hair as he sat on the first step. "He is a study, Ezra Banks is. He's got some hard ways. But he takes good care of Hannah, feeds her good, and I believe he'll do right by his new young'un, Zeb. That's my first grandson." He blew a ring of smoke from his pipe. "I know if I ever hear different, he'll have hell to pay."

"They say he's good at apples."

"Best I ever seen, Hiram. He's got natural talent, and he'll go far if the weather'll let him. Speaking of weather, remember that harricane that tore all my good trees up by the roots?"

"I sure do. We lost a bunch that fall, too."

"Tell us about it," said Jake.

"Not much to tell," said Will. "It was the fall of sixty-six, right after the war. About the only thing still growing around here was apples, and we hoped we'd sell them for a little cash to get us through the winter. Them trees was full of apples, and one night a monster wind come from the top of the gap and stripped damn near every tree from there to the post office. I had two apple trees standing out of forty or fifty after it was over, and they didn't have a Limbertwig on them. Mighty lean winter, let me tell you. Apple makes good firewood, sweet-smelling smoke. But, Lord, I hated to burn them trees." He looked at Jake. "Boy, you best hope you don't never see nothing like that."

Hiram peered at Jake over his pipe. "Son, I wasn't much older'n you are now when that happened. Your papa's right—it was a pure mess, that's all there was to it."

"Was you hungry that winter?"

"We got by. I expect your papa's folks were worse off than us."

Will stared toward the old cabin. "We was living down there back then. We ate so dad-jim many turnips that winter I can't eat them no more."

Kate and the girls came out on the porch. "You've come a far cry from that, Will Carter," she said, as she arranged herself in the rocker Hiram vacated for her. "You eat good nowadays."

"If you eat like that all the time, I might have to move to this side of Noland Mountain," said Hiram.

Kate cocked her head at him. "Mary might have something to say about that. She's got a reputation for her kitchen, you know."

Ezra's house sat a hundred yards up the road around a small bend in the creek. In the morning Hiram and Jake bounced together in the wagon seat to the front yard, then Hiram backed the wagon to the porch and braked the wheels.

Ezra came out with a bag of nails and a piece of trim in one hand and a hammer in the other. He laid the board against the wall and put the hammer handle through the loop on his overalls.

"Morning, Hiram." They shook hands. "Boy, it's about time old

Will got some man's work out of you," he said to Jake. Ezra looked at the desk. "I see you got it padded right stout."

"I've hauled a thing or two on that old road, Ezra. I take pains to protect my work. Last winter you said we'd have all kinds of help here to unload. Where's it at?"

"I thought them Davis boys would have been here by now. They been helping me trim things out, but you can't keep nobody decent."

"You mean the three of us got to get that thing in there by ourselves?"

"More like two."

"What do you mean?" asked Hiram.

"Throwed my back out the other day lifting shakes to the roof. But I can help guide it inside."

"Guide it," Hiram muttered as he went to the front door. "Mind if I see where it's going?"

"Help yourself," said Ezra. "In the left-hand room yonder. Kindly in the center."

The odor of newness stung Hiram's nose as he walked through the front door, which, in his opinion, was hung the wrong way. They barely had room to straighten the desk before making an immediate turn into Ezra's office. "Wish I hadn't glued the legs on," he said, and walked outside. "Might need to take that door down."

"It'll likely be all right," said Ezra.

"I'd feel better if we could take the door off."

"Just keep the blankets on it," Ezra insisted.

"Suit yourself." Hiram untied the legs and stowed the rope before scooting the desk away from the side of the wagon.

"What you want me to do, Cousin Hiram?" asked Jake.

"Take it by the legs and lift it on the porch. Then we'll turn it over."

As they lifted and turned it Jake grunted proudly. "You boys act like that damn thing's heavy," Ezra said.

Hiram wiped his brow. "Ought to be. I don't cut no corners when I make something." He looked at Jake. "Now let's pick it up. You take them two legs through the door and I'll straighten to you. I hope we got enough room to get my end inside and turn, too."

They made it in the front door without incident but the interior doors were narrower. Ezra stood in the office doorway with a hand on the top leg to guide it. "Careful now," he said to Jake.

The front legs slipped in, and Hiram began to straighten until he heard Jake's feet shuffle fast and felt the desk jerk sideways. Ezra's hand caught the leg as the desktop hit the door jamb. Hiram tried to correct on his end but heard the blanket rip on the metal lock. "Damn, boys, pick it up," he yelled. They righted it and slowly wormed it through until they could set it in the middle of the floor. Hiram cut the twine with his hawksbill knife and unwrapped the desk. Jake panted beside the window.

A gouge the shape of the corner of the lock gaped at them. Hiram's face was red and he grimaced as he ran his thumb over it. "Banks, if I wasn't so mad you'd see a growed man cry over this." He straightened up and looked at Ezra. "I can fix this, or I can tell you how to do it, one or the other."

Ezra put his fingernail in the gouge. "I'd sure looked forward to having this desk perfect."

Hiram pursed his lips. "If we'd had some help we wouldn't be in this pickle. Besides, I can fix it so you'd never know it."

"I'd know it 'cause I seen it."

Hiram studied the place, running his finger over it. "I can get a piece of the sister board to that one and inlay it. Once it's finished, you'd never know it."

Ezra shook his head. "Listen here, Hiram, I got to live with it. But you're right, it's my fault for relying on the boy here."

"Mr. Ezra, I 'pologize," Jake quavered.

"Don't fret, son. I'll take it out of your pay so you won't feel too bad on my account."

Ezra carefully shook money from a black leather pouch. "Let's see. This started out a five-dollar desk with fifty cents boot to haul it. I give two dollars down. That leaves three-fifty, but there's that gouge. I figure that makes it a four-dollar desk. Sounds like I owe you two-fifty."

Hiram crossed his arms. "You think I'll take a whole dollar less for something that ain't my fault?"

Ezra folded two dollars around a fifty-cent piece and handed them toward Hiram. "Either that, or go back and get that sister wood you was talking about and fix it. If I can't tell, then you'll get your three-fifty."

Hiram hesitated. "Three dollars and let's call it done."

Ezra smiled. "Hiram, I pay what things is worth. If you think you can make it worth another dollar by another round trip, then feel free."

Hiram pocketed the money, folded Mary's blankets, and took them to the wagon. Ezra leaned against the column and tamped his pipe. "You ain't going away mad, are you?"

Hiram stowed the blankets and sat on the wagon seat. "Let's put it this way, Banks. Somebody told me there wasn't but two sons of bitches in Cataloochee. If that's so, you're both of them." He did not turn to watch Ezra grin at him.

10

SANCTUARY

Hannah gave Ezra three more sons in four years. Then, after a stillborn girl in 1890, she ceased to let Ezra in her bed, declaring what pleasure she derived from their congress insufficient to allay the potential sorrow of losing another child. She moved his things to the room across the hall, where he slept on a cot. He was confident she would not keep him out of her bed for long. Wakeful, he paid close attention to her footsteps, but they never turned toward his bedroom. After six months he morosely carried the cot down to his office, figuring there was no longer reason to climb the stairs.

Sunday mornings he liked to take his time, dress, eat plenty of eggs and bacon, sausage and apples, biscuits and gravy, and drive the family to church in the buggy. But this April Sunday Hannah was in bed with her worst cold in years. She had sent her least ones—George, five, whom folks called a handful, and his brothers Crate and Rufus, three and two—to her mother's. She would have packed off the entire brood, except Zeb pleaded to stay to help take care of her.

Ezra split leftover biscuits with a knife, laid a glob of butter inside, and warmed them in the oven. That, with a dollop of applesauce, was breakfast. As they dressed for church he watched Zeb squirm into his blue chambray shirt and best overalls. At the rate Zeb was growing, Hannah would have to make him new clothes before fall. The boy's cowlick did not bother Ezra, but Hannah would not hear of him leaving for church with it sticking up.

"How in hell do you get this boy's hair to lay down?" yelled Ezra from the front room.

"Quit using that language around my Zeb." Hoarse and weak, she sat up to project her voice downstairs. "Take a wet washrag to it. If that don't do it, find a little lard." She lay back down and tried not to cough.

Zeb was almost seven, skinny, usually quiet but capable of a normal boy's noise and sputter. The rest of Ezra's sons looked like their father, George especially so across the eyes and nose. Zeb looked more like Hannah, rounder of face and lighter of skin, with a dimple in the middle of his chin. He suffered his father to plaster his hair to his forehead with water. Ezra wiped the white shirtfront with his handkerchief. "Stand straight, son. Nothing worse than a slouch." Zeb's hair slowly sprang back. Hannah had made him a short-billed cap with a forward rake to the crown, like Ezra's wartime forage cap. Ezra put it on his son's head. "There, boy. Snap to attention." Zeb grinned and clumsily clicked his heels like his father had taught him. Shoes felt awkward but he liked how they sounded on the floor.

"Go pass your mother's inspection."

Zeb started up the stairs but didn't lift his foot high enough to make the first step. As he tripped, Ezra caught him by the gallus. "You all right?" He straightened his son's cap.

Zeb, more embarrassed than hurt, nodded. "Yes, Papa."

"Then don't kill yourself getting upstairs."

Zeb came quietly into Hannah's room. "Remember to take your cap off in church," she said. "Let me look at you." She sneezed, and blew her nose into a soft rag. "Here." She handed him an Indian head penny. "It's for the collection. Don't let your Papa see it until the basket comes by."

"Thanks, Mama, I won't," he said, shoved the penny in his bib pocket, and kissed her cheek. "I hate you're feeling bad."

"Run along now. I'll be better when you get home."

The Baptists built their church on land the Davis family donated, at the top of the first western ridge past Ola. The ground would grow nothing save catbriers, but did afford a view of the road snaking toward the confluence of the Cataloochee creeks. The back door faced southwest, and down the hill lay a carefully tended cemetery, graves facing east.

Zeb asked if they could walk to church instead of riding in the buggy. "No, son, you'll get your shoes dirty. Get in." Zeb picked up a stick and sat by his father, pointing it at birds and squirrels, emitting noises he imagined guns of various calibers would make as they killed Yankees. When they rounded the corner below the church, Zeb's Sunday school teacher waved from the window. Last Sunday she had promised a treat for perfect attendance.

The boys met in the back left corner of the sanctuary, where, after a head count, prayer, and Bible recitation, the teacher produced a pan of fresh fudge. Ezra remained in the churchyard with the men, whittling, spitting, and talking about weather and the news of the week. The bell announced the end of Sunday school, and Zeb and his cohorts bounded past the men into the cemetery.

Cassius Davis was a tall, walleyed man with a dry wit. A widower, he lived with his father, whom the neighbors referred to as Old Man Davis, so Cash came to be known as Old Man Davis, Junior, even though he was in his forties. Cash grinned at Ezra. "Young'uns got the energy, don't they?"

Ezra nodded and watched Zeb zigzag among the headstones, neither fastest nor slowest, just a boy full of sugar and chocolate. Ezra yelled for him but if Zeb heard he did not let on. Ezra strode into the cemetery and caught Zeb by the shoulder. "Boy, what's got into you?" Ezra took out his handkerchief and wiped Zeb's chin. "What truck have you been eating?"

"Fudge, Papa. It was real good."

Zeb's arm felt taut as fence wire. "Get a drink of water. And don't lose no time getting back."

Zeb raced to the south corner of the graveyard, then whistled and roared like a locomotive as he sped by his father up the hill. Ezra looked the cemetery over slowly, then walked back to the churchyard. In a minute Zeb presented himself, took off his cap, and sputtered.

"Boy, don't start that racket. We got to be quiet in church." They found their place, on the aisle toward the front on the left, where men and boys sat.

The pews, wooden benches about as new as the preacher, were all right angles, with backs that hit adults in places that rendered sleep impossible. Reverend Grady Noland, himself an angular red-haired creation with a turned-up nose, had begun caring for their souls in Little Cataloochee three years before, in 1888. Folks still called him "the new preacher." The pews had been milled about the time he preached his sixth sermon, and still had acquired no comfort or smoothness.

Nor, for that matter, had Brother Noland. Like most Baptist preachers of his day, he had no schooling past the seventh grade. God called, and he answered. From the pulpit he rarely spoke of politics or, for that matter, of religion, unless one considered a tenacious grasp of biblical text a religion. His method was to worry meaning from a passage of Scripture over the space of an hour. A text like "Noah found grace in the eyes of the Lord" was easy—the world was simple, black against white, good against evil, Noah against the rest, God in charge. The Ark floating on the waters became the Ark of the Covenant, both turned into the Cross of Christ, and all bounced back and forth from Genesis to Revelation in relative harmony. On the other hand, if he felt the Lord calling him to preach on "ye shall make images of your emrods, and images of your mice that mar the land," he and the congregation were in for tough slogging.

Ezra's role in church was to keep order among his boys, not to listen to sermons. This morning he hoped to have it easy, with only Zeb to shepherd. Zeb at first knelt on the pew facing backward. Ezra leaned toward his son's left ear. "Straighten up and fly right or I'll wear you out."

Zeb faced front, legs dangling, kicking to some unheard rhythm. Ezra pinched his son's leg just behind his left knee, stopping further motion. Noland and Cash Davis stood. Davis took great pleasure in leading the congregation in song. They first sang "He Leadeth Me," then "My Latest Sun Is Sinking Fast." Noland strode to the pulpit. "Friends, today's scripture is from the Sermon on the Mount, Matthew, chapter six: 'Lay not up for yourselves treasures upon earth, where moth and rust doth corrupt, and where thieves break through and steal: but lay up for yourselves treasures in heaven, where neither moth nor rust doth corrupt, and where thieves do not break through and steal: for where your treasure is, there will your heart be also. Let us pray.' "

Noland began with thanks for the Word of the Lord, then launched into blessings on all the sick and infirm, each by name and circumstances. Zeb no more kept his eyes closed than he was mowing hay. Ezra pointed a warning finger, closed his eyes, and bowed his head. Zeb imitated his father.

Noland started blessing the missionaries in the foreign fields. He began to list countries, Arabia, Belgium, Cameroon, and so on through the alphabet. Zeb decided to hold his breath. When the prayer jumped from Rhodesia to Saskatchewan, Zeb startled Ezra with a loud exhale and sputter. Ezra glowered at the boy, who, in the pause between Turkey and Uruguay, hiccupped, then giggled. Ezra pinched Zeb's shoulder. The boy drew up, and as he did, a splinter of appreciable heft and sharpness plowed into the back of his leg.

Zeb's immediate anguish drowned out Noland's "amen." All eyes were on Ezra, who snatched the screaming boy by the arm and carried him far enough into the cemetery to punish him without everyone hearing.

"Son, what in hell's the matter with you?" he hissed. He shook Zeb's shoulders while the boy yelled bloody murder and grabbed at the back of his leg.

"Papa, it hurts. I didn't do nothing it hurts oh it hurts," Zeb screamed.

Ezra knelt, back straight, and whacked Zeb's butt hard with the flat of his hand. The more racket Zeb made, the harder Ezra, red-faced and furious, bent to his work.

Ezra did not notice Cash Davis, who, after Noland's prayer, had started the congregation singing "There Is a Fountain," then walked to the graveyard and caught Ezra's hand. "You'll have to beat me before you hit this young'un again." Ezra glared at Cash, who pointed at Zeb's overalls leg, marked by a bloody spot the size of a hen egg. "A man draws blood whipping a boy ought to be whipped his own self."

Ezra paled. "I didn't . . ." He knelt and hugged Zeb. "Son, I'm sorry, believe me, dear God, I wouldn't . . ." Zeb wet the shoulder of his father's jacket with tears and snot. Ezra pulled a handkerchief and wiped Zeb's face and nose. "Here, son, blow. Let's have a look."

He pulled Zeb's overalls down to uncover fiery buttocks and an inch-long splinter shoved in the back of his right leg. "My God," said Ezra. "No wonder you were raising Cain." Ezra unclasped his pocketknife as Zeb shook violently and grabbed his father. "If we don't get it out it'll fester. Here, Cash, hold this young'un a second."

Cash took Zeb by his shoulders. "OK, little man. It won't hurt no worse than it already has." He folded Zeb's face into his overalls.

The splinter's blunt end did not stick out enough for Ezra to pluck with his fingernails. Ezra, hand trembling, stretched toward the back of Zeb's leg with his knife.

"Banks, you're shaking like a leaf." Cash, his own knife at the ready, with one hand clicked his fingers in front of Zeb's face, and with the other quickly yanked out the splinter. Zeb barely had time to notice the pain before Cash handed him a keepsake. "Here, boy, take it home. It's big enough to start a fire with."

Cash looked toward the church windows, where he saw no curious faces. "Now we got to clean that out." Turning his back to the building, he pulled a glass flask from his front pocket and poured whiskey on Ezra's handkerchief. They washed the back of Zeb's leg until the handkerchief no longer showed pink, then Ezra pulled Zeb's overalls back up.

The men stood as Zeb wiped his nose and face on his arm. Cash looked at Ezra. "Now then. I reckon you best take the boy home. He smells like a brewery and so does that nose rag." Ezra's hands trembled. "You want a little snort for them shakes?"

"Never touch it." Ezra held out his hands. "They're all right now. . . . I knew I hadn't drawn blood." He saw an Indian head penny in the edge of the grass, walked around so he faced the Indian, and picked it up.

"Be careful with that temper of your'n. I'd hate to hear you really hurt the boy."

Ezra's face clouded. "I reckon that's our bidness."

As Cash came back and stood along the back wall, Noland's sermon wandered somewhere between the riches of Solomon and the desolation following the Day of the Lord. When the preacher paused for breath and looked out the window he saw Ezra, holding Zeb's hand, walking toward the buggy. Noland barely missed a beat. "As the prophet said, the fathers have eaten a sour grape, and the children's teeth are set on edge, amen." If his flock wondered what that had to do with his sermon, no one let on.

"How was church?" Hannah asked when Zeb bounced upstairs to give her three dandelions he'd picked beside the barn. "My goodness, that's pretty. Makes Mama feel better. Zebulon Baird, look at me. Your eyes are red as can be." She sat up in bed.

"Mr. Cash pulled a big old splinter out of my leg, Mama. See? Then he washed my leg with some awful smelly stuff."

"With this cold I couldn't smell nothing. Where'd you get a splinter? Those new pews? Let Mama see."

"It's OK, Mama, it don't hurt now or anything."

"Let me see, young man. That's a mighty big splinter for a skinny leg."

He frowned and Hannah pointed a finger at him. "*Now,* Zebulon Baird Banks."

He squiggled out of his overalls and turned around. "Lord, child," she gasped, "has your papa beaten you?"

Zeb said nothing.

"We'll put some ointment where that splinter was. But the rest of that . . . Get your clothes on and tell your papa to get up here."

In a minute Ezra walked upstairs and leaned against the door frame.

"Mr. Banks, tell me what happened."

"I had to whip him." He ran his finger aside his crooked nose.

"A whipping's one thing. But it looks like you near about killed him."

"He wouldn't be still. Then he got the hiccups."

"Ezra Banks, you don't beat a boy within an inch of his life over the hiccups."

"It ain't nothing to worry yourself about."

"You've got your daddy's temper, or worse, and it's going to be the death of somebody one of these days. Maybe you, if you beat my boy again. Get downstairs and fix you and him something to eat. There's cold chicken and such in the springhouse."

Outside Zeb ran circles around the barn. Ezra's hands no longer trembled. When he picked two sticks of stove wood off the back rail, some of the stack collapsed onto the porch. "Shit," he muttered, restacked the wood, then went in to warm up their dinner.

11

SAVED TWICE

Ezra Banks hated idleness as much as he loved tending to apples and lending and collecting money. He worked his four sons hard. If they finished their regular chores he had them harvest windfall kindling or grub rocks from the pastures. Year-round he made them sweep the yard free of pine needles or walnut hulls. Winter nights he set them to whittling toothpicks. Once when he had run out of things for them to do, Hannah suggested with tongue in cheek that he give them all buckets, and make them carry water from the branch to the creek. He actually considered it.

In September of his twelfth year, Zeb finished a trench for storing cabbages over the winter. He leaned the shovel against the porch and sat like a lizard, soaking in sunshine. A yellowhammer spiraled around a dead maple limb, alternately calling and pecking. After a morning rain, even yard dirt smelled rich.

Hearing Ezra's boot heels strike the floor inside, Zeb, quick as a ground squirrel, slipped underneath the porch.

Ezra yelled for his sons but only three showed. Ezra hollered again for Zeb, eyeing the shovel. "You boys know where your brother's at?" His nose cut a sharper angle than ever.

"He was out back a bit ago," said George, ten. People said Zeb looked like his mother, down to the dimple in his chin, but there was no mistaking George for anyone's but Ezra. His nose bent leftward even though it had never been broken, and he could even glare at a fellow like his father.

"It's going to be mighty hard when I find him. Go clean up the rest of the pasture yon side of the apple house. I'll holler at you for supper."

They pulled a small wagon holding a mattock and hoe to the pasture, where they dragged the hoe blade across the ground. When it clanked on a rock they grubbed it out with the mattock and tossed it in the wagon. Arrowheads went in their pockets, hoarded against Ezra's trips to Newport or Greenville, when their mother let them play wild Cherokees.

Ezra called again. "Well," he said, "I don't know where he's at, but it'll be hell to pay when he gets back." He went to his office and opened a ledger on his four-dollar desk, while Zeb peeked from under the east end of the porch like a groundhog.

Making sure his brothers looked the other way, Zeb sidled around the house and ran up toward his grandpa Will's place. Barefoot, brown hair cowlicking in the breeze, he figured a little freedom was worth a whipping.

Ezra saw just enough of Zeb's leaving out of the corner of his eye to close the ledger and pull his rifle from the rack above the door. It was a new rifle, at least new to Ezra, a model four .32. Ezra's neighbor John

Bennett had gotten rid of it because his oldest boy had leaned it, loaded, against the porch column. Some Remingtons had safety hammers but this one did not. It fell and discharged into the face of Bennett's only daughter, barely a head taller than the porch floor. After she was buried he asked Ezra if he wanted the weapon, and Ezra traded him even for his old Colt's, which Bennett vowed to keep hidden from the rest of his brood.

The standard .32 load was fine for varmints but Ezra had filed the points off a dozen bullets in case bigger game presented itself. He put four in his pocket, chambered one, and stood on the porch, wondering what his oldest son was up to.

Little Cataloochee Creek headed above Will's farm, at the big spring on Jake Carter's place. By the time it flowed through Will's property it was just wide enough for Zeb to jump across. He turned up creekbed rocks for a while, looking for crawdads and snails. Then he headed north toward their orchard, running to dry his overalls, zigzagging among the trees to the rhythm of a katydid. Suddenly he heard apples drop. Stopping dead still, he shaded his eyes.

In the center of the orchard one tree held a cub bear bending an apple-laden branch like a bow toward its mouth. When he bit an apple the branch sprang and flung the rest to the ground like cannonballs.

Zeb took cover behind one tree, then another, searching for the sow, which seemed to be nowhere. He found two apples on the ground and walked closer to the cub. Looking around, seeing nothing, he threw one of the apples at the cub, and missed. The bear paid him no attention. Zeb shifted the other apple to his right hand, and hurled it at the bear's snout. The animal snorted, pawed its nose, and looked weakly toward the boy.

Zeb was so absorbed in deviling the cub he didn't hear its mother. When she raised on her hind legs and clamored, Zeb turned and froze. Three hundred pounds of black anger bid fair to kill him.

He knew a bear could climb faster than he, but he might be able to outrun her. He shouted and fired his last apple at her snout. The apple hit true and she clawed the tip of her nose. Zeb took off like his overalls were on fire but tripped on a rock and went tumbling into a tree trunk. Scrabbling up, he saw the bear coming for him like a locomotive.

As he screamed, "Mama, help me!" a bullet from Ezra's Remington entered the she-bear's forehead and tore a sizable patch out of her head on exit. Two strides later she fell beside Zeb at the base of the apple tree. Breathing odor strong as heat off a road, Zeb shook all over. The warm wet in his overalls was from his own bladder.

Ezra took a whimpering Zeb by the arm. "Get up, son. Your mama couldn't have helped you with this. Don't know why I brought this gun, but I'm glad I did." Bark, dirt, and ants clung to Zeb's clothes. Shaking, he wiped his upper lip on his arm. Blues already flittered about the bear's head.

The other boys ran into the orchard, pointing at the bear and laughing at their big brother. Ezra scowled. "Get back to work. The ruckus is over."

"Papa," said George, "when you whip Zeb can we watch?"

"He might get worse than a whipping."

George pointed to the center of the orchard. "Papa, there's something in that tree yonder."

Seeing that every time the cub moved, apples dropped, Ezra chambered a round and raised the rifle, but realizing he faced toward Jake's place, he thought better of firing. He frowned at Zeb. "Son, you know we won't get no harvest from this tree." He moved to the other side for a safer shot at the cub, which fell in the cradle of the lowest limb.

Ezra hugged the rifle, rubbing the octagonal barrel with his thumb. "Zeb, I ought to wear you out. Sometimes I wonder where your mama found you. Any son of mine ought to have sense enough not to mess with a bear cub."

"I won't ever do it again, Papa."

"Damn right you won't. And so you'll remember, it's your job to get these varmints down to the house so we can dress them."

Zeb looked at eighty pounds of bear meat jammed in the crotch of the tree and about four times that laid out on the ground. His brothers giggled.

"You damned rascals get back to the pasture before I cloud up and rain all over you," Ezra said, then looked at Zeb. "I'll see *you* at the house." He turned and walked down the hill behind his other sons like a roadside guard, nestling the rifle in his arms.

Zeb was too big to cry but sure felt like it. His mother was across the mountain with her sister Tildy, who was having another baby, and there was no disobeying his father, so he brushed his overalls and skinned up the tree. The cub's dead eyes mirrored nothing and the back of his head was a mass of gore. Zeb shoved and poked the bear, which fell like a sack of cornmeal. Flies and yellow jackets followed it down.

Zeb was fixing to go for the mule to drag the bears home when he remembered a tenant was snaking deadwood with it. Grabbing the cub by its hind legs, he jerked it a couple of feet, then in frustration kicked it hard enough to hurt his ankle.

Hoofbeats echoed down the mountain. Soon Jake Carter turned into the orchard. His horse shied at the she-bear's odor but he talked her still. Zeb's uncle, still unmarried at twenty-five, tied and patted the horse, then looked at the skinny boy and dead bears.

"I heard shots," he started, and shook his head. "Son, I'd have let them bears have a snack." He looked toward the house. "Or is your old daddy so poor he couldn't stand to lose a couple of apples?"

"Uncle Jake, I was throwing apples at the little one and the mama nearly got me. Papa shot them dead. Now I got to drag them both down to the house and he won't let me have no help."

Jake wiped his glasses slowly with a plaid handkerchief. "I can tell by your face you've learned a lesson. Listen. Locust here'll drag them if I can talk him into thinking a dead bear won't hurt him. Your daddy'll want me to help with the meat, anyhow, so I might as well get going." He held his glasses to the sunlight, put them back on, and stowed the handkerchief in his overalls.

Tying a rope around the big bear's middle, he pulled it taut behind her forelegs. Knotting rope to saddle horn, he mounted the horse and backed him gently down the hill. "I'll be back in a few minutes."

Zeb watched his uncle coax the horse to drag the dead weight. Standing in sunshine, Zeb pulled at damp denim sticking to his itchy legs, then chewed at his thumbnail. A crow seemed to laugh at him. Kicking the cub in the belly, he started a swarm of insects that quickly returned to their feeding. He suddenly shuddered. "I just about got killed," he muttered.

When they returned for the cub, Locust seemed easier. "I'd let you up behind me," Jake said, "but I don't know if he can handle a bear and a pissed-pants boy at the same time." He grinned at Zeb, who managed a wan smile.

"What did Papa say?"

"Wanted to know why I was doing all your work. I told him he was mighty lucky you wasn't laying up here dead. He didn't say nothing to that. Your daddy's a hard man, Zeb. Stick close and I'll show you how to dress a bear. Maybe when we get some meat ready your daddy'll cool off."

"Thank you, Uncle Jake." Zeb's brow wrinkled. "I just realized, I've got saved twice today—once by Papa and now by you. I'm much obliged."

"Think nothing about it. We'll chalk it up to kinfolk helping each other. Maybe Ezra'll let you help me run cider next month."

Zeb knew that would be a stretch, since they had their own cider to press. Yet, as he walked beside Jake and Locust, the idea gave him some comfort. He tossed an apple from one hand to the other.

"Uncle Jake, what it's like to be dead?"

"I'd expect you'd be poorer than the poorest man alive, but I reckon a body wouldn't care. Why?"

"I just wondered. I nearly found out this afternoon."

"Son, I hope it's many a year before you know how being dead feels. I know a couple of things, though."

"What's that, Uncle Jake?"

"Them that knows how it feels don't come back to tell us. And I ain't seen a corpse yet that looked happy."

"But I've been baptized, so I'm going to heaven when I die. Wouldn't that make me happy?"

Jake stopped the horse and looked at his nephew with a grin. "Boy, you ask too many questions. But I can say this: if half what the Bible says about heaven's true, happy's too sickly a word for what it'll be like."

12

WORTH A TRIP TO KNOXVILLE

Ezra and Hannah made a bargain early on: no one was to be in his office except at his invitation, and he was to stay out of her kitchen except at mealtimes. Their largest room, the kitchen took up the west side of the house behind the front room, running to a pantry that had been a back porch before Ezra closed it in.

He kept accounts in his office and she hid butter and egg money in the pantry. Over the years she had accumulated about fifteen dollars, which she counted every few days. Mostly nickels and dimes, the money sat in a half-gallon Mason jar wrapped with part of a feed sack.

A week after Ezra killed the bears, Hannah sent Zeb to the post office. The weather still held a hint of summer, and he was delighted to have a furlough from the cider press.

The post office and general store was the center of Ola, a half mile toward the Mount Sterling road from Ezra's place. The road twisted beside the creek, and every rock and stick Zeb found got thrown in the water.

Ruby Parham, pregnant to the bursting point, glanced up from sorting mail when she heard Zeb on the front step. She laid her hands on her belly and smiled. "Child, did your daddy go off somewhere? I'd a thought you'd been working apples."

"No, Miz Parham, he's at the house." The mail lay in wooden boxes in the north corner, one for Wright Branch, another for Banks Branch, and so forth, all the way down to where Little Cataloochee Creek joined Cataloochee Creek. The rest of the place was a general store, coils of rope on pegs, bolts of fabric on shelves, and a hoop of cheese on the table. A tater bug mandolin hung by a strap beside a calendar for 1896. Zeb had saved a dollar and a quarter toward the instrument's five-dollar price, hoping one day to take it home and learn to play with his uncle Jake. Ezra was about as musical as a crow, but most Carters had talent. "We get any mail today?"

"Matter of fact, you did, and you best be stout." She fished out a large parcel wrapped in brown paper.

Hannah had seen a Sears, Roebuck catalog at her cousin Hiram's house back in the spring. "If they ain't got it, you don't need it," Hiram had said. Hannah had copied the address, thought about it awhile, then dug a quarter out of her jar. She'd sent it to Sears three weeks ago. The book was big as a Bible. "Is this a catalog?"

"Yes, and, Lord, clear as Cataloochee Creek, it's going to run me out of business."

"How can that happen, Miz Parham?"

"When you get that varmint home, you'll see all kinds of things, and find out they sell their stuff cheaper'n I can sell it. You know that mandolin?"

"Sure, Miz Parham."

"Well, they got one just like it for a dollar and a quarter less'n I got to have for it. Even paying postage it's cheaper."

"Miz Parham, I promise when I get the money I'll buy it from *you*."

"Zeb, you're sweet like your mama. Now take her catalog to her."

He decided to see if he could run all the way home with the heavy package. He quickly slowed to a trot. When he hit the yard he saw his father sitting on the front porch, fanning at a yellow jacket with his handkerchief. Zeb cradled the catalog against his chest and walked slowly toward the house.

Ezra probed his pocket for his pipe. "I saw you running, boy. What's the all-fired hurry?"

"It's mail for Mama."

Ezra struck a kitchen match and lit his pipe. "Give that here."

"But, Papa, Mama said bring it to her."

"Never mind what she said. Give it here. Your brothers are stacking stove wood in that near shed. They likely could use some help."

"Yes, Papa."

Ezra stared at the catalog like it was a box of snakes. Brown wrapper, "Sears, Roebuck and Co." printed in the corner. "Mrs. Ezra Banks, Ola, North Carolina," machine printed, stared back at him. He lifted it and scowled.

In the kitchen, while Hannah stirred a run of applesauce, he laid the book on the table and put his hand on her shoulder.

"That must have cost me a dollar, Hannah. Maybe more. What's got into you?" He inhaled with vigor. "Them apples smell mighty good. Can I have some?"

She walked from under his hand, got a bowl, and spooned him a helping. "I ain't run them through the colander yet, so watch for seeds." As he sat at the table she pushed the sugar bowl toward him and handed him a spoon.

He took a tentative bite and nearly burned his lip. "How'd you get them damn things so hot?" He stirred a bit of sugar in, then blew on the bowl.

"First, you can't cook without heat, Mr. Banks. Second, that there catalog didn't cost you a penny. I paid for it with my own money. And third, you quit cussing in my kitchen."

Ezra ate, and watched Hannah's back as she stirred. "Woman, I thought you had ever thing you needed."

She pushed the pot of apples toward the back of the cookstove. "Mr. Banks, it's just a wish book, is all."

"Woman, a body don't pay cash money for something just to wish on. What is it you think you need?" He took another spoon of applesauce.

"All in good time, Mr. Banks. I got to find out myself, and I'll thank you not to complain no more about it."

He finished the apples and left the kitchen shaking his head. Hannah put the catalog on the shelf under her jar of money. After supper Ezra tended to the fireplace and Hannah darned socks while the boys did homework and chores. They did not mention the catalog nor glance at each other.

At breakfast Ezra wiped his mustache with the corner of the tablecloth and announced he was going to see Hannah's father. She watched him walk out the door and disappear past the big chestnut.

As she walked back to the kitchen she removed her apron and put the catalog and a glass of springwater on the table. Carefully tearing the wrapper, she folded it and put it in the pantry to use later.

She opened the catalog at random, to a page full of vises. Thumbing past buggy tops and carriage poles and pipe pullers and toilets and sinks, she stopped to gaze on each page. She took a drink of water, then moved the catalog closer and wondered if they sold eyeglasses. Then her eye fixed on a beauty, a sewing machine with six drawers and a drop leaf on the left, useful for putting together long frocks or quilts, and a box to cover the machine. The treadle said "Sears, Roe-buck and Co." and the machine said "Burdick." The cabinet could be either oak or walnut. It came with instruction booklet, oilcan, screw-driver, quilter, cloth guide, six bobbins, and a pack of needles. Looked more substantial than the New Queen on the opposite page. Twelve dollars and thirty-five cents, plus shipping. For an extra seventy-five cents she could get an attachment kit—ruffler, underbraider, tucker, binder, shirring plate, and short foot. "Let's see," she said, "that would come to thirteen dollars and ten cents. If freight ain't higher'n a cat's back, I can manage."

She turned to the shipping tables. The machine weighed a hundred and twenty-five pounds. She ran down the columns with her finger. "Land's sakes," she said, "this print's teeny." She wiggled her head back and forth until her eyes focused on North Carolina railheads. Waynesville was not one. The closest she'd heard of was Shelby but she did not know how far away it was.

She sipped again and turned to the Tennessee headings. Newport wasn't there but Knoxville was. She went to the freight section. "A dollar and a quarter'll get it to Knoxville—that makes fourteen dollars and thirty-five cents for the whole shebang. That won't quite clean me out. Then I got to get it to Cataloochee."

She thumbed through the back half, looking at ladies' clothes and hats and shoes. The front part displayed guns and tools and musical instruments. The index in the middle showed her eyeglasses came right after mantel clocks and silverware. A pair cost less than two dollars. She could barely manage to add that in.

She laid the catalog in the pantry next to her money jar, put on her apron, and went to the back porch. She came back pushing a bushel basket of apples with her foot. As she started peeling she remembered saving two tins of pineapple for an upside-down cake—Ezra's favorite—which she could turn into her ticket to Knoxville.

When Ezra got to his father-in-law's place it was not quite eight, too early for a drink, even for Will. They sat in the front room, the table cluttered with coffee cups and a W. W. Williams cigar box with a picture of a sulky and horse on the lid.

"Well, son, that last wagonload made the year's crop a couple of thousand bushels. Not bad for an old man, eh?"

"I didn't get that many, but I ain't got as many trees."

Will chuckled. "Son, the way you grow apples you could get a bushel off one of them menny-ture trees in a pot. Time I pass on to my reward, you'll be producing twicet as many's me."

"You must've made right at eight hundred dollars."

"Yep. I traded some, of course, and give some away. Polly Rogers don't do no good with her trees so I always give her some—let's see, I got it right here." Will opened the cigar box and removed a slip of paper. "Come to seven hundred eighty-six dollars and forty-two cents." He looked at Ezra. "Of course, it ain't all me by any means. I got me a hot-shot son to help me. That's worth ten percent."

"Ain't that fifteen?"

"Son, I bargain in tens, not fives. If it was more'n ten it would have been twenty, and I ain't about to give nobody, not even you, twenty percent. You know, you try that ever year. Looks like you'd give up one of these days."

Ezra shrugged and sipped his coffee.

"Tell you what, I'll round that seven hundred-something up to eight. You'll get eighty dollars, and I got something in the barn to sweeten the deal."

Will ratted around in the box and found four Liberty twenty-dollar gold pieces that looked like he had polished them lovingly. He started to hand them to Ezra.

"Will, how come you give that meddling Polly Rogers apples?"

"Son, she's kin, her daddy was cousin to my mama. She's been poorly, and it never hurts a man to share. Now then. Here's your money—in gold. Reminds me, what do you think about them presidential candidates wanting to do away with our good old American gold standard?" Ezra stared at the coins and put them in his pocket, then looked at Will like he had asked about Leviticus.

"Don't keep up with it."

"Son, you can't vote right if you don't."

"Will, you know I don't care for politics. I vote for who you tell me to, like ever body else in this part of Catalooch."

Will shrugged. "This election's the worst I ever seen to figger out. You got gold Democrats and silver Democrats, Republicans, too, that's four parties, and about fifty-leven others to boot, one of them's the Prohibition party, if you can imagine such. I like that Bryan fellow. I hear when he come through Asheville last week he really give a humdinger of a speech. I like speechifying as much as any a man, but Bryan's against the gold standard, and when you get down to brass tacks, I'm partial to gold money. Besides, some of them Republicans support him. So I don't know. I do know the government's getting too big for its britches."

"Well, when you figure it out, let me know. I need to get home." Ezra stood and fingered the coins in his pocket.

"They's something in the barn, remember?" Will pulled his canvas jacket off the peg by the front door. "Kate, we're outside for a little while," he shouted toward the back of the house.

In the barn Will pulled out a quart bottle filled with fluid the color of dark straw. "Here, son. I took a little sup but didn't care none for it. I'll stick to liquor either I made or know where it comes from."

Ezra hadn't had much to do with whiskey since his army year. He loved how it used to make him feel, expansive, full of energy, but it also made him want to fight men twice his size. So he had quit.

After he came to Cataloochee he'd have to take a drink with his father-in-law every now and then—it was difficult to tell Will Carter no—but though Will made smooth apple brandy, and his corn liquor wasn't bad, Ezra had no taste for either.

Ezra wiped hay dust from the bottle, which sported a federal tax stamp over the cap. "I never seen a square bottle except for medicine."

"The boy in Newport said it's the first year for them. It come from one of them stilleries in Tennessee. Claims it's sour mash but it's too sweet to suit me."

Ezra shook it and held it to the light. "Good bead." Embossed in the middle of the glass was "No. 7" in a circle. "Why you reckon they call it by a number?"

"I think maybe they age it seven years. He said they filter the damn stuff through charcoal, too. Seven years is a awful waste of time, if you ask me. Whiskey's liable to go bad if you put it up that long. I wouldn't chance it."

"Ever buy a bottle of government-bonded whiskey?"

Will rubbed his chin. "No. I stole one when I was in the army, but when a man's thirsty enough to steal, he takes what he can get."

"Never hurts to have some around for a cold." Ezra cradled the bottle. "Much obliged. Reckon I best head home and try to get some work done. See you Sunday if not before."

Ezra went straight to his office and set the bottle behind the front right leg of the desk. The bottle was too tall for his desk drawer, but he figured to decant it into some half-pint Mason jars that he could lock away there.

That evening when Hannah called him to supper he came in and ran his finger behind George's left ear. "Son, you could plant taters back there. Get cleaned up before I take a switch to you."

Hannah looked behind each set of ears after she set a dish of beans on the table. "Now, Mr. Banks, he just forgot, is all. Honey, run do as your papa says. We got a surprise tonight."

"What kind?" asked Zeb, a boy his mother figured would one day make a fine figure of a man.

"The kind that makes your tongue slap your brains out. Pineapple upside-down cake."

Ezra, smiling, put an end to the cheers from the boys. "I don't mean to make you mad, but it has been a while since we've had much besides apple pie," he said to Hannah, who winked and nodded.

They polished it off after supper along with a big bowl of whipped cream. As Hannah and Ezra watched each other from the ends of the table, the boys cleared the dishes and went to do their lessons.

Ezra stifled a belch. "Lord, Hannah, that was the best cake you ever baked. Makes me think you're fattening me up for the kill."

"Well, not exactly." She put her hands together like a prayer. "Mr. Banks, how would you like to go to Knoxville?"

"Why? The crop's done sold."

"It could save me some money."

He put his elbows on the table. "Woman, what's this all about?"

"Ezra, promise me something."

He shifted and looked at her on hearing his first name. "When a woman says that, a man's fixing to be in trouble, no matter what he says. I promised to provide for you when we married, didn't I?"

"Has that got you into trouble?" When she pursed her lips the dimple in her chin deepened.

"No. Ain't I done it good?"

"Can't say you haven't."

"Well, why make me promise more?" He moved the saltcellar absentmindedly from one hand to the other.

"Because—oh, Ezra, let me show you something in that Sears, Roebuck catalog."

She laid it at his place and turned to the sewing machines. "That's the one, that Burdick. Ain't she a beauty? Think of all the clothes I could make with that. Shirts for you and the boys, a dress ever now and then for me." She put her hands on his bony shoulders. "Well, Ezra, what do you think?"

His eyes rested on the price. "Hannah, what makes you think we got thirteen dollars for such a contraption?"

She squeezed his shoulders. "Ezra, it ain't 'we' we're talking about."

"What do you mean?"

She came around to face him. "Ezra, I got the money. And I can't think of a thing to do with it that would give me more pleasure. I could make a shirt in nothing flat, or piece a quilt in a day or two—why, I could make clothes to sell down at the store. It'd pay for itself pretty quick. Look at me, Ezra."

The message in her eyes said he was doomed. "Hannah, you started out talking about Knoxville. What's this got to do with that?"

"They ship it from Ohio, and the closest place they'll bring it is Knoxville. Hiram goes there right regular, but I'd feel like I'd have to pay him. I thought maybe we could pick it up, just us two, make it a lark."

"Hannah, I got to make ends meet around here. We can't go spending that kind of money."

She looked him straight in the eye. "How much did you lay out on that cider press year before last?"

"That's different. I needed that machine."

"So. A man needing a machine is different than me needing one?"

"Apples is how we live around here, woman."

"Mr. Banks, you bought that press without asking me a thing about it. Well, I *am* asking you about this machine, which would make *my* work easier, and it's *my* money that'll pay for it. You got no cause to object."

"Well, promise me you'll make things to sell, then I might think about it."

"Ezra, promises work both ways. You wouldn't promise a few minutes ago and I ain't going to neither. But I will say this." She put her hands toward his on the table. "You and me been together a long time. We got four fine boys and a mighty nice roof over our heads. But if you tell me I can't do this, it'll sour that."

He took a deep breath and closed his hands over hers. "You sure you got the money?"

"Yes."

"Well, then, I reckon I might like a trip to Knoxville."

She squeezed his hands hard. "Do you mean it? Do you really?" She trotted around the table and hugged him from the back. "Ezra, thank you, thank you. Wait till you see it. You won't be sorry, not a bit. Why, you might want something out of here for yourself." She turned it to two pages of weapons.

"Woman, I got a shotgun. But I reckon it won't hurt to look."

She danced on the balls of her feet and wrung her hands. "I haven't been this excited since I was a little girl."

He picked up the catalog and closed it. "I'd hate to have to bury you over a damn sewing machine." She hugged him again. "Thank you, Ezra," she said into his shoulder. It had been a long time since they had touched like that, and he moved his hand to the curve of her backside.

"Ezra Banks, you cut that out. I'll tend to the young'uns, and you tend to your own knitting. If you're still frisky when they're asleep, why, then, we'll see about that."

He closed the office door, put the catalog in the middle of his desk, and lit his pipe. From behind the desk leg he got the Daniel's, uncorked it, and turned the bottle up. "Damn," he said. "That's mighty fine." This man's whiskey had no rough edge and he turned the bottle up for another long swallow.

He spent a while with the catalog. Women's foolishness toward the back. A desk for seven dollars that looked half as nice as his, even with the gouge. He noticed he had paid too much for his door locks, passed with impatience through the horse and buggy section, and was about to call it quits when he found pages of pistols.

Lately there had been some thieving down past the post office. Two of Cash Davis's hogs had disappeared. Someone had filched a scythe and two sledges from the Parhams. Ezra had thought about looking for a pistol in Waynesville, had even said something to Hannah about getting one, but here were two pages full of them.

Poring over the columns of calibers and prices, he felt his lip becoming slightly numb. That made him smile but still he frowned at the book. "Jesus, they think a lot of these things. Thirteen dollars for a thirty-eight Smith and Weston?" They even had a Colt's pearl-handled single-action "six-shooter" for twenty-two dollars.

He turned the page to revolvers by Stevens, Iver Johnson, Harrington & Richardson. None cost more than five dollars, and they even had a .22 tip-up pistol, a single-shot target .22, for less than two. He took another drink. An "automatic revolver" for three dollars from Iver Johnson stood out. "What in hell is an automatic revolver?" he asked himself. But it looked good, nickel plate, three-inch barrel, .38 caliber, "every one warranted." It used smokeless center-fire cartridges, which cost a bit over a penny apiece, but they wouldn't mail explosives. To get a hundred cartridges by train would cost more than the ammunition itself. "Piss on that," he said. Will had a .38 Smith and some store-bought cartridges. He might give Ezra a box.

On the other hand, it cost only a penny an ounce to mail the pistol, and that would make eighteen cents postage plus a nickel to insure it. So he could land the pistol for three dollars and twenty-three cents. Not quite ten bushels of apples. He could grow ten extra bushels with no trouble.

Once Hannah herded the boys upstairs for bed, Ezra figured he'd root around for a couple of Mason jars for the liquor. He walked out in the hall, lurched into the kitchen door frame, and cursed out loud. Uninterrupted footsteps upstairs told him they hadn't heard him. He came back to his office and shut the door.

His earlier desire for Hannah had vanished like a whipsnake, and he decided to lie down on his cot. He closed his eyes but instantly heaved himself bolt upright, wide-eyed, hand against the wall to stop the motion of the room. He was warm and swirly and full of cake and he hoped like hell to keep it all down. He'd drunk a third of the bottle.

Hannah mailed the order the next day. She had misgivings over the pistol, but wanted to take no chance Ezra'd renege on the sewing machine. It would be shipped from Dayton to Knoxville, while the pistol and eyeglasses would come to Cataloochee by mail.

Hannah was good at waiting, but after two weeks passed, whoever went to the post office got a grilling from Ezra when they returned without a package. "That damn woman's lost it, by God. Or she's give it to somebody else," he said. He strained to hear someone fire a new weapon.

Monday the ninth of November, it promised to snow before dark. The order had been mailed over a month before, and Ezra, who had taken back up with his quart of Mr. Daniel's No. 7 against the chill in the air, decided to go for the mail himself.

Ruby Parham heard the horse and buggy, then Ezra's boot on the step. She looked him over. "Howdy, Mr. Banks. What brings you here this windy old morning?"

"I come for my package."

"Mr. Banks, all you got was this circular about voting, and that should have got here a week ago."

"Woman, what in hell do I want with this? I voted last week like Will told me to. I come for my package." He threw the wadded paper on the floor.

"Mr. Banks, I told you it ain't here. If they don't bring it to me, I can't give it to you." She put her hands over her belly.

"It's bound to be here somewhere. You've dropped it or put it in the wrong box." His eyes darted from one corner to another.

"You're welcome to look all you want, Mr. Banks. I swear, a body'd think you was looking for a shipment of gold."

"It ain't none of your damn bidness what I'm looking for. Just because you're kin to Will and he got you this here job—I want my goddamned package." She clutched her belly more tightly. "When I come back tomorrow it better be here. Or if you find it this evening, bring it to the house. It's likely with them magazines you read before you give them out."

"Listen here, Mr. Banks. I don't read nobody's mail. Now you get out of here."

"Don't order me around, you sow. When I come tomorrow you best have that package."

He left the door open, and she waited a full minute before closing it. How in the world, she thought, does Hannah Banks put up with him? And him smelling of drink. I never knowed him to drink, but maybe old Will's won him over.

The next day Ezra opened the post office door to find Tine Parham, Ruby's husband, a round fellow in faded blue overalls. Despite his name—short for Valentine, he'd been a February baby—he looked like a loggywoods boy wearing a gunbelt with an outsized Smith & Wesson like some dime novel character. Parham threw him a package. "Here's your mail, Banks. It come this morning. You and your old daddy-in-law might think you own this settlement, but you don't talk to my woman like you did yesterday, I don't give a shit *who* you are."

Parhams had a reputation for meanness. Their father used to tie cats together by their tails and sling them over clotheslines just to see what happened.

Ezra touched his hat brim and nodded to Ruby. "Miz Parham, I'm sorry if I was rough on you yesterday. I didn't mean no harm in what I said. Tell you the truth, I can't even remember. . . ."

"You still think I'm a sow?"

"That what I said?"

Tine came a step closer. "You calling her a liar?"

"Mr. Parham, if I said that, I'm mighty sorry." He turned toward Ruby. "Miz Parham, I won't do that no more."

Tine fingered his pistol. "If there's a next time I'll use this on you, Banks, sure as the world. Now get out of here."

When Ezra pulled the package from under his arm a postcard fell to the ground. He put it in his inside pocket, and hurried home. Bouncing up the front steps, he grabbed the doorknob. Locked. "Well, shit." Unlocking the door, he turned into his office, laid the package on his desk, threw his coat on the peg, put another stick of wood on the fire, and sat.

He tore off the paper and twine to find two boxes, one with eyeglasses and the other a pistol. He took the gun out of the box. It was shiny, nickel-plated, but the prettiest thing was the ebony, or at least black, handgrips. In a circle at their apex was the head of some creature. He knew it was an owl from the drawing on the box. He turned the weapon to look the owl in its eyes and noticed when he did so the weapon pointed straight at his chest. The closer he stared the more the owl looked like a round-headed, big-eyed cat. "I hate a damn cat," he muttered.

He spun the freewheeling five-cartridge cylinder, then removed it and examined it like it was a curiosity from Madagascar. He put the gun back together and cocked it. It didn't half-cock, which didn't suit him much, and his little finger wanted to curl underneath the butt, which didn't suit him at all. "Damn it, this thing don't feel right." But the proof would be in the firing.

He put some of the cartridges he borrowed from Will in his pocket. As he laid the gun in his coat pocket and stepped into the hall, Hannah called from the kitchen.

"That you, Mr. Banks? Did it come?"

She was rolling out dough for fried apple pies. "Yep. So did these." He handed her the postcard and eyeglasses. She wiped her hands, opened the box, and put on the glasses. She almost jumped as she read the card.

"Lord, Mr. Banks, you know how long it's been since I could see good? And look here. We got to figure out when to go to Knoxville."

"I hope when you get that infernal machine you won't be disappointed like I am with this pistol."

"What's the matter with it?"

"Butt's too little, and it don't half-cock."

"Well, try it out. You might need to get used to it, is all."

His footsteps sounded like gunshots in the hall. Out in the yard he loaded the owlhead and with it blew into pieces an empty square bottle. By the time he had totally obliterated it he started to think maybe they'd go to Knoxville the next day so Hannah could get her machine and he could get another bottle.

13

A NICKEL OR NOTHING

Zeb Banks had known Mattie Carter forever but had paid her no mind except to wonder if she really had killed a wolf the summer they turned eleven. Zeb's grandfather Will told the story to anyone who would listen, how his great-niece Mattie and her cousins, stringing beans on Hiram and Mary's back porch in Big Cataloochee, saw a wolf come calling on the hog pen. Mattie's uncle Hiram was up at Uncle Andy's and Aunt Mary was down in the garden. The wolf, too hungry to care about sneaking in after dark or even minding Hiram's penned and yelping dogs, jumped the fence and commenced to kill shoats.

Mattie, a rail of a girl, ran into the front room for Hiram's goose gun, a single-barrel Long Tom taller than she was. She had to stand in a chair to get it off the rack over the door, and in the yard took a while to steady the barrel. The recoil knocked her into the dirt, and she wasn't happy until Aunt Mary, running from the garden, picked her off the ground and showed her she had plastered that wolf with a load of number two shot.

The next summer, Mattie visited Ezra and Hannah's place to see the brand-new Burdick sewing machine, and quickly learned to use it. She wandered down from Will's often to sew with Hannah, learning to make the blue shirts Hannah's boys all wore, and even made herself a couple. Zeb talked to both of them in the front room, fetched bags of quilt scraps, and ran to the store for thread. After that summer he missed Mattie something awful.

One June afternoon in 1898, Will and Ezra composted trees in the upper orchard, a task they hadn't gotten around to because of the wet springtime. Ezra aerated out to the drip line first with a short-handled shovel, then a trowel. Will followed with a wheelbarrow, scattering compost with a pitchfork.

Mattie and Zeb had just finished school—Haywood County only had seven grades, and they had started a year late because of the awful 1890 winter when both Cataloochees gave up on school—and Will had taken the cousins to the high pasture. Will had been going on about their trip when he wasn't talking politics. He'd told his son-in-law about the cattle, and that chestnuts weren't blooming yet at that elevation. The she-balsam had a lot of bloom, which the old-timers said meant a rough winter.

"You know, Ezra, them young'uns beat anything I ever seen," said Will. "Like two peas in a pod. They get along good, like they wasn't no difference a-tall, you know, one being a girl. Up on the yellow bald, they got to shooting at rocks and such for targets, and Mattie's as good a shot as Zeb, if not better."

"Horsefeathers. A girl never outshot a boy if he's any good. Not even that one with that rodeo show, what'd they call her, Annie something. You know *that* was rigged. Zeb may look like his mother but I taught him how to use a rifle."

"Bet you a nickel." Will grinned as he forked compost.

"You know I ain't a betting man, Will."

"You sound mighty confident. Why not put your money where your mouth is?"

"Tell me why you think she might could beat Zeb."

"Zeb's a natural shot like you; he don't put concentration to it, he just shoots. She's steadier, she studies it, like she was lining up rows. Remember how her pore old daddy'd stretch a tight string before running bean rows? She's just like him. She hates to miss, too, grits her teeth and stomps if she does. And you know how she killed that wolf."

"Yep, and I'm getting pretty damn tired of that story. A wolf out in daylight's either foaming at the mouth or starving to death, so it ain't got good sense. And even a gal could kill a wolf with that old Long Tom. Barrel's damn near four foot long."

Will scattered mulch behind Ezra's digging. "Son, you sound like old Doubting Thomas, but I'm here to tell you, she's a humdinger of a shot. Maybe we ought to let what you might call an impartial jury decide this."

Ezra straightened and wiped his forehead with his arm. "You mean a shooting match?"

"Yes, sir, that's the ticket. A match just for the under-sixteen crowd, though, or we'll be there all week. Mighty fine idea. We'll need a prize."

"How about that white-faced heifer with the brown patch around her left eye you was going on about a while ago?"

Will chuckled. "Son, that ain't like you, giving away something worth money."

"I ain't giving nothing away, Will. Zeb'll win, sure as you're standing here."

Saturday, folks from both Cataloochees headed for Cash Davis's farm, where shooting matches in Little Cataloochee had been held for years. Three wagonloads came from Big Cataloochee, and the area between the Davis house and barn looked like town on court Saturday.

Kate and Hannah were especially delighted to see Hiram and Mary, with whom they got together once a year at most. Mary had lost three children, one at birth and the others at age three, and had nearly given in to melancholy for a time. Kate questioned her niece thoroughly about how things were with her. Mary's sons, Manson and Thomas, thirteen and twelve, looked hale and happy and so did their mother. Hiram was building them a big frame house and told everyone of his progress and bruises.

Youngsters loaded tow wads in shotguns and fired in the air like it was Christmas. Most everyone, even Ezra, had modern rifles, but for a shooting match they used old-time weapons, the only concession to modernity being percussion caps instead of flint and steel. Hiram brought his hog rifle for Mattie, a relic said to have been fashioned by a descendant of the Gillespie who made a long rifle for Daniel Boone. Ezra's boys planned to shoot their father's single-trigger Sharps. It was old—clearly not possessed of its original barrel—but its chief charm for Ezra was it had come with the price of his old Edneyville farm. And it would put a .52 ball where a man aimed it.

Back of the Davises' new barn beside the horseshoe pit stretched a field of some seventy yards ending at the base of Noland Mountain, where two empty hayricks stood. Ezra, with Hannah, her brother, Jake, and his new wife, Rachel, toured the Davis farm. Ezra admired the barn, while everyone else took a shine to Rachel, a young woman Jake had courted and won that spring, no one could quite figure out how. She was a town girl, a Thrash from Clyde, considerably younger than his twenty-seven years and pretty, everyone said, as a speckled pup. The barn was twice the size of Ezra's, and he told Cash Davis he meant to have one that size one of these days.

A half dozen hemlock boles about four feet long lay on the ground beside it, roughly sixty yards from the mountainside. Cash spread bearskins behind two of the trunks. Those youngsters who shot prone would lie upon them while they steadied the barrels on the trees. He also provided worn-out jackets for them to fold and lay on the trees, to lessen the recoil that might spoil the shot.

Cash recruited young folks to carry tables to the shady side of the barn so women could lay out baskets of fried chicken and jars of pickles and jugs of tea and coffee beside cakes and pies galore. Men unloaded bass fiddles and other instruments while their wives fussed with the tables like they were competing at the county fair.

Two hours before supper Will gathered everyone, laughing and rubbing young people on their heads for good luck. "Now listen," he yelled. "Write your names on this paper. Mandy Lou here will cut them up and put them in this hat. Cash'll draw two names. They'll shoot three shots apiece from back here on these bearskins, then Cash'll score their targets. Then he'll draw one more name to shoot against the winner. Last one standing wins Ezra's heifer."

"Where's she at?"

"The summer pasture. You win, you go get her in the fall. Course, Ezra says he don't look for it to change hands. May the best man— or gal—win. Oh, I about forgot." He walked ahead some twenty yards to a skinny, barkless dogwood log fairly stamped into the ground. "You can shoot laying on them bearskins, or you can stand on this mark and shoot off hand, your choice."

Contestants fitted percussion caps and tamped powder and ball with priming rods. They aimed in turn at paper targets pinned to boards leaned against the rick supports. After an hour and a half it was down to George and Zeb and Mattie, waiting to shoot against Cash's great-nephew, who had just scored one and a half. Cash called for "the gal" to shoot.

Mattie was not quite fourteen. With short hair and loose overalls, from behind it was impossible to tell she was a girl. She primed and tamped Hiram's rifle, lifted the front sight, lay on the bearskin, and stuck her shoulder into the half-moon-shaped butt. She cocked the hammer and sighted down the barrel that rested on the padding atop the bole.

The paper targets were marked with an X as close to the center as Cash could draw. Mattie's first shot lay a half inch high and a bit to the right. Her second hit even with the X but a half inch to the left. She took her time with the third. Hiram silenced the crowd with an uplifted finger. Mattie centered the X. After she stood, Cash examined the target. "That's a half, a half, and zero. That makes one." Her opponent, head down, tried to disappear into the crowd. Hiram whooped, "Atta gal."

Cash called George Banks.

Even at twelve George swaggered, like Ezra in a good humor. He took the old Sharps, leered at Mattie, and stepped toward the dogwood. He held the gun on the ground butt first with his left hand and shoved a shock of hair out of his eyes with his right. Shouts of "Hurrah, George! Show that gal what's what!" came from Crate and Rufus. The air was thick with black powder smoke. George picked up the weapon and wiggled his hips like he was up to the plate in the ninth inning of the World Series. Taking no particular pains, he fired.

His shot hit up and to the left a good inch. He reloaded and fired, with no better results. A perfect third shot gave him a score of two. George passed Mattie, muttering something she neither heard nor cared to understand.

Prone, she shot two dead center and one a ball's width to the left. Ezra picked a stick from the ground. "Mighty good luck," he said to Will and Hiram.

"Luck, my granny," Hiram said. "Banks, you want to bet on the winner? You beat me out of a dollar over that dern desk fourteen year ago, and I'd like to make it back."

"I'll bet a nickel on my boy Zeb."

"Make it a dollar and you're on."

"A nickel or nothing, Hiram Carter."

"You always were John D. Rockefeller. But if that's all you'll wager, you're on. Will, hold the bet. Here's my nickel."

Hiram gave Will a Liberty head coin. "Come on, Ezra, ante up," said Will.

Ezra put the stick in his shirt pocket and reached for a leather pouch. Counting out five Indian head pennies like they might have been his grandfather's teeth, he growled, "Here, damn it all. Zeb'll win it, or I'm a monkey's uncle."

Cash called Zeb, who grinned at Mattie and took the gun from his father like he was picking up an old friend. He moved out to the dogwood, put the butt on the ground, turned his body so the barrel was under his left arm, and smoothly stuck the priming rod down it with his right hand. An observer might have thought he was dancing with the rifle. Then with hardly more attention than a fellow would give to a passing gnat he raised the weapon, cocked, and fired. Folks clapped and hooted. The ball hit beside the X. He took a little more time with his next two, one slightly left and the other dead center.

For the first time Mattie stepped to the mark instead of shooting prone. The crowd hushed as she nestled the butt into her shoulder and waited for the barrel to quit moving. The center of the X disappeared.

The youngsters looked at each other, she with a shy grin.

"You couldn't do that again in a million years," George yelled at Mattie.

Zeb turned to his brother. "Let me do the talking, son. I'm shooting, not you."

"You're talking big for a body losing to a girl," George said.

"I reckon a possum beat you?"

George drew back to hit Zeb but yelled when his mother pinched his earlobe and raised him nearly off the ground. "That's enough out of you, young man," Hannah said. "Leave your brother alone." George, rubbing his ear, sat down with the rest of the family.

Mattie shot twice more and Cash walked to the targets. His tall frame bent as he examined them like they were pieces of Scripture. "Boys, they ain't no difference in these here targets. Both scored a one."

"Hot-toe-mighty," yelled Ezra, "look again. You ain't blind, are ye?" He strode to the rick.

"Ezra, look for your own self, there ain't no difference here a-tall."

Ezra peered at the targets. "Well, you might be right. That gal sure is lucky."

The next round Zeb shot first for a half, which Mattie matched perfectly. Then Mattie led with three shots high and a bit to the right, for one and a half. Ezra yelled, "Son, you got her now." Zeb placed three high and left, and Cash called the score even.

Zeb led the next round with a bull's-eye. His second shot was barely to the right and his third covered the first. "Beat that now," yelled Ezra, waving the stick over his head.

"You can do it, gal," yelled Hiram.

Mattie primed her rifle, turned to the target, and plugged it dead center. Then twice more. The crowd stood silent. Cash held up Mattie's target. "She's the winner, folks. Neighbor, you're going to lose a heifer come fall."

The crowd cheered, and more hats than Hiram's sailed into the air. Hiram and Will hugged Mattie, who rubbed her right shoulder and grinned. People lined up to shake her hand.

Ezra, yelling, "Wait a damn minute," hurried to the targets, peered at Mattie's last, and poked the edges of the hole with his stick. "Looky, Cash, this's outside by a cat hair."

Trying to take the stick from Ezra, Cash managed only to rip the target. "Damn it, Ezra, we'll have to shoot this'n over." He glared at Ezra, best as a walleyed man could. "Do me a favor. Keep away from it this time." He put up two clean targets. "All right now, you two, it's one shot to decide this."

As they reassembled, folks made way for Ezra, who had broken the stick and thrown it away. Cash tossed a penny, caught it on the back of his left hand and covered it with his right. "Call it, young man."

Zeb called heads.

"Heads it is. You shoot first."

He steadied his weapon and fired a perfect shot to scattered applause.

Mattie stepped to the dogwood, raised her rifle, then lowered it and went back to the logs. She lay prone, put up the sight, and steadied the rifle. Folks coughed and scraped boots and bare feet in the dirt. Her shot took the left-hand foot of the X. She stood, rubbing her shoulder, a perfectly neutral expression on her face.

Will embraced both shooters. "I'm proud of both of you. I got a grandson and great-niece that's both crackerjacks." He cocked his head toward Mattie and whispered, "Girl, why did you let that boy win?"

Mattie blushed and shook her head. "Papa Will, you know better'n that."

"Well. Whatever you say, gal." He looked at the crowd. "Now let's put on the feedbag and dance a round or two. I'd hate for all this chow to go to waste, not to mention having all you women's feelings hurt."

That day Ezra took Hiram's nickel and kept the heifer. Between ages fifteen and sixteen Zeb and Mattie's friendship turned to something altogether different as Mattie bloomed into a woman. That summer they courted while Mattie stayed with Will and Kate. The following winter Zeb ran to Big Cataloochee every chance he got. Ezra opposed the match but Hannah abetted Zeb in his suit, and the couple married in the spring of 1901. Ezra insisted they move into the cabin Will had built right after the war, halfway between Will's house and his. Until Zeb could build a new house, he was under Ezra's constant eye.

14

The Rattlesnake Farm

During fifty years of living with Will Carter, Kate kept the house just so, and Will didn't trouble her. Kate made wine, starting with dandelion and rhubarb in spring, then strawberry, elderberry, blackberry, and finally Concord grapes as the season advanced. Will drank no wine, said it made his head ache. He kept corn whiskey and apple brandy in the barn, and Kate didn't trouble him. Kate said she'd just as soon drink coal oil as whiskey. They had a good marriage.

Hannah had talked her father into a golden anniversary hoedown, even though nobody paid anniversaries much attention in the family. Will scoffed at first, but when Hannah batted her eyes he melted, always did.

Hannah, black shawl over a housedress against the cool morning, headed out to help her mother get ready for the gathering. Halfway there she picked a handful of galax for decoration, its leaves glistening in the sunlight, a new shade of green with each bounce in her step.

Hannah found it hard to believe her parents had been married fifty years, until she reflected she and Ezra had been married thirty-five. Her boys were grown and married, and life with Ezra had settled into a pattern—a few days' drunkenness after harvest on his part, followed by her threat to throw him out and his promise to do better. Then a cool but comfortable truce the rest of the year. Not ideal, she knew, but better than the lot of many widows.

A jaybird shrieked like she was an intruding cat. Hannah looked for her mother, who was not on the porch nor in the front room, where Hannah laid the galax on the table. Kate wasn't in the kitchen either so Hannah went out back and shouted. She walked to the barn and yelled again and Will emerged, wiping his hands with a piece of feed sack. "Howdy, little gal. What's the matter?"

"Can't find Mama."

"You look in her flower garden?"

Kate's garden was maybe fifty feet by twenty. Perennials on three borders bloomed nearly the year round. Yellowbells and bridal wreath, peonies and lilacs, snowballs and butterfly bushes, attracted bees and hummingbirds and butterflies. During dog days praying mantises swayed with the stalks in the breeze. The season inside the borders marched from pansies and violets to snapdragons and columbines, roses and Sweet Williams, marigolds and sunflowers, asters and mums. Many varieties of ferns peeked from under the bushes. She always said the first thing God made was a garden and she could do worse than raise one herself.

Hannah came around the corner, Will just behind, still wiping grease from his fingers. They'd just finished the first hay cutting and he was sharpening the mowing machine. Hannah'd called "Mama" but heard only a squirrel in the walnut tree. Turning to the open side of the garden they saw Kate's body flattening a row of poppies.

Hannah screamed and ran to her mother while Will stood in his tracks. "Papa, go fetch cold water, hurry, Mama's hurt!" Will seemed uncomprehending until Hannah turned again and told him to bring the bucket. When he sloshed over with it Hannah sprinkled her mother's face. Kate slowly revived, trying to spit out dirt. Hannah cleaned her face with the corner of her shawl.

Kate opened her eyes. "Lord, I'm a foolish old woman."

"Mama, don't talk . . . what happened?"

Kate tried to move but only managed to groan.

Will knelt beside his wife. "Mama, take it easy, now. You're going to be okay."

"I broke it."

"Broke what, Mama?" said Will.

"My hip. I heard it crack when I twisted around. Lord have mercy, it hurts. I was just walking and next thing I knowed I was falling. I heard you all calling but . . ."

Will stood. "Hannah, we got to get her in the house."

"Papa, stay with her and I'll get Ezra. He can help us get her inside."

"We can use the stretcher we made when Jake broke his leg in the upper pasture."

"Promise not to move her before we get back, Papa."

Will took a deep, rattling breath. "I promise, honey. You fetch him lickety-split." He reached for an uncrushed poppy. Kate smiled faintly as he placed it in her right hand.

Hannah hadn't run so fast since she was a girl, and in a trice flew into the barn lot. "Mr. Banks, Mama's broke her hip. She's laying in the flower garden and Papa and I can't move her."

Ezra drew himself up straight. "Damn, Hannah. You got to be joshing."

"The only 'got' is, you got to move Mama right now." Ezra dropped his wrench and hurried after his wife.

They found Will sitting by Kate, head cocked toward hers and the back of his hand stroking her hair. His lips moved but they heard nothing.

Hannah grabbed Ezra's arm. "Looks like she ain't breathing."

They walked closer and saw her open eyes mirrored nothing.

Hannah screamed and knelt beside her father. "Papa. Papa, what happened?" She started crying.

"She's my sweetheart, Hannah. She's my sweetheart, this old gal is."

Ezra walked to Kate's other side and put his hand in front of her nose and mouth. "She's gone."

"Ezra, she's just resting a minute."

Ezra found the brandy jug in the barn and brought it to the garden. "Here, Will. This'll help."

"No, son, put that back. She sees it she'll raise Cain with you."

"Will, she's dead, don't you understand?"

Will put his arm around his wailing daughter. "It's okay, Hannah, she's just resting a minute. Ain't you, sweetheart?"

Ezra handed the jug to his father-in-law, whose hands shook as he raised it to his lips. "Son, thank you. I always did make good brandy. Kate, she makes real good wine." He looked at Kate's body in the riot of flowers. "She's my sweetheart. Fifty years tomorrow. I'll dance with her then. She's resting up, that's all."

That was June 11, 1915, a Friday. They buried Kate the next day. Will made it through the funeral without alcohol, a fact Ezra thought better than to point out to Hannah. Will stayed sober that fall but went downhill fast.

At their elevation they were used to the skinny creek icing over but that winter the big creek at the bottom of the mountain froze solid, huge icicles hanging from laurels like daggers pointed at the creek's heart. Jake woke one morning as wind whipped the house. Rachel had been up for a while. They had been married seventeen happy but childless years. He put on boots and a denim jacket, and an overcoat, and opened the front door. The wind took his breath, caught the door, and slammed it shut. Sidling along the wall to the west edge of the porch, he looked down the valley. No smoke from either of Will's chimneys. Crablike, he went back inside.

Rachel handed him a cup of coffee, which he held to his face. "Thanks, honey. I got to check on Papa."

"I hate you have to go out in this. Want me to go with you?"

His coffee tasted of coins, or shell casings. "Not unless you want to. I'll saddle Lilly. If a mule'll go out on such a morning. What time is it, anyhow?"

Rachel pulled the gold-plated Elgin her father had left her from her apron pocket and flipped open the filigreed cover. "Quarter till seven."

"If he was up he'd have a fire. I hope to hell he ain't out in this."

He covered his boots with tow sacking laced and tied with strings of groundhog leather. His cold-weather hat was made of otter Will had trapped when such creatures still inhabited the creeks. Jake thought the hat made him look like a varmint was trying to suck his brains out, but it kept wind out and heat in, so he didn't care.

On the porch, still no sign of smoke, so he saddled Lilly, who seemed willing enough to move. On the way down he kept looking at his father's chimneys. No smoke. No lamplight. To breathe deeply hurt his chest.

He hitched the mule and stomped on Will's porch, both to make a racket and to warm his legs and feet. He opened the door and hollered. Snow dusted the front room floor. In the back bedroom he found Will under a pile of quilts, themselves under a thin sheet of snow, empty brandy jug like a failed heat lamp beside the bed. Two days before, Will had allowed he'd like a sup of brandy again. Jake had fetched a fresh gallon from the barn. He took a deep breath. "Papa, wake up now," he whispered.

At the Baptist church they dug five or six graves each October against a hard winter. Will's body had frozen in a fetal position so they had trouble fitting him in a casket. It was a month until the pile of dirt thawed enough to cover him decently. The family decided the weather was too bad for a funeral so they gathered at the graveside while the men lowered Will into the grave and covered him with hay and rocks until the ground thawed. That was the fifteenth of January, 1916, seven months and four days after Kate's burial.

Just after Kate died, Will had gathered the family and told them who would get what land and who would get the big corner cupboard, so when they convened after the burial to read the will, Ezra expected no surprises.

Hannah, the eldest, got the home place and fifty acres, which suited Ezra to a tee. It made him the largest landowner in Little Cataloochee, with the fifty acres he already owned. Ezra had already promised to buy Hannah's sister Sadie's share, which would add another fifty, and he had that morning talked to her sister Matilda, who said she would think about selling her share, too. Both lived in Waynesville and didn't need the property. Selling to Ezra would at least keep it in the family.

They gathered in Will's front room, and Ned, Sadie's husband, got the envelope from the family Bible. A town man with a vest and watch fob, and a gap-toothed smile, Ned had trouble with Will's old-fashioned script at first, but soon droned through the sound mind part and the property part and then: "To my son-in-law Ezra Banks, married to Hannah Carter Banks, I bequeath the Rattlesnake Farm, bounded on the west by the big spruce at the corner of the Davidson Gap road, north by the top corner of the rock clift, east by a arn pin setting next to a laurel slick, and south by a pile of boulders on the side of the road, then back to the spruce tree."

Ezra turned to Hannah. "You know about this?"

She put her finger to her lips. He pretended to listen to the rest of the will, but his mind raced every which way.

Ned told him Will had won it in a card game right after the war. Ezra asked him how it lay. "Like ever thing up yonder, straight up and down. No water, no dirt, just rocks and laurel and ivy and snake holes. To make pasture you'd have to dynamite the rocks out and haul in dirt and you still couldn't put nothing but goats on it."

"Why you think he willed it to *me*?"

" 'Cause he loved you, I reckon." Ned chortled, finger in watch pocket.

Back home, Ezra declared he wanted to walk the new piece of ground.

"Lord, Mr. Banks, you'll freeze to death. Why don't you wait till spring?" said Hannah.

"It's got to be worth something or your daddy wouldn't have given it to me special. I mean to find out what it is."

Ezra put on two extra shirts and two pairs of wool socks, tied a bandanna around his head, jammed his hat tight, and went outside. Hannah threw a log in the fireplace and uncovered her Burdick to piece a quilt.

It had snowed four inches the night Will died, but wind had mostly drifted it off the road. After trudging up two switchbacks he passed Jake's place on the right. A snowbird in the holly was the only sign of life.

Past Jake's orchard the grade steepened, and the icy road made Ezra stop and hunt a walking stick. He trimmed a deadfall limb best he could with his cold hands. Without it he might slide back down the road, if indeed a man wanted to dignify the trail by calling it a road. Too tight for switchbacks, it went straight up to Davidson Gap, a quarter mile of pain and suffering.

He saw the boulders after a while, too big to have been piled by any humans save ones of biblical proportions. That was the southern call, which looked straight up the mountain to a black spruce, the western call. The huge spruce, within fifty feet of the mountaintop, looked like a giant Christmas tree.

The north corner cliff was obscured by a maze of laurel and ivy. How could a man walk through all that? Climbing around the boulders, Ezra tried to peel back the laurel leaves, curled in tubes against the cold. As they broke away he looked into impenetrable dark.

At the back corner of Jake's upper fence he found a stob of rusty iron pipe. From there he could see the top of the cliff. This was the shortest line, a little over seventy-five feet. Maybe three-fourths of an acre.

Ezra feared he might freeze, but he had to get to the top. He came back to the road and made it halfway to the spruce when he stopped, totally out of breath. He looked to the north and spied a boulder on one side of the laurel hell that marked the edge of the one flat place on the piece. The flat might accommodate a cabin big enough to cuss a cat in if a fellow didn't mind hair in his mouth. Otherwise snow and rocks and laurel and two or three gnarled junipers. Ezra shivered and muttered "Hellfire" over and over.

Returning, he nearly slipped a couple of times before he reached Jake's place. He was heading by the house when Jake whistled and motioned him inside.

The heat in the front room made his face tingle. Rachel brought coffee, which hurt his hands as he held it.

"What in the world made you go up yonder in this weather?" Jake asked.

Ezra put his cup on the mantel, took out a handkerchief, rubbed ice out of his mustache, and blew his nose. "Jake, when you get a piece of ground you go see it."

"Anything worth a chance at frostbite?"

"I might see something when snow gets off it."

"Years ago, after Papa got it, he took me up there. I thought it was a bodacious place for a house, but, of course I wasn't but ten, and all I was thinking about was how far a man could see."

Ezra sniffed. "If a view was worth a damn, any man in Cataloochee would be a millionaire. Will kept it for a reason, and I got to figger why." He gulped his coffee.

"You want a little liquor to go in that brew?"

"You know I don't touch it."

Rachel turned around to keep back a giggle.

Ezra glared at her and drank his coffee down. "I'll come back when the snow's gone. Got to be something a man can do with it." Ezra retied his bandanna, jammed his hat back on, and tromped out.

Rachel watched him trudge homeward. "Jake, why did your sister marry him?"

"Only thing I can think is, she was young and he was there."

15

SEVENTH VIAL

Levi Marion Carter had been three when his father was killed by the burning tree. Named for his grandfather Levi and his father, Marion, he'd been raised to remember both as tough workers quick to help a neighbor. His mother, Lizzie, would not let them forget the men who settled, then tamed the Cataloochee valleys.

She died of a stroke the day after Levi Marion turned eighteen—that was the summer of 1899—so Levi Marion had no great hopes for the new century. But it soon brought Valerie Brown into Cataloochee. Auburn-haired with a crooked smile, she was what they called a tomboy, six weeks short of Levi Marion's age. The Browns moved into Cataloochee in 1900 and stayed a year, and Levi Marion and Valerie spent as much time together as their families would allow. He had no idea he was in love until the Browns moved back to Jonathan's Creek. The couple was only six miles apart as the crow flies, twenty or so by the old road, but to Levi Marion it might as well have been a thousand.

He found no other to fill Valerie's place in his soul. Meantime he kept busy, farming his father's acres. In the summer of 1912, a bachelor of thirty summoned to the county seat for jury duty, he found himself on the plank sidewalks of Waynesville looking into Valerie's eyes. She wore no ring. They married a week later, and moved into the old cabin in Lucky Bottom his father had begun and his uncles had finished for Lizzie.

Levi Marion had heard his uncles Hiram and Will talk of the "harricane" that uprooted practically every apple tree in Little Cataloochee in 1866, but he never expected to see such himself. The night of July 16, 1916, after it had rained every day for nearly six weeks and showed no sign of stopping, he inspected every seam and crack where water came in. "I'll swear, I'm going to seal this whole place with tar when it dries out," he said.

Valerie rocked in the chimney corner looking full as a cloudburst. "Maybe by the time this young'un comes you can. Sure hope it won't be much longer."

"Valerie, don't fret. It'll come in God's good time. We just want him healthy and strong, like his big brother, Hugh, asleep back yonder." He paused, listening to the rain's steady beat. "Just not tonight. Couldn't nobody get here to help." He squeezed her shoulder and she put her hand on his.

"I'll keep my legs crossed." Suddenly she gripped his hand. "Lord, Levi. My water's broke." Water upon water, he thought. Hold on.

Hiram always said Mary could sleep through a war, and that night she snored softly beside him as lightning and thunder simultaneously shook the house. He got up three times, each time lighting the bedside lantern and taking it into every room, checking for leaks. There were none despite the wind's serious attempt to denude the roof of every shake.

The wind kept shifting, so one time he pissed from the east end of the front porch, another the back porch beside Mary's canning room, the third toward the corner where the gallery took a right turn and faced west for the length of the front room.

Any more he had to get up at least twice during the night to relieve himself but he refused to use the slop jar under their bed unless he was sick. Mary couldn't get much to grow close to the porch, and had even stopped planting daffodil bulbs when her idea that maybe something yellow would grow there proved invalid.

Inside he gave thanks for a dry house and wondered how wet his mother, Granny Lib, was getting. They had buried her a month ago, dead at ninety-nine. She had known nothing during her last years, kept alive through some strength unknown to them. He gave thanks for her, then thanks for his sons, Manson and Thomas, upstairs snoring like rip-saws, having inherited their mother's ability to sleep. Although past twenty, they showed no signs of courting women, but somehow their father thought that might be a blessing.

Folks in both Cataloochees spent that night listening to water run wherever it wanted. Grim jokes about fish jumping back into the creek to dry off alternated with gritted teeth. People took inventory of hogs and chickens and wondered how many would be there when it quit rain-ing. Apple trees fell, and up toward the big poplars lightning struck a hemlock top, which tumbled into what had been a road and ditch before the deluge made it a flume. The nineteen-foot hempine spear coursed down the mountain like a malevolent juggernaut. When the road turned sharp right on a rise above Henry Sutton's place, the tree kept straight. Henry heard it hit the barn about three o'clock. He got up and stumbled to the back porch but could see nothing except a sheet of water pouring from the roof edge.

Up the creek from Henry, Silas Wright heard a crash in front of his place, lit the lantern, and headed for the porch. When he opened the door, wind tore it from his fingers and slapped it against the side of the house. He set the useless lantern inside and reached for the door. The top hinge broke but he finally pulled the door back and latched it. He realized his springhouse sat a good hundred feet from where it should have been. He cursed and slammed around in the kitchen, built a fire in the cookstove, and set pots around the house. Rhetta came downstairs and they drank coffee to a cacophony of syncopated notes from the pot bottoms.

Over the mountain in Little Cataloochee, Hannah woke Ezra with the news their hogs were hollering. He cursed her silent, lit a lamp, and went to the bedroom window. His scowling reflection stared back at him from the glass. Locomotive wind carried horizontal rain. Thunder shook the house and lightning revealed rushing water bearing apple limbs. The rest of the night he paced and muttered to himself about having to move to the poorhouse come October.

In Big Cataloochee, Henry Sutton was glad for morning light. He and Callie sat at the kitchen table with coffee while she stared at the tabletop. "It's the devil," she said.

"What's the devil?" Callie hadn't been right since their only child, a boy, had died three years before. Lately she was given to intense broodiness punctuated by such pronouncements. He saw little of the bloom that had attracted him when they were courting.

"This here weather. The Lord's backed out of the world for a time, mark my words. He's give it to the devil, like they say in Revelations. The sixteenth chapter. This here's the seventh vial. They won't be nothing left standing."

She didn't look up when he got his hip boots. He wondered if she was walking in some bright field somewhere with their dead son. He stomped to set his feet in the rubber boots. "I'm out to check on the barn and see can I milk."

Henry came out the door buttoning his slicker. Rain had let up, or at least fell straight down. In the yard brown water rushed over his boots like his feet were rocks in a stream. No living thing in sight, save night crawlers tumbling in the current.

He peered through water pouring off his hat brim. Normally he would have seen a hundred feet of path through the yard, then a creek maybe four yards wide crossed by a footbridge leading to a barn. That morning he slogged in a good fifty yards of creek. Water hid the footbridge except for its railing, hanging by one upright, canting toward the downstream side. Crossing it gingerly, he knew anything big as a drowned cat coursing down the creek would knock him off and someone would find his body down about Hiram and Mary's place or even farther.

The back end of the hempine stuck out of the barn, black soaked bark surrounding a cluster of yellow-white splinters. Best he could tell, it had flown off that rise and impaled the barn. He figured the cow wouldn't give milk for months.

In the barn Henry shook water from his hat. Hearing the horse, he hung his slicker on a peg and looked left. The cow, switching her tail, glanced big-eyed at him. He removed his hat and hung it on a peg, nodded at her, and put his arms on the top rail of the mule's stall.

He couldn't tell if the tree had toppled Old Sal and she had drowned, or if it had killed her outright. Her head was half underwater and cocked at an odd angle, tongue drooping like a washrag in the water. The tree hung over her side and filled half the stall. A resiny aroma rose over the dank water. He scratched his head.

"They God," he muttered. He could rig a pulley to the ceiling, but how would he swing her out? Or he could tear out the exterior wall, but that seemed a lot of trouble, consonant with this storm and its aftermath.

His father had been in the war, and had told of mule steaks enjoyed around campfires. Henry wondered how long an animal could lay dead before a man couldn't use it for meat. Then it hit him. A dead mule was only the start of his problems.

He couldn't work a farm without a mule. Nobody had bred mules in Cataloochee since Uncle Andy died, so that meant a trip to the stock market in Newport, if he had cash money, which for the most part he didn't. Old Sal cost fifty dollars back then, and a mule might be ten times that now. He wouldn't trade the horse and they couldn't do without the cow. "They God," he said again, slow as smoke off a fresh cow pile.

He sloshed into the stall. The cow bellowed faintly. "You'll have to wait, old gal," he said. Pushing past hemlock needles and splinters and limb ends, he squatted beside Old Sal and dimpled her haunch with his fingertip. His mouth quivered. He waved off two blowflies walking the perimeter of her eye.

With the back of his hand he rubbed her neck, smooth on the visible side, but underneath a limb an inch thick protruded into the water. "I reckon that limb done it. At least she didn't suffer," he muttered.

He'd bought her from Uncle Andy the spring the creek stayed frozen until April and they'd had snow Easter Sunday. Spring of '83. Thirty-three years ago. "Old Sal, I wonder how many miles me and you has plowed." He looked toward the ceiling of the barn. "Feels like I orta say some words over you, but it don't seem right to recite the Twenty-third Psalm over a mule." He couldn't think of anything else except "Jesus wept," so he turned to try milking the cow.

Over the mountain, Ezra had come close to a conniption fit by daylight, pacing from one corner to the other, noting where water came in. He would ask Zeb and Jake to fix the roof. As the light grayed, then pearled, he knew he couldn't get to the orchard until the rain slacked. He put on boots as Hannah got up to start breakfast. "Where you going?"

"Out to the barn," he snarled. "Got to check the livestock." As muddy water ran like a river between house and barn he cursed each floating apple. Drenched and muttering, he came into the middle of the barn. A stream deep enough to carry many years' worth of accumulated hay stalks and bits of manure raced through.

He kept money, counted daily, in a Mason jar in a lidded basket hidden underneath a manger. The lid was gone and the basket was damp but not sodden. A clutch of baby copperheads big around as his little finger and half a foot long writhed in the jar.

"I hate a goddamn snake," he yelled. But for the money he would have heaved basket and all at the side of the stall. Reaching for a pair of leather gloves, he put the basket down as if the snakes might run away with his cash. Gloves on, he reached into the basket.

One snake tried to strike but he flung it onto the driest part of the barn floor and stomped it. "That'll fix you, you son of a bitch." The next one he beat against the wall until it was dead. He was used to killing copperheads with a hoe or his owlhead but this was new, a kind of grim dance. The stall was soon splattered with gobbets of snakeskin and blood. He stomped all except the last, which somehow wrinkled under the wall before Ezra's crashing boot.

He counted the money and looked for something to cover the basket. A filthy piece of cheesecloth from the cow stall and thread raveled from an ancient blanket made do. He stashed his money, came to the cow stall, shoved her, threw the stool to the floor, and sat to milk.

Levi Marion built a kitchen fire to boil water, and shoved a hatchet under their bed. He held Valerie's hand, and stood behind the bed and rubbed her shoulders when she would let him. By four-thirty the next morning she gave birth to a son, whose head Levi Marion caught in a piece of towel. Valerie gave one last push and his son squirted into his arms. He wiped him as she slumped on the pillow and said to clean out his mouth so he could cry. He did so, then cut the cord with a clean knife and tied it. She named him James Erastus.

As baby suckled and mother dozed, Levi Marion put on his denim jacket and gray felt hat and stepped to the porch. It was barely daylight and he was numb tired.

A two-acre bottom lay between house and creek, full of hay soon ready for a second cutting. In the morning gloom it looked more like a lake, except with current, clotted with trash and limbs. A shoat floated by as water lapped the porch corner. The barn seemed all right except a branch of ochre water poured from it. At the other end of the porch he craned his neck to look up the mountain. He saw no standing corn and feared his tobacco was destroyed.

Something caught the corner of his eye toward the south. A yearling doe walked slowly from the far side of the barn. He hadn't seen one in years. She stopped at water's edge, put muzzle to water, snorted, and lifted her head. He imagined nostrils widening, trying for his scent.

Slowly she maneuvered to the other side of the barn and disappeared. "This storm's a sign," Levi Marion said. "What kind, I don't know, but it's what they call a harberger. Wonder what it means when a man-child's born during a plumb harricane?"

16

A DIADEM BETWEEN HER EYES

When Henry Sutton came back in, Callie still stared at the table. Seven o'clock and no breakfast. He came to the cookstove and chafed his hands over it. "You want your coffee warmed up?" She nodded. "Something to eat?"

"Don't feel like it. Ham and cornbread's in the warmer."

"It's a plumb mess out there. We got creek water dang near to the house. Old Sal's dead in the barn."

She looked at him in disbelief. "Sal's dead?"

"Yep."

"Sal? Dead? How dead?"

"Dead as a mule can get, best I can tell."

"Henry Sutton, you know what I mean. I never seen no dead mule and I want to know how she got that way."

"Well, this broke-off hempine come clean through the side of the barn. Kindly like a spear."

She looked for any sign he might be pulling her leg. "What're you going to do, Henry?"

"Callie, I don't know. I thought about carving her up for steaks."

"Henry Sutton, you can't eat no mule, specially her. A body can't eat nothing the devil's laid his hands on."

He went to the kitchen window. "First thing, I got to get her outen the stall. Ain't room to dig a hole and push her in. Might could get Maggie to drag her out that side wall but I don't know if a horse'll pull her. She might spook."

"Well, you got to bury her quick. The old devil might come get her."

He went back outside to check the farm. Aside from the mule and the barn, they had little damage. The tobacco patch, sheltered from wind by a piece of hill, was mostly intact. They'd have time to replant and harvest corn before frost if weather cooperated. The top of the footbridge across the creek was by then emerging from the flow, and he stepped on it carefully.

Henry had felled a straight chestnut trunk maybe thirty years ago, shaved two sides flat, and set it into place to span the creek. "Who was it helped me with that?" he muttered. "Likely Marion Carter and Silas Wright. Me and Callie moved in four years before Marion got killed, 1880. Time sure does get away from a man." He got hammer and nails, righted the railing, and began to nail it upright.

Henry heard hooves slopping up the road, and stopped to see a neighbor, Jim Hawkins, twelve and smart as a whip, on his new mule, Sally Ann. His family lived a half mile up Carter Fork and had been in the valley about as long as the Carters. "Howdy, Uncle Henry," said Jim. "Looks like you got a job of work."

"Sure do, son. It's mighty good to see you. That mule of yours don't seem to mind water on her feet. Hard to find one like that."

Jim smiled. "Yes, sir, she'll step lively most anywhere, that's why I named her for a fiddle tune." He looked around. "I come because we didn't get hit too bad and I wanted to see was there anything I could help with. Uncle Levi Marion said he had a bad feeling about your place. This bridge the worst of your luck?"

"Son, I wish it was. But it ain't. I just got to take care of this first. I'm trying to get this dad-gum railing back where it belongs."

"Can I help?"

Jim was tall for his age, spindly, with a bounce to his step. He was always into something. Folks said he ought to make a doctor or lawyer, he was so curious about things. He played a fiddle with the best of them.

"I sure could use some. Why don't you hold this while I nail it down?" They made short work of the railing. "Much obliged," Henry said.

"Glad to do it, Uncle Henry. You said the bridge wasn't the worst of it. I got all day."

Henry frowned. "Son, you know Old Sal?"

"Sure."

"Well, she's dead."

"You don't mean it, Uncle Henry."

"It's a fact, son, and I got to take care of her somehow."

Jim cocked his head and stroked his chin. Henry couldn't help but smile, because Jim's daddy, Mack, fingered his beard when he was "studying" things, and Jim had mimicked him for years. "I never heard of a dead mule. Can I see?"

"Sure, son. Maybe you can help me get her out."

As they walked into the barn they doffed their hats. As Henry peered over the edge of the stall, Jim put his foot in a hole in the wall and stepped up to see.

He whistled two long notes. "Uncle Henry, I never seen nothing to beat this. You reckon that tree killed her?"

"I reckon so. There's a stob on yon side of her neck." He paused, then put his hat back on. "I sure am going to miss that old gal."

"What you going to do with her?"

"I'll have to bury her. She's got so stiff I don't think we could eat her."

Jim's blue eyes flashed with alarm. "Shoo, Uncle Henry, you wouldn't eat a mule, would you? That'd gag a maggot. Mind if I get a closer look?"

"Help yourself. She sure can't kick you."

Jim entered the stall carefully, like an Egyptologist entering a tomb. A small army of flies surrounded Old Sal's eyes and mouth, traveling from head to fundament. Jim wormed his way to the back side of Sal's neck and touched the impaled piece of limb as if it were a dagger. He scratched his chin.

"I bet it broke off here. I bet when we raise her, the butt end of yonder limb will match this piece."

Henry nodded. "You think that's what killed her?"

"I'd bet a nickel on it. She was standing right there when it hit, and I expect this limb broke her neck. Never knew what hit her."

"That's a blessing. What did you mean when you said 'raise her'?"

"Uncle Henry, we can't get her out that stall door—she's too stiff and the door's too narrow—so we could cut away enough of this wall to drag her outside. But you still got to raise her over that foundation log."

"How 'bout we get some planks and pull her out over them?"

"That might work," Jim said, still studying. "But first thing, we got to get shed of this treetop."

"Son, I'll go get some tools." He hung the claw hammer on the rail and headed for the toolshed. Meanwhile, Jim poked the mule's carcass, lifted her limp tail, and stuck his finger into the available ear. When Henry got back Jim whistled "Erie Canal" with an eye toward trying it on his fiddle.

Henry carried a two-foot pry bar, a bow saw, and a handsaw. A small sledgehammer hung from the loop on his overalls. "It's about quit," he said of the rain.

Jim stopped his whistle in midnote. "Uncle Henry, I just figured out how to get her out without knocking out that wall."

"How?"

Jim held out his hand. Henry looked puzzled, then nodded and gave him the saws. Jim tucked the bow saw under his arm, fingered the hand-saw for sharpness, then laid it on top of the stall rail. He tested the bow saw, then nodded. "This'll do it."

"You mean we orter cut this door out?" The stall door was framed with six-inch locust posts. "Son, we'll be the better part of a day sawing this door out."

"I ain't talking about the door frame."

"Well, then, what?"

Jim began to grin, slowly, like the sun coming up. Henry didn't see much to smile about. "You going to tell me or not?"

"Uncle Henry, you got a dead mule, right?"

Henry nodded.

"Stiff as a board and legs stuck straight out, right?"

Henry nodded, faint light in his eyes.

"Well, we got two choices. We could open up that outside wall and drag her out that-a-way." He paused to see if Henry followed him.

Henry's face began to catch up with his eyes.

"The other choice—" Jim started.

"You mean, t-t-to use that saw on my Sal?"

"Yes, sir. Saw them legs off and we can drag her through the stall door just fine. Ought not take but a few minutes," Jim said. "What's wrong?"

"You can't saw Old Sal. It wouldn't be right."

"Uncle Henry, you was going to cut her up for steaks, didn't you say?"

"That's different."

"How?"

"Well, it just is. Now step back, son, and let me study this." Henry walked to the stall rail and balanced his face on it. Jim went around to the end of the stall where the hemlock stuck out.

When he came back Henry faced him. "Son, I admit it makes a heap more sense than knocking out a wall. But . . ."

"Yes, sir?"

"I just can't do it."

"I can, Uncle Henry. You wouldn't have to watch or nothing."

Henry's fists balled. Jim saw his knuckles turn white and his eyes fill. "Uncle Henry, she was your friend, won't she?"

Henry nodded and took a deep breath.

"What if we wrap her legs in a tow sack and bury them with her?"

"Son, that'd make me feel better. It's a fact." He considered the saw and his young neighbor. "Okay, we'll do it like that. But let me get away before you start. I don't want to hear it."

"She ain't going to holler at us."

Henry grunted. "I didn't mean that. I don't want to hear no sawing."

"I'll give you a minute, then I'll start. Let me get a couple of tow sacks. You go find your guinea hens or fetch Aunt Callie some kindling or something. It won't take long."

Henry put his hand on Jim's skinny shoulder. "Son, you're going to make a fine 'chine-a-trician one of these days. Holler when you got them wrapped up."

Jim gave Henry a couple of minutes, then began cutting hemlock away from the mule, throwing wood out the hole in the wall to clear a path to Old Sal. Soon she lay legless except for stumps exuding blood and rheum. He cut a tow sack into fourths and covered and tied them with twine. He'd sure have something to tell when school started.

When Henry came back in, blood had not yet stained the burlap. He put his hand on Jim's shoulder. "Son, I thank you. I couldn't a done it a-tall. She'll go out now, don't you think?"

Jim nodded. "Yep, Uncle Henry. You want to drag her?"

"I reckon. We'll bury her in the middle of the cornfield. She'll make right good fertilize. But it's going to take a heap of digging to get her in a hole."

"I can get us some help. Everbody in the valley'll want to see a dead mule."

Jim mounted Sally Ann and dragged Old Sal to the middle of the ruined cornfield. Henry followed with the sack of legs, a hoof sticking out of the left-hand end, and placed it beside the animal with the gravity of a town undertaker.

Behind the mule the field looked like a broad-beamed boat had sailed through it. In front of the mule's carcass mud was piled like her body was a scrape blade. Cornstalks stuck out from under her and she had picked up a horse nettle, its white and yellow flower a diadem between her eyes.

17

TWO MILE FROM PROVIDENCE

Folks from both Cataloochees flocked to Henry Sutton's farm the day after the cloudburst. Simply to see a dead mule would have been fine, but they also got to help dig a hole, bury a legless equine carcass, and visit with Henry and Callie to boot. Silas Wright then moved them up the creek to his place, where he and Rhetta fed a multitude after they put his springhouse back and cleaned flotsam from the creek. Everyone then returned home except Jim Hawkins's brothers Fred and Troy, who stayed with Silas to work on the creek bank, and Ezra Banks, who, after seeing the mule, left straightaway, having been to the Wright place in 1880 to no personal profit. Townfolks from Waynesville who showed up the next day on rumors of a bona fide dead mule were flat out disappointed to find only a mound of earth crowned by a wilting nettle.

Silas Wright had just turned sixty-six, and, mostly at Rhetta's urging, no longer resisted paying money for extra help. He figured he and
Fred and Troy might as well take down the rest of the trees along with
the storm-snapped hemlocks on the far bank. He would not clog his
chimney by burning hemlock, but the band mill would buy them, along
with a poplar, straight for eighty feet, limbless for forty.

Silas had ordered parts to fix Rhetta's buggy, and the day before the
storm the postmaster had sent word they had arrived. After dinner
Rhetta looked at him. "You forgot that Sears order, didn't you?"

"I'll get to it this evening." After a nap he saddled his horse and
headed down the road.

Silas had inherited from his father, Jonathan, about a hundred acres
bisected by the Rough Fork of Cataloochee Creek, to which he had
added another hundred. The house was nearly a mile from Uncle Andy
Carter's place north of the creek and Henry Sutton's to the south. The
land climbed from the valley to the top of Big Fork Ridge, then formed
a huge amphitheater around the peaks to Horse Creek Gap and halfway
up Spruce Mountain. He figured never to have a close neighbor unless
the Cherokees rose up again.

His farm was mostly pasture and cropland but a stand of woods on
the east buffered against a growing Cataloochee. He was perfectly happy
to see no one save Rhetta for weeks at a time. If it were up to him he
would stay at home, except for church on Sundays and trips to Waynesville in the spring and fall.

Rhetta, on the other hand, was gregarious as a crow. She insisted
they keep boarders, mostly vacationing fishermen, and when not caring
for them had worn her buggy's suspension out "traipsing," as Silas
called it, all over Big Cataloochee, visiting folks both well and sick, taking food, news, and her own brand of comfort to anyone in need of it.
Silas could have postponed his trip to the post office, but it meant
Rhetta and her little dog could get back on the road tomorrow and he'd
have more peace and quiet.

After fording the twisty creek and coming into the woods, Silas
reined his horse Maude up short to stare at a large white bird preening in

a dead sweet gum. He shook his head and squinted. Half the size of a blue heron, but white. He sat the horse and watched the bird's bill sweep through its wings like a comb. "By God," he said, "I must be seeing things."

After convincing himself it was real, it occurred to him that those feathers would make a fine hat for a fancy woman. Then he eyed the bird, leaned in, and whispered, "Maude, ain't that just like a man, thinking to make something foolish as a hat out of such a creature. There used to be so many birds around here they named the Pigeon River after them. Why, when me and Hiram went to look at that train, we seen clouds of passenger pigeons on the way. Now, not fifty year later, they're extinct, like them dodoes they tell about in school."

He waved at Henry as he passed his place. The mound over Old Sal still pocked the ground and a fresh wooden cross stood at its head. Callie sat on the porch, book in hand. Silas waved but she paid him no attention. Down the creek, Hiram's field was springing back from the storm, and it looked like he wouldn't lose his oats. Silas didn't plant oats anymore—too much handwork to brier them. He passed no one on the piece of road between the empty church and the post office.

Soon the little frame building, its steep roof peak belonging on a much larger structure, appeared. Weather gave the raw structure a patina of age. A sign hanging over the front door read, in large block letters, POST OFFICE above and ᴎELLIE, ᴎᴄ below. Years ago a Cherokee had painted it that way, whether as a joke or in ignorance no one knew. Nelson Howell's daughter Nellie told him to leave it that way. She let her father think he ran his life, the post office, and store, but folks knew Nellie ran all three.

Silas tied his horse, stepped onto the railless porch, and went in. Behind the counter, Nelson, a paunchy man, removed and folded a dirty apron, revealing a necktie that stopped six inches above his belt. "Howdy, Silas. You got a package from Sears." He turned to a chestnut standup desk with pigeonholes atop the back. Across the front was stenciled DO NOT HANDLE OR MESS WITH THE MAIL ASK AND IT WILL BE HANDED OUT. He gave a parcel to Silas, who rattled it like a Christmas present.

"Much obliged, Nelse. Say, you know about critters. Guess what I seen at the edge of the woods."

"Maybe a porky-pine?"

"Might's well have been. A big old bird, kinder like a long shitepoke, but all white. Black legs. Setting in a gum tree just back in the woods."

"How big?"

"Maybe two foot tall. Long neck." He looked around for women in the room. "When it took off it shit a big old wad."

"Sounds like an egret, or maybe a white heron. Storm must have blowed him in. Got a brother in Wilmington. They got the damnedest birds down there, setting in salt marsh like it was natural. You know, Silas, they could make us into one of them Audubon places if such would stay around instead of flying back home."

"I don't know who *they* is, but they can stay out of here. Storm do much damage?"

"Not here. Home, that's different. It ripped up most of our apple trees. Tobacco's gone. I still ain't found one of my barn cats."

Silas grunted. "If all the livestock you lost was a dad-jim cat, you ain't in too bad a shape. One I feel sorry for is Henry, losing a mule like that."

"Well, that's right, neighbor. First they lost their boy, then he's near about lost his wife, and now his mule's gone. Hard for a man to manage under all that."

Silas took his package, paid Nelse a dime for a tin of sardines for Rhetta, and started home. As he approached the church he spied a person sitting on the little porch he had trod nearly every Sunday since he had moved to the valley. It was odd to see someone idle this time of day.

A man and a dog came into focus. A big man with wide shoulders, body tapering to a slim waist. A hound—or was it a mastiff?—beside him stood silently bristling. Silas knew a dog that wouldn't bark at a stranger would just as soon rip a piece out of his leg as look at him. As Silas reined the horse, the man straightened and spoke to the creature.

Silas stayed atop his horse. "Howdy, stranger," he said. The man put hands together, elbows balanced on knees. A pistol butt showed at the edge of a bedroll beside the steps.

The man stared at Silas with deep brown eyes set into a ruddy face almost flat except for high cheekbones hinting Cherokee or Melungeon. He wore a silver ring on his left little finger but was otherwise devoid of decoration save a red bandanna. His hat, the paling green of timothy hay the day after it is cut, caved in at the sides. The man nodded. "Howdy yourself." Tobacco-and-whiskey voice. The man looked from Silas to the dog, and put his hand on the dog's head.

The canine was bigger than a Plott hound, with almost curly chestnut fur on his haunches. One eye was clouded blind and the other was clear and yellow as a cat's, or a round-pupiled goat's. As Silas moved in his saddle, the dog's eyes shifted with him. Black gums outlined bared teeth. Nape hair stood like soldiers but the animal made no sound. The man pulled a pack of Fatimas, shook one out, and put it in the corner of his mouth. "Smoke?"

"Thanks, but I'm a pipe man. Smoking cigarettes is burning money."

The stranger scraped a wooden match on the porch. "A man's got to waste something, and if it's only money, then he's all right." He waved the match and held it between his stained fingers until the heat left, then put it back in his pocket and took a deep drag.

"Mind if I get down?"

"If you're worried about getting dog-bit, don't be. Old Dan won't mess with you long as you don't mess with us." He pointed his finger and the dog relaxed.

Silas dismounted and tied Maude to a sapling. He took out a leather pouch and pipe. Packing it full of loose tobacco, he stretched to his full six feet four. "Don't believe I ever seen you before." He lit the pipe and threw the match behind him.

The man nodded and looked down the road. "I come over the mountain night before last."

"Which one?"

"Mount Sterling. Been living in Knoxville. Kind of hopped my way here through east Tennessee. Stayed awhile at Cosby. Come over Sterling day before yesterday. Slept in a little lean-to up there. Cold of a night." He dragged on his cigarette. "Sure is pretty country."

"Born and raised in Knoxville?"

"Naw. Out a ways, in the country. Two mile from Providence. Ever been there?"

"Can't say as I have. Sevier County?"

"Blount. Just across the county line."

"What's your name?"

"Harrogate. Folks call me Bud." He finished and stripped his cigarette. Flecks of machine-cut tobacco scattered into the churchyard.

"You plan on staying, Bud? Mine's Silas, by the way. Silas Wright."

Bud stood and shook Silas's hand. "Don't know. Might if somebody's got work."

"What made you leave Knoxville? You ain't running from trouble, are you?"

"Not over here, I ain't."

"If you're getting away from the law, you come to a good place. They used to hide all kinds of varmints in here, outliers, Indians, runaway niggers, fugitives, I don't know what all. But if you make trouble here it'll not go well for you." He hitched his suspenders.

"Mr. Wright, if I'm hiding from anything, it's a woman."

"Many a man's done that. You do farmwork?"

"I can do most anything. You got a tractor or motorcar, I can keep it running."

Silas smiled. "They ain't no tractors in here, automobiles neither, but I heard our neighbor Hiram's thinking about getting one. Myself, I ain't got money enough to throw at something unreliable as a motorcar, not when I got Maude here. I got a mule-drawn mowing machine if you want to work on that. If you ain't too proud to cut trees and grub underbrush, I can pay you a little and put a roof over your head for a spell."

"I'd be much obliged, Mr. Wright."

"Mr. Wright was my daddy, dead twenty years now. Call me Silas. What kind of dog is that anyhow?"

"Airedale. Chow dog. Mostly mutt. Long as he gets fed he's fine."

"You want to ride with me?" Silas walked over and untied his horse.

"Naw, point me and I'll be afoot. I'd hate to miss any of this country."

"Then follow this road. Don't take no right or left. When you ford the creek you're getting close. Two-story frame house on the left-hand side."

Silas mounted and touched his hat brim to the stranger. Bud and the dog started walking westward toward the schoolhouse.

At home Silas handed Rhetta her tin of sardines, then told her about the bird. "Silas Wright, you ain't old enough to be seeing things. My papa lived to ninety-one and he had a clear mind until way past eighty."

"Nelse says he's seen such things on the coast. Storm must've blowed it in here."

"I wouldn't tell nobody. We got to keep our heads up." She forked the sardines onto a saucer and nodded for Silas to share with her.

He ate one and wiped oil off his chin. "By the way, I met a stranger at the church. I told him he could help clear that hill. Said he was Bud something, from over next to Knoxville. Harrogate, that's it."

"Sounds like a name in a story."

"Could be. I told him he'd be welcome long as he didn't cause no trouble."

"He look like a ne'er-do-well?"

"Didn't get his life history, Rhetta."

"Well, I won't be shy." Rhetta had always been what some folks called curious and others called nosy. They finished the sardines, and Silas went to the shed to work until Rhetta called him for dinner.

That afternoon Silas pulled the buggy out, jacked up the rear axle, and removed the right wheel. He meant to install the new anti-rattlers from Sears so the thing wouldn't shake out his wife's eyeteeth. He was taking off the left wheel when Bud and the dog rounded the bend.

Right away Rhetta's little dog, Chigger, started raising hell. She came outside to see what the animal was upset about. Silas halfway hoped the big dog would kill Rhetta's Chigger and be done with it. He'd board Bud for six months for nothing just for that.

Rhetta's sister Viola had lived in Clyde, a hamlet between Waynesville and Canton, for years, and somehow started breeding little town dogs. Silas never called them Chihuahuas. He said any dog of that size was a "broom-handle dog," no use for them except to stick a broom handle up their ass and clean the floor with them. But he didn't say it around Rhetta, whose sister's Chihuahua bitch had gotten out when she was in heat. Chigger was a pup from that brief encounter, his father a rat terrier. Chigger was sullen, quick to bite, and Rhetta was the only person he trusted.

Silas watched, wondering if the big dog would strike, but Rhetta kept Chigger behind her with a broom. Bud clapped his hands, ordering Dan under the shade of an apple tree.

Every now and then Silas looked to see Bud, listening to Rhetta, polite, shifting from foot to foot, occasionally lighting a cigarette. Rhetta stood in front of him, arms swinging and pointing. After half an hour Silas looked up to see Bud and his dog.

"Well, did you pass muster?"

"I reckon. Meaning no disrespect, Silas, but, lordy, that woman can ask questions."

Silas lit his pipe. "You're telling me? If she'd made a lawyer we wouldn't have no criminals walking around. They'd all be under the jailhouse."

Bud lit a cigarette. "Well, Silas, now that she knows every thing I ever done, I might as well stay awhile. That is, if you're still willing."

"You can start by helping those boys across the creek. Going to terrace it—keep rainwater on it long as I can. Something might grow up there."

At supper Rhetta talked a blue streak at Silas, the two Hawkins boys, Bud, and Mr. Camel from Cosby, a boarder, who came twice a year to fish and hunt. Bud kept his eyes on his plate and only looked up when asked to pass a dish. Supper was potatoes, pickled beans, soup beans and spareribs, applesauce, cornbread, and biscuits. Bud had eaten pickled beans before but never any mixed with corn. He kept the dish close by his plate for a second or third portion.

When he became aware Rhetta had stopped talking he looked up—all eyes were on him. "Ma'am, did I do something wrong?"

"I just asked if the cat'd got your tongue. And if you was so partial to them pickled beans that you wasn't going to let the rest of us have seconds."

Bud's face reddened as he passed the dish. "Sorry." It went around the table and came back to him empty.

"Maybe he don't have nothing to say," Silas offered.

"Silas, that reminds me of my sister Zera's girl Flora. Remember when she was about ten and quit talking? Zera got so worried she asked Doc Bennett to take a gander at her."

Rhetta poured molasses on her plate and mashed a hunk of butter into it with her fork. "Old Doc Bennett, he's a big man wears a black suit. He come in and kinder squatted down by Flora and talked to her but she didn't say nothing. She hadn't made a sound in two or three months. He felt her forehead and looked in her mouth. About the time he took to tapping her chest Flora looked at her mama and said, 'Mama, tell this old man to get his hands offen me.' " Everyone guffawed as Rhetta covered half a biscuit with molasses and butter.

"Well, sir, Zera hugged Flora and fussed over her something fierce, and then asked Doc Bennett what she owed him. 'Not a thing,' he said, 'Flora just didn't have nothing to say.' Is that you, Mr. Harrogate? Nothing to say?"

"I reckon not, ma'am. I kinder keep to myself."

"Well, around here we talk. Silas might work you for money but you can pay me for your victuals with a story, Mr. Harrogate." She finished her dessert and sat back in her chair.

Bud pursed his lips. "Okay, how's this . . . I was in the fourth grade. They was some boys ahead of me, you know, seventh graders. Some of them was shaving, they'd been kept back so much. I was scared of them, mostly Billy Turner. Billy, he'd up in the morning ask the teacher if he could go, you know, to the outhouse. He'd go and come back, and by and by another'n'd do the same. They was going out to the creek where we kept our dinner buckets and eating the young'uns' dinners. We was too scared to tell on them, so they had a good business going."

Harrogate drank buttermilk and wiped his mouth on his sleeve. "One day I told my old man I didn't get no dinner. Well, he knowed the teacher, Mr. Burris, he was a red-headed man with freckles all over his face. So Pap went over to his place and said somebody'd smouched my dinner.

"Next morning, Mr. Burris sat on the edge of his desk and stared at us for a minute or two, tapping his britches leg with a ruler, seemed like forever. Then he started telling us a story."

"Well, now, Mr. Harrogate, that's more like it," said Rhetta. "Keep it coming!"

"Said when he was a pup he done time in the penitentiary. For stealing. Well, I looked at Billy Turner and his face screwed up proper. Then Mr. Burris told it, kinder like this:

" 'First thing was when I was ten, I started stealing lunches from the young'uns at school. I'd go out and eat me a sweet tater and come back. Then I'd get bold and clean out the whole bucket, ham, beans, taters, and all. Got away with it, too. Pretty soon that wasn't enough. I'd steal crackers at the store. Or snuff. Or a thimble, any old thing laying around. Then it got to be shotgun shells or a pack of cigarettes. And then I thought, well, sir, stealing is pretty good. I'd done left school by then. So you know what?

" 'My place was pretty ratty, so I figured I'd fix things up. I come upon a farm that was handy and that night I got the hay out of the barn. Took it home and hid it. Next night I come back for the barn. Put the hay back in it. Made several trips, but I got the house and the corncrib and the smokehouse and the outhouse and put them over at my place. I got the cornshocks and the pitchforks and the bee gums and ever heifer, sheep, and chicken. Most trouble was the hogs. The last night I got the well. Dug it up and put it on my shoulders and you know what? I was carrying it home when the high sheriff shined his light in my face and said, "Boy, it's all over for you." I did years at hard labor for that. And it won't a bit of fun. But you know what I learned in them years?

" 'I learned there ain't nothing worth stealing, not a cracker, not a farm, not a man's land, nothing.' Then he sorted us into grades and started teaching. And not a one of us got our dinner stole after that."

Rhetta clapped. "Mr. Harrogate, I declare, that was a fine story!" She stood. "Now, if you menfolks are finished, get out to the porch and I'll clean up."

They sat in chairs or on the porch itself, lighting tobacco and listening to the murmur of the creek. Silas looked at Bud. "Son, she'll make you do that ever evening now, like them A-rab nights."

Bud sucked on his cigarette. "Silas, I got plenty of stories. It's finding one to tell when women's around that's a problem."

"Well, you best think about that. You know, boys, we got work to do in the morning. Best turn in pretty soon."

Silas produced a quart Mason jar from the box in the corner of the porch. The men were mostly silent except for guesses about tomorrow's weather. From inside they heard dishes clatter and Chigger's toenails click on the floors. They drank one last round to their new friend Bud Harrogate, who told Silas that terrace they were working on would grow fine watermelons. When Rhetta got to the porch, the jar was back in the box and the men were stretching, scratching, and beginning to head for bed.

18

THE WORLD WOULD BE BETTER OFF

Ezra woke one August morning in 1916, thirsty, not for water, as might be expected after a supper of salt-cured pork, but dry-lipped in remembrance of last fall's binge. Then he shuddered with the memory of his first drink, stolen from his old man's jug the summer he broke Ezra's nose. It had tasted more like kerosene than liquor but it had made him feel better than he thought a man could, or probably should, feel.

He licked his lips and sat on the edge of the bed in his office, thinking for a brief moment to search his desk for a square bottle, though none nested there yet. Crops were not made, cattle not sold, apples not graded for market. In a month or two he would allow himself a drink.

Ezra never thought it abnormal that he took no alcohol fifty of fifty-two weeks, nor reflected that before 1896 he spent thirty years of his adult life stone cold sober. He would have as soon wondered why the sun came up or the moon changed. It was the way things were and the business of no other person, nor even of the God Grady Noland preached about every month at the Baptist church.

A bite in the air, promising the smell of working cider mixed with woodsmoke, fresh cow manure, and frost, made him eager for harvest. He dressed and clomped into the hall, heard Hannah cooking breakfast, and stepped to the front porch. It was good to see a few sourwood leaves scarlet already. The night temperature had been in the sixties lately but this morning it was a dozen degrees cooler.

After breakfast he hitched his mule, Huldy, to the wagon, in which he had put a ladder and handsaw and ax, and drove to the edge of the road. The old chestnut at the corner of the lane into his farm was slowly dying. It still bore leaves, thick in the top but patchy down through the branches. The two bottom limbs, big around as a man, were dead as hammers. He meant to cut and haul them to the house, then get his sons to work it into firewood.

He braked the wagon under the south limb and patted the mule, who was unusually hard to spook. In the wagon bed he leaned the ladder against the tree's huge trunk. He bounced on the bottom rung to see if the wagon would move. Saw in hand, he climbed the ladder, grabbed the top of the limb, and steadied himself.

The saw was in midstroke when the ladder moved. He whistled at the mule to stay put, but it was too late. As the ladder fell in the wagon Ezra let the saw go. He swung on the limb with both arms and saw a motorcar chug up the road. Cursing first mule, then vehicle, Ezra moved his head to see if he could let himself down.

A Model-T of a color between black and dirty, driven by a man of about thirty years, stopped ten yards from the mule. Ezra dropped into the wagon bed, then grabbed Huldy's reins and calmed her. He glared at the driver, whose Adam's apple reminded Ezra of a turkey wattle. The man wore a hat of a kind not seen in Cataloochee, with a high crown and narrow brim. The man switched the motorcar off and got out, dusting his suit with his hat. Ezra couldn't decide if the fellow was an insurance peddler or a politician.

"Morning," said the stranger. "Are you Ezra Banks?"

"Who's asking?"

"My name is Grover Cleveland Moody. Revenue agent." He put his hat back on and displayed a badge in a leather wallet. His coat opened to uncover his service revolver.

"What do you want?"

Moody smiled mirthlessly. "Sir, I think there is a whiskey operation close by. I want two things, three, really. One is a man named Harrogate. Two, I need permission to search your land for this man. And it would be helpful if you would guide me."

Ezra's eyes brightened. "You and me got nothing to talk about."

"Must I get a warrant?"

Ezra walked close enough to the agent to smell his pomade, and poked his bony finger in the man's chest. "Look all you want. But if you looking depended on me helping, you'd never see another thing in this world."

"Can you at least tell me which direction to go?"

"You can go to hell for all I care."

Moody put his hand on his weapon. "Sir, cooperating with the law could help you in the future."

"Is that a threat?"

"Call it a suggestion."

"Take that damn hand off your gun, then."

When Moody relaxed Ezra stepped toward the road. "OK, then. Up this way is my boy Zeb's on your left. My brother-in-law Jake's straight yonder. That's all farmland. After that it's nothing but a rattlesnake farm at the top of the mountain. Now leave me in peace."

There's one to keep a weather eye open for, thought Moody as he left Ezra, who was climbing back into the wagon. If he doesn't break his neck first. Moody walked past Jake's place because the mountain rose precipitously past it and was thickly wooded to the northwest. He saw no woodsmoke but one would have to be careless or even luckless to fire a kettle with green wood. Still, he thought the area worth checking.

He climbed to the top and satisfied himself no paths led to secret places. Nothing smelled of mash. Coming back down, he admired the view, but grew impatient. He fingered his inside pocket, which held a wallet with a substantial amount of cash. Some folks would talk for as little as a fin. In Tennessee the week before someone had ratted out Harrogate for thirty dollars.

He cranked the car and drove back through Ola and down the mountain to the road into Big Cataloochee. He stopped by the creek to eat his tin of sardines for dinner. By late afternoon he passed the Bennett place, wondering where he might lay his head that night. He crossed the bridge over Cataloochee Creek and started up the road. At Lige Howell's he pulled in beside two cars parked in the turnout.

A short man with a large white beard came to the porch to greet him. "Howdy, stranger." Lige put out his hand. "Need a square meal and a room? Best of both right here."

Moody shook his hand. "Don't mind if I do, Mr. . . ."

"Howell. Lige Howell. And you?"

"Moody. Grover Cleveland Moody."

"Pleasure to meet you, sir. Where you from?"

"Born in Dellwood."

"Well, now, you're a neighbor. That's mighty fine."

Over supper Lige discovered his neighbor was a federal revenue officer, which did not please him until he figured being polite might stand him in good stead someday if any of his sons needed a favor. One or two of his boys likely made liquor, but when they brought him a jar he never asked where it came from.

"You know a man named Harrogate?" asked Moody.

"Sure. New face around here. Boards with Silas Wright. Why?"

"Let me ask the questions, Mr. Howell. Have you seen Mr. Harrogate lately?"

"Not in a couple of weeks, maybe three."

"Does he make liquor, Mr. Howell?"

Lige lit his pipe. "I wouldn't know. He ain't been in the valley long enough for me to talk to him but once, and that ain't a question you ask a man you just met."

The next morning Moody drove up the valley to the post office. When he asked about Harrogate, Nelson pointed to a tall man with receding hair and a droopy mustache coming through the door. "That's Silas Wright. Harrogate boards at his place."

Moody showed his badge. "Mr. Wright? Grover Cleveland Moody. May we talk?"

Silas looked down at Moody, then at the postmaster. "I got any mail, Nelse?" He started around the agent but the man sidestepped into Silas's way.

"Mr. Wright, please cooperate."

"Put that damn refugee from a tin can down and I might."

Moody complied. "I am told you know a man named Harrogate. Goes by Bud."

"What do you want with him?"

"Just a few questions."

Silas regarded Moody with disdain. "Son, let me save you some work. First place, Harrogate's gone fishing."

Moody opened his mouth but Silas raised his hand. "Don't say nothing, Mr. Federal Agent. I'm about to answer your nosy questions before you ask, then I expect you to let me alone. Second place, Harrogate don't make liquor, or my wife would have worried that fact out of him and he wouldn't be eating at my table. Third, I'll know he's back when I see him coming. Now get the hell out of my way." Nelse handed Silas a letter and Silas nodded thanks and left.

The postmaster grinned. "Mr. Moody, I heard there's a still up Deadfall. Way up toward the Big Poplars. Yes, sir, there's been talk, lessee, seems like Hiram said he'd seen a man with a hundred pound of sugar the other day, I don't know." Nelse rolled up his sleeves and adjusted his necktie. "I doubt your Mr. Harrogate has anything to do with it, but you might find something to bust with that ax you carry around. You *do* have one, don't you? If you don't I got some in the back. Good lawman like you, I'd sell you one cheap."

Moody's Adam's apple rose and fell like a bouncing ball. "Deadfall, eh? Where might that be?"

Nelse pointed him past Hiram and Mary's, told him to turn left when Deadfall Branch came into the creek at Henry Sutton's place, "then travel straight up the mountain. Even if you don't find a still, the poplars up there are worth seeing."

Outside it became clear he wasn't going to find Harrogate this trip. He knew Nelse was kidding him, but something might present itself between Sutton's farm and the top of the mountain. He drove to the Sutton place, where a woman on the porch rocked slowly and read from a book. She paid him no attention and no one else seemed to be around. He checked his weapon, then started walking. He thought this road would, if taken over the mountain, carry him to Carter Fork, an area where he'd be surprised not to find some illegal whiskey.

Halfway up he felt something watching him and stopped in midtrail. He was past Sutton's pasture now, into a woodlot. Toward the top huge trees loomed like silos. The section was aptly named. Tulip trees, chestnuts, and hemlocks littered the ground like broken fence posts after last month's storm. Nothing moved but a squirrel. He fingered his holster. Maybe he had sensed an animal but he didn't think so.

After another half hour's climb he rested on a rock. He stilled himself, eyes moving only occasionally. This was nothing like the feeling on a hunt when game was close. He was the quarry. Maybe it was a wild hog, for he had seen signs of their rooting and gouging the land.

He moved his right leg when he felt an ant bite his calf. He crushed it and stood. Might as well go to the top, he thought. Although still apprehensive, he knew he could shoot his way out of most anything, and he wanted to see those big trees. Much of the Smokies was becoming cutover, but neither the northern companies or the paper mill in Canton had yet gotten a toehold in Cataloochee.

At the top he found a place used by generations of Cataloochans and

Cherokees to rest their animals. A hitching post, dead charcoal in a hollowed rock, a dessicated rattlesnake, its buttons no doubt drying, meant for the inside of a fiddle.

The path veered to the right and steeply down. He had seen nothing speaking of anything save normal travel, no sudden side paths or dropped locust bark or spilled mash. He was debating whether to head for Carter Fork, which would add five or six miles to the journey back to his car, or to return the way he had come, when he heard a stick crack.

He cocked his weapon. A man-sized figure scuttled northwest along the ridgetop. "Halt," Moody yelled, "or I'll shoot." No longer attempting stealth, the person started down, angled sideways against the grade. Moody yelled again but the man—a big hulk carrying a rifle—did not slow. The agent fired his pistol twice and ran toward the figure.

As he sped toward the man his left leg jammed into a hole and he pitched forward. The sound of his leg snapping seemed loud enough to wake the dead. He didn't know if he had passed out but when he lifted his head the man he chased was nowhere in his vision. Moody's hat hung in the brush and his pistol lay a dozen feet down the mountain. He tried to sit up and lift his leg out of the hole, but the pain was too great. Spitting leaves and twigs, he kept jerking his head to keep himself conscious. "Boy, I'm in a damn fix," he muttered.

"You bet your sorry ass you are." He had not heard the man circle behind him. "Who in hell are you anyhow?"

Moody beheld a man of about thirty years with piercing blue eyes, body and clothes innocent of soap. "Federal Revenue. Grover Cleveland Moody." He pulled out his badge.

The man laughed. "Throw that shit away, Revenue. You ain't never going to need it again." Moody waved the badge like a shoofly stick but the man knocked it from Moody's hand with his rifle barrel. "You son of a bitch. I'd wring that chicken neck of yours, but you've done spooked the game. So I might as well blow your damn brains out." He calmly shot Moody between the eyes.

Willie McPeters, one of Rafe McPeters's many sons, lived on Carter

Fork and often hunted boar at the top of the mountain. He never made whiskey himself but had about as much use for a federal agent as he would have had for a canopy bed. Less, really, for he could have used the bed for firewood.

He tidied things up without haste. Moody's badge went in his shirt pocket. He cleaned the revolver and put it in his jacket. The spent rifle cartridge went in his hat brim. He hefted the limp agent and extracted his leg from its prison. His boot toe nudged blood and brains into the hole. "Look at that," said Willie. "Hog rooted that sure as hell. I might've killed one if this bastard hadn't showed up."

He lay Moody's body on the forest floor. Within a minute he transferred a knife, six hundred thirty dollars in bills, and a tortoiseshell comb into his overalls. Grinning, he hoisted Moody's body onto his shoulder. "I reckon that's better'n a hog," he said. He picked up his rifle, toted the dead man over the hill, and threw him in a pit hollowed centuries earlier by animals or Indians, which for ages had hidden things best not exposed to the light of day.

Hannah liked to walk to the post office in late summer, for her favorite roadside flowers wore the delicate blues of chicory and aster. August had been dry, and the usually shiny galax was covered with dust. Orange and black butterflies lingered on thistle blooms. When she returned one Thursday morning, Ezra sat on the porch sharpening a scythe.

She plopped in the rocker and fanned herself with a circular. "Lord, Mr. Banks, it's got warm again." She had taken her hair down but now pulled it off her neck.

Ezra dragged his file down the blade twice. "Won't be long till we wish it was this hot."

"You're right." She extracted her reading glasses from an apron pocket and looked at the pamphlet's drawings advertising patent medicines and cure-alls. "They've got something for everything, Mr. Banks. Here's a kidney pill, and here's something for the rheumatism. Oh, and this'n'll grow hair on a bald man. You sure don't need that kind of medicine." She fanned again and looked to the opposite ridge, where two buzzards circled. "Oh, listen, Mr. Banks. You'll never guess what I just heard. Them buzzards reminded me."

He looked toward the ridgetop, then fingered the scythe and frowned. "What?" He absently trailed the file down the blade again.

"You know that revenue man?"

Ezra grunted.

"He up and disappeared!"

Ezra felt the blade again, then put down the file and reached for his whetstone. "Good riddance. Them rascals ought to go back where they belong."

"No, Mr. Banks, you don't understand. He didn't just leave. Wasn't it a week ago Monday you talked to him?"

Ezra nodded. The sound of whetstone on metal made Hannah shudder.

"Well, after he was here he went to Big Cataloochee, spent Monday night at Lige Howell's. Then he went to Silas Wright's looking for that Harrogate fellow. He left his car at Henry Sutton's place a week ago Tuesday and ain't been seen since."

"Seems like a man would come for his auto."

"Well, he didn't. They sent three revenue men back this Monday. Searched the woods two days, never found hide nor hair of him. So they left yesterday with his car. Mr. Banks, what do you reckon happened?"

The edge seemed to please Ezra. He lay the scythe down and looked at his wife. "Don't really care. Maybe that damn popinjay found out a tin star won't help a man meddling where he don't belong."

"You reckon somebody killed him?"

"Wouldn't be surprised, Hannah. And wouldn't blame them a bit. The government ain't got no bidness taxing liquor. They work men like that to enforce the law. I bet not a year ago he was making it hisself."

"What do you mean?"

"That's who they get to work the revenue. Men that ain't smart enough to make money on whiskey themselves, but say they know how a stilling man thinks. Most ain't got the sense God give a goose."

Hannah pulled her hair into a ponytail and let some breeze hit her neck before letting her hair go. "Well, I feel sorry for his wife—or I suppose widow—or whatever you call a girlfriend when the boyfriend dies. If he had a wife, or girlfriend, I mean."

"Don't know why a woman would stay with such a man, myself."

Hannah focused on the soaring birds. "There's no accounting for tastes, Mr. Banks."

Ezra smiled. "That's right. Some like that homemade stuff he was so hot to find. It ain't for me."

Hannah stared at her husband and started to speak, then turned to the advertisement again and rubbed the back of her neck. "I . . . oh, never mind."

"Never mind what, Hannah?"

"Nothing."

"No, I mind that tone. What is it?"

"I just don't know, Ezra."

"Damn it, woman, *what*?"

"The world would be better off without it."

"What?"

"Liquor. It's nothing but a curse." She put her glasses back in her apron and took a deep breath. "You've heard Preacher Noland. It's ru-rined many a man, and woman, too, and—God help me, I never thought I'd have to say this—it's about to be the rurination of you."

Ezra picked up the scythe. "Woman, save such talk for drunks. I don't touch it but once a year. My old man, that's different, he was drunk ever day he had money."

"Yes, and one thing about you when we first married was you didn't touch it. So different from my own father. Oh, Ezra, why did you take it back up?"

He set the scythe handle end on the ground and leaned over the blade. "Hannah, I'm warning you, don't start in on me. I work hard. I keep you up, don't I?"

She looked him in the eye. "Yes, but it's different now." She reached for extra words. "When you're drinking you ain't yourself. You get . . . mean, and I'm afraid . . . why can't you let it alone?"

He threw the scythe straight down as hard as he could. It clattered and bounced but somehow did not break. "Damn it, woman, I told you not to go on like that. It ain't fair."

She stood and folded her arms over her chest. "Fair? Fair to who? Ezra, it ain't fair for me to have to tiptoe around you a week or more a year. You don't remember your meanness. You even set the bed quilt on fire last year. I'm afraid you're going to kill somebody one of these days."

Red-faced and snorting, he slammed his hat in the yard and stomped it. "Damn it, woman, I'll drink when I damn well please. I built this house and I'll make the rules until they carry me out in a box." He turned toward the barn, then back to Hannah. "Now don't give me any more of this shit," he yelled. Picking up his hat and scythe, he strode to the barn, cursing every breath.

Hannah went to the kitchen and wept for a short time. Then she prayed, "Lord, keep us safe. Keep us safe, in Jesus' name."

19

A SIMPLETON

Ezra visited his rattlesnake farm two days later. He'd been there twice, the day after Will's funeral, and again a warm day that January, when he'd discovered nothing to make him think any better of it. This time he told Hannah he was going to stay there until he figured out what to do with it.

She watched him emerge from the shed with a hoe laid on his shoulder like a Continental soldier's musket. As he headed for the road it was all she could do not to laugh as she went to her Burdick. He's a fool, she thought, if he thinks anything'll grow there besides catbriers and trouble. For his part, Ezra figured a walking stick that happened to have a hoe blade on one end would help him both conquer the elevation and find dirt—if indeed any dirt existed.

Just past Zeb and Mattie's gate the grade steepened, and he reached Jake's front corner puffing and red-faced. At the corner of his property he stopped, raked mud from his boots with the hoe, then studied the lay of the land as he caught his breath.

Perusing the plot did not bring happy thoughts. Maybe a mountain goat could walk the north corner. A man could hide a still under the laurel, but he'd have to haul in hardwood and water, so he might as well build a house, but then there wouldn't be room for a still. He struck a flat spot about the size of a kitchen table with the hoe blade. Sparks. Chopping the hoe at the nearby laurel stirred a puny spider.

A glint beside an eight-foot-high boulder caught his eye. Ezra wormed his way to the rock, briars catching his trousers. He stretched the hoe toward the object and dislodged what proved to be a bottle.

Maybe a traveler between the two Cataloochees had dropped it, or maybe his father-in-law had come there to figure out the value of this patch of ground and had thrown it away in disgust. Dirt, spiders, and sunlight had turned the glass chalky. Ezra set it in a niche on the boulder, pulled his owlhead from his belt, and backed away, careful to shoot at an angle with little chance of ricochet. The bottle disappeared, leaving white dust where the bullet hit. He put his boot toe in the niche and skinnied up the side, sitting atop the boulder like an outlandish cormorant, peering first one way, then the other.

The top of Cataloochee Mountain rose to his east. Several chestnuts had broken in July's storm, their splintered limbs scattered like a giant's toothpicks. To the south Noland Mountain divided both Cataloochees. To the west Indian Ridge's peaks spiked like an old comb's broken teeth. The solitary black spruce loomed behind him on the north.

He surveyed his ground with dark eyes. No timber nor water. No dirt—except what he'd brought on his boots. No mammals, unless a bear denned in the laurel, and it would be a runt. Ragged cylinders of snakeskin made him keep watch about his feet. No place save one on which to build, and not even a fool would want to live there. Nothing to tempt a man to do anything except leave. Old Will was likely laughing in his grave at making a fool of his son-in-law.

At home Hannah called as he came down the hall, "You plant your fall garden, Mr. Banks?" She looked up from the sewing machine and smiled sweetly.

"Woman, what do you mean?"

"You took the hoe, didn't you?"

He stomped down the hall and slammed his office door.

That afternoon Ezra saw a man turn into the lane toward Zeb and Mattie's place. Slightly over six feet, he wore a plaid long-sleeved shirt, denim britches, and a hat reminiscent of a toadstool. Soon there was a knock at Ezra's door.

Ezra stuck his head outside. "Howdy, stranger."

"I search for Mr. Ezra Banks."

Ezra had never heard such a brogue. "You ain't from around here."

The man smiled, showing straight yellow teeth. "No, *mon ami,* I come from far away. Canada."

"What would make a man come down here from there?"

The man took off his hat. "Excuse my manners, sir. Are you Mr. Banks?"

Ezra nodded.

"*Bon, bon.* Your daughter of law, Mrs. Banks, she told me to come here. To answer you, sir, I work as foreman over the mountain at Crestmont. I supervise the men logging. Are you familiar with our workings?" The man's hands were scarred like those of Cataloochans who worked for Crestmont, but his clothes bore no patches and he smelled of store-bought soap. Tufts of coarse, wiry hair peeked from under his cap.

"I heard of it. You all are taking every last tree in Tennessee."

"Yes. Just the big ones, really, to Big Creek, then off to the Pigeon."

"What's your name, anyhow?"

"Pardon, sir, I forget my manners again. My name is LeClerc. Neil LeClerc."

"What kind of a name is that? Lee Clerk did you say?"

"LeClerc. It's French. My Crestmont men call me Neil Canadian."

"By God, you mean I got a real live frogeater on my porch?"

LeClerc frowned. "No, sir, I was born in Canada. My parents are French."

"That counts. A French foreigner in Little Cataloochee. I'll be damned." Ezra released the screen door and held out his hand. LeClerc's hand felt calloused as it looked. "Mr. Neil Canadian Lee Clerk, set down."

LeClerc sat on the edge of the porch. "Mr. Banks, I am much impressed with your mountains. Quebec has short mountains, not tall like these. It would be excellent to own a place here. With a view, high to see in many directions. Understand?"

"You mean to build a house?"

LeClerc nodded. "*Oui,* a small cabin. I first thought close to a stream, but I found no willing one to sell such a place. So I next thought to find something high."

"You mean something at the gap?"

LeClerc nodded. "What I mean is I like to be a fisher when I get away from my occupation. But everybody farms the—how do you call it?—bottoms land. They will not sell land near a brook. But from a high place I could walk to water soon, and when I enjoy the view I could think about fish catching."

"You want something to drink, Mr. Canadian?"

LeClerc quickly shuffled to his feet. "I learned long ago to drink and to lumber do not mix, Mr. Banks. But thank you."

"I was talking about water, Mr. Canadian. We're Baptists."

"Oh, I would like very much some water, then."

"We keep it in a bucket in the back."

Ezra gave LeClerc a gourd dipper of water. He drank deeply. "Sweet water."

"Part of that's the cedar bucket. Never had nothing in it but water. Now then. What makes you think I got land to get shed of?"

"The postmaster told me you had—how you call it, inherited?—land that is high up, not good for farming."

"Like it's any of his damn bidness."

"Pardon, Mr. Banks, I did not mean to be offending."

"It ain't you, Mr. Canadian. That meddling rascal's what raises my dander. But the more I think about it, he might be right. You got family?"

"No, just myself."

"So if you was to build a house it'd be small."

"One room. A quiet place, far away from the crashing trees and the saws and locomotives of my work. A retreat."

"A what?"

"Retreat."

"A ree-treat. So you can think about fish."

"About anything, Mr. Banks. Fish. Maybe look at the clouds and not think at all."

Ezra grinned. "I believe you're tetched in the head, Mr. Clerk. This storm rurint my apple crop. But if you was to buy this piece of ground it might keep us out of the poor house."

"May we walk the land?"

"Let me tell the wife."

Ezra knocked on the kitchen doorsill.

"Who's that, Mr. Banks? He's a sight."

"Says he's Neil Canadian Lee Clerk. He wants to look at that piece of ground your daddy willed me. I think he's crazy enough to buy it."

"Lord, Mr. Banks, what for?"

"A ree-treat."

"What's that?"

"Damned if I know, except for what a army does. He talks like he'd live in it and think about fish and clouds and sh—stuff."

Hannah smiled. "Sell it. A simpleton only comes by ever now and then."

Late that afternoon in the office Ezra dragged a straight chair for LeClerc in front of his desk. He pulled paper from the right-hand drawer and dipped his pen. LeClerc looked around. "You are a man with money and land."

"Hmp." Ezra scowled. "Don't talk while I'm writing."

"I am sorry. I was just reflecting that there are no books in here."

"What in hell would I want with books?"

LeClerc raised his hands. "I did not mean to offend. I will be silent."

Ezra turned the paper to LeClerc. "Okay, Neil Canadian. This here's the deed. Them's the calls, the corners like we walked them. Here it says you give me two dollars cash money. We'll sign it—I'll get the wife to witness—and I'll get it put in the book at the courthouse in Waynesville."

"A handshake would not be—how you say?—OK enough?"

"No, sir, property is property. Sign right there." He yelled for Hannah.

LeClerc signed with a flourish.

"You learn that fancy writing in school?"

"My signature I teach myself. In school they make you make everything look the same, you know? But I want my name to look different." LeClerc smiled with satisfaction.

"Well, it sure does." Hannah signed where Ezra pointed. Ezra then crabbed his name on the paper and started waving it to dry. "Now then. My money."

LeClerc stacked eight Liberty head quarters four to a pile in front of Ezra, who stared at him intently.

"Mr. Banks, is something wrong?"

"When I record this they'll charge fifty cents. The buyer pays that."

"The courthouse makes *me* pay for that?"

Ezra nodded.

"You mean I cost two dollars for a beautiful piece of land with a view and they get—what is that, a fourth?—to register it? That seems *très cher.*"

"It's the same if you sell half an acre or a thousand."

"Well, then, if I must, I must." He stacked five Liberty head dimes beside the quarters and looked pointedly at Ezra. "Excuse me, Mr. Banks, but you would not make advantage of me?"

Ezra opened the drawer, cupped his hand, slid the money into the drawer, and locked it. "Mr. Canadian, I wouldn't take advantage of a man. Hell, even if they didn't charge for it, it'd be worth fifty cents for the trip. It's a hard day's ride to the county seat."

LeClerc pumped Ezra's hand, making a formal bow. "As you will, Mr. Banks." He bowed to Hannah. "A pleasure to make your acquaintance."

Ezra rested his hand on LeClerc's shoulder. "Tell you what, Lee Clerk, if they don't charge me nothing, I'll give your fifty cents back."

LeClerc smiled. "*Bon,* good, that is—how you say?—deal. Must I wait to begin my building?"

"Put a artillery battery up there if you can find room."

20

SQUIRREL SKULL

Ezra departed early the next morning, bound for the courthouse in Waynesville. He first stopped at the store to let Ernest Parham, the current postmaster and storekeeper, know he'd outfoxed that Canadian fellow. Parham got along well with all his customers except Ezra, whom he enjoyed needling, especially about his rattlesnake farm. Ezra stopped to see him before he left Little Cataloochee. "Didn't even argue with me over the price," Ezra said, grinning. "You'd think he'd have had better sense than that."

Parham wiped his hands on his apron. "Well, Banks, don't I get a finder's fee since I sent him over? A nickel maybe?"

Ezra's face clouded. "Finder's fee. Shit. I don't know why I even come in here. Only mail I ever get is circulars." He turned on his boot heel and slammed the screen door.

Ezra got to Waynesville about three, in a drizzle that started at the Frog Level bridge just before the depot. He felt in his saddlebag for his slicker. A man on the depot porch, the left side of his face the color of a strawberry, raised his hand at Ezra but was not greeted in return. At the top of the hill up Depot Street, Ezra saw two automobiles parked behind the courthouse. "Must be damn lawyers," he harrumphed. The clock atop the building said four-thirty. Ezra knew that wasn't right but in the rain could not tell the exact time. He considered getting his slicker out but decided it was more important to hurry.

In the courthouse basement his eyes strained to adjust to the dim light of electric wall sconces. "Darkest place I ever saw," he muttered. He made out "Register of Deeds" lettered in white on the frosted glass of a door, "George C. Haynes" toward the bottom of the panel.

The register of deeds was in Clyde at a meeting, and his secretary, Miss Smathers, took a while to convince Ezra she could take care of recording the deed. It was nearly dark when Ezra left clutching his official receipt and cursing rain that had by then turned cold and copious. He briefly thought of getting a room, then put his slicker on and headed for home.

He and his mule, Old Huldy, made a sorry pair coming back over the mountain, slogging for hours, like drenched fugitives bound for a grim encounter. At three in the morning they got to the barn. In spite of his slicker Ezra was soaked and his hat brim had come unmoored in front. He kept dry matches in a box near the lantern. By its light he checked his pocket—the ink on his receipt had bled clean off the paper. He wadded the paper and stomped it into the dust of the barn floor, then fed and watered Old Huldy.

On the front porch he threw the soggy hat on the floor and rattled the doorknob. He turned his soaked pockets inside out but the only key was to his desk, where his door keys, tied by a rawhide string, were locked.

Twenty years ago Hannah had been a heavy sleeper but over the years Ezra's binges changed that. In the early years of his drinking she lay awake just a few nights a year, fearful he would hurt himself. Then she worried that he would hurt the boys, or burn down the house. She had not yet come to fear for herself but figured to with time. And the change of life had murdered sleep during large portions of her nights, so when she heard Ezra bang at the door she had been awake a half hour listening to rain on the roof.

"I've a good mind to let him stay out there," she muttered. Rolling onto her side, she pulled the blanket over her head but the noise persisted. "He can sleep in the barn." When she began to feel his kicks and knocks as well as hear them she pulled the covers back and sat on the edge of the bed. The thought of a furious Ezra smoking his pipe in the barn made her light the lamp and descend the stairs. She flicked the latch and opened the door.

"Damn, woman, what in hell took so long?"

Out of its bun her hair shone yellowish in the lantern light. "Mr. Banks, I'll thank you not to curse me this time of morning. What in the world are you doing out here anyhow? Are you drunk?"

As he brushed past her he nearly knocked the lantern from her hand. "Woman, I'm half drownded. You know I don't drink this time of year and I don't need you fussing after you done locked me out of my own house."

"You're touched in the head, Ezra Banks. You know good and well nobody locks anything around here but you. And clean up all that water before I have a conniption." She went upstairs and disappeared into her bedroom.

Fumbling a dry match from the tray on his desktop, Ezra lit the lamp. He piled his sodden clothes on the floor and as he sat at his desk his long johns squished audibly. On a piece of ledger paper he recorded the details of the transaction and hoped they would not lose the original at the courthouse. He chuckled to himself. "I sure foxed that Frenchman."

LeClerc returned in a wagon laden with tools, logs, and lumber. Two men dark of skin and eye sat with him. They spoke a fast, musical language and sang while they rode, stopping at Ola for cheese and crackers.

"Where in the world you fellers from?" asked Ernest Parham.

"They were born in Italy, my friends were. They are carpenter and mason. They have come to help me build retreat."

"Build what?"

"My small house on high land."

They stayed long enough to borrow two sleds. The road past Jake's was too steep for a heavily loaded wagon, so they split their team, hitched a mule to each sled, transferred the wagon's contents, and headed up the road.

When they came by Ezra's place he and Hannah were fixing the rail fence. A section needed replacing, but Ezra wanted one more season out of it. They tamped rocks around the bases of the posts and Hannah helped hold one end of the rail while Ezra nailed the other back in place. LeClerc stopped his odd circus. "Good day, Mr. Banks," said LeClerc. He removed his cap. "And to you, Mrs. Banks. I hope you are well in health."

Ezra put his nail jar on the ground. "What kind of a hat do you call that? I meant to ask you the other day and forgot."

"It is a beret, Mr. Banks. I think your people call it a tam?"

"We don't call it anything," said Ezra. "Nobody in here would wear nothing like that. What you got on the sleds?"

"These are, how to say, materials for the retreat. We will build it starting today."

The two other men nodded. "Them two look worse'n you, Lee Clerc. Where'd you find them at?"

"They, too, work for Crestmont, building the shanty houses for the loggers. They are from Italy, my friends, Luigi this one and Stefano this one."

"Lord, Hannah, you hear that? Next thing you know, Cataloochee'll have a Chinese laundry."

Hannah smiled at the men, who grinned and nodded. "How long you expect it'll take to build your ree-treat, Neil Canadian?" asked Ezra.

"We have a week off. I think to have it finished during that time."

"If these boys will work I don't see no reason you can't do that."

"Then, Mr. Banks, we better get to work. Again, I thank you for the sale of the property." He put his beret back on. "Did they charge you at the courthouse the fifty cents?"

"Hell, yes, and then some. I had to pay them to notarize us and get exercise tax stamps and I don't know what all else. I'm a good mind to make you give me an extra fifty cents."

LeClerc shook his head vigorously. "*Non, non,* Mr. Banks, I have paid out all my money for these materials. You can't get—how you say it?—blood from a *navet.*"

"Around here it's a turnip. Don't expect no help if you run out of money."

"No, sir. I won't. Good day to you both." Luigi and Stefano quirted the mules and started up the mountain.

A regular pilgrimage passed Ezra's place that week. Folks caught up their farmwork and rode to the head of the valley to watch the "ree-treat" get built. They tied their animals the best places they could and offered to help so they could listen to the foreigners.

First the Italians, who knew stone, cleared the laurel and chiseled a level place fifteen by thirty feet. They laid out the house and hacked a foundation that would admit no water. As the logs went up language was no barrier. When LeClerc wanted *solives* atop the walls, it was easy for the Cataloochans to figure "joists" and they got lifted. When he would say, "We need *couper* for the *châssis,*" a saw got fetched and the cut was made. LeClerc called the panes of glass *les vitres,* which the Italians made into *la finèstra.* The Cataloochans installed this "winder-light" on the west side opposite the chimney. The natives at first didn't understand LeClerc's insistence that interior logs be *carré* but after they squared them they saw it added a full foot to the inside of the structure. Some vowed to go home and "car-ray" their own walls.

On the third day they put a porch across the front deep enough for one straight chair. LeClerc thanked the neighbors for their help and promised them *hospitalité* if they wanted to visit. The next Friday, LeClerc returned in his wagon loaded with a couple of straight chairs, a small table, a rope bed and mattress, and a small box of books. He stayed until Sunday afternoon. Folks soon got used to him coming over the mountain to spend the weekend. After a while they no longer went out of their way to see him sit on his porch admiring the mountains and inspecting tackle.

One September Friday, LeClerc showed up at Ola in the late afternoon, a warm day just before weather gets cold enough to turn leaves. In the store he nodded to four or five loafers sitting, whittling, spitting, and lying about one thing or another.

He asked Parham for cheese and crackers. "What else, Mr. Canadian?"

"Maybe some tinned, how you say, sardines?"

"Coming right up, Mr. Canadian. That all?"

"*Oui,* yes, how much?"

"Let's see, that's soda crackers, twenty cents, sardines is a dime, the cheese's forty cents, that'll be seventy cents in all."

LeClerc counted coins from his money pouch, which he laid on the counter. Something shiny peeked out the opening.

Parham whistled through his teeth. "Mr. Canadian, I ain't seen a gold nugget in a coon's age. That's what that is, ain't it?"

"*Oui,* yes, you want to look?"

The loafers muttered to themselves when LeClerc held it up. The size of a buckeye, it had worn smooth in the pouch. The storekeeper stuck out his stubby hand and LeClerc put it on his palm. "That's the real thing, I do believe," said Parham. "Know what it's worth?"

"Can you tell me?"

Parham took it to his scale. "Right at two ounces. They figure gold in different ounces than American, I think they call them troys, but I'd give you forty dollars cash money for it right now. Where'd you get it?"

LeClerc smiled. "Let us say I found it."

"Well, where at? A man might want to go find him one, too."

LeClerc looked at the group, who had stood to look at the nugget like it was the holy grail. "I would not want to make Mr. Banks unhappy."

Not a half hour passed before Ezra heard boots on his front porch.

He looked out the window, saw the storekeeper, and sighed. Ezra swung the door open.

"Howdy, Banks. Thought you'd like to know a little something."

"What do you know that I need to hear?"

"Well, you know that Canadian fellow?"

"What about him?"

"He was down to the store a while ago."

"I know. I seen him come by."

"Well, guess what he had with him?"

"Parham, if you got something to say, say it."

"He had him a gold nugget, Banks. A genuine gold nugget the size of a squirrel skull. And you know where he found it at?"

"Where?"

"Up yonder." Parham nodded his head toward LeClerc's property.

"The hell you say."

"Well, I asked him where he got it, and he wouldn't say. Said you'd get mad as hops if you knowed about it."

Ezra came all the way out on the porch and scratched his face. "Parham, that ain't right. They ain't no gold in this country or ever foot of it'd be dug up."

"All I know is it sounded like he found it up yonder and didn't want you to know. And if I was you I'd not be happy I sold a man a two-dollar piece of ground that had a forty-dollar gold nugget on it."

Ezra slammed the doorsill with the flat of his hand, then turned toward Parham. "You damned scoundrel, get back to your bidness and let me run mine."

Parham put his palms up as he scooted toward the steps. "Yes, sir, Mr. Banks, I didn't mean nothing. I just thought—"

"You son of a bitch, you ain't happy unless you're meddling in everybody's affairs. Git, before I kick you halfway down there."

Inside Ezra took five or six turns around his desk, fuming, slamming his fist on the desktop. "Goddamn! What if it's true?" Opening the desk drawer, he looked at the receipt he'd made. He paced to the window and back, took his owlhead from the desk drawer, and shoved it into his belt.

Ezra was sixty-six that summer but made it to LeClerc's place quick as a stripling. LeClerc sat on his porch in a straight chair, an empty one beside it. "Mr. Banks, what a pleasure. Please come to sit and see the view."

"To hell with your view, you cheating Canadian son of a bitch. Any truth to what Parham tells me? You found gold up here?"

LeClerc shook his head and frowned. "I was afraid someone might tell of this. I tried to keep it, how you say, a secret."

"Then it's true?" Ezra's right hand fingered the butt of his pistol.

"Mr. Banks, some things are not worth the telling of them. It is sufficient that I have a piece of gold. Let us leave it at that. Now please, let us be friends and have some water to drink."

"You saw it, didn't you? That day we walked it. You saw it and swindled me out of this place for two damn dollars. I ought to kill you."

"Mr. Banks, Neil LeClerc may be many things but he is no swindler."

"You're a goddamn liar, too. I ought to blow your damn head off." Ezra pulled his pistol out of his belt and put his thumb on the hammer.

LeClerc stood, his right hand in the air, fingers pointing to the sky. "Mr. Banks, so help me God, what you say is not truth. You sold me this land fair and square. I paid for it what you wanted. If you need to shoot me, then remember I am a man with no arms." He walked to the western edge of the porch and Ezra raised the owlhead as he went. "I ask of you, let me gaze at this majesty once more before you shoot poor Neil LeClerc."

LeClerc took several deep breaths as he looked to the ridgetops. He glanced at Ezra, whose hand trembled too badly to aim the pistol. LeClerc let out a long sigh, walked slowly back, and sat.

Ezra stood in front of the porch, the grade making his head level with LeClerc's knees. "You goddamn scoundrel. You got to give it back."

"Give what back, Mr. Banks? I do not understand."

Ezra came a step closer and leaned forward so he was square with LeClerc's chest. "You stole this here property from me."

"Mr. Banks, I bought this ground. You said yourself we made it legal."

"Looks like I *thought* I was selling you a two-dollar piece of ground. Now I changed my mind. If I have to go back to Waynesville to get that deed annulled, I will. So you might as well give it back now. I'll even give you back that two dollars."

"That I cannot do, Mr. Banks. *Voilà,* look, what I bought was wildness but now, here is the house that was not here before. You see the porch, the door, the roof. I plan to be here as long as the lumbering lasts. Three, maybe five years. Then I might sell it back to you. But not for two dollars any longer. It is now a worthwhile property. I am sorry."

Ezra raised to his full height and hitched his trousers. "Mr. Canadian, we'll see about that. I might can't shoot an unarmed man but I can still get this property back. You'll hear from me."

Ezra rode Old Huldy all night. Looking like a nightmare, he came to Waynesville, burst into the register of deeds office, and slammed the door. He looked wildly at Miss Smathers. "Where's Haynes?"

"Mr. Banks, he is in a meeting. What can I help you with?"

"You know that piece of ground I sold to that Canadian?"

She nodded.

"We got to annul that deed."

"Mr. Banks, do you mean cancel it?"

Ezra waved his hand impatiently. "Whatever you call it. I got to get that land back."

She saw the owlhead and glanced toward the door. "Mr. Banks, it belongs to Mr. Clerk. If he wants to sell, that's fine. But he has to dispose of it, not you."

"What if he swindled me out of it?"

"What do you mean, sir?"

"He found gold up there—didn't tell me about it and bought it for two dollars. That's my gold, damn his hide. And I mean to get it back."

"Mr. Banks, I can't help you with that. Perhaps a lawyer—"

"I hate a damn lawyer! I want to see Haynes right now."

She opened the door and caught the eye of Sheriff Sam Leatherwood. He saw Ezra and quickly walked in with his hand out.

"Banks, good to see you. Met you politicking over in Catalooch. Remember?" They shook hands. "You ain't bothering Miss Smathers, are you?"

"Damn it, Leatherwood, I'm trying to get a piece of land back from a swindling Canadian."

"I handle swindlers in this county. Why don't you come over to the jail and we'll talk about it?" said Leatherwood.

Ezra explained the situation on their way down Depot Street. They turned onto Montgomery and stopped on the jailhouse porch.

"That woman said to talk to a lawyer, but I don't know."

"Banks, here's some free advice. Go back and either forget about it or try to buy it back fair and square."

"What about my gold?"

Leatherwood hitched his pants and took a Camel from his shirt pocket, offering one to Ezra, who shook his head and filled his pipe. "Far as I can tell, it's his gold—if it is gold. But I never heard of gold over there, nor over here, for that matter. I bet he got it somewheres else. Did he tell you he found it on the property?"

Ezra frowned and shook his head.

"Well, there you go. Tell you the truth, Banks, he's likely having some fun with you. If I was you, I'd go home and forget about it."

They smoked in sunshine, Ezra's expression cloudy. Leatherwood looked at him as he mashed his cigarette butt with his boot toe. "You've never been on this end of a deal, have you?"

"What do you mean?"

"From what they tell me, you come years ago with plenty of money and bought a farm and then inherited a bunch more land when Old Will died. You're as rich a man as there is over there. Right?"

Ezra concentrated his gaze on the balsams ringing the town to the south and west.

"Then first time you get hold of something that won't worth nothing you found a man crazy enough to give you cash money for it." Leatherwood smiled. "And now he's done convinced you he's found gold up there. Hell, Banks, you got beat either way. Either you sold a gold mine for two dollars or he only made you out for a fool. I was you, I'd go back home and forget it."

Ezra tapped out his pipe and shrugged. "Much obliged. But I reckon I got to handle this my own way."

"I better not hear about no Canadian with a owlhead bullet between his eyes. You got another pistol?"

"Nope. Used to have a Colt's Army but I traded it off."

"Then keep that little old owlhead where it belongs."

21

No More Power

Henry Sutton never claimed any particular gift except an ability to breed fighting roosters. Mean-tempered, they had to be housed in separate pens or they would tear each other apart. He no longer fought them himself but sold them to men who did, and he was known as a fellow who would breed a champion.

Sometimes they started crowing at three in the morning and kept up until after dusk. One year when he had two dozen, several disappeared until he stayed up with a shotgun, shells loaded with rock salt. Late in the night Henry fired at a retreating backside. No one admitted a thing, but old George Carter, Hiram's brother, didn't sit for a week.

Henry had no further reflections about a fire sale on roosters until the morning Silas Wright rode up on his black mare Maude.

"Howdy, Silas."

"Damn it, Henry, quit grinning like a mule eating briers. Them birds are getting me up too damn early, and I live a mile from you. I'm getting damn tired of it."

"What do you want me to do?"

"What ever body within earshot of these cussed mite factories wants—get shed of them before we all end up in the asylum."

"Silas, I got money tied up in these birds."

Silas hitched his trousers. "Either get shed of these varmints or I'll give you fifty cents a piece, wring their fool necks, and leave them for the damn buzzards. You hear?"

So he decided to sell most of the birds. He only had ten traveling coops but folks were happy to lend him extras. The morning he left for Cosby his wagon sounded like a circus in hell. School stopped to let everyone wave at Henry, frowning on the wagon seat, staring straight at Old Sal's backside. That was three years before the cloudburst of 1916.

Now, in 1917, he was down to two roosters, and Callie was convinced the devil had gotten into both of them. He figured they would need to stew for two days to get them tender enough to eat.

First thing was to whet the ax head, for, tough and mean as those birds were bound to be, he didn't want to have to chop at their necks more than once. His mother always wrung chickens' heads off but as far as he knew she never killed a fighting cock.

He'd bolted an old mower seat to the grindstone frame, and turned the wheel with a bicycle crank and chain, so when he sharpened his tools he looked like he was riding slowly to nowhere, showering the way with sparks.

"Here we go now. Wonder how things got this way, Callie seeing the devil behind ever green tree. I think she'd be all right if Tom hadn't died like he did. Bless him, he was a fine boy, only seventeen when that boar's tush ripped his leg and he got blood poisoning. His mama's only boy, and a favorite one if he'd had brothers. Lord, when was that? May 1913, he died, the twenty-fourth, I mind it was a pretty Saturday when I found him dead in Callie's arms. She was sitting on the bed telling him he'd be all right. I took that rag she'd been wiping his forehead with and cried my own tears on it and dabbed it on him but it didn't do no good. My fine boy dead. Liked to have killed me, but I made out, that's what you do, you put one foot in front of the other and go on but she started talking about seeing the devil ever where after that." He turned the ax head and honed the other side.

"That's getting more like it, it's about sharp enough. Got to grind that nick out of the edge, looks like I cut a fence wire with it. Oh, Callie'd been talking about the devil since that Kerlee woman killed her two-year-old grand-young'un. That was 1913, too, the old woman told folks she was taking the girl to the county home 'cause she couldn't afford to keep her, but instead climbed clear up Ad Tate Knob and stuck her in a hole and covered it up with rocks. I don't know if she knocked the girl's head in or she just covered her up and left her screaming. Somebody noticed they never showed up at the county home, so we got to hunting for her, must have been five hundred men and boys, found her after a couple of weeks, bad business. To think a body could do that to her own flesh and blood made a man think about the devil, sure made Callie talk about it, and Preacher Will Smith preached about a snake slipping into our Eden here in Haywood, and that must've made a big dent in Callie's mind, 'cause that evening she read me about Jesus making them demons jump into all them hogs. Who I felt sorry for was the farmers. Did Jesus pay them for their livestock? Anyhow, even that Kerlee woman, a man could tell she won't smart, or clean, or for that matter any account, but she won't no devil." He stopped pedaling and held the ax to the light. "As pretty an edge as I ever put on an ax." He dragged his chopping block to the rooster pens. "Mean as these things is, a man don't want to be carrying them any farther than he has to." The birds started counterpart crowing with appreciable menace. "Maybe they do have some devil in them. But when you get down to it, I don't believe in no devil. I'm near seventy and ain't seen him yet. I mind when I was a pup up on Hemphill, me and one of them Brown boys, Woody I think it was, come by the schoolhouse and there sat a bucket of rocks somebody'd left aside the road. We flung ever one of them through the winder lights and afterward Papa said the devil'd got into me, so he'd beat the devil out of me, but I still didn't see him."

He circled the rooster pens, admiring the color of their feathers and bright eyes. "Makes a fellow wonder about Jesus, too. I ain't saying I don't believe in Jesus, but I sure ain't seen him neither. Didn't feel him when I got baptized in that there creek. I was nine, some Baptist revival preacher from Milledgeville, Georgia, name of Peacock, baptized me and said Jesus had come into my life, said I'd got saved, but all I remember getting was wet. Soon's me and Callie was married I become a Methodist like she was raised. They don't—what's that new word?—zero, that's it, zero in on what you ortent do as much as Baptists. Baptists always holler how you ortent drink or frolic. I don't know what frolicking is exactly but it sounds like a man could enjoy himself at it.

"Just wish Callie'd let me keep liquor in the house. I asked her once if she'd let me, just in case of snakes, but she stubbed up like an old heifer. Winter nights it feels like it's a half mile to the barn for a drink. But I don't blame her, her daddy was a drunk and her brother kept up the family business, you might say, and both died early with bad livers. Course, she never thinks that patent medicine she takes is drinking, no, sir, it's *medicine,* but the first time I got her a bottle of Lydia Pinkham's I took a whiff and figured it to be forty proof. Licorice and rotten hay. She got to taking so much I started boiling chamomile and dandelion and licorice whips and pennyrile all together, then lacing it with whiskey. Put it in her empties and she didn't hardly miss a beat. She's, Lord knows, worse hooked on it than I am on my drink of a night, I just like mine 'cause it gets me all limber to sleep, but she's getting to where she's shaky in the mornings."

He reached into the first rooster's pen. "Got to grab this old rascal just right or he'll flog the shit out of me. Up, old man, you're in the stewpot soon's I chop your head off." Henry had the bird by the wings and feet but it still had a mind to peck Henry's eyes out or at least mangle his hand. When it lunged its neck to strike, Henry cut his head off with a clean blow. "There now. One down, one to go. Damn, look at that. No devil, just showers of blood, he'd have made a good fighting cock."

So he killed his last fighting roosters, scalded them down to pinfeathers, scraped them, cut them up, and stewed them. Life got quiet. He ran the farm and made the kitchen garden and did most of the cooking. Callie got up mornings and once in a blue moon made breakfast but usually went to the porch in warm weather or the front room in cold and read her Bible, coming in for medicine, until Henry made dinner. He thought reading something besides the Bible might do her good, so when folks went to Waynesville he gave them a little money to buy newspapers. She learned about the war in Europe, and the troubles with Prohibition, and the government creating national forest in the East from private lands, and concluded the devil's forces were winning. She went back to her Bible.

One spring afternoon he said he was going to the tobacco patch. "Henry," Callie said, "you be careful. I seen the devil this morning behind the tulip tree. He's laying for you, sure as the world. You're all I got now." She looked at her lap and wrung her hands, and he patted her shoulder and told her not to worry.

It got worse through the year. She found no comfort in November's news that the World War was over. And then January was cold as blazes, unusual even for Cataloochee. This time of year Henry usually longed for spring, but now he didn't know. At this rate spring would find one of them in the lunatic asylum.

One night she went upstairs early, about seven, and he walked to the barn for a deep draft a bit thereafter. It was clear, a bit windy, and the ground crunched underfoot with ice. Going to the barn, normal rhythm, forty-two steps to the footbridge. Back in the house the beadboard ceiling creaked. He found her upstairs in her rocker, tears falling in her lap, muttering about the devil and Jesus mixed together. He persuaded her to get to bed, then went downstairs to sit by the fireplace with no hint of coming sleep. The wind picked up and the west end of the house popped. His legs tensed and chest tightened, like when he ran out of tobacco.

He walked around the room, pausing at Callie's picture on the mantel. "She ain't smiled like that in years." Sighing, he laid a piece of locust on the fire and listened to it crackle. He figured another dram wouldn't hurt.

Putting on his coat, he went to the porch, taking care not to bang the screen door. The Dipper had rotated a bit since his last trip. He crunched the forty-two steps, haltingly crossed the creek, and leaned into the shelter of the barn.

Even in cold weather the barn smelled of comfort. Little Sal, the new mule, moved in her stall and Petunia the cow lowed at him. "Hello again. I know this is twice but I ain't crazy. I just need some sleep." The cold fluid went down his throat and a rivulet spilled down the corner of his mouth. He sat in the shelter of the hay, cradled in the warmth of the whiskey.

He didn't know how long he had been there when he started awake. Clear-headed, but unsteady as to legs, he capped the nearly empty jar, reached the barn entrance, and leaned against the doorpost with deep, painful breaths. He had never seen stars so bright.

Halfway across the bridge his right foot sailed out from under him. He yelled, "Jesus!" as his body lurched to the right. When he hit the poplar railing it snapped, and he flipped and fell, it seemed forever, before his head hit a rock in the creek. His body settled like a sack of cotton batting. In the frigid water, scattered thoughts buzzed toward the back of his brain. "Orion's near about behind the mountain, so spring ain't far off. Feels warmer. That red light's Callie, coming to help, the devil, too, and, looky, here comes Jesus."

Mary Carter was finishing the breakfast dishes when she heard steps on the porch and a soft but insistent knock at the front door. Hiram had gone back to bed after breakfast. Mary grabbed a dish towel and walked to the front door drying her hands. "Lord, child, get in here. You'll freeze plumb to death!"

"Thank you, Aunt Mary." Callie hadn't been seen off her and

Henry's place in a year or more. But here she was, face shining clean, fresh calico dress, hair brushed straight under her head scarf, wearing a coat not nearly heavy enough for the weather.

"What on earth?" Mary shut the door and took Callie by the shoulders. "You look nice, Callie Sutton. But what are you doing down here? Is something wrong?"

Callie smiled and nodded. "It's Henry, Aunt Mary. He's—I don't—he's froze to death in the creek. I can't get him out by myself."

"You can't mean it!"

Callie looked at the floor and nodded. "It's true, Aunt Mary. I got up this morning and couldn't find him. I'd slept good for the first night in months and I wanted to tell him. He wasn't nowhere in the house or the springhouse or the back part of the place. I thought he might be in the barn, so I bundled up and started out there. On the footbridge I looked down and seen him laying in the water, looking up at me. I tried to pull him out but couldn't. I need some help."

Mary went in the hall. "Hiram. Get down here quick."

She hugged her neighbor. "I sure am sorry, dear. I'll pour you some coffee. Soon as Hiram gets here we'll see what we can do. I can't believe it."

Callie sat by the fire and listened to the old hall clock marking time for all but Henry. Mary went to the kitchen for coffee and as she came back Hiram clattered down the stairs.

In the morning light Mary noticed Callie had better color than her own husband. Hiram's prostate had been bothering him, and he was falling off. But urgency put a spring in his step.

"Well, Callie Sutton, what a surprise," he said. "We don't expect company on cold mornings. What's the trouble?" The hall clock chimed the half hour, rich and true.

Mary handed Callie a cup. "Henry's froze to death in the creek, Hiram Carter, that's what. We got to help her with him." She gestured to the other cup. "You want this coffee?"

"No, sweetheart, I don't need nothing else to run through me this morning. Henry's dead? In the creek?"

Callie nodded. "I found him about an hour ago. I tried to get him out but them rocks is so slick I couldn't budge him without falling in. I hate to ask, but I need help."

"Well, let me put my boots on and get a coat. Sweetheart, you come with us, too. I ain't as strong as I used to be." His old boots were still wet from his early trip to the barn. He sat beside Callie and put them on slowly.

"You say he's in the creek?"

Callie nodded and sipped her coffee daintily.

"Face down or up?" Hiram laced the right-hand boot first.

"Up. Looking straight at me, it looked like."

"How long's he been there you reckon?"

"He went out about nine last night. I remember hearing him trying to be quiet, but you know Henry, he couldn't be quiet if he tried. I never heard him come back in. When I got up, there wasn't nobody in the house but me."

Hiram laced the left-hand boot but beforehand patted Callie on the shoulder. "So he's likely stiffern' a board."

Callie nodded. "I hate to get you out on a morning like this, Uncle Hiram. But there ain't no help for it."

"Don't you fret, Callie." They bundled against the cold. "You ready?"

Callie took another sip and put the cup on the mantel. Hiram went to the shed for gloves and either a cant hook or a pick he hoped he wouldn't have to use. He decided on a mattock with a pick on one end.

They walked up the road in silence, their breath swirling white in the sunshine. After a minute or two Callie started humming "Amazing Grace" and Mary joined her on the second trip through, just under Callie's soprano. The last snowfall was mostly gone, but under the trees by the creek drifts lay gray-white in the shadows. Snow stays three days, it's waiting for more, the old people said.

Hiram saw half the railing hanging off the footbridge and knew immediately what had happened. At the edge of the creek an empty Mason jar lay overturned beside a cracked slop jar. Henry's body lay just out of reach. The back of his skull seemed wrapped around a rock and his open eyes stared at the bridge as if to condemn it. Ice bunched on his shoulders like epaulets.

"We need to get on the other bank and pull him out that way," Hiram said quietly. Mary barely heard him over the noise of the creek. She put her arm around Callie and pointed for her to cross the footbridge. It was only wide enough for one, so Callie went first and Mary held on to the back of her coat. They reminded Hiram of a pair of young possums. He let them get across, then made it over himself. There was no ice on the bridge but it was wet in the sunshine.

At the edge Hiram told Mary to take Callie to the house. He didn't want Callie to see him use the pick. After he watched the women halfway to the house he extended the tool and caught the back of Henry's coat collar. He set the pick and pulled downstream, so Henry's coat wouldn't come off. The stiff body tried to float when Hiram freed it from the rocks but the pick held and Hiram slowly pulled his neighbor to the bank.

Hiram tried unsuccessfully to close Henry's eyelids. He saw Mary on her way with a blanket. She laid it beside Henry's body and together they put Henry on it, and folded it over once. Hiram looked at the Mason jar and then at Mary. "She say anything about that?"

"Said the devil'd got to Henry, him drinking and all. But this is the beatenest thing, Hiram. Said this morning after she found him she poured all her Lydia Pinkham in that slop jar, then got Henry's liquor from the barn and sloshed it in, then threw it all in the creek. Said it washed around Henry's body and cleansed the devil out of both of them. Kind of like a baptism, she said."

Hiram looked at his wife like now he had heard everything.

"Yes, I know it sounds quare, but Callie's always been a little that way, even before Tom died. This's the first time in two years I've been around her that she don't smell like a brewery. Maybe she's going to be all right." She felt Hiram's coat sleeve. "Honey, you're wetter'n a frog. Let's take him in and get you by the fire."

They carried Henry to the back and set his body on the porch. Mary cleared the cooling board in the back room where Callie used to do her canning. Inside she put a half dozen or more Lydia Pinkham bottles, empty and uncorked, under the counter. She and Hiram carried Henry in and laid him on the board. Mary shooed Hiram out. "You go stand by the fire. I've done this many a time. Go keep Callie company."

Mary and Rhetta Wright sat up with Henry that night. The next day was pretty and warmer as wagons full of neighbors gathered. Hiram gathered everyone in the front room to read Scripture and pray. Henry had been fond of "In the Sweet By and By" so Levi Marion and Jim Hawkins played it slowly on banjo and fiddle.

At the end Callie gave Levi Marion a pressed rose out of the big Bible. "Here, son. Lay this in his coffin before you shut it up. He give it to me when we were courting. It might make him feel better." Levi Marion laid it like a relic on Henry's chest before they screwed the lid tight and laid the coffin in the mule-drawn sled. He took the reins and walked beside the mule up the path to the cemetery, to bury Henry beside Levi Marion's own father, killed by a tree thirty-four years before.

22

HANGOVER

For years Bud Harrogate had drunk his share of whiskey and beer—he never touched wine, said it would give a man the bust-head—and his body rarely rebelled. But on a cloudy late March morning in 1924 his head felt like his skull had shrunk two hat sizes. It hurt worst behind his eyes, which he opened and shut slowly.

Something, he thought, was wrong with the whiskey Ed Camel gave him last night. He'd drunk far less of it than he had the corn whiskey two nights ago, and that bout hadn't bothered him. He sat on the edge of the bed, corn shucks in the mattress rustling. Upright did nothing for his headache.

He reached for the bedside quart, only a fourth gone—or maybe a third. He wished they still had labels, as if that would help. Bonded Tennessee whiskey used to be good herbs, but since the state went dry in 1910 a man couldn't depend on it. Harrogate took a drink and grimaced when it hit his stomach. His head pained sharply, then slowly eased. After another swig he corked the bottle.

Ed Camel boarded at Silas and Rhetta Wright's farm several times a year to fish and watch birds. He lived in Cosby, Tennessee, nearly thirty miles by the twisty road Cataloochans called the turnpike. Harrogate thought him a strange duck, but he brought a bottle or two each trip so oddity was well tolerated.

Camel was slight and prim, with a bit of a limp. Well dressed, he drew a Spanish-American War pension, always brought gifts for Rhetta, and doled out Bennett's Milk-Bones to Rhetta's Chigger, a contrary fice tending to walk on three legs. "He's my ciphering dog," she would say proudly. A puzzled look would bring, "You know. He puts down his three and carries his one." Chigger showed Camel no devotion but at least didn't nip his heels when Rhetta wasn't looking.

Harrogate decided if he could get through breakfast without puking he would take Camel fishing as they had planned. He donned shirt and overalls and looked in the mirror. Dipping his comb in the pitcher, he smoothed his prematurely gray hair, listening to Rhetta downstairs in the full throes of finishing breakfast.

In the kitchen Rhetta, whose height and width lately were not so much proportional as approaching equality, insisted her hired girl check the biscuits. "But, ma'am, you're right in front of the oven," said the young woman.

"Child, I can't quit stirring these eggs now. Mr. Camel's due any second and he likes them just right. You just—morning, Mr. Harrogate— do the best you can. I ain't never served burnt biscuits and I ain't starting this morning." The hipless girl pushed the door handle down with a potholder as Rhetta moved enough for the girl to declare the biscuits not quite brown. "Now put out the meat and stir that gravy, then pour it in the bowl. Get them apples in a dish and where's the butter? And jelly? Lord, child, do I got to do ever thing around here?"

Silas, reading a month-old Asheville newspaper at the head of the table, nodded to Harrogate. Camel came downstairs just as Harrogate's chair scraped the floor. Chigger sniffed disdainfully at Bud's legs. If Rhetta hadn't been close he'd have told the dog not to piss his leg or he'd stomp its scrawny ass through the floor. Chigger walked three-legged to Camel, who greeted everyone and sneaked a dog biscuit under the table.

The women served food, poured coffee, and sat. Silas prayed over it, his usual thanks to God for the day, the food, and the hands that prepared it. As they spooned out eggs and grits and apples, Silas started first the bacon and pork loin, then followed with the butter print, apple butter, and blackberry jam.

After a small wave of nausea the food smelled good to Harrogate and his headache was becoming a bad memory. They all ate with relish. Chigger, like most dogs an eternal optimist, hopped from place to place hoping someone would drop a morsel.

Afterward the men went to the porch. Silas filled his pipe, looking into a cloudy morning. "You boys going to the woods?" Curved pipe stem matched the angle of his craggy nose. A man of a hand more than six feet, he looked down at Harrogate with head cocked.

"Thought to take Ed up Indian Creek, maybe all the way up Spruce Mountain." Harrogate picked a Fatima from his shirt pocket and looked at Camel. "What do you think?"

Camel lit a Pall Mall and blew smoke toward the creek. "Long as we're in the woods, I don't really care, Bud. I'm happy on a warm morning like this."

"You want to take supper or catch it on the way?"

"Tell you what. We'll fish on the way up. If we end up staying awhile we might kill a squirrel or two. I haven't made squirrel stew since the last time I was here."

"Fine with me. Your stew's as good as I ever ate. Silas, you ort to go with us."

"Getting too damn old for that. Ain't slept on the ground in five year, maybe more. And it'll get cold again tonight. Hope so, anyhow, it's way too warm for this time of year."

"You don't care to camp, do you?" said Camel.

"I got a perfectly good bed in the house."

"You know, a lot of folks, like me, love the outdoors so much they want to be in the backwoods constantly," said Camel. "They'll go to Yellowstone or one of the other national parks to hike and fish and ride horses. I might go all the way West, too, if I didn't know about this place."

Silas chuckled. "No offense meant, Mr. Camel, but people like that ain't got enough work to do. And, speaking of that, I'm going to get our taters in the hole for winter. You boys be careful."

Harrogate and Camel saddled mules and tied bedroll and baggage. Out in the yard Chigger yapped at them while Dan, Harrogate's yellow-eyed part Airedale and mostly something else, walked silently beside Harrogate and his mule. Camel kept a spyglass close in case he saw a new bird. He had logged over two hundred species and aimed for many more. Harrogate, for his part, knew a turkey buzzard from a humming-bird, but didn't know a warbler from a wren, and saw little need to.

Past the schoolhouse they crossed the creek and turned up the road following Indian Branch, a trail lined by low, moss-covered stone walls. Up a small rise they went by the mill on the west bank. Mountains arched close to the creek on both sides. This time of year no sun touched the deep valley road until eleven or after three-thirty.

Past the mill, the mountain on the left stayed steep as a mule's face but the right-hand mountain took an eastward turn, allowing space for a farm in the hollow. A furlong later Camel reined his mule. "I caught fish here last time. Want to try our luck?"

Harrogate stopped and nodded. "Whatever you want, Ed. It's your week off."

Harrogate's homemade cane pole was cut short for skinny water. He baited with a red worm and immediately had a strike. Camel had a long split-cane Granger. He attached his reel and sent leader through the guides with a high ratcheting noise.

Harrogate caught and released three by the time Camel tied fly to tippet. Camel finally stroked his fly in an eddy a foot from the west bank. "Damn, Ed, that was pretty. You just missed decorating a laurel bush." A trout claimed the fly and headed up the creek. Harrogate brought his line in.

Harrogate took Camel's ash-framed net—mail-ordered from up North—while Camel played the fish. A two-pound rainbow soon graced the net. Camel's smile seemed three feet wide. Harrogate asked if he wanted to keep it for dinner. "Something so magnificent ought not to be eaten. There's plenty more."

Within an hour Camel had caught and released a dozen. Harrogate didn't see much sense in fishing unless he was hungry, so sat on a rock and smoked. Camel looked at the trees as much as the creek, for he heard now one bird, then another. After he dropped his spyglass in the water he reeled in. "Too many birds to fish right now," he said. "We'll try it closer to supper." He cleaned the spyglass and stowed his tackle.

Harrogate heard a birdcall, musical with an emphatic ending. "What you reckon that was?"

"It came from over there." Camel searched with his spyglass. Suddenly he stopped moving. "I have it, my friend. It's a bird I've never seen. A chestnut-sided warbler, perhaps. Come see."

Harrogate moved beside Camel, who showed him where to look. Finally he located the bird. "Looks like a sparrow."

"They all look like sparrows to you. But see the brown streaks below the wing? And a sparrow was never that musical. Listen." He took the spyglass. "These birds enjoy open country. The chestnuts are dying, and the loggers are clearing trees everywhere hereabout, so birds have more opportunity. Yes, it's a migratory chestnut-sided warbler. How marvelous."

Across the creek the mountain tore sharply upward and bare rocks jutted from its face. Harrogate stared like he expected a bobcat to slink out and pounce. Camel noticed his partner's trance. "Bud, do you want to climb? We could probably get a fine view of the valley."

Harrogate broke out of his reverie. "Ain't lost nothing up there. I was just wondering what them rocks was good for."

"God put them there for a reason. They support lichens and moss. And over time they wear down and become dirt. Nothing in this life is wasted. As the poet says, 'Nothing we see, but means our good.' "

"What in creation does that mean?"

"Everything in nature is useful and good, whether we know it or not."

"Even poison oak?"

"Even that."

"Don't hardly see how."

The sky began to clear. Bud swatted at a deerfly. Up the trail they came to a three-way junction. The right fork snaked up to Little Cataloochee, the middle prong went to Mount Sterling, and the left crawled up to Spruce Mountain.

"Let's stop here for dinner," said Harrogate. "I mean to go toward Spruce Mountain later. We'll get some speckled trout for supper up higher. I like them better'n rainbows, don't you?"

"Yes, the brook trout *is* a better meal. Did you know it's native? Rainbows are beautiful but they were introduced from elsewhere." While they tied their mounts and spread out dinner, Camel gave Bud a history of trout and their allies. Rhetta had packed deviled eggs and ham and biscuits and apples. There were now no clouds and the sky bled blue into the coming green of budding leaves. The temperature had dropped a couple of degrees. Camel pointed out butterflies, pale blues the size of dimes, on mule droppings. Harrogate was not much interested in them, nor in ants on their boots or flies shooed from their food, but Camel told of their habits.

"You learn all that in school?"

Camel smiled. "No, but I read. And I watch. It's just as interesting to read the book of nature as it is to read nature books. You know that, too. I have seen you pick through bear sign and tell where it has been lately. It's but another step to seeing what ants are up to."

"I reckon you're right. I just never been around nobody could do it good as you. Still don't see no reason to pay a pissant much mind."

Ed laughed. "They will tell where you spilled the sugar."

They headed up the left fork after dinner. As the trail started sharply upward they were surrounded by forest. The creek narrowed and its murmur diminished. No loggers had found this forest. Hemlocks six feet through vied for sunlight with poplars of similar proportions. Dead chestnuts had dropped skeletal limbs. Camel, spyglass ready, sighted birds Harrogate only heard. Through the trees they saw freshly gashed formations from which boulders had fallen. A half mile later they found a plateau near the headwater of Lost Bottom Creek. Around a left-hand bend Camel pulled up. "Here, my friend. This is perfect."

A huge rock overhung from the mountain like a canopy awning thirty feet above a fancy storefront. The rock face was black with the remains of fires, many started long before white people came. Forgotten names carved in the rocks told of men who spoke English, and runic shapes burned in the rocks spoke of prehistory. "The Cherokee, or whoever was here before them, took shelter here," Camel said. "So will we."

"OK. I'll make camp while you catch supper."

Harrogate laid out bedrolls. The air was noticeably cooler now so he scoured a pile of deadfall wood. Building a fire in a ditch in the bedrock, he backed it windward with stones and logs. Camel returned with three fine fish, which they gutted, filleted, and fried.

They ate, then smoked and talked quietly as dark fell. Camel threw a butt in the fire. "You know, Bud, I didn't say anything to Silas this morning, but there are folks talking about the government making an Eastern national park."

"That so?"

"Yes, and it's a fine idea. It's so expensive to get to the West, for one thing."

"Where in hell would they put it?" Pulling a bottle from his pack, Harrogate drank and offered it to his friend, who declined. He'd brought some corn whiskey he knew wouldn't hurt him.

"Oh, I don't know. Maybe the Shenandoah, maybe in these mountains here."

Harrogate took another swig. "Only problem is, people live there. How you going to persuade them to move?"

"Good question. It would be difficult, I grant you, to get such a large amount of property into government hands. But if they wanted to do it badly enough, they could."

"How? There ain't enough money in the world to make some folks move. Take Silas, for one. You think he'd move if the government said to?"

Camel laughed. "You have a point, Bud. It will in any case be interesting to watch what happens."

Harrogate took another drink, set his bottle off to the side, and lit a cigarette. They watched the fire in silence awhile. Finally Camel stretched and yawned. "My friend, it's time to turn in. I'm glad to be in such a beautiful place. I plan to sleep well under this overhang. Tomorrow we'll see more."

Camel bedded down close to the fire, which sent cherry red sparks upward, then slowly down like light snow. Camel lay on his side and watched for a while, then turned on his back and within a minute snored softly.

Harrogate walked outside the overhang for a piss and a look to the heavens. Up this high they had a view of the whole sky, and the spring star, Spica, hung just over the eastern horizon. He stretched and buttoned his britches. A fresh log on the fire intensified it before it settled into an all-night rhythm. He lay hat over face, and went to sleep a body's length from Camel, feet to the fire.

Two hours later a force more felt than heard bounced Harrogate vertically two feet or more like a rag doll. Coals zinged like tracers in the night. Crashing back on the bedrock he looked stupidly at the blanket. "Damn, Ed, what the hell happened?" He rubbed the back of his head, then started to beat his smoldering blanket. Dan was nowhere to be seen. He looked to Ed. All he could say was "Oh, my God," over and over.

The outcropping above them had expanded and contracted with fire and weather one time too many and had fallen straightway atop Ed Camel. His only visible parts were the right forearm and hand. His fingers moved, clawlike, reptilian. Harrogate threw the useless blanket off, scuttled through the remnant of the fire, and tried to budge the boulder big as half a freight car.

He knelt and tried to look under the rock but needed more light. He almost reached for Camel's hand but was afraid to touch it lest Camel grab him and keep him there for all time. He yelled at the rock and told Camel to hold on.

Five feet his way and Harrogate would have been under twenty tons of rock. He called for Dan but no dog came. His whiskey bottle was wet shards. He got his gloves and picked up coals and put them on the bedrock. Trembling hands piled kindling atop the embers. Firelight cast hellish shadows and showed nothing he wanted to see.

He called again for the dog, then screamed in the night. "God," he yelled, "help me. Help him. Help us all."

Harrogate knelt at the side of the boulder where Camel's head had been. "Hang on, buddy. I'll be back soon's I can. We'll get that off you somehow." He wiped his nose, banked the fire, and went for his mule.

In the clearing beside the schoolhouse he caught his breath and inspected his face for cuts. There had been places the mule would not go in the dark and he was suddenly glad. Libra hung over the mountain, so it was a bit after midnight. He found the bell rope. The clang tore through the night, at the same time frantic and mournful. Lights soon illuminated windows, and men ran to the schoolhouse, heard Harrogate's story, and went back for tools. Dan showed up with Silas. By one-thirty a torchlit crowd headed up Indian Creek.

At the camp Camel's hand was blue and motionless. The fifteen of them stood under the lip of the boulder and heaved to no avail. They cut small trees for prize poles and placed bait rocks beside the boulder but could find no leverage. Like unsuccessful ants they moved to all corners of the unmoving boulder.

They worked for an hour before Silas called them to the fire. "Boys, we need more men. Me and Bud'll set with him till the sun comes up—somebody go over the mountain to tell Little Catalooch, and the rest get back and ring the bell at sunrise. If it takes a hundred, we got to move that rock."

Harrogate sat near Camel's head and Silas leaned near his feet and added wood to the fire. Dan lay opposite, stretched, and closed his eyes.

At first light they made breakfast in the frosty daylight, thankful that neither Harrogate's nor Camel's kit bags had been crushed. Soon, men, and boys, too, for they had decreed school out that day, appeared with ropes and axes and iron bars and whatever else they conceived to be of use.

By eight-thirty they were in place with more poles and rocks. On Silas's count of one, two, three, heave, they brought the boulder up perceptibly, and boys rushed to shove rocks and limbs into the interstice. Another heave raised the boulder a bit more. Within a half hour they slipped Camel's crushed body out and lay it on a blanket. But for clothes in the shape of a man nothing besides the forearm was recognizable. All removed their hats as they stared at the body.

"Boys," said Silas, "Ed was as fine a man as ever put feet under my table. A little quare, but a good man. I take comfort, and maybe his widow will, too, in knowing he never knowed what hit him. He woke up with the Lord, and no man here would wish for less. Let's get him home."

Some amened, others just grimly put hats back on and headed home. Silas and Harrogate wrapped Camel's body with one fresh blanket, then another. They laid him over the saddle and tied him on like a carpet. Harrogate hung his kit bag, fishing gear, and spyglass on the saddle horn. They left his bloodstained blankets beside the rock. Songbirds flittered as though nothing untoward had happened. Butterflies sucked moisture from the fabric that had lately covered Ed Camel.

23

A FOX CAUGHT IN LANTERN LIGHT

Sunlight streamed over Hannah's face as she lay on the kitchen floor. She grimaced when a fly lit on her cheek. She listened hard—no Ezra. He'd been drinking ten days, the 1924 version of his annual fall jag. Tensing her left arm made her wince. Moving finger to face, she asked herself whose blood she tasted.

She heard the silence of her new mantel clock. Two years ago he had thrown her old one through a closed window. Now when he was on a bender she turned the clock off until he sobered. The breeze was cool. One chair lay on its side. She pulled herself to the closest upright chair, grabbed it, and stood creakily.

Rearranging her apron, she felt her hair bun. On the way to the front room mirror she remembered Ezra filling up the back door frame, blocking the sun. She had asked what was wrong. The rest was confusion, him yelling, crashing racket, then nothing.

Liquor had made Hannah's father happy but it made Ezra mean as hell. A quart lasted him two days, sometimes three, days in which he would kick cattle, beat the boys when he could catch them, and curse her savagely. A body could bear three days of his rage a year, but something in Ezra broke the year the Canadian showed the gold nugget around. Ezra bought a gallon that year, 1917, and this year he had gotten two.

At the mirror she gasped. A bloody cut full of dark nastiness on the point of her left cheekbone traveled toward her jaw. She made her way back into the kitchen.

The lace doily hung off the edge of the round oak table and the salt-cellar lay on its side. With a piece of paper she pushed spilled salt back into the cellar. The wooden bowl of apples she had been cutting up lay upside down next to the counter. Shooing flies off the apples, she threw them in the slop bucket for the hogs. She set the chair upright, repositioned the doily, and found her eyeglasses.

She got water and lye soap and a hand mirror. Clotted blood sloughed in front of the washrag, which she rinsed and sudsed again as she took a deep breath. As tears came she cleaned out solid flakes of blackened blood. Patted dry with a clean washrag, the cut showed pink. At the window she raked some clean spiderweb and daubed it into the wound.

They had four press-back chairs with the table set they ordered from Sears years ago. Hannah had wanted six, one for each family member, but Ezra said four would be fine, the young'uns didn't care whether furniture matched. The golden oak finish had darkened with time, and the varnish on the overturned chair was the same color as the matter in her wound. A new scar showed on the edge of the chair back. She wondered if she had fallen, or if Ezra had knocked her into the chair, or outright hit her with it. She could summon nothing past him yelling and her waking on the floor, everything clamoring in a blur of images and noise.

Usually he hit her on her arms or torso, places easy enough to hide from her family. And those she remembered. This time she was frightened, like a wren in a bedroom.

At the back porch the screen door spring dangled, eye hook pulled from the door frame. Ezra's boot print twisted like he had lost his balance. Quiet, not even a crow hollering. She followed his crooked steps to the barn.

Inside, a riot of manure, hay, sour milk, and apple leavings hit her nose. Old Huldy snorted in the lot but she heard no steer in the far right stall.

In July, Ezra had found a yearling in the high pasture considerably skinnier than any in the herd, and cut it out to find it covered with ticks. He led it home and every couple of days rubbed the calf down with arsenic water. Hannah fed the animal a handful of hay or a piece of apple every day, and it gained weight. She called her new baby Ticker, even though Ezra refused to name anything meant to be eaten or sold.

She pushed the stall door open, hinges screaming. "Lord have mercy," she said. An ear dangled from a shred of cartilage at the side of the beast's bloody head. An eye socket was empty. As she turned in revulsion something moved in the corner of the stall.

Ezra perched on the foundation log, a bottle, corked and half empty, beside him. He moved his head slowly. Manure and blood covered his britches and his sleeves were bloody and torn. In front of him lay a broken scythe, and next to it the snath with its gore-covered tang.

Ezra jerked awake, fumbled for his bottle, uncorked it, and turned it up. If he noticed his wife he gave no sign. She squinted at the bottle. The brand was impossible to tell. Liquor bottles hadn't been labeled since what she called "the Probation" started.

The steer's back leg skewed at an odd angle and patches of skin were missing up and down its side. Green bottleflies, horseflies, blackflies covered the bare places. Ezra moved every now and then when one lit on his nose.

"Mr. Banks."

Her voice made him move not at all so she tried a bit louder. This time his eyes opened and he raised his hand to swat at a fly and knocked his hat off. The sunlight reflected red from his eyes, as if he were a fox caught in lantern light. It slammed into her consciousness that Ezra had killed the steer in a rage she somehow started in him. Or killed it instead of her. "You sober up," she said. "I'm going to Zeb's."

Walking the fifty yards to the hickory at the road, she realized she was scared to let Zeb see her, but staying with her husband would be worse. Hannah turned toward Zeb's and soon saw Mattie in the kitchen garden, pulling seed pods from her marigolds.

Mattie always planted flowers among her vegetables. She said she did it just to make her feel better, but Mattie's beans and, for that matter, her whole garden, always looked better than Hannah's. Maybe they kept the bugs out.

Mattie's back was to Hannah, so Hannah shuffled her feet on the path to alert her daughter-in-law. Mattie's knees popped as she stood. "Mama Banks, what . . . ? Did that man do that to you? Let me see." She wiped her hands on her apron and stepped toward Hannah.

"Child, I don't know. It's all right—just a cut. Don't touch it."

"What do you mean you don't know?"

"Well, he come to the kitchen door and started yelling. Tell you the truth, I didn't pay him much mind. Thought he'd get it out of his craw and be done with it. Next thing I knowed I woke up on the kitchen floor and he'd gone to the barn."

"How'd you know he was in the barn? Lord, you didn't follow him out there after he hit you like that?"

"I had to see where he was. And something killed that yearling he brought down from the high pasture. He was setting in the stall with it laying out dead as a hammer."

Mattie stomped her foot in the path. "The something was Ezra Banks. Lord, Mama Banks, I'm a good mind to go kill him my own self."

"Horrors, child, don't talk of killing. Right now I'm lucky to be alive. I could have fallen, you know."

"Mama Banks, he may be your husband and Zeb's daddy, but I've said for years—he ought to be put up somewhere when he's drinking." Mattie hugged her mother-in-law. "Mama Banks, you're staying with us until he's over this bender. The young'uns is at my sister Charlotte's so we got room aplenty. I'll get Zeb. He's worrying with that back fence."

"Maybe I better get back. What if Mr. Banks falls and breaks his leg?"

"Then he couldn't get to you as fast. Now come in and get something to eat." She led Hannah to the house and hollered "Zeb!" until she heard him answer. "Come quick. Your mama's here."

A minute later Mattie met him at the back door. "Zeb honey, your mama's in the front room and he's hit her, I swear it. They's a cut on her cheek she says she don't remember nothing about."

"My God, Mattie."

"I'm fixing some nerve-root tea. I'll be there in a minute."

In the front room Hannah sat in the rocker, patting her cheek with a washrag. Zeb bent to kiss his mother. "Mama, what in thunder happened? Let me look at that."

"You young'uns fuss too much over me. I'll be all right."

"You let us judge that, Mama. How'd this happen?"

"Son, I've been trying my best to remember. I was in the kitchen and all of a sudden your daddy showed up yelling. There was a big crash and next thing I knowed I was laying on the kitchen floor like a sack of taters."

"He hit you. Mama, I said if he ever did anything to you I'd kill him. And I meant it." He gnawed on the side of his thumb.

She grabbed Zeb's arm. "Son, don't talk like that. I honestly can't say whether I fell or not. He's still your father, mean as he gets. I've been hurt worse'n this."

Mattie handed her mother-in-law a cup of tea. "Not by him, you ain't. Mama Banks, you're going to stay until he sobers up."

"Child, he ain't got but the one bottle left and it's about gone. I've got to go back home. He's got to eat sometime."

"Mama, I'm going down there." Zeb looked toward his father's place. "Mattie's right. You stay here tonight."

"We'll see about staying when you get back. Last I seen him he was in the barn with that dead yearling."

"What dead yearling?"

"Ticker. Least it was in Ticker's stall."

"You mean he killed that steer?"

"Something did."

Zeb and Mattie exchanged glances. "Mama, that just as easy could have been you."

Zeb headed for the kitchen, picked his Remington from the rack over the door, and went out the back. He looked to the sun for the time, then headed toward his father's house.

Last year Ezra in his cups had offered to sell Zeb the rifle, the old model four Ezra had used to teach all his sons to shoot, for two dollars. Instead of getting mad at Ezra for selling it, Zeb's brothers all bristled at the buyer. Zeb cradled the rifle in his right arm and bit the nail of his left pinky as he walked, face clouded as the day was pretty.

As he entered his father's property his chest tightened and he heard his heartbeat over the breeze in his ears. Swallowing hard, he chambered a round and walked quietly toward the barn.

At the back stall on the right he looked over the railing and whistled low and mournful. In the stall the calf was covered with enough blowflies to pick it up could they coordinate themselves. His father was nowhere in sight. Squatting beside the dead animal, he shuddered, and threw the scythe handle in the corner. "It's a wonder before God he didn't kill Mama, too." Rifle ready, he went out of the barn toward the back porch.

Zeb heard Ezra crashing around upstairs. The step creaked like always. Kitchen chairs were scattered. Ezra's bottle stood uncorked on the counter with two fingers left. The table sat a good three feet off center.

His father's voice came into focus. "Hannah," he cried, "Hannah honey, where are you at? I didn't mean it. I'm sooooorry."

Zeb walked to the bottom of the stairs and readied the rifle across his midsection, like a Confederate soldier in a daguerreotype. "Papa, get down here."

Ezra poked his head out of Hannah's bedroom like a long-necked bird, wiped his nose, and staggered to the stairs. "Zeb? That you? What they done with Hannah?"

"*They* ain't done *nothing*. What in hell did *you* do to her?"

"Thank God. I thought she'd got carried off."

"Papa, get down here. I got to talk to you."

Ezra stumbled and propped himself against the wall. He focused on Zeb, then pulled his pipe from his pocket. He eyed the Remington. "*You* got to talk to *me,* eh? You with my rifle and me a poor unarmed man? Do you think you're half the man I was when I went to the army in sixty-four?"

Zeb looked at the weapon. "Just insurance, Papa."

"Insurance, my ass. I left my old man, damn his hide. Least I didn't try to shoot him."

"Papa, get down here. I got to get you sober."

"Shit, I need another drink. Where's my bottle?"

"Down here."

"Well, why don't you bring it to your poor old daddy?" Ezra fumbled for a match and lit his pipe.

"Why don't you see if you can get down in one piece?"

"You think I can't?"

Ezra put his right foot out to test his vision. The boot came down reasonably well on the first step. He clung to the wall and thumped downstairs without doing much damage except to track manure. "There, you was hoping I'd break my damn neck. Where's that bottle at?"

"Papa, the last thing you need is that bottle."

"Where is it, boy?"

Zeb backed a couple of steps. "Right where you left it."

Ezra and Zeb maneuvered in the hall, Zeb gripping the rifle tighter and Ezra making as if to hit his son. "Now stay the hell out of my way. You sure as shit ain't getting my liquor."

"I'll show you where it's at."

"That's more like it."

In the kitchen Ezra leaned on the doorsill sucking on his pipe while Zeb picked up the bottle. "Here, Papa. You can have it on the porch."

Ezra lurched toward his son. "You ungrateful stinking pismire, give me that."

On the back porch Zeb held the bottle out. "Come on, Papa. Set in this chair."

Ezra laid hands on the kitchen table to steady himself, then lurched toward the back door. His shoulder hit the door frame hard and turned him toward the screen door, which he grabbed at and missed. His other shoulder hit the porch column, which spun him as he fell like a stone to the ground, his pipe sailing into Hannah's butterfly bush.

Zeb made no motion to break his father's fall nor to help him afterward. Ezra lay trying for breath, then pushed himself up and looked at Zeb, who stood on the porch, rifle in his right hand. With his left hand he held the bottle up, then turned it upside down. Ezra screamed as liquor headed groundward.

"Nooo, don't I beg of you don't you bastard you shitass goddamn I'll kill you!" Ezra got his legs underneath him and leaped on the porch before Zeb could figure whether to let go the rifle or the bottle. Father's fist caught son's stomach. Zeb shoved the rifle out of reach, then crowned the back of his father's head with the bottle. Transferring the bottle to his right hand he prepared to whack his father again but when he saw Ezra was unconscious he flung it hard toward the hog pen, where it shattered on a fence post. "Now, damn it, maybe we're done for this year." He propped the rifle against the wall.

Ezra breathed in a labored but steady rasp, and Zeb dragged him to his office. He laid his father on the cot and covered him with a wool blanket, then fished for the desk key in his father's shirt pocket. No whiskey in the desk. He put the key back, satisfied himself no more liquor was on the farm, then remembered the slain steer. "I'm a good mind to leave it for him to bury," he muttered. He held his hand straight, fingers trembling. "Damn, I guess he scared me more'n I thought." By the time he made the barn he decided he'd bury the animal himself. Anything like that, Ezra got the neighbors to do anyway, and Zeb wanted no one else to see business this bad.

24

CLOSER TO JESUS

Monday, March 1, 1926, Uncle Hiram Carter's left hand lay palm up
on the coverlid, fingers moving slowly, reaching for a thing invisible.
His breathing was shallow, irregular. He lay in a downstairs bedroom
that had slept boarders until Aunt Mary commandeered it when her
husband could no longer walk up the stairs in their big frame house.

He had enjoyed the sound of the clock. It had been far too big for
their first place, the two-room cabin built by his father, Levi, ninety
years before. But it had sounded fine in the new house, echoing loudly
in the bare hall before Mary could hang even a picture. It had kept
nearly perfect count of the hours for forty-six years.

Hiram always told Mary they would fill a big house with children, but
from her point of view that was quite uncertain. Her first, Ada Pearl, was

stillborn in 1881. She had a son, George Henry, in 1882, and a daughter, Mandy Elizabeth, in 1884. Another son, Manson Levi, came in 1885, but that same year little George Henry succumbed to whooping cough. She heard "the Lord giveth and the Lord taketh away" far too often, but Hiram was ever sanguine, so they kept at it. A fourth child, Thomas Marion, in 1886, proved to be their last, the year before Mandy Elizabeth died of influenza. The boys lived to adulthood and never married nor left the farm, which they now ran as efficiently as their father had.

Hiram had started the house in 1898 by tucking a foundation into the foot of the mountain. He worked on the house as he and the neighbors had time, for five years, when he hired a carpenter from Waynesville, who camped onsite for a month. The fall of 1903 he had a finished house with two stories and nine rooms. He said to the carpenter if he couldn't fill it with children he meant to take in boarders, but dared not say that to Mary's face.

So the house rose, central hall running front to back, a gable peak over the right-hand bedroom upstairs facing north and another facing west. The front porch started on the northeast and ran the width of the structure, then turned south for half the length, and offered a perfect view of their old cabin and the big field behind it.

The interior was paneled partly with tulipwood from the place, sawn by a portable creek-powered band mill, and the rest with pine beadboard trucked in from Waynesville. Each wall was uniquely trimmed, fancy arches graced doorways, and, perhaps most remarkable, floors were plumb and smooth. Mary said she'd be forever falling down until she got used to that, but it didn't take long.

Hiram's cancer had started in his prostate. That was in 1922, when Doc Bennett said he could have surgery for it in Asheville. When Hiram heard what the doctors wanted to cut, two things off and one thing out, he would have none of it. Rhetta Wright swore by honey for such ailments, so Hiram happily ate locust or sourwood honey by the quart. He thought for a while things were better but ultimately nothing helped. Now, at seventy-eight, with a color between yellow and gray, he no longer awakened when the clock chimed.

Mary sat beside the bed, holding Hiram's right hand, while his left slowly gathered small clumps of air. On the east side at three in the afternoon, no shadows marked the time. Clock and breath instead told its passage.

The muted shuffle of people bringing food and best wishes had punctuated Mary's consciousness all day. Kitchen and springhouse were full of fried chicken, potato salad, string beans, deviled eggs, nut breads, yeast rolls, pies, and cakes. Callie Sutton made an apple stack cake, the dessert Hiram always requested on his birthday. Penny Howell brought a wiggly salad made of newfangled lemon Jell-O. Mary had given Rhetta command of the household. Mary wanted to be alone with Hiram, but would welcome his oldest friend, Silas, or the preacher, if he chose to stay an extra day in the valley. She also asked that no one leave without eating a little something.

Just after three Silas Wright showed up, hat in hand. In the hall he looked at his wife hopefully but she shook her head. Silas glanced at the clock as Rhetta, in her fancy apron with rickrack outlining the pockets, opened the bedroom door for her husband.

Tiptoeing in, he looked down at the man with whom he had shared a lifetime of working and hunting and fishing. They had known each other since 1861, farmboys with no eye toward leaving except the one time when they were twenty-two. Silas had stayed closer to his farm after that trip, while Hiram had branched into the teamster business. Rumors said he had put a sizeable sum of money under the mattress despite having paid for a truck, an automobile, and a big house. Silas touched Mary's shoulder.

"Silas, how are you?" she asked, putting her free hand on his.

"Fair to middling. Question is, how are *you*?"

"This morning about three a mockingbird sang in the backyard. I reckon it came back early on account of Hiram. So I know this is our last time together. Silas, talk to him. He can still hear." She patted Hiram's hand. "Sweetheart, someone's here to see you."

"Afternoon, buddy," said Silas.

Hiram's eyes moved behind their lids as though he might be watching a slowly moving animal across an expanse of field.

Silas looked at a yellow and white daffodil in a glass bud vase on the mantel, then at Hiram. "Partner, me and you go back a ways. Remember that train?" His sandpaper voice caught, and he swallowed hard.

"It's all right to say good-bye, Silas. If he never wakes up, you'll be glad you did. If he does, you all can laugh about it."

Silas walked to the other side of the bed. "Hiram, I'll see you. You hear?" He turned to Mary. "What's he grabbing at, you reckon?"

"I don't know, but it's peaceful. Like he wants it, whatever it is."

Silas came closer to Hiram. "Friend, you bet I'll take care of this lady best I can. We won't let no national park hoodoo us, neither."

Rhetta opened the door again. "Preacher's here," she whispered.

"Preacher" was what Methodists in Big Cataloochee called Reverend Will Smith. A South Carolinian born in 1880, he had preached to western North Carolina Methodists since 1910. His first charge was Dellwood, which included the little church in Cataloochee. Then he bounced around for a tour in Buncombe County, then Kings Mountain, and back and forth until he finally found himself where he had started.

Hiram had been delighted Smith would again be their preacher. Smith enjoyed Hiram and Mary's company, and split his boarding time between their house and Lige and Penny Howell's place. He would never say which table he enjoyed more, although both women tried to trap him into stating a preference.

When he entered the room Hiram stopped breathing. Silas put his hand to his mouth as Mary squeezed her husband's right hand with both of hers. After what seemed an eternity, he breathed again, then resumed a slow rhythm.

There was nothing remarkable about Will Smith except a sincere smile and hair that disobeyed gravity. Most men his age were either bald or gray but he still had wiry brown hair that frizzed according to humidity and temperature. "Mary, how are you?" he asked, placing his hand over hers and Hiram's.

"I'm bearing up, Preacher. With God's help, we'll be all right."

"Yes, bless you. Silas, good to see you."

"Same here, Preacher. You got to excuse me. I need some fresh air."
He shook Smith's hand, gave Mary a hug, and left, clearing his throat.

The clock chimed the quarter hour.

"How is he?" asked Smith, pulling a chair to the side of the bed and
scratching the back of his neck.

Mary raised first one shoulder, then the other, in younger days a signal to Hiram she needed a neck rub. "He's slept the better part of two
days. Mostly breathes regular except sometimes he almost pants, like
he's after something. Then it gets quiet. He don't seem to be in any pain,
praise Jesus. But Preacher, did you ever see someone reaching with his
fingers like that?"

He quietly took Hiram's right hand in his. "It means he's on his way,
Mary. Not quite there yet, but he sees it and wants it. Mind if I pray
with you both?"

"I hoped you would."

"Lord, look down on your servant. We thank you he is in no pain.
We praise you for your Word, in which your Son promised to make a
room for Hiram. Lead him gently home, I pray, into that grand man-
sion prepared for all who believe. Hiram, my brother, don't be afraid.
Reach for Jesus' hand. He'll lead you over Jordan, dry as can be, into
paradise.

"And Lord, be with this good woman, help her to know your comfort in the days and months and years to come. Create in all her family
gathered in this home a strong desire to care for her in the coming times.
For it is in your Son's strong name I pray, amen."

He put Hiram's hand on the coverlid and stood. The hand moved
slightly, then stopped. Hiram took a short breath. Mary would say later
his soul left on it. That she saw it drift to the ceiling, look back at her,
then vanish. For now, she looked at her unbreathing husband with the
gentlest of smiles, tears welling, and held his hand.

Smith opened the door. "It's time," he whispered. One by one folks
walked as silently as possible into the bedroom, led by Hiram's oldest

living brother, John. Levi Marion and several other nephews shuffled in with their families, and soon the room was full. They stood reverently until the half hour chimed. Manson then stopped the clock, which would stay idle until they buried its maker.

Meantime Silas leaned against the porch column smoking his pipe, wondering how it was with his friend and who would go next.

25

YOU COULD HAVE GONE ALL DAY

Over the years Silas Wright got used to Harrogate's ways. With his mongrel, Dan, Harrogate had come to Cataloochee after the 1916 cloud-burst, worked for Silas a couple of years, then one morning didn't show for breakfast. "Where's Mr. Harrogate?" Rhetta asked. Her husband stepped upstairs to find the bed made and a note on the dresser, which he studied as he came downstairs. "Gone."

"Gone? Gone where?"

"Home. Says he'll see us but he don't know when."

"You figure he got tired of my cooking?"

"You know that ain't it."

Spring saw him return, and that became his pattern. Stay a year or more, leave, then reappear like a sheriff up for reelection. Silas's own roots were so deep he reckoned it would take a combination hurricane and earthquake to move him ten yards. Other folks, he figured, didn't put down roots, like the seeds Jesus said fell in the rocks.

In the early fall of 1926 Harrogate had been gone the better part of six months when Silas looked up from the cider press and spied a man in a blue plaid flannel shirt, pack on his back, walking into the lane leading to the barn. A dogless Harrogate. Silas wiped grease from his hands with a rag. "Look what the cat drug in. Son, it's good to see you."

They shook hands warmly. "Good to see you, Silas. How's everything?"

"Not bad. Where you been this time?"

"Oh, I went home a spell, then to Knoxville, then up to my sister's in Asheville. Ever now and then I got to get close to bigger water than this skinny creek. But I got to missing Rhetta's cooking is the truth of it." He fumbled in his shirt pocket for a pack of Camels and offered it to Silas.

"I ain't desperate enough to take up cigarettes." Silas fished his pipe from his pocket. "Did you quit that dancing gal kind?"

"Fellow on the train gave me a Camel. Lot smoother than Fatimas. Cheaper, too. Supposed to have Turkish tobacco in them."

Silas puffed his pipe. "Where's old Dan?"

Harrogate glanced up at the trees. "Had to put him down, Silas. About the hardest thing I ever done. You remember how creaky he was. In Tennessee he hurt bad, got to where neither of us could sleep. I'd had him thirteen year. I sure miss that old boy. How about Chigger dog—he go to his reward?"

"Hell, that sumbitch can't hardly walk but Rhetta keeps his mangy carcass in a box by the kitchen stove. Snarls at anything that ain't her. Dog'll probably outlive me." Silas slapped at a deerfly on his arm.

Harrogate looked around. "Got anything a man could help with?"

"You're always welcome at my table. The older I get the worse I need help."

"How old are you, Silas, if you don't care for me asking."

"Born in 1850. Be seventy-six come October, Lord willing. I'm still spry, but seems like any more I start something and can't get it finished."

"Silas, you ought to take it easy."

"Son, I hope to fall over dead working these fields. I've tried setting. Can't do it. Lige Howell, since he started taking in boarders, just sets on the porch and talks. I couldn't any more do that than fly."

"What you going to do when the national park comes?"

Silas looked at Harrogate in disgust. "You could have gone all day without saying that, Bud. I've told you, they ain't going to put no park in here."

"That ain't what they say in Tennessee. They're talking serious in North Carolina, too."

"We'll jaw about that later. I got the Cagle boy shocking corn. You can help him till suppertime. . . . Park, my ass," he muttered.

Harrogate grinned when he saw the table Rhetta had set. "Rhetta, you've outdone yourself," he exclaimed. She in fact had fixed a normal meal—a bowl of ham hocks in their own juice, another of soup beans cooked with a slab of salt pork, some fresh applesauce, and a pone of corn bread—but she had sliced three extra tomatoes in Harrogate's honor. The Cagle, Norman by name, a pleasant young man of eighteen who passed food promptly, came from Hemphill. They hosted one boarder, a man named Thomas from Asheville by way of Charleston. Whether Thomas was a first or last name no one said. He wore a white shirt with a newfangled collar and a yellow bowtie.

"Mr. Harrogate, you say you was in Knoxville and Asheville." Rhetta's voice sounded rusty. "Would you mind telling an old woman why in creation you went to a noisy city when you could have stayed in God's country?"

Harrogate took another bite of corn bread. "Rhetta, sometimes I miss the commotion. It gets my blood to stirring, trolley cars clanking and the policeman blowing his whistle up in that perch in the middle of the street. Truth is, I enjoy that as much as the quiet over here."

Rhetta harrumphed. "Pass the beans if you ain't too busy."

Thomas sent the bowl around. "I know what Mr. Harrogate means," he said. "Sometimes I'll take the train from Asheville to Charleston just to walk around the harbor and listen to the machinery. I call it the music of commerce." Thomas, slightly hard of hearing, did not hear Silas mutter "Bullshit" under his breath.

"What's happened over here since I been gone?" asked the wanderer.

Rhetta dabbed at her lips with the corner of her apron. "Mr. Harrogate, it's been right quiet, unless you count them boys of Mack Hawkins's, they come to Lige Howell's house late of a night, took his buggy apart, carried it to the barn roof, and put it back together. You should have seen the look on Lige's face, sir! Oh, and them twin boys of Ratcliff Carter's, up at the head of Carter Fork? They got into a nest of yellow jackets two weeks ago and got stung something fierce. One died. Silas, was that Tom or Tim?"

Silas sopped his plate with a piece of corn bread. "Tim, I think."

"Oh, and old Chloe Howell, you know who I'm talking about, she busted her hip last month. Felicity's her girl that never married, and I think Chloe is perfectly happy to let Felicity wait on her hand and foot for the rest of her life. She ain't got out of bed, I hear, since the doctor was there. Gentlemen, a wise man once said applesauce on corn bread makes a fine dessert. That's all you get tonight."

"How's Hiram Carter?" asked Bud.

"Well, you know, that's right, Silas, you should have reminded me, he was sick when Mr. Harrogate left. His prostrate finally killed him. That was about the first of March. Died in his sleep. Mary's doing pretty well, considering."

"I hate that about Hiram. Was it painful?"

"At the end it was right peaceful, wasn't it, Silas? Him just laying there and sleeping."

"That's good," said Harrogate. "Anything new from old Banks?"

"Same old mess. It's September, so his yearly spree's about due. Mattie's sent the young'uns to her sister's."

"Hannah Banks is a good woman," said Silas. "I was her I'd a killed him years ago or run him off, one. Fact is, I'm glad my daddy run him off from here back in 1880."

"Is this Banks a problem?" asked Thomas.

Silas looked at his guest. "Two weeks ever year he lays up drunk, and he ain't a man that drink makes happy. Mean as a striped snake and twicet as dangerous."

Rhetta pushed her plate toward the center of the table. "Well, at least he stays to himself. Lord, if I did cook it, that was mighty fine. Mr. Thomas, are they still selling ever foot of ground in Asheville quick as they draw a deed for it?"

"Mrs. Wright, it's quite amazing. A lot that sold in August for a thousand will sell in September for two. I don't know where it will stop."

Harrogate looked at Thomas. "Are you in property?"

"I'm an attorney, specialty, property law. I speculate a bit, too. Everybody does. Even a shoeshine boy will give you real estate tips."

"They say there's a brand-new Kress's coming in," said Harrogate. "They talked like it would be five or six stories."

Thomas nodded. "It will be a nice addition to the town, if Mayor Cathey and Ottis Green can quit arguing. The Kress company wants Lexington Avenue to stay narrow so their store can be bigger, and the mayor, of course, is on their side. Green and his cronies want the street widened. They nearly came to blows the other day. Wonderful meal, Mrs. Wright, as usual."

Rhetta stood. "Thank you, sir. Now, if you menfolks are through, leave and let me clean up."

Silas stood. "Rhetta, can I help you?"

"I reckon I can still do it myself. Go on."

On the porch Silas leaned a chair against the wall and lit his pipe. Thomas sat in the other chair and Harrogate perched on the edge of the railing. Norman cut a chew from a plug of tobacco. The men turned their ears to the creek.

"Silas, you know what I got to thinking while I was gone?" asked Harrogate. "This water we're listening to goes from right here in Rough Fork down to Cataloochee Creek. Then you know where it flows?"

"Into the Pigeon."

"That's right, then that Pigeon River dumps into the French Broad yon side of Newport. And from there it joins the Holston at Knoxville to make the Tennessee."

"What makes you think an old man needs a geography lesson?"

"No, listen here. I've been sitting there fishing the Tennessee River when I've thought, Well, right by me goes a piece of water that went by Silas's place in Cataloochee. Wonder how long it takes for it to get from here to there?"

Silas blew a smoke ring. "I don't know, a week maybe, but I bet you by the time it gets there it ain't clear like this. It's got tires and dead dogs and a man don't know what all floating in it."

"I got to admit that."

"And the river down there don't smell right. It's flat as a pool table and you got to get right on it before you hear it a-tall. I can't figure why a man would want to get close to it like you do here. This creek gives me good fish and water, and sings me to sleep of a night. It and me gets along fine. You might say we're old friends." Silas took a deep breath. "Bud, this gets me thinking about that damned park. Got any news that ain't just rumor?" Silas's head was wreathed in pipe smoke.

Harrogate dragged deeply on his Camel. "Well, Silas, one of these days we might be living smack in the middle of it."

Harrogate heard Silas's chair come down on all four feet. "You wouldn't kid an old man, would you?"

"No, Silas, they're talking it up big in Tennessee. Young'uns is bringing pennies and nickels to school to send to the state to buy land with. They've had parades and banquets and I don't know what all. Governor Peay says it's going to be great for the state."

Silas fiddled with his pipe. "What's Tennessee got to do with us?"

"It's what they call a joint venture—between North Carolina and Tennessee. The states will buy land and turn around and deed it to the federal government."

"I heard about that. But they ain't decided where the North Carolina part'll be."

"Tennessee thinks they have. I brung newspaper clippings. And an Asheville paper. In Tennessee they passed a law back in the spring to get it rolling. Why, you can even get a founder's certificate if you give them a dollar."

Silas leaned back against the column. "Same foolishness over here. But I still say it won't be right here. Couldn't be."

"Why not?"

"Well, the idea is that people in the East need to go see wilderness like folks does out West, right?"

Harrogate nodded.

"Look around. You see any wilderness?"

"Can't say that I do."

"That's because they ain't none, except up Hell's Half Acre, and nobody except a punch-drunk bear would go there." He puffed his pipe and straightened himself. "They got plenty of wilderness over toward Linville way, they could put it there. See, the way I figure, the only land around here that's still wild's getting cut over by them Northern timber companies. And you know what a mess they leave behind. Hell, over in Big Creek when I was a pup you could find trees big around as this house, but they done cut them all and shipped them north. Big Creek now looks like they had an apocalypse, there's so much desolation. Even the government ain't stupid enough to think ever damn body on the east seaboard's going to take a vacation to look at cut-over timberland." He knocked his pipe out on the column.

Thomas cleared his throat. "Mr. Wright, if you will pardon me, the idea of an Eastern national park is exciting, and it makes sense for North Carolina and Tennessee to share it."

Silas looked at Thomas like he was an imbecile. "Mr. Thomas, do you want to keep eating at my table?"

"All I meant was this place is so beautiful, Mr. Wright. And convenient to the population centers. Government ownership would assure that future generations could experience this same beauty."

Silas snorted. "You sound like one of them chamber pots of commerce."

"In fact, I belong to the chamber, Mr. Wright. We have had several informative programs about the proposed park." He adjusted his bowtie.

"Oh, why didn't you say so? That makes a big difference."

As sarcasm seemed not to register on Thomas, Silas pointed to the terrace on the other side of the creek. "Mr. Thomas, does that look to you like I've spent seventy-five years ruining this property? I ain't put three-fourths of a century into this farm just to give it to the damn government so ever Tom, Dick, and Harry with the price of gasoline can come over here and lollygag."

"I apologize if I have offended you, Mr. Wright. You have a beautiful farm. All I meant was that decisions about location have probably already been made. And the North Carolina portion will necessarily join the Tennessee side. I have seen maps with the eastern boundary in Haywood County. Perhaps there might still be time to lobby for Jackson or Swain counties instead. But it will be in one or all of those areas. Wherever, I do think it would be good to set aside land for public use and enjoyment. Make government a benefactor."

"They said years ago it was going to benefit me to pay income tax but I ain't seen no damn good come from it."

"Mr. Wright, are you totally against an Eastern national park?"

"Mr. Thomas, if they're dead set to have one, they ought to put it in Virginia. Up in the Shenandoah. It's closter to Warshington, where all them folks that want to walk in a park live. Farmers there want it 'cause they've done wore out their land. It makes sense."

"What makes you think the government's got any sense?" Harrogate asked.

Silas smiled. "You got a point, Bud. But even them scoundrels ought to have better sense than to put it here. Tell you what. If this park comes around here, me and you'll go to the gaps—I'll go to Cove Creek and you go to Starling and we'll pick them off one by one. I can still shoot the eye out of a squirrel at fifty yards."

"Sounds good, Silas. By the way, is Rhetta all right? She seemed quiet tonight."

"Son, she had a spell a while back. Woke with a pain in the side of her head. She couldn't talk right for a few minutes, but by that evening she was fine. Ever since she's been slowing down. She says nothing's wrong, but a man can tell."

"None of us is getting any younger, are we?"

"No, for a fact, we ain't. Now, gentlemen, I got a little hot a few minutes ago. I don't apologize for that, but I think old Paul in the Bible said let not the sun go down on your wrath. Let's take his advice and have a little drink." They passed the Mason jar around, and Silas returned it to the box in the corner. Bud went inside and Norman headed toward the creek. "I didn't mean to make you angry, Mr. Wright," said Thomas. "I do apologize."

"You just didn't think before you started talking, Mr. Thomas. If they'd hang a man for that we'd all be swinging."

Thomas started inside and doffed his hat when he saw Rhetta heading for the porch. "Evening, Mrs. Wright."

"About to turn in, are you? I hope you sleep well, Mr. Thomas."

"Thank you, ma'am. That was a fine dinner."

She looked at him like there was no hope. "How many times do I have to tell you, we ate *dinner* six hours ago. What you just ate was *supper*. That's in the Bible."

"Excuse me?"

"It says Jesus and his disciples gathered in the upper room for a meal, right?"

"Yes, ma'am."

"Well, don't it say it was evening?"

"I believe so."

"Well, then. They don't call that the Lord's *Dinner*, do they?"

"No, Mrs. Wright, they don't. I'll remember that. And your supper was delicious. Good evening to you."

Rhetta sat fanning her face with her hand. "I declare, is it hot or is it me?"

"It's a bit warm. You been in the kitchen too long."

"You menfolks solve the world's problems?"

Silas leaned against the column. "That Thomas fellow just about made me mad."

"That dear little man? What in the world did he say?"

"We got to talking about that national park. He said it was all but decided. I just didn't like how he said it."

"Maybe he knows something you don't."

"Maybe. Shoot, I got enough to worry about without that."

Harrogate returned. "Here's that newspaper, Silas. You want me to read you that article?"

Silas reached for the paper. "I reckon I ain't too old to read." He stared at the headlines. "Tunney beat Dempsey. Never would have thought that would happen."

"Silas, I didn't know you was a boxing man. Thought you kept up with baseball."

"Lots of things you don't know, Bud." He rustled the paper, scanning the smaller headlines. "I reckon this is what you was worrying over. 'Tennessee to Acquire Big Tract for Park.' " He rustled the paper impatiently. "Says old Townsend, I've heard of him, he's the chief cook and bottle washer over at Little River Lumber Company, complained the state hadn't taken title to that eighty thousand acres over there. That got Governor Peay's dander up." He looked up. "That must be more of that cut-over timberland I was talking about."

"Actually, that tract hasn't been cut yet, but it will be if the state doesn't buy it quick."

Silas pished at that. "Says some people from the Department of Interior said 'much of the anticipated glory of the Park is going to be stolen and despoiled before North Carolina and Tennessee get busy.' Anticipated glory, my ass." His eyes narrowed. "Boy, listen at this horse manure. 'When Mark Squires, chairman of the North Carolina National Park Commission, heard this news he is reported to have gotten into action so suddenly and boisterously that the phone operators in Lenoir have not yet recovered from his bombardment of long distance calls.' Says it's unknown how many acres North Carolina has purchased. Hell, Bud, I know for a fact no property's been bought around here."

Rhetta reached for his hand. "Silas, they ain't going to run us off, are they?"

He squeezed her hand. "Long as I got breath and buckshot they ain't. My God, listen to this, will you? Says here a white family in Stokesdale got six cases of typhoid fever. Well water stunk so bad cattle wouldn't drink it, but they kept on at it. Some people ain't got good sense."

She smiled. "We've always had springwater. Maybe wells is different."

"You're right, water here is what makes whiskey good and if them park critters come here they'll have to pay us a premium. But don't worry. We been here too long for them to get us."

"Promise?"

He put the paper down and smiled. "Long's I've got breath I ain't leaving here. You can mark them words."

26

I Reckon You Killed It

Rass Carter's father, Levi Marion, kept as fine a farm as anyone in Haywood County, but Rass wanted no part of it when he grew up. Born in Big Cataloochee the year the cloudburst killed Old Sal, Rass was not exactly lazy but, as his father put it, kept his head in the clouds or his nose in a book. The summer he turned twelve he was sent to the high pasture by his great-uncle John to check on the cattle. A boy felt grown up to be by himself so far above the valley, just himself and Columbine the mule, getting ready to spend a night under the stars. Rass fancied himself an author, and had lately written some three- and four-page stories about cowboys. For weeks he had anticipated this trip. He might even make a story out of it.

As he listened to the clopping mule he realized how noisy the valley had become. The creek made a constant racket, people shouted to one another across the fields and stopped in the road to chitchat, grain mills ground to the slow squeak of water-turned axles, mowing machinery clattered behind teams of equines, blacksmiths pumped bellows and beat red iron into shape, and, in 1928, six or seven automobiles and Lige Howell's Model-T pickup putted around, stirring dust and scaring horses. He reined Columbine to a stop. Up here was breeze, an occasional cricket chirp, and the twisty, unwinding sound of what his teacher, Mr. Frazier, called cicadas, but the old folks called jarflies.

He really noticed a difference when he rested Columbine. As she snorted he patted her haunch. He stopped, totally motionless, listening to what at first, to a second of seven children, sounded like absolutely nothing. He heard no rushing water but noticed the green sound of wind in the tree canopy. It was likely ten degrees cooler up there than down in the valley.

He'd come up along the road that followed Cataloochee Creek to the turnoff at the Bennett place. When he passed the Bennett house he remembered the story about his great-grandfather Levi and his great-uncle Hiram, captured by the Yankees sixty-four years ago now. He'd heard that story a hundred times—in fact, had tried to tell it on paper but it didn't sound good told with proper grammar.

Past there the road rose for a half mile, dropped to its lowest point at the confluence of Little Cataloochee Creek, then climbed sharply toward Mount Sterling. He and the mule had left a world cultivated on both sides of the road for woods on one side and steep drop on the other. Sun cut through first from one direction, then another, as the road switched back and forth like a cat's tail before she pounces. As they rose he saw more white pines and hemlocks, some too enormous to cut save with machinery. Every now and then he heard the whickety sound of surprised doves but nothing louder since about halfway up.

The mountaintop pastures, large areas bare of trees, were called yellow balds because from a distance the short grass and huckleberry bushes looked more yellow than green. Rass's teacher had told them no one really knew how balds formed. Some figured fires caused by lightning or the Cherokee kept them clean of trees, but others both white and red attributed them to the finger of God at creation. For three generations Rass's people had pastured beef cattle on the Sterling bald in summers.

He and the mule went over the gap and a hundred yards down to the northeast, where they had turned out the cattle in the spring. He ate dinner—his mother had packed him a feast of cornbread and ham, cold sweet potatoes, chicken, and fried apple pies—then tied the mule in the shade and walked out on the bald. Coming into sunshine he couldn't help but sneeze, scattering grasshoppers of every color and size. He found the chestnut lick log embedded in the middle of the field, its dozen empty holes notched out by some forgotten cattleman. Rass filled the holes with salt and hollered. Before long he heard a bell cow. Then in no time white-faced Herefords and roans and Anguses surrounded him, licking salt, picking grass, teeth clicking, nostrils blowing. One of John's cows had lost part of an ear and showed a pinkish scar down her haunch. Rass brushed it with tar. He wrestled calves to the ground and shoved worm capsules into their mouths. Some cattle were content to lick salt and go after water. Others investigated Rass with creamy breath. He sat cross-legged in the sun while they circled and nodded at him like Joseph's sheaves, picking, snorting, and shitting.

He refilled the lick log and put the empty bags in his saddlebag, then headed to the road as the cattle ambled toward water.

At the gap the roadbed snaked down and north into Tennessee but he turned northwest up a switchback trail to the top of Mount Sterling, where balsam woods were full of squirrels and feasting birds. Rass rode east atop the mountain to a spot where his great-grandfather had camped on such expeditions as this.

He led the mule to the springhead and while she drank he put out oats. Tying her, he went to the mountain's edge and sat in sunshine like a lizard, more than a mile above sea level. In the woods a pair of birds his mother called "wood hens" and his father called "Lord God birds" and Mr. Frazier called "pileated woodpeckers" yelled.

Hearing a three-noted keen, Rass looked at a golden eagle flying overhead. Rass wished he could soar like that, but then considered having to eat raw mice and squirrels. He looked back to the valley and wondered when he would leave this place.

He had heard of the national park since he was eight but had no clear idea of what that might mean for him. Rumor shifted places with information when it came to park news. Some said you could stay after the government took over and some said everyone would have to leave right away. Moving sounded like an adventure, and he had imagined himself in a big place like Asheville or even New York.

On the other hand, he was afraid moving might kill his father. His devotion to Cataloochee soil shouted from every crease in his face. After the initial uproar about the park, neither North Carolina nor Tennessee had raised enough money to buy more than a shirttail's worth of land, and that had given Levi Marion heart. But in March, J. D. Rockefeller had pledged five million dollars, after which news his father spent an unheard-of day in bed. Now every new boarder in Cataloochee was asked whether he worked for the park commission, which was known to be looking at all counties bordering Tennessee. The Carters still hoped Haywood County would be spared.

Rass picked a sprig of grass and sucked the sweet end. No wonder cattle like grass, he thought. A fellow could get used to life up here. But park or no park, one of these days he planned to go somewhere. His cousin Clyde made ten dollars a week at the paper mill in Canton and didn't work half as hard as Rass's father.

In his high fantasies he went to New York, or even Hollywood, having written a book that became a moving picture. Mr. Frazier said that Burroughs fellow who wrote about Tarzan was a millionaire. Rass had just finished Zane Grey's *The UP Trail,* which Mr. Frazier loaned him, saying Grey just fished, and only wrote when he needed more money.

His imagination spent money on a European car for himself, a grand piano for his mother, and a new farm far removed from the threat of a national park for his father. Or if he made enough money maybe he could persuade the park to go elsewhere so his father could keep the farm intact.

Something manlike but heavier crashed in the woods to his rear.

Columbine brayed and pulled to get loose. Rass shook off his reverie, ran to the mule, patted her, and surveyed the woods. A blue jay shrieked overhead. Ten yards in, it was much cooler. He stood listening. "It's a bear," he whispered, "and I bet it's still watching us, girl."

He backed out of the woods and patted the mule again. "Whatever it was, it isn't interested in us. Let's pitch camp." By the sun it was nearly five.

A circle of fire-charred stones marked the camp, where he had imagined generations of men like him had lain their bodies down for a good night's sleep. He led the mule toward the springhead and tied her. As he put down his bedroll near the circle he heard the rattle before he saw the snake stretching to his left eight feet behind him. Not coiled, tongue flicking, making racket like a jar of rocks. As Rass moved his head, the snake, five feet of power, flat thick head, solid black tail, coiled upon itself. Rass traced the steps he would need to get the rifle. Warren Neale, his new Zane Grey hero, would just shoot the snake and cook it for supper. He thought he could do that.

Then his legs got shackly and his heart pounded under his blue shirt and overalls. Rass picked up bedroll and saddlebag and sidled away from the reptile in a wide arc. The snake's head followed his motion but its body did not move toward the boy. Rass's legs were still rubbery as he stowed the saddlebag, tied the bedroll, and began to lead the mule away.

Then he sat down beside the mule and bawled for a full minute. "What's the matter with me? Why can't I kill that snake? I'm acting like I was six." He hiccupped, wiped his nose and face, mounted, and turned the mule. The snake stared at him still. He and Columbine started back into the balsam, heading home.

When men went to check the high pastures they always stayed a day or two. Yet he checked off everything Uncle John had asked him to do. He'd counted the animals and wormed the calves and doctored a wound or two, put out salt and medicine, and had finished in a couple of hours. Then it dawned on him. The men never stayed alone. There were always at least three and sometimes as many as a dozen. "They don't *want* to come home," he said to Columbine, who snorted as if to agree. "They sit up drinking and telling tales. We'd have been by ourselves with a dead snake if I'd had guts enough to kill it, and a live bear, and Lord knows what else." Sunlight faded halfway down the mountain. A screech owl started up behind him as bats flitted. He wondered if there were whippoor-wills this high. When he got to the valley he came into daylight again. Riding beside the creek he urged Columbine to trot, to keep up enough breeze to fend black gnats from his eyes.

Lige Howell, a roundish man with a halo of white hair and beard, stood behind his house watching a man fish the creek. Rass halted Columbine as Lige walked over and patted the mule. "Howdy, Rass. Ever body's cattle all right?"

Rass brushed his hands across his face. The fisherman, a fellow named Pendleton who had told Lige he lived in Knoxville and worked for the paper mill in Canton, wore a hat with a veil, such as a woman might wear to a fancy funeral. "Yes, sir. One cow got ambushed, but she's healing. Rest are fine."

"That's good, son. Reckon this fellow's going to catch anything besides a cold?"

"I don't know. Why do you think tourists make it so hard on themselves, with artificial flies? I never had trouble catching fish with worms."

"Yankees are downright strange, son. But they won't get all my stock fish that way."

"I better run, Uncle Lige. I thought I'd stay on the mountain but now I better get on before they all go to bed."

Lige stepped back. "I wondered if you'd stay the night up there. I wouldn't by myself, I tell you. Too many bears and such."

Rass wished he had a fancy horse so he could rear it up like Douglas Fairbanks. But at least Columbine's pace was fast enough to keep most of the gnats out of his face.

Uncle John, sweat trailing down his cheek, came out of the shed when Rass rode up. "I thought you was staying up the mountain. What's wrong?"

"Everything's fine, Uncle John. I got through, so I just came back. Truth is, that rattler I nearly stepped on helped make up my mind."

John wiped his brow and nodded. "Nothing like a buttontail to hurry a man. Say you nearly stepped on him?"

"Close as from me to you. And I think I heard a bear before that."

"Don't blame you for coming back. Only reason I stay is to get away from the old lady awhile. How's my cattle?"

Rass accounted for livestock and gave him his empty salt bags and medicine kit. "Rass, I'll tell Levi Marion you done a fine job."

"Thanks, Uncle John. I better get. I'll scare everybody to death if I come riding in after they're in bed."

Jarflies chattered in the trees over Columbine's hoofbeats. Rass was aware of the creek after the silence in the forest. He saw no early color in the trees. It was not time for katydids, and Rass was glad, for the old folks said when the first one hollered it meant six weeks till frost.

Red, Levi Marion's ancient bear dog, barked twice. Two younger dogs snuffled through the field to greet mule and rider, and accompanied them to the barn. Rass fed Columbine, rubbed her down, shed the dogs, and came outside.

As he walked to the porch Rass studied his father. Levi Marion's nearly white hair was haloed yellow by the coal oil lamp inside. His overalls were at what Rass called half-staff, one gallus off, one on. Bare feet tough and burnished as the knots in the porch floor. The left big toe mostly gone, victim of an ax. "Evening, Rass," he said. "I thought you was staying on the mountain."

"Well, sir, I got done early. I counted cattle and wormed calves and put out salt. I just figured I'd come back home."

"Never knowed a boy not to lay out of a night when he had leave." Levi Marion didn't move his eyes from Rass's face.

"Papa, I didn't want to camp by myself." Rass's eyes scanned the porch as if for help. "Truth is, I got scared. I nearly stepped on a rattler."

Levi Marion's blue eyes narrowed. "I reckon you killed it."

Rass paused and took a deep breath. "No, sir. I—"

"Rass, your people spilled a lot of sweat and blood to make this valley safe. Then you tell me you walk off and leave a man-killing snake like it was a hoppy toad?"

Rass's cheeks burned. "Yes, sir, but I knew it wouldn't hurt me if I gave it its territory."

Levi Marion stood. "Son, I'm surprised at you. Now get on to bed. We got lots to do tomorrow." He squeaked the screen door open and went in, banging the door loud as a shotgun. It was enough to get a twelve-year-old boy to think once more about leaving.

27

STAND YOUR GROUND

Ezra had thought about a new barn for years, but put it off until 1928, when he took a notion to build a combination barn and apple house in the middle of the summer, never mind there was no time to finish it before harvest. Any more he jumped at things. He'd bought Hiram Carter's old T-model from Hiram's sons, Manson and Thomas, for fifty dollars, despite the fact it had been sitting in their barn for two years and Ezra did not know how to drive nor even if it ran.

Zeb had told his father he didn't need a whole new barn. "Papa, you can take the T-model out of the old barn and the wagons out of the side sheds. It's no trouble to board up the sheds."

"Son, I want a new barn, and that's what I mean to have. Besides, I don't want my new car to rust."

"Papa, that 'new car' is fourteen years old. And you know the national park's going to buy us out. There ain't a bit of use in all this
work."

"Park be damned. If I want a shit-fired barn I'll build it whether you
help me or not." Ezra laid the foundation using rocks Zeb and his brothers had stacked over the years. Neighbors helped Ezra raise the roof
beams over the weekend. Zeb stayed home, pleading a sore back.

Monday morning a steady beat started slowly, a hammer sounding
like someone down the road was trying to unkink a shoulder. Zeb slept
through the first few, but as they got faster he woke. Five or six quick
hammer blows, then quiet. Then again. Son of a bitch, Zeb thought. It
ain't even daylight.

Mattie stood looking toward Ezra and Hannah's place as Zeb laced
his boots and felt for his blue shirt hanging on the ear of the bedside
chair. Walking toward Mattie he jerked his head suddenly like he had
walked into a spiderweb. She put her arm around his waist. He winced
when she tickled his side. "Sound sure carries when it's about to rain.
He's going to build that barn if it harelips Herbert Hoover."

"Reckon so. He needs it like I need another hole in my head." He put
his hand over Mattie's to keep her from digging her fingers into his ribs.
Pretty good, he thought, to marry a woman, live with her seventeen
years, and still like having her around.

He pulled away. "You want me to build the fire?" The hammer re-
frain was joined by another hand.

"No, I'll get the fire going and fix breakfast. Sounds like Jake's over
there now."

"Bad as Papa's treated him over the years, Jake's a good man to be
there. I'd not be helping if he wasn't my father." Zeb bit the end of his
thumb and headed toward the barn. Louder outside, the two hammers
rang first in offbeats but soon echoed together, Jake altering his rhythm
to fit Ezra's. Zeb would add his hammer after breakfast, and Arvil and
Wilbur Wright, Silas's nephews, had promised to help today, so up in
the morning there would be five hammers ringing through the valley.
He wondered how long they would stay. When Ezra hired help, they

would usually work a couple of days, then he would threaten to blow them to kingdom come with his owlhead over nothing, so they would leave.

When Zeb got to Ezra's place, sun backlit the mountain and colored the cirrus pink. On this early September morning, Zeb waved to his mother, who was hanging dishrags to dry on the back porch. A flock of stubby-tailed black birds half the size of crows circled in unison, and perched in a sweet gum down toward Ola, where they skreaked like rusty hinges.

"What you reckon them birds are?" he asked Jake. "I'd call them blackbirds but they ain't hardly got tails."

"Only bird you need to worry about is old Tom Turkey." Jake pointed at Ezra with his hammer. "Never seen a man with such a short fuse."

Zeb nodded. Carter tempers, themselves substantial, held no candle to the Banks variety. He had seen his father beat a mule with a trace chain until its ears bled, so he had no trouble imagining the old man in his cups killing Ticker. After they had started having mailmen, one got a black eye and lost a tooth trying to collect a penny postage due.

Ezra meant to dry in the east side of the barn with a trailer load of poplar and oak boards sawmill cut in eight- and six-foot lengths. He had gotten the mill to pile the leftover slab—bark on, cut into stove wood—atop the lumber. Arvil and Wilbur arrived—lanky young men in overalls and slouch hats, smelling of filthy socks and stale whiskey—and soon they had thrown all the slab in a pile close to the woodshed.

"Now, boys, let's get them six-footers over here," said Ezra, stepping back to light his pipe. They piled the boards beside the building, set up a scaffold on sawhorses, and shortly closed that side up to the loft's floor.

Midmorning they took a break as sunshine peeked over the mountain. Zeb approached his father. "Papa, why don't we work on the other side till this afternoon, then come back and finish here? That way we'd be in the shade all day."

Ezra lit his brier with a kitchen match, dragging flame deep into the pipe. When the cloud of smoke cleared, Ezra's dark eyes stared at Zeb like he was the dumbest human in the county. "Lumber's laid out the way we'll work. It ain't so damn hot you'll melt. And I ain't paying you boys to set in the shade."

Zeb shook his head but said nothing. By dinnertime they had worked up a good sweat. While Ezra went to the house, they got dinner buckets from the springhouse and squatted under the yard maple.

"Old man's a study, ain't he?" Wilbur wiped his brow with the back of his arm.

Jake looked at Wilbur. "Just eat. Won't be five minutes before he's back out here." He held a half-eaten cat-head biscuit stuffed with pork. Sure enough, they soon heard the screen door slam. Ezra looked at the sun, checked his pocket watch, and adjusted his hat.

"Now boys," he said, "don't rush yourselves. Wouldn't want you to get the bellyache." Wilbur leaned back against the tree and pulled his hat over his forehead. Zeb couldn't help but smile. Arvil started to lean against the tree when Ezra poked Wilbur with his boot.

"While you boys rest, how about splitting that slab wood? That'll help settle your dinner." Wilbur looked at Arvil and they headed to the woodpile.

"Now, let's get going on this here barn." Zeb and Jake shrugged and started in with the old man.

The Wright brothers joined them an hour later. By supper they had finished three-fourths of the next side. Ezra had gotten a good day out of them, and stove wood split and stacked to boot. "Don't you two stay out helling around all night," he said to Arvil and Wilbur. "I want you back here before daylight."

When they stowed tools and left, Ezra turned to his son. "Zeb, you got the sleeping sickness? You showed up way after sunup this morning."

"Papa, I ain't going to milk in pitch dark to build a barn for the park to take over."

"Don't sass me, boy. I ain't too old to whup you."

"I ain't sassing, I'm telling. I got my own farm to run. See you in the morning."

He walked deliberately up the hill till Jake caught up with him.

"Don't let him get your dander up."

"One of these days I'm going to get up the nerve to tell him to go straight to hell."

"Now, Zeb, he may be ornery but he's still your papa."

"Ornery." Zeb snorted. "I could stand ornery. But that old man's going to bust hell wide open—that is, if he ever dies. I get so damn mad I could kill him."

"Take it easy, Zeb. At his age it can't be too awful much longer."

"God may have to knock him in the head Judgment Day." They both laughed with little mirth.

They finished siding the barn the next day. When Zeb got home, William, oldest of his four children, met him on the porch. He looked more like his mother every day, brown eyes at once piercing and flighty, like a bird that might either take off or sit on your shoulder. At fourteen he was nearly tall as Zeb.

"Mama's in the bed with a sick headache. She says don't stomp around."

Zeb sat in the rocker and took off his boots. "Where's your sisters?" They were anywhere from twelve to eight and looked like Carters, except little Alice, who was black-headed like Ezra.

"At the barn. They're stringing a mess of beans for leatherbritches."

"What's for supper?"

"So far it's a pot of beans, and leftover chicken. I'm about to get the girls to stir up some corn bread."

"You do that, and I'll check on your mama."

William headed to the barn while Zeb tiptoed to the back bedroom. Mattie lay under the coverlid, eyes closed, cloth over her forehead. He shut the door and went in the kitchen. William had beans boiling and chicken in the warmer. Zeb peeled and cut up Irish potatoes and threw them in the bean pot.

In a few minutes the four children came in the back door. William toted an armload of stove wood. Doris, Lizzie, and Alice all carried beans strung together, slung over their shoulders like bunting. They hung them in the loft to dry. William laid the wood in the box by the stove and Doris started making corn bread. Zeb looked in on Mattie again.

This time she peeked at him. "Hey, honey," she said so quietly he might have made it up.

"You feel like supper?" She shook her head slightly. "All right. I'll look in on you in a little bit." He squeezed her hand and got faint pressure in return.

They were cleaning up after supper when the bedroom door creaked open and Mattie shuffled out in her house shoes. William pulled out a chair for her at the table. "Mama, you want to eat?"

"Yes, son, I think a little bite would help. It smelled so good in here I had to get up."

The children rushed to fill her plate. Zeb had finished eating but poured sweet milk in a glass and sat at the table with Mattie. He slowly crumbled a piece of corn bread into the milk.

"Glad to see you feeling better. I hate it when you have them things."

"Don't hate it half as bad as me. Beans are good. We got butter to go on this corn bread?"

Doris apologized and set the print of butter, minus the cloverleaf on top, beside her mother. "I bet Alice scraped the top off that," Mattie said, and looked at her least daughter, who giggled. "Child, when are you going to learn that ain't polite? Now get in there and fold them clothes before bed. You hear?"

The children took the clothes basket to the front room. Mattie looked at Zeb and smiled weakly. "How's things down the way?"

"'Bout the same. Nothing suits Papa and Arvil stinks to high heaven, but we about got the thing sided. Tomorrow we start on the loft floor. Might finish this week if it don't rain us out."

"How's Jake?"

"Barked his knuckle, but he's all right. We both got to work our own apples. But sure as we're done with the barn Papa'll want us to help him with his'n."

"Why don't you tell him you got to tend to your own business?"

"You know Papa. He'd pitch a fit and then some."

Mattie scowled. "Zeb, you know one of these days you're going to have to stand up to him. You can't let him bully you forever."

"I know. Right now he's wound tighter'n a two-dollar clock over this barn."

"When did you ever seen him not wound up about something or another?" She pushed her plate away and wiped her mouth. "Zeb, if you don't care, get these young'uns to bed. I'm going back myself. Eating makes me think I can sleep, and I'll weather this headache." He took her plate to the sink and looked out the window, his reflection staring back at him, flickering in the coal oil light.

Zeb woke the next morning before daybreak to the sound of a critter scratching through the yard, probably a fox or a polecat. He sniffed but smelled no skunk, only the wine scent of apples. He'd heard of forty cents a bushel this year, and probably had a thousand bushels, winesaps and Romes and sheepsnoses and Golden Delicious.

He padded to the back porch, careful not to bang the door, and sat on the edge of the porch. Crickets chirped. Smelled like rain. He studied out there for a half hour, rehearsing what to tell Ezra. In gray dawn he began to distinguish the shapes of outbuildings and orchard. "I'll give him today but that's it. We all got to harvest our apples else none of us'll make a nickel off them. We can't waste what we've worked so damn hard for."

Zeb heard Mattie get up, and saw the lamp in the back of the house. "Might have a hot breakfast after all," he said to himself. In the kitchen he hugged Mattie. "Morning, honey. You sleep good?"

"Thank the Lord that sick headache's gone. I washed down a couple of aspirins with a cup of pennyroyal tea and slept like a corpse." She lit the fire. "You going to talk to your daddy?"

"Yep. I been studying over it."

"Good for you." She cocked her head and grinned at him. "You remember that shooting match you won when we was fourteen? Or at least the one you didn't lose?"

Zeb nodded. "Sure. Only you let me win, I've always known that."

"That's not why I brought it up, silly. I just remember how determined your daddy was that you'd win. He's always been like that, used to getting his way. Get down there and stand your ground."

Leaving, he looked at the old .32 Remington in the rack over the back door and remembered the time he could have shot his father with it. He started down the hill and heard a single hammer begin to drown out the birds. Soon he saw Ezra lay a piece of one-by-eight across the loft floor joists, tap the board into place, kneel, and nail it fast. His father laid another board out and fingered his shirt pocket for a nail as he saw Zeb. "You're out mighty early."

"Papa, we got to talk."

"Can't work and talk at the same time."

"Then don't work. I got something to say."

Ezra straightened.

"Papa, I'll work today but tomorrow I'm starting to pick my apples. You got to, too. Our crops'll ruin if we don't."

Ezra laid down his hammer and squatted at the edge of the loft. "Well, son, you think that's what you're going to do?" He eyed Jake, who was dismounting. "Jake Carter, come here! I got something for you to hear."

"Morning, gents. It's mighty early for a palaver."

Ezra stood to his full height. "This boy just said he ain't going to work on his daddy's barn no more."

"That so," said Jake.

"You ever hear the beat of it?"

"Fact is," said Jake, "we all got to tend to our apples."

Ezra ignored him and stared at Zeb. "I never thought to see such a thankless child. I brought him into this world, fed, clothed, and schooled him. I sold him his place, which he's still paying on. And now he won't help an old man that ain't got many winters left. I reckon blood ain't thick as it used to be. You always was your mother's boy anyhow. And you turned around and married that gal that damn near beat you shooting. Go, damn you." He stooped and picked up the hammer. "I don't need the likes of you around here."

"Wait a minute, Ezra," said Jake. "We got three farms full of apples. Ain't no reason we can't help each other do what needs doing for a couple of weeks, then finish this barn."

Ezra's expression would have fit well on a man whose legs had been sprayed by a tomcat. "So, you think we can just stop. Goddamn. I thought Hannah's people had better sense. Throw away two whole weeks' work?"

"Ain't throwing away nothing. This barn ain't making us no money. Apples do. Let's get our crops in and then we'll finish your barn."

"Then goddamn both of you. Get the hell back to your shit-fired apples and I'll finish this barn my own self. If I ever need to see either one of you again, I'll let you sons of bitches know." He found his nails and hammer and addressed the floor once again.

Jake walked to his mule, put the dinner bucket back on the saddle horn, and mounted. Zeb started home on foot. Jake caught up with his nephew.

"Want a ride?"

"I got to walk this off."

"He'll get over it."

"Maybe he will but I won't. He's beat me and cussed me before but this time it's . . . I don't know what the word is, meaner'n usual. Before I left I had a notion to bring my rifle. It's a damn good thing I didn't."

"Zeb, that's your father you're talking about."

"And what was that bullshit about me still paying on my place? I paid it off two months ago."

"He's old." Jake sat the mule. "All he's got on his mind is his own sorry self, and we can't do nothing about that. Now we got to get our business tended to. Then we'll help finish his damn barn. Okay?"

Zeb shrugged, spat on the road, and kicked a couple of rocks. "I'm obliged to you for standing up for me."

"I'd left my place with the same thing on my mind. Rachel was after me last night about it. See you tomorrow."

Jake nudged Lilly and headed home. Zeb looked to the heavens as if for consolation, but all he saw were short-tailed black birds coming once again over the ridgetop.

28

BY THE RIVERS OF BABYLON

The morning of September 30, 1928, Preacher Will Smith woke at four in the upstairs back bedroom of Lige and Penny's boardinghouse. Even in bitter weather he cracked the window a hair to hear the creek. But the night before it had kept him wakeful. A dream of an emaciated woman crying beside a creek in a forest, carrying a soaked blanket covering an unmoving infant, the pair meandering from tree to tree, woke him. He got back to sleep but dreamed it again.

He sat up, mattress rustling. White veneer covered the field. Last night Lige had said it would frost, but Smith had said it was too early. But there it was. Cold in there, too. Penny's girl had laid a fire in the fireplace, but no more time than he'd be in the room this morning, he'd not light it.

As he dressed, his spirit was troubled. He thought about last month's talk with Harris Pendleton, another of Lige and Penny's boarders. Some folks called Pendleton "Red," although it was no longer because of his hair, gray since he'd turned forty. Natty was the word for him. Every hair in place, every item of clothing matching. He was from middle Tennessee but along the way the drawl had been educated out of him.

Smith liked about everyone he met, but when he first shook hands with Pendleton it was all he could do not to make sure his Masonic ring was still there. Pendleton told Lige he was cruising timber for Champion Fibre, the truth, had he told it ten months ago. Then he apprised Smith in confidence that he worked for the park commission. Smith did not appreciate the irony. The timber company wanted to buy forest for nothing, cut it down, and ship it off. The commission said, at least, it wanted to buy the same forest to keep as wilderness. Smith thought Pendleton a turncoat on some level, like playing most of a career for the Browns, then suddenly wearing pinstripes, becoming Ruth's colleague. And telling it one way or the other depending on the company one kept.

Pendleton had requested the preacher's company on a walk after dinner. While they strolled toward the bridge, Pendleton told him who he worked for, and that in a short time Cataloochee would be part of the Great Smoky Mountains National Park. All residents would be bought out, one way or another, and would have to move, sooner or later. Pendleton told it with as much emotion as if he were reporting the price of wheat.

Smith inwardly blanched but thought Pendleton probably told the truth. Rumors had flown about an Eastern national park since the early twenties, and a late push by newspapers and politicians had put such a plan in the public eye. Smith looked at his companion. "By 'one way or another,' do you mean you expect trouble?"

"I don't know," said Pendleton, with an odd smile. "We will get the land regardless. The State of North Carolina will condemn it if we can't agree like gentlemen on a price. Then it will be out of our hands. Courts will fix the price, lawyers will take their cut, and owners will get a fraction of what they would have gotten had they cooperated in the first place. So you can see it is important to preach to these people about co-operation."

Smith stopped and stared at Pendleton. "Me? Me preach? Preach about—"

"Who better than the shepherd to advise the flock? The sheep believe what they hear from the pulpit." Pendleton's smile chilled Smith, who watched the blue flame of a kingfisher dipping toward the creek, yelling in midflight.

"You call me friend, but we are only talking because you think I can help you."

"Well put. I do expect confrontation. These people are backward, and have weapons. But you—see, they trust you."

Smith scratched his ear. "So you want my pulpit to make it easier for the park commission to uproot these people?"

"You might say that." He started walking again. "Doesn't 'relocate' sound better?"

"Call it what you will, Mr. Pendleton. Many of them have held this land for generations. You ask me to preach that it's God's will for them to give up their land to the government?"

"Precisely."

They paused briefly at the bridge, watching the sun turn the creek to gold and silver coursing around slick rocks. Smith thought of Melville. He'd never gotten through the big book about the whale but had copied the line about meditation and water being wedded forever. A glance at Pendleton told him all Red wanted was to own the creek.

As they started back the slight breeze tickled their faces now and turned up white wisps on the side of Pendleton's head. He licked a finger and smoothed them, then put his hands behind his back. Smith, walking just shy of him, saw a deerfly light on Pendleton's bald spot. Pendleton knocked it away but a red welt rose immediately.

"Damned flies. Pardon my language, Reverend Smith. They breed around these run-down farms. Where was I? Oh, yes. The park commission will pay fair market value for these people's worn-out land. That's more than a timber company or a mining operation would pay.

These folks can then buy better land elsewhere. Under the park service the land will return to pristine wilderness so future generations can enjoy it. These people will benefit—so will hardworking Americans who want a vacation. I'd think you would want a significant role in that process."

Since that evening, the preacher had turned Pendleton's words over every which way. The park would happen. Rockefeller's five-million-dollar pledge had sealed the deal. Talk of siting the North Carolina portion of the park around Mount Mitchell and Linville had died. He knew he needed to say something to the congregation, and he would naturally have preached a sermon of compassion and comfort had the news been announced already. This way, he had to bring the tidings, and that angered and frightened him a bit. King David, he knew well, had killed messengers.

Over the next two weeks his anger turned to anxiety. He tried to pray but no answers came. From Scripture nothing jumped at him. One evening he pushed food from one side of his plate to the other with his fork. His wife put her hand on his. "Will, you're going to worry that poor bean to death. What's wrong?"

He smiled at Edna, his mate for nearly thirty years. "It's that business about the national park." He told her of Pendleton's conversation. "You have any ideas, dear?"

"I've been thinking about those poor people. You've got to preach to them."

He turned his hand over and squeezed hers. "How to go about it? What I mean is, must *I* be the one to tell them?"

"Here's the nutshell, Will. If they hear this news at a meeting at the schoolhouse, or get a notice in the mail, they'll have time to get really mad and do something foolish. Mr. Pendleton, no matter how much you don't care for him, is right about one thing—mountain people can be violent. Revenue men disappear in these hills all the time. Remember that poor Moody boy? If you tell them in a sermon they won't dare explode on the spot. But, listen to me, Will, aside from that, the important thing is, after you tell them, you *have* to give them something they can put in their hearts."

"What would that be? They're getting uprooted from land they've known for generations. . . ."

"That's right, dear. They'll be exiles. The Bible says a lot about them."

So he had spent three days immersed in the Bible, and one evening wrote a sermon on foolscap, folded now in the inside pocket of his jacket. He wasn't happy with it, but Sunday morning gave no time to start anew. He tied his black and gold bowtie, hoped his hair wouldn't stick up too badly, and wondered why he had dreamed about the woman and the dead baby twice.

He liked to be out before other guests appeared for breakfast. He walked downstairs and off the dogtrot and turned left toward the kitchen, smelling warmth amid sharp air. The cold would make leaves turn soon. Sticking his head inside the kitchen, he waved at Penny and said he'd see her at church. He picked up the grease-stained brown bag and headed up the road. She always left him a sausage or ham biscuit in a paper poke with a flask of springwater.

He drove his black A-model into the valley but liked to walk to church in all but the worst weather. Two and a half miles gave him time to collect his thoughts and eat breakfast. When he first came, people would try to get him to ride with them, but now they paid him no mind. Tourists up early saw him drink from a flask. Lige told them it was preacher whiskey, made special so he could drink and still preach. Angular, black-suited, he resembled an old crow walking up the road.

Several wagons and a couple of buggies were already hitched beside the church when he arrived. Sunday school was still half an hour away, but Uncle Will Carter, who ran the mill up Indian Creek, was already there, tuning fork protruding from his overall pocket. There was a time old folks called him "Mill Will" when they needed to distinguish him from "Apple Will" in Little Cataloochee. But since Apple Will, Hannah Banks's father, had died, most folks simply called this one Uncle Will.

He shook Preacher Smith's hand with a hand rough and grooved as millstones.

"Morning, Preacher. Hope it ain't too cold for you."

Smith shook his head. "No, Brother Will, I like cool weather. Frost burning off makes a pretty mist."

"Lige says you got a good message and I'm raring to hear it."

"Well, I don't know so well about that. I don't quite know *what* I'm going to say."

"Preacher, Lige's told ever body it's important matters you'll talk about this morning. Set down in our buggy and pray. Draw them side curtains if you like."

As Uncle Will walked him to the buggy, Smith asked him to lead the congregation in "By the Rivers of Babylon." That puzzled him, but Will had never known a preacher without odd ways.

Lige looked like a prophet, the preacher thought, with his halo of white hair and white beard, and had in fact predicted frost last night. Maybe if he asked Lige to lead a prayer, Lige would go ahead and preach so Smith could sneak away.

Folks greeted each other with a mixture of talk about the morning message and the cool snap. A voice he didn't recognize drawled about taxes going "higher'n a cat's back." He heard Sunday school start in the sanctuary, older adults to the right of the pulpit and younger adults left. Children met at the back of the church, which was noisy as a Chinese fire drill. As they sang and droned Bible verses Smith's chest tightened. He could walk back to Lige's, get his Ford, and leave, but he'd run into Lige bringing his boarders to church. Lige would not let them stay at the house on Sunday mornings, saying anybody who would fish with a store-bought fly would rob a man blind.

He got out of the buggy knowing only that what he had written would not preach, did not adequately speak to this mob, a crowd bigger than he drew at Easter. He saw unfamiliar mounts, men he hadn't seen in years, and some not at all. Uncle Will announced it was time. The preacher put his hand to his chest, where his breakfast biscuit had not moved a bit. Please, God, he prayed, let it move down, not up.

The clapboard church with three double-hung windows on the east and west sides seated maybe a hundred comfortably, but today everybody hunkered together. Men stood all the way around the walls, five deep along the back. Uncle Will tapped his tuning fork on the pulpit and hummed the key for a chorus of "On Christ the Solid Rock I Stand." Levi Marion and his family sat near the west wall crowded together like refugees. Lige had brought his usual wagonload of boarders, who stood outside. Three dark men in the southeast corner stood out like porcupines at a fancy wedding. Dirty, unshaven faces and hobnailed boots bespoke loggywoods boys, drovers, or just plain trouble.

After "Solid Rock" they went into "Rock of Ages" and finished with "Amazing Grace." Uncle Will had chosen well, from the congregation's shared foundation. Smith closed his eyes in a silent prayer: "These are their life, their creed, their deliverance. These people are going to need a lot of Jesus to get through this. So am I." When they sat and shuffled feet and coughed, Preacher Smith stood behind the pulpit, bowed his head, then opened his Bible.

"Today's text is from the Old Testament," he said, in the steadiest voice he could muster. "It is the One Hundred and Thirty-seventh Psalm."

Outside, men and women looked through the windows, straining for a glimpse of the preacher through the bodies of the people standing inside. He took a deep breath and read:

"By the rivers of Babylon, there we sat down, yea, we wept, when we remembered Zion.

"We hanged our harps upon the willows in the midst thereof.

"For there they that carried us away captive required of us a song: and they that wasted us required of us mirth, saying, sing us one of the songs of Zion.

"How shall we sing the Lord's song in a strange land?"

He stopped there. The rest of the Psalm, about dashing babies against stones, was too much. He laid the Bible on the pulpit. "Let us pray." He bowed his head with them. "Almighty God, we thank you for this day and for these people gathered in your name. We ask you to bless us with your bounty. Grant us wisdom, strength, courage. Your Son promised a Comforter, the Holy Spirit, to help us. We claim that promise this morning. With the ancients, we call on your Holy Spirit to descend and guide us. We are bound on a journey. May it be to a Promised Land, guided by your Spirit and your Son, Jesus Christ, in whose name we pray. Amen."

He nodded to Uncle Will, who rapped his tuning fork and led them in "By the Rivers of Babylon." Levi Marion had a fine tenor voice, but it was silent this morning. Rass kept watch on his father like he might explode.

After the hymn Smith stepped to the pulpit. He tended to ramble without a written text, but shoved his written sermon in his jacket pocket, turned to the One Hundred and Thirty-seventh Psalm, and started telling about David and Psalms in general. He turned to Genesis and talked about the Garden of Eden and how Adam and Eve had it made for a long time, but then had to leave. He went back to Psalms and told about exile, and how after Adam and Eve the Hebrews were never strangers to it. He spoke of Moses and the wilderness and how God through Joshua finally led them into a Promised Land. God, he thought, this talk is wandering all over the wilderness. He drank self-consciously from a glass of water.

He told how desolated the Hebrews were when they were carted off to Babylon, to a land that would not grow familiar crops or feed cattle or yield trees to their axes. He lifted his Bible and read to them again, slowly, with emphasis: How shall we sing the Lord's song in a strange land?

He laid the Bible back on the pulpit. "Friends—and I call you that from the bottom of my heart, for I have known you a long time—I have rejoiced and suffered and eaten and drunk with you. And now I have a thing to tell you, so I might as well get on with it." He looked straight at a glaring Silas Wright.

"Friends, it is official. This valley will become part of the new Great Smoky Mountains National Park." He paused, bravely hoping to look them one by one in the eye, but could not. Silas said, "God Almighty," under his breath.

Tears sprang to Levi Marion's eyes as he lowered his head into his hands. Valerie put her arm around him and took his hands in a tableau repeated throughout the church.

"Soon, people will survey your land and buy it. You will have to leave, and no one regrets telling you about it more than me. It will not be tomorrow, nor next week, but it will be soon. They will offer you a price. You can take it and buy a farm somewhere else and continue your life there. Or you can take less and stay on this land for the rest of your life, then when you die it will become part of the park. You could contest it in court. You might get more money but you will still have to move eventually. If you refuse to sell, the state can condemn your land, and you can take or leave their price. Those are your choices."

Silas pushed his way outside, where his neighbors asked if what they had heard could possibly be true. Preacher Smith banged the water glass on the pulpit as hard as he dared.

"Friends, you have a great choice. When you find yourself on your new farm, or your new job, you will be in a strange land like the Hebrews. Your choice is to choose the sunny side, as the song says, to sing the Lord's song in spite of exile. You can sing for Jesus or you can sing for bitterness and revenge. You can sing for new life or you can sing for sadness and death. You can sing for family or you can sing for hatred and hurt. You can sing 'Rock of Ages' or you can throw rocks. It's your choice. I beseech you, this morning, make the right choice. Choose to sing with angels, not with the devil. There is a right way and a wrong way. I pray you will choose the right. May God watch over you. Amen."

He picked up his Bible. Uncle Will tried for a closing hymn but folks were either stunned and sitting in place or streaming outside.

When the preacher walked the aisle people gave him room to leave. He stopped beside Levi Marion, and put his hand on Valerie's arm, still anchored around her husband. They said nothing. He stepped into the yard.

Three dark men stood under the maple talking to Silas when the preacher came outside. After his eyes adjusted to the light he saw one wore a pistol.

Folks clamored after Smith. Even matriarchs, who had spent yesterday getting Sunday dinners ready, seemed in no hurry to go home. He went to the steps and spread his arms for quiet. "Folks, if you have questions, please ask one at a time." He kept his arms up like a statue pleading for mercy.

Someone in the back yelled, "Is it true?"

"Yes, my friends, I'm afraid it is."

"Preacher," shouted John Carter, "my family's been here since the 1830s. We ain't leaving without a fight." Cheers flew.

"John, I appreciate how you feel, but I had hoped you would listen to me today. Remember, Jesus turned the other cheek."

"Jesus didn't have nobody trying to steal his farm," yelled Verlin Moody, and received a chorus of "amen's" louder than any Smith had ever gotten. Some women started for wagons and buggies. Old Mrs. Rathbone put her hands over her ears.

"Friends," Smith shouted, "please let this be a time for cool heads."

John Carter laughed derisively. "It's them park people that need cool heads. You ain't no better'n them, Preacher. I hate to say it, but you ain't a bit better."

Several people agreed but the crowd quieted when Levi Marion, Rass on one side and Valerie on the other, appeared on the church porch. "How much time do we have?" Levi Marion's voice was shaky.

"I don't know. Tennessee has optioned the Little River tract at Elkmont, and North Carolina is beginning to talk to Suncrest Lumber Company up at Mount Sterling. I'd guess within six months appraisers and surveyors will be here."

"What about spring planting?"

"If you decide to stay, plant. Even if you don't, it ought to take at least a year to get everything signed and paid for, so you can make next year's crops."

Silas strode from the shade of the maple, his tall frame casting a large shadow on the roadbed. "Preacher, I got an idea," he shouted. The crowd got quiet again. "We ought to have a proper meeting, up at the schoolhouse, this evening. Nobody ever made a good decision on an empty stomach."

There were general murmurs of assent and a couple of stray "amen's."

"Silas, are you offering to lead this meeting?" asked John Carter.

"If nobody else will. Right now my belly thinks my throat's been cut. I'll be at the schoolhouse at four if you all want to talk about this mess. That all right with you, Preacher?" The preacher nodded. Instead of breaking up, the crowd clustered in several places, people flowing from one group to another like ants.

Lige patted the preacher's shoulder. "I knew something was heavy on your mind when I seed you leave. You had the whole world setting on your shoulders. You'll ride back with me, won't you?"

"Yes, thanks," said Smith. "You knew about this, didn't you?"

"Well, sir," said Lige, fussing with his pipe, "let's say I read the papers and I seed you talking to Red Pendleton last month and I seed you this morning. It don't take Einstein to figure some things out." Smoke haloed his face.

"What are you going to do?"

"I'm an old man. My young'uns has got young'uns and some of *them*'s about to have young'uns. I figure to get what it's worth and buy a place in Dellwood or Maggie and finish my years there. Ain't no sense for an old man to go off shooting federals. Me and Penny'll be all right." He motioned for the preacher to ride beside him and turned to see if all his passengers were in the back.

Levi Marion and his family pulled their wagon past them and headed up the valley. "Preacher," said Lige, "if you're a mind to fret about somebody, try Levi Marion."

"I'll see him this afternoon. Should I come to that meeting?"

"Preacher, if I was you I'd let us Catalooch people work out our own way to deal with the government. Ain't that what you preached last month? Out of Paul to the Philippians? 'Work it out with fear and trembling?' "

Smith nodded. "After I visit Levi Marion I'll just leave. I've done enough damage for one day." The preacher shook his head. Fear and trembling, indeed, he thought. Some people really do listen to sermons.

29

ABUNDANT AND INAUSPICIOUS

Riding back from church, Silas Wright remembered the one time he had moved, from Spring Creek to Cataloochee, when he had vowed never to move again. He had just turned eleven, and picked up a horrible case of poison oak after their wagon overturned into a tangle of briers and vines. Folks in Cataloochee thought he had the worst case they'd ever seen. Hiram Carter's mother, Lib, said he might lose an eye. Sixty-seven years later Silas had managed to keep out of poison oak and stay put.

Silas sat his horse tall and worked harder than much younger men, including his niece's husband, Carl. Carl and Ruby, his sister's youngest girl, had moved in after Rhetta died of a stroke the winter before. None of Rhetta and Silas's three daughters lived in North Carolina. They had no sons, unless they considered Harrogate such, which Silas practically did, especially when Harrogate found Chigger dead, and buried dog and box beside Rhetta.

Fording the creek Silas remembered Rhetta's dream of a retirement house in Waynesville. She used to say a little house wouldn't be much trouble to clean, all on one level, central heat, coal-fired furnace, hot water radiators. He used to say when they took him out of Cataloochee it'd be in a pine box, but she'd still talk about it. Then she went first. If she had not already died, he thought, she'd likely have croaked at church this morning. National park. He figured the park to be another sign of the times, like the latest Haywood County tax collector, a man with a stainless steel hook for a right hand. Signs lately were abundant and inauspicious.

At seventy-eight he could no more separate himself from his land than he could fly. His father lived to ninety, and his grandfather was in his eighties when he died. Silas expected to stay on his place ten years longer, maybe more, park or no park.

When he was eleven they had moved into a one-room cabin on two cleared acres. Now he owned nearly three hundred, all field and pasture except for timber on the ridgetops, and not a sprig of poison oak. He had made the land his—and now the preacher said the government wanted to give his sweat and sinew to "the people."

His father had settled this end of the valley because there were no close neighbors or traffic. Silas was no misanthrope but enjoyed his relative isolation. He kept boarders only because Rhetta had wanted them, but now no new ones need apply. The more he thought about it, this park threat had really started with the train. Fifty-five years ago he had ridden with Hiram Carter to see one. He'd told Hiram every flatlander in creation would want a piece of mountain land once the tracks got to Asheville. Sure enough, "the people" had seen the mountains, and wanted them.

As he stabled his mare he realized no one in government had asked a single Cataloochan what *he* thought about a national park. Head down, fuming, he stomped toward the house. Noticing a glint from the ground, he prized out a flint arrowhead, its point broken but translucent edges still sharp. His father used to tell of Cherokees hiding from Andy Jackson's men trying to round them up and march them to Oklahoma. Some secreted themselves in caves in the far ridge, in that driest of summers, the old men remembered, the same place they hid horses from Kirk's raiders in the war. Maybe Silas would have to live in one himself.

Ruby greeted him at the front door. "Uncle Silas, you look like you seen a haint."

He put his hand on her shoulder. "Ruby, the preacher told about the park."

"What do you mean, Uncle Silas?" She was a foot shorter than he, and looking up at him she reminded him of a wren.

"Park. They really aim to put the national park in here."

"That's foolishness. They've been talking about that for ages and nobody's done a thing about it. Eat some dinner. You'll feel better."

Ruby had fixed slaw and corn bread and boiled potatoes and green beans to go with a dozen fried trout. A plate of sliced tomatoes graced the middle of the table, around which the Bradleys, boarders from Morristown, Carl, Harrogate, and Norman sat.

Silas nodded at everyone. "Folks, let's pray over this meal. Lord, thank you for this food and the hands that prepared it. Let it put strength into our bones to get us through this day. And the days ahead. All of them. Here. Forgive us our sins. Amen. Dig in."

As they passed platters and shooed flies Ruby asked him what the preacher said. "All I'll say," Silas said, lifting a slice of corn bread, "is I got to digest it a little. He rattled on about Hebrew Jews, and then said the park was going to take this land. Didn't make much sense."

Carl perked up. "You mean we're going to move?"

Silas looked at him, not for the first time, like he was a fool. "Never said that. They'll make an offer and then we'll see who's a better hand at dickering. If we don't move, we can stay, but only until we die." He raked potatoes onto his plate. "Come to think of it, that's about as long as I'd want to stay anyhow. Pass them fish."

"That don't sound right," said Harrogate. "Out west nobody lives in the parks except wardens and their help."

"Well," said Silas, "it ain't right any way you sound it out. But I aim to stay here until they carry me out. Ain't no damn—my apologies, Mrs. Bradley—dern government going to tell me where I can or can't live. Now somebody change the subject so I can eat dinner without getting the bellyache."

After a short silence and forks scraping plates, they spoke of the weather, and Mrs. Bradley told of her daughter, who was in boarding school. Spoiled little bitch, Silas thought, as he patted his mustache with his napkin and excused himself for a nap.

Lying on his back, staring at the ceiling, he tried to relax enough to sleep, but for a long time all he could think of was that revenue man, Moody, waving his badge with the manners of a polecat, a dozen years ago. They never found a trace of him, not even that stupid hunk of tin. After Rhetta died, Silas had asked Harrogate whether Moody had a case and Harrogate had grinned and said he had no idea where the agent got that information.

Levi Marion picked at his dinner, excused himself, and headed for the porch. He sat down in a straight chair, unlaced his Sunday shoes, took off his socks, and stretched his feet in the warmth of the sun. But he was disturbed by his guinea hens hollering. He turned to see Preacher Smith's A-model chugging up the road. Levi Marion told Rass and his big brother Hugh to mind the dogs, sighed, and put on his socks. The preacher got out and greeted them. "Folks, you didn't look too well this morning. I just wanted to see how you're doing."

Levi Marion got a chair for the preacher, who allowed he'd rather stand in the yard. The screen door opened and Valerie and the rest came out. Levi Marion gave Valerie the chair, and two adults and seven children sat looking at the preacher like they did the battery-powered radio at Aunt Mary's on Saturday nights.

Smith smiled nervously. "Folks, I know you need to hear some good news this afternoon, but about all I have is that Jesus loves you."

Levi Marion sniffed and stared at the preacher. "Reverend Smith, nobody here doubts that a bit, but we're still hurting. That this morning hit me like a locomotive. I knowed it could happen someday but I never in a million years thought I'd hear about it in church."

"What will we do, Papa?" said Hugh.

"I don't know, son. Preacher, you got to help us think through this perdicament."

"I'll try my best. Lord knows, it's hard. Like a death in the family."

"It's worse'n that. When a body dies you mourn and bury them and then they get to be part of the ground you're working. You talk to them when you're plowing or hunting or picking beans. This is different."

"I'm sorry, Levi. I know this hurts."

"Preacher, my great-granddaddy came here in 1836. We've worked this land nearly four generations. We've bought it with our own gristle and we've listened to that creek till it's in our blood. I doubt I could sleep a wink without hearing that water."

"Levi, you can stay here," said the preacher. "Red Pendleton said the park commission would let you stay for the rest of your life."

"I knowed that man wasn't what he said he was. . . ."

Smith shifted his weight from his right foot to his left. "I personally think lots of folks will elect to stay their lifetimes."

"Then tell me this, Preacher. What good is it to stay your life out if you can't leave nothing to your young'uns?"

"Then you can use the money to buy property you can hand down to these boys and girls."

"Where in creation am I going to find a farm half this fine? Ain't nothing in most of Haywood but wore-out places, except that bottom-land on Jonathan's Creek, and the Leatherwoods that own it don't sell property. I don't know what we're going to do." He looked at the ceiling. "Preacher, do us a favor," said Levi Marion.

"Anything you say."

"Could you pray over this family?"

"Of course." They held each other's hands in a circle spilling into the yard, bowing their heads. Little Ned grabbed his mother's leg and wouldn't let go.

"Lord Almighty, smile on these people, workers in your kingdom, and take them under your wing. Bless all neighbors wrestling with the same demons this Lord's Day. Guide and direct us, now and forever more. In your Son's name. Amen."

"Amen," they chorused.

As he put his car into low gear, Smith nodded at the Carters, who waved in a row like ragged sheets hung on the porch to dry.

After a nap Silas got his old Colt's Army revolver, a .44 converted to cartridges, from the closet where it hung in a buckeye-colored holster. At shooting matches he would come close to shooting as well with it as younger men with rifles. He didn't like handling a weapon on Sunday but figured his would not be the only pistol at the meeting. Then, too, a man never knew when he might see a snake.

He rode into sunshine at the edge of Uncle Andy's place and stopped. There the valley opened into a rich field looking toward Aunt Mary's. Six or seven shocks of hay surrounded by rail fences waited for cattle. Jessie Ridge and Noland Mountain rose like a cradle hood at the end of the valley. He sat his horse and gazed at the mountains surrounding him.

Silas always said government was of no particular use except to keep the peace, and wasn't hardly any good at that. The world war Wilson said would straighten Europe out had done no permanent good. He followed a crow from halfway up Jessie Ridge over the ridgetop. That old boy, he thought, doesn't have any more idea than a rock that the government wants to own him. All he's got to do, though, is be a crow and he'll be all right. Maybe all a man has to do is be a man.

In the school yard several men stood in the shade, their mounts hitched next to the branch running into Indian Creek. Cigarette smoke hung like a wraith. Silas patted Maude and tied her.

"Hey, Uncle Silas." Arvil Wright's reedy voice floated toward him. Silas had had no particular use for Arvil from the time he was an unruly boy. "Howdy, fellows. Arvil, that you?"

"Sure is, Uncle Silas. I thought you might be going to let Maude run this meeting."

"That horse's got more sense than all of us put together."

Silas stared at a line of folks riding their way. As he turned, his coat swung open to reveal the Colt's.

"Damn, Uncle Silas, who you going to shoot?" Arvil shifted so his pistol wouldn't show.

"I mean to keep order this evening, and this here is friendly persuasion. How about you? I seen yours this morning. Wilbur's likely got his."

Arvil shrugged. "A man needs to defend hisself."

"From what?"

Arvil scratched the side of his jaw. "Old Ezra Banks is on the warpath. He's just finished that damn barn over yonder and he don't want the park to get it. Talking about shooting federals and us, too, if we're on their side."

"That's drink talking. Besides, he ain't been in a church since he sold that high ground to that Canadian. If I was you I'd put them pistols in your saddlebag. And we need to move down to the church. There's already too many folks for this little schoolhouse even if we take the desks out."

They stowed weapons and by four-thirty everyone had been herded to the church. Folks parked wagons close to the outside wall for bleachers. Silas entered the building, where a steady murmur drowned the noise of the creek. He strode to the front.

"Folks, I want this meeting to last as long as need be but no more. We got to milk and feed." He looked at Lige. "Could somebody open us with a prayer?"

Lige stood, hat in hands, and cleared his throat. "Lord, thank you for another day in this valley. Give us strength to face this hour. In the name of Jesus. Amen."

Silas fiddled with a coat button. "Folks, you heard the preacher this morning. You know the park is about to come. They say they will give us a fair price. They say we can stay after we sell. Looks to me like we ain't got but one choice: sell and leave or sell and stay. Or they will condemn it and take it anyhow. Anybody got anything to say?"

"I got another choice." From the back, Rafe McPeters's rheumy voice. A tall, broad-shouldered man, he was normally quiet, like a mean

dog or a copperhead snake. "I ain't going nowhere, I ain't selling nothing, and if anybody tries to take it they'll die like a stinking skunk."

This brought cheers from some but the sudden report of a pistol made
folks duck and jump. Horses whinnied and a child was launched from a
wagon seat where he'd stood a second before. Silas rushed to the door,
where men grabbed animals, women soothed babies, and children in the
yard trees checked themselves for bullet holes.

Ezra Banks had gotten Zeb to drive him to the meeting in their old
Ford. Pulling into the churchyard late, Zeb had jerked the car to a stop
while his father stumbled from it. He'd dropped his owlhead, which had
gone off and come within a hair of wounding him through the lip. Silas
saw him fumbling with the weapon, finally getting it in his jacket pocket.

Silas holstered his pistol and returned. "It was an accident, folks. Old
men ought not carry loaded pistols. Rafe, do you mean to shoot these
park people?"

McPeters's sixty-five acres up Carter Fork were largely straight up
and down. He had thirteen children and was on his third wife, a girl in
her midtwenties no one had ever called pretty or even plain. His first
two wives had died in childbirth, worn to death, folks said, and she
looked to no better fate. One of his sons, Willie, stood beside him.

"Silas, they's revenue men come here and never come back out. These
park men ain't no different. I'm for shooting ever slap-dab one of them."

Zeb and Ezra entered the back of the church, Zeb trying to lead his
ornery father by his arm. Silas had not seen Ezra in a coon's age. He remembered the morning Ezra had come to their house back in 1880. Back
then Ezra was ramrod straight, dressed all in black, not a hair out of
place. Now he was bent, unshaven, wearing dirty trousers ripped at the
knee.

Ezra focused on Rafe McPeters. "I'll help you, brother. You and me,
we'll kill ever damn one of them whore-hopping bastards."

Zeb tugged his father's coat sleeve. "Papa, sit down. You're in a
church."

"Leave me alone, damn it. I got you to carry me over here, not give
me a damn Sunday school lesson."

Lige rose. "Rafe, you ever kill a man?"

"I've killed foxes stealing hens and I've killed bear trying to raid my smokehouse. This ain't no different."

"Talking ain't the same as doing."

Ezra laughed at the ceiling. "I killed a Bluecoat in sixty-four, up toward the gap at Old Starlin'. I've shot game that give me more pain of conscience." Seeing Ezra's owlhead protrude from his coat pocket, women tugged their husbands' sleeves, whispering to be taken home.

Ezra took a deep breath. "These park services work for that same damnyankee government that come sixty-some year ago to take our ground." Again Zeb tugged on Ezra's coat sleeve but Ezra yanked his hand toward heaven. "My boy here says there ain't no Yankees no more. That's horseshit. Yankee lumber companies buy up our timber for nothing, then pay us a dollar a day to help them haul it out, then tell us how rich we are. They set in our boardinghouses eating our food, and kill our deer and catch our fish. Now they want our land outright. They might as well wear blue and tote Henry repeaters. Let's kill them all."

Silas put up his arms against the commotion. "All right, Banks, we know where you stand. I'd like to see if anybody in our side of the valley got other ideas." Silas saw pursed lips and worried brows. Men normally unafraid to wrestle a boar rooting up their potatoes seemed dog-hobbled.

Lige stood. "Boys," he said, "we're all in this together. Now, it's one thing to say you're going to shoot a man, or two, or a dozen. But if the whole United States of America wants this land, we can't stop them. As for that war he was talking about, meaning no disrespect, I was a short-pants lad in Cataloochee then. Those were hard times, no men around except broke-down old coots. Banks yonder come in a lot later. From outside."

Silas started toward Ezra as an older couple stood to leave. Ezra began to rush Lige but Zeb grabbed his shoulder and slammed himself and his father into the pew where the couple had been. Mothers gathering their broods to go home glanced over their shoulders at the front of the school. Silas pulled his pistol and half cocked it as Ezra tried to get up. "Banks, stay right there. You've said your piece. Lige, you done?"

Lige grabbed his galluses. "Only choice is to stay or go. I'm going, myself. I couldn't bear to see what happens around here when the government gets hold of it." Lige fixed his eyes on McPeters. "Rafe, you got a passel of young'uns, all the way from that growed one by you to little tykes. If they take you off to the hoosegow, them chaps get nothing. Kill the park men if you like, but you'd be better off to shoot your own self. Then your boys can get money from selling your land." Rafe and Willie stared stonily at Lige.

After more scraping of boots and clearing of throats, Jim Hawkins, home from college in Cullowhee, stood. "I agree with Mr. Howell. I see the papers every day. The whole nation will be looking at us. We would be the laughingstock of the country. And if it got serious, they'd send the army."

Ezra wrenched himself from Zeb's grip and fumbled for his pistol. "Boy, you ain't old enough for your piss to stink. You keep out of a man's business."

"Papa, you can't talk that way in here. Besides, if the government wants it, they'll get it." Zeb looked at his father's pistol. "Hand it here, Papa. You're going to hurt somebody."

"Only one I orta hurt is you, you turncoat Jezebel. If I'd have known that day I killed that sow bear you'd turn against your father like you've done, why, by God—"

Zeb reached for his father's pistol but Ezra lunged toward the center of the pew. Silas caught his wrist. "Okay, Banks, give me the damn gun before you and me have a falling-out." Silas caught the pistol and handed it to Zeb. "Get out of here, Banks. I mean it."

"You bastard, I'll be outside. Anybody wants to talk sense, come on out."

Ezra got as far as the door frame before he had to rest. He skulked out the door as Zeb broke the owlhead and dumped the cartridges in his lap, apologizing. Silas uncocked and holstered his weapon, searching the room. "Anybody else?"

Harrogate stood but quickly sat as his eyes filled. Silas looked everyone over. "Here's a parting thought, folks. We all got to figure out what we're going to do. Me, I'm staying put. And unless anybody's got anything else to say, I'm going home."

On his way home he thought that things had gone well. No one had gotten shot, and no one had made much of an ass out of himself except Ezra Banks. He'd look forward to staying in Cataloochee, if for no other reason to see what would happen.

30

PERFECT ALIGNMENT

Ezra's old car only had one working headlight, which pointed, instead of straight and out, crooked and more than slightly up. Zeb had to drive slowly, startling red-eyed owls and possums. They turned into Ezra's lane two hours past midnight, and when Zeb slowed the car it backfired and woke Ezra.

"Shit fire, boy, you finally decide to start shooting Yankees?"

"It's the car, Papa. Get out and go to bed."

"Where's my damn bottle?"

"You threw it out empty back at the Bennett turnaround, remember?"

Ezra harrumphed, fumbled for his keys, and stumbled to the front door. Zeb put the car in the barn and walked home. The last time he had been out this late was on possum hunts years ago. Inside he fell immediately asleep beside Mattie.

Zeb woke to the smell of perking coffee. He stretched and went in the kitchen and kissed the back of Mattie's neck. "I'll get bedsores sleeping this late. What time is it anyhow?"

She smiled and returned his hug. "It's seven-thirty, honey. What time did you get home? I didn't hear a thing."

"I think it was about two. Got any bacon?"

"Sure. Since the young'uns are gone to my sister's, let's have a good breakfast and take it easy the rest of the morning for a change. How about it?"

"Well, I've got to fix that back fence, but taking it easy sounds mighty tempting."

"Bacon sure beats side meat. And I can tempt with the best of them."

They put the latchstring inside and went back to bed. They had to reperk the coffee before breakfast but Zeb allowed that was all right. "Not bad for a couple of old folks," he said, as Mattie cooked. They puttered around the rest of the morning, and got a late start on mending the fence.

Zeb had meant to fix a section that had gotten down to two strands of sagging barbwire, but Ezra's barn had taken up most of the late summer and early fall. About four they stood in the backyard with a roll of barbwire, a beat-up coffee can containing rusty steeples, a wire stretcher, and a claw hammer. Zeb, wearing a straw hat Mattie had mail-ordered for him, pulled the wire taut as Mattie set the steeple. Zeb was about to hammer it in when he heard a commotion in the front yard. He stopped, looked at Mattie, and quickly set the steeple.

The racket sounded like a small army but was only a single mule and rider. The animal twisted and reared. "Goddamn you," shouted Ezra, holding on for dear life, "it's an outrage, come out and take your medicine, you ungrateful bastard."

"He must have found another bottle," Zeb said. He rounded the corner of the house to see his father on Old Huldy, sawing her reins and waving his owlhead. Seeing Zeb, Ezra dismounted, steadied himself, and quickly fired at his son, knocking his hat off. Zeb hit the ground and felt the top of his head, relieved to find it still there and unbloody. He ran to the backyard yelling for Mattie to get in the house.

Zeb had been cursed and beaten by his father but never shot at, and he knew if Ezra got another shot he was dead. As Ezra rushed him with menace in his eyes Zeb leaped, swinging the claw hammer at his father's head. A blow just over the ear knocked off Ezra's ratty felt hat.

The men fought without finesse. As Ezra reeled and Zeb grabbed his father's pistol hand, the gun went off. Ezra sagged to his knees, dropping the weapon and clutching his mouth. Zeb stomped the pistol into the dirt.

Ezra shook his head like a wet dog, blood and spit flying everywhere. He screamed unintelligibly at Zeb, who scuttled to get behind his father. Ezra tried to pummel Zeb with his fist. As the men struggled, Zeb got his hammer hand free and lifted it to hit Ezra in the head again. A sudden shot brought Ezra to the ground.

Zeb looked first at his father, then toward the report. Mattie stood spraddle-legged on the porch, chambering another round. "Get back," she yelled, and Zeb rolled away from his father. She steadied the weapon, pulled back the hammer, and shot again.

"Mattie, for God's sake, stop!" Zeb scrabbled to his feet and knelt beside Ezra, who tried to talk over the rasp of a chest wound. Ezra smelled of whiskey and had pissed his pants. "What is it, Papa?"

"You . . . shit-fired . . . sorry . . ." Ezra groaned.

"Papa, don't talk."

"No son of mine . . ." Ezra wheezed. "No son . . ." He stopped moving his mouth except to take in a shallow draft of air.

Zeb looked at Mattie, then at his father. "Dear Jesus," he muttered under his breath and stood. He walked to the porch, where Mattie handed him the rifle and two cartridges. He loaded and cocked the weapon. "*I* shot him, honey. Remember that." Moving to a different angle, he aimed the weapon and fired, shaking Ezra's body. He trembled so much his next shot missed his father by a foot. "God help us all," he cried, taking a handkerchief from his pocket and wiping the gun. He gave Mattie the handkerchief. "Get shed of this somehow. It smells like cordite." Then he flung the gun into the well like a spear.

Mattie put her arm around her husband, who hugged her. "This day started so good," she said. "Let's just bury him and be done with it."

"No, if folks heard all this commotion, they'll come." He erased the last shot's track in the dirt with his boot. "Throw them shells in the well, then get in the house. Remember, you didn't see none of this."

"Lord, Zeb, do you think I care if anybody thinks I killed him? You know he needed killing. Has for years."

"That ain't the point, honey. If anybody goes to jail over this it'll be me. *I* killed him. That's what happened. I did it myself."

"Zeb, once you start lying it don't stop."

Zeb took her by the shoulders and touched his forehead to hers. He looked at Ezra. "Ain't nobody lying. He was still breathing when I shot him. Now do what I say. Get in that house and stay there. I love you too much for you to get mixed up in this."

Mattie kissed him, threw the shells in the well, and went inside. Zeb chewed the side of his thumb and rearranged the yard. After ten minutes he began to hope no one had heard the shots, but he soon heard a mule clop down the road and turn into his place. He came into the front yard fumbling with a cuff button and saw his uncle, who had dismounted from Lilly. "Jake, I just killed Papa."

"Damn, son, you didn't."

"He come over here and tried to shoot me. I don't rightly know what happened but he's laying dead out back towards the well."

Jake grabbed his nephew's hands, where dried blood clustered in half-moons around the nails on his left hand. "You really mean it. You really killed him? Stay here, Zeb." Jake walked slowly to the back, where Ezra lay on the ground, hawksbill nose plowing dirt, blood seeping into his dark hair from a cut above his right ear, left arm folded underneath his body. Jake knelt. "Well, old man, now you can rest," he said, "but not us, not yet, anyhow. This is bad business." Jake came back to the front yard. "Son, don't move nothing till the sheriff gets here. I reckon you ain't got down to Ola to get word to the law. We got to do that."

"But what if they think I killed him? Can't we just bury him and be done with it?"

Jake turned so he could look Zeb in the eye. "If he'd died in his bed we could. Now we can't. Anyhow, I thought you told me you *did* kill him."

"I did. Or I reckon I did. I mean, on purpose, they might think I did it on purpose, Jake, and I couldn't stand to be in jail."

Jake walked Zeb to the front porch. "Sit down and tell me what happened, slow, like you'll do it for the sheriff."

Zeb's trousers said he had been on his knees and his collar was ripped in back. Zeb laid his elbows on his knees and wrung his hands. "Me and Mattie was out back fixing fence. I had the hammer and she had the can of steeples and we was about to stretch the wire when we heard Papa's mule. Papa was yelling to high heaven for me to come out so he could kill me. I come to the front and I seen him get off that mule with that pistol cocked."

"What did you do?"

"Didn't have time to do nothing. He turned and shot, just like that. Knocked the hat right off my head. I run back to tell Mattie to get in the house but she had skedaddled. Papa followed me back there. When I saw he was fixing to shoot I remembered I still had that hammer. I run and hit him on the head and we wrestled for that pistol. It went off, more'n once, next thing I knowed he was laying there dead."

"You sure about all this?"

"Jake, would I kill my own papa if I didn't have to?"

"I reckon not. You'd done it a long time ago if you'd been a mind to murder. Now we got to get word to the law and I better tell Hannah, too. Stay out of that backyard, you hear? Mattie, too." Jake intercepted Ezra's young neighbor on the south side, Lon Davis, who had rushed up the lane as fast as his father's old mule would carry him. "Lon, do us a favor."

"Sure thing, Jake."

"Find your daddy and tell him Sheriff Leatherwood needs to get here quick. Ezra Banks is dead. You got that?"

Lon's eyebrows arched like springs. "Old Man Banks? Dead? How dead?"

"Shot, dead as hell, damn it all. Now go tell your daddy." As Lon rode off, Jake grabbed Lilly's reins but thought better of putting another set of mule prints in the yard. He looked around and saw Zeb's hat by the back fence. There were already so many footprints it looked like they'd had a barn dance around the body. Jake walked to the front porch where Mattie sat beside Zeb, arm around his drooping shoulders.

"Jake, you got to help us."

"Mattie, I can't help till I know what happened."

"What happened is what he said. Ezra came on that mule and yelled at the house till Zeb came from out back. The old man shot at my Zeb and liked to have killed him. I run in the house, heard the gun blasting. When I came back out, the old man didn't get back up. I'd swear it on my mother's Bible."

"How many times did the gun go off, Mattie?"

"Once when he shot Zeb's hat off. Oh, I don't know. . . . there might have been three, four shots. Scared me so bad I put my hands over my ears and couldn't look. I just knowed Zeb'd got killed but when I opened my eyes Zeb was getting up and Ezra was laying on the ground."

"You know this is a heap of trouble. I hope you're telling it straight, 'cause that means Zeb killed him in self-defense."

"Course he did," said Mattie. "That's what I seen, and I ain't afraid to tell nobody that. You got to make sure Leatherwood hears that."

"I will," said Jake. "Right now I need a drink of water. Then I'm going to Hannah's. And I got to get people to watch both places till the law gets here."

Jake went back to the kitchen for a drink from the cedar bucket by the back door. As he drank he saw Zeb's Remington was not in the wooden rack over the door. Jake shuddered like someone had just walked on his grave.

On the porch Jake asked Zeb about his rifle. "You think he killed him with it, don't you, Jake?" Mattie shot back.

"I'm just asking what the law might ask if they knew there used to be a gun over the back door."

Zeb looked up. "Somebody pilfered it. About two weeks ago."

"Oh. News usually travels faster'n that around here."

"I just hadn't told nobody," said Zeb.

"Jake," said Mattie.

"Yes."

She pursed her lips. "You know the world's better off with him dead."

"You're likely right. I just don't want nobody going to the penitentiary over it."

"We ain't going nowhere," said Mattie.

At Hannah's front porch Jake took a deep breath, then decided to check things out back to delay facing his sister with the news. Nothing seemed amiss at the barn but at the house the back door had been opened with enough violence to jam it against the porch soffit, broken glass littering the floor. He wrestled the door shut and nudged the shards to the wall with his foot.

In the kitchen sat a round oak table with a crocheted doily in the middle. A cobalt salt and pepper set stood beside a green glass bowl holding four apples. Sitting in a press-back chair, Hannah dealt a game of solitaire. She was not wearing her wire-rimmed eyeglasses. He took off his hat and waited for her to acknowledge him.

She laid the game out like so much depended on perfect alignment. Her hands neither shook nor fumbled. He couldn't think how old she was, did the arithmetic in his head, decided she was sixty-two, five years older than he.

Without looking up she said, "He's dead, ain't he?" The question darted and hovered like a dragonfly.

"Yes, Sis, he is."

"I heard the shots." She absently picked from the hand the top card, blue-backed with a cherub riding a bicycle in both directions, examined it, and put it back. "Which one killed him?"

"What do you mean, Sis?"

"You know good and well what I mean." She stood and faced him. "Somebody was going to do it sooner or later. God knows I dern near did it myself one night. I snuck that pistol of his and was standing next to him with it cocked, when, I don't know, I just couldn't." Her right hand fingered a silver brooch, a present from Ezra after the time he set fire to one of her quilts. "I bet it was Mattie. Zeb's not got enough sand."

"Why'd he go over there?"

"He was drinking, getting broody. Saturday George came to see him, and you know George can't stand Zeb, and them brothers, you know, it's a shame before God. George and Ezra had some liquor and after that Ezra got madder'n fire at Zeb. He set in that so-called office the best part of Sunday stewing, until Zeb showed up to take him to that meeting they had about that park. They was arguing last night when they got back but I didn't hear nothing clear.

"This afternoon I heard him yell, 'By God, I'll kill him for this,' and he went out the back door, and I think he might have broke it. Not three minutes later I heard shots. The first was from the owlhead and I didn't know. Then another from the owlhead and I still didn't know. Then them four others wasn't from the pistol so I figured they'd laid into him. I come to his office. The desk drawer was open and his pistol was gone, real estate papers laying on top of the desk. I got the cards out beside where the pistol stayed and laid out this game." She smiled at her brother. "You remember me and you used to play cards all the time when we were little? He wouldn't let me play. Said a woman oughtn't do foolish things like that. Now I can play it when I want to."

Jake pulled out the other chair and sat it backward. "Hannah, the sheriff will ask you about all that. Not the cards. The other. I'm going to get some men to stay the night, to make sure you are all right and nobody disturbs anything until Leatherwood comes."

"I don't need nobody," she said. "You never told me who killed him."

"Hannah, if I knew I'd tell you. What I do know is I heard shots from two different guns and Zeb's rifle ain't over the back door."

"Was Mattie there?"

"Said she was in the house when it happened."

Hannah sniggered. "That sheriff better check for bullet holes in the winder lights. I bet a Sunday hat she shot him."

"That's for the law to find out. Look, Sis, I'm sure Rachel would be happy to come stay with you."

"I'll be fine, Jake. You know, there was a time I'd have been sad about this, early on. But now, just knowing I'll never get a cussing again from that man, or get hit, for that matter, makes me feel like I was all wrapped in a feather tick."

"Well, then, I'll get back over there. If you need anything, let Rachel or me know." As Jake stood and put his hat back on, she turned three cards faceup. On top was the jack of diamonds. It would play on the queen of spades next to it. She looked at her brother.

"Is that all?"

"I'm sorry about Ezra."

"Thank you," she said, and played the jack on the queen. That brought up the ten of clubs. "And you ain't a bit sorry except we got to get the law mixed up in it."

31

Dead Man on My Hands

Lon Davis tied his father's mule to a tree and ran barefoot to the post office with the news about Ezra. Velda Parham, Ernest's daughter, drove the dozen twisty miles to Miller's store at Cove Creek, the closest telephone to Cataloochee. Too late to get Sheriff Sam Leatherwood at his office in Waynesville, she found him at home. After asking a few questions he hung up the phone, then called his deputy Rafe Shuford. "They say old Ezra Banks is shot dead over yonder. Round up Ned Bradley and go over the mountain in the morning. Maybe by then they'll have tidied things up. Folks over there won't help you find a liquor still, but maybe they'll solve an old-fashioned murder for us."

Tuesday morning Shuford and his brother-in-law Ned found Jake had built a small fire in the yard and camped on Zeb's back porch. He said nothing was disturbed. The lawmen took statements from Zeb and Jake, and told Zeb he'd have to come to town with them. Rafe talked to Hannah while Ned picked up evidence—hats, Zeb's hammer, Ezra's pistol—which they loaded into their truck.

Zeb rode between them to Waynesville, occasionally turning to look at Ezra's corpse, wrapped in two quilts tied with twine but bouncing and rolling in the back of the truck like some cast-off burden. They left the body with Ted Maney at the furniture store for the coroner to examine and the Maneys to prepare for burial. Zeb they deposited in the county jail on Montgomery Street.

After he got the coroner's report late that afternoon, Leatherwood sat at his desk, reading, fidgeting. Rubbing the wart on the left side of his flat nose, he threw the paper on his desk, then read Zeb's handwritten statement for the tenth time. He got his key ring and clomped back to the cells.

"Banks, you there?" he yelled into the narrow hall, which divided four cells, two right, two left. If Zeb replied Sam didn't hear. Leatherwood fumbled for the key to the second cell on the left. Zeb, in a clean chambray shirt, looked at him, catlike, from the pull-down cot. "Banks, have you told me everything?"

"Yes, sir."

"Let me get this straight." He opened the cell door and sat on the other end of the cot. "Your seventy-eight-year-old daddy rode over to your place and started yelling he was going to kill you?"

Zeb nodded, gnawing the side of his raw thumb.

"And you and your wife were in the back fixing fence?"

Zeb nodded again.

"And when you came around front to see about all the commotion, your daddy up and shot your hat clean off. Then you ran to the backyard and he come after you. You knocked him in the head with a hammer. You all struggled. Gun went off a few times. He might have shot himself. Is that it?" Leatherwood looked at him sideways.

"Yes, sir. I've been trying, but I can't think of nothing else. It all happened too quick."

Leatherwood shifted on the cot. "I got a dead man on my hands whose son says he may have killed him but don't know. I got a thirty-eight owlhead with two spent cartridges and a barrel full of yard dirt. You say he shot at you once, when your hat got knocked off. That's one." He held up his right index finger. "Then the gun went off you don't know how many times and your daddy ended up dead."

He stood and hitched his belt. "Now then. Your daddy's got four bullet holes in him." He held up four fingers on his left hand. "If I'm counting right, we got one shot fired at you and we got four bullets in your daddy. That's five you'd like me to think were from a five-shot revolver that's not got but two expended shells and a bunch of yard dirt in it. Means we got three unaccounted-for bullets and no cartridges they used to be in. And you said you didn't have a gun."

Zeb's eyes darted. "I don't own a pistol. I did keep a rifle and a shotgun."

"Did."

"Did?"

"Yes, dammit, *did*. You said you *did* keep a rifle and a shotgun."

"I still got the shotgun."

"What went with the rifle?"

"We keep it over the back door. I noticed a couple of weeks ago it was gone. I looked all over. Reckon somebody stole it."

"What kind was it?"

"Thirty-two Remington model four. Papa sold it to me years ago."

"So I got a dead man with four bullet holes in him, of maybe thirty-two caliber, and you had a thirty-two Remington up and leave and you don't know where it's at?"

"That's right." Zeb wrung his hands. "That ain't good, is it?"

"Son, that's liable to send your scrawny ass to the electric chair. I think you knocked him out with that hammer and then shot him in cold blood with that rifle." He rocked on his heels. "If we was to find that rifle, and it hadn't been fired lately, that would be in your favor. If we can't find it, that coroner's jury's going to ask where it's at, and then I got to say I don't know. By the way, can you back up that you was hunting for it?"

Zeb shrugged.

"I didn't think so."

Zeb shivered. "Sir, I don't know where the rifle went and I can't re-member what happened except what I told you."

"Son, let me give you some advice. Write me another statement. All I want is the truth." He went out and locked the cell. "I'll leave you paper and a pencil, so if suddenly you remember you loaned your nephew or somebody that rifle to shoot tin cans with, you can write it down."

Zeb stood. "I've told you the truth."

Sam shook his head. "You're not holding anything back?"

"You keep the light on all night? It's giving me the headache."

"You all don't have electricity over there, do you? Don't fret about that lightbulb. Just worry about that statement." After Leatherwood left the steady tick of the sheriff's wall clock put Zeb to sleep.

Wednesday morning Sam looked in on Zeb, who sat beside a blank tablet. In the office Sam poured a cup of coffee, shook a Pall Mall out and tamped it against his thumbnail, then reread the coroner's report.

The night before, Sam had told his wife about the Banks business. She said he ought to give Zeb the benefit of the doubt. "When I was lit-tle, Mama used to say she'd give me to old Ezra if I didn't straighten up and fly right. You know, Sam, there was a time he didn't drink. They say he was a hard man back then, but wasn't mean. I don't remember that. All I ever heard was to stay away from him, especially fall of the year."

Sam looked at her. "So you don't think I need to worry I got a dead man under what you might call strange circumstances?"

"They say Ezra's been asking for a killing for years."

"I got to tell that coroner's jury something tomorrow. You want me to say the old man shot hisself once up close, and three times from a dis-tance, and it was a sewercide?"

"Happens in Mississippi all the time," she said, turning to her knitting.

He read the report a third time, lit another Pall Mall, drained his coffee, and looked out the window. He wasn't honor-bound to tell the coroner's jury about the missing rifle, because it wasn't in Zeb's written statement nor did Jake Carter mention it. But the jury had the coroner's report and Doc Bennett would also testify. He threw his cigarette out the window. Somehow he would have to explain how a man could be shot four times by one weapon fired twice, and that might make him look pretty stupid. He needed to find that Remington.

In only half an hour the six jurors voted to bring murder charges against Zeb. Solicitor Osborne ordered Zeb to be arraigned at two for a Monday trial. When he got back, Leatherwood went straight to Zeb's cell.

"Son, I got to get you to court so they can arraign you."

"What's that?"

"They're going to charge you with first-degree murder."

Zeb softly pressed his head against the bars.

"I'm going to go over your place like stink on shit until I find that rifle. You might as well tell me where you hid it."

"I'd tell you if I knew where it was at." Zeb let go of the bars and slowly sat on the corner of the cot.

Sam opened the cell and sat on the other end. "You know, Banks, I remember my daddy telling about your daddy back when my daddy was sheriff. Said he had that old owlhead pistol back then. Said he was thinking about killing some Canadian over some gold or something. You remember anything about that?"

"A little. He never did, though. That man still comes up there ever now and then. I kinder like him."

"Banks, level with me. Why would your daddy want to kill you?"

"We didn't get along much good. He was drinking, and he was a mean drunk. I reckon he got some notion in his head."

"You all argued lately?"

"Well, a month ago I was helping him build a barn. Told him I needed to get home and make my apple crop. Got him madder'n hell. But after I made my crop I helped with his and we even got that barn finished. I thought he'd got over that."

"He threaten you then?"

"Not that I remember. Least nothing like wanting to kill me. But then there was last Sunday evening."

"What happened then?"

"They had that meeting about the park. I didn't want to go, but nothing would do but I drive him over there. He couldn't drive, you know."

"I heard about that meeting. What did your daddy think about the park?"

"Lord, he was dead against it. By the time I got him over there he was mouthy, talking about killing federals."

"How about you? Are you for the park?"

"Well, I don't think it'd hurt none. Me and him didn't agree on that no better'n on anything else."

"Did he threaten to kill you that night?"

"Not as I remember. But he threatened me with about ever thing else."

"What about your wife?"

"What about her?"

"Did she get along with him?"

"She put up with him, like ever body on Little Catalooch."

"Would she have wanted to kill him?"

Zeb put his thumb to his mouth and gnawed on it.

"What's the matter, son?"

"Leave Mattie out of this. She didn't have nothing to do with it."

"Is that right?"

"I told you she wasn't near us, and anyhow I said I killed him."

"What you told is you don't know how he got killed. And I don't either. But before Monday I aim to find out." Sam headed back to his office for his hat and jacket.

"What now, Sheriff?" Rafe sat reading the newspaper at the desk in the corner.

"Get your coat. We ain't coming back till we find out who killed old Banks and what with." He threw one of their battery flashlights in a canvas bag along with rope, a grappling hook, a field shovel, and a magnetized bar. "Get a coal oil lantern or two, Rafe. I don't trust these new-fangled lights. It'll be dusty dark time we get there and I damn sure don't want to run out of light."

Mattie was washing dishes when she heard the sheriff's car. She dried her hands, took off her apron, and sat in the rocker by the chimney.

The sheriff knocked on the doorsill. "It ain't latched," Mattie said. Leatherwood took off his hat and entered the dimly lit room.

"Evening, Miz Banks. I wonder if I could talk to you a minute." She nodded but did not offer him a chair. He looked around the room, his gaze settling on a pine knot on the mantel, with five huge cones around it like a radial aircraft engine. "I wanted to see if you might make a formal statement about Mr. Banks's death."

She smiled. "I told you all I know about it. I want my Zeb back something awful."

"Miz Banks, this morning the coroner's jury said to try your husband for first-degree murder." Her smile disappeared, and she stood and looked out the window.

"I told you. I was in here. I didn't see nothing. I heard yelling and fighting and next thing was some shots. That's all."

"Do you remember any exact words from all that?"

"Something about an outrage—that was it, he was going to kill Zeb over this outrage."

"You have any idea what that was?"

"It likely had something to do with the property. Zeb and his brothers was always yammering and fighting about it. Zeb never talked much about it."

"You mind if me and Rafe look around?"

"There's likely the same nothing to find today as you found last time."

About midnight Sam and Rafe cranked the Ford for the trip back. They had gone over the house inside and out, examined the barn and other outbuildings from smokehouse to outhouse to corncrib to apple house. Sam thought he had found the Remington in the well when the magnet clanked but all he pulled up was a rusty grappling hook. He found an unopened box of .32 ammunition in the chest in the back bedroom.

"Damn it all, Rafe, I know we missed something." In the glove box he found a batwing flask of clear whiskey, turned it up, then offered it to his deputy.

"You can have it all, Boss. I got to get us the hell out of here in one piece." Sam took another pull and silently went over all their tracks, but could think of nothing they'd left out. They had found no rifle, no spent shells, no nicks in the outbuildings, no fresh-dug dirt. Even probing the outhouse hole had revealed nothing.

Sam dozed fitfully after they finally came to a macadam road, and Rafe poked him in the shoulder when he pulled in front of the jail. "It's three in the morning, Boss. Want me to take you home?"

Sam looked around as if he had never seen such a place. "No, hell no, I ain't going to wake the wife this time of morning. I'll sleep in here." Sam went in, sat in his chair, covered himself with his long coat, and fell into a dead sleep.

32

~~~~~~

A Lawyer with Ambitions

Oliver Babcock was a lawyer whose ambitions included the statehouse in Raleigh. Born in the tiny town of Moyock in Currituck County, he made his way to the university, graduated cum laude, and entered law school, where he excelled at playing bridge and hosting parties. He had done well in the classroom, too, and passed the bar examination on his first try. In Raleigh he had landed a job with the park commission, which sent him to Haywood County as part of the property settlement team. He was staying at Lige Howell's when word came that Zeb Banks finally got up the gumption to kill his old daddy.

Oliver dressed in a boiled white shirt and a black suit and fedora, with a silk monogrammed handkerchief in his left jacket pocket. This gave him trouble in Cataloochee. He might go to inspect a farm, and the owner would put a dirty hand on his shoulder and lead him straight into the hog pen. Discussing business with some old man in a slouch hat and overalls was difficult in slop up to his shoe tops. When he heard a native son had been accused of murder, he saw an opportunity to gain some respect.

At seven-fifteen Thursday morning, Sam Leatherwood woke to an insistent knock. He looked at the clock and muttered to the door. When he opened it Oliver stood expectantly in the morning light.

"May I introduce myself?" he asked, smile shiny as a counterfeit coin.

"If I knew who in hell you are I could issue a warrant for disturbing the peace. Do you know what damn time it is?"

Oliver produced a card that declared in raised black letters that the bearer was "Oliver W. Babcock, Esq., Atty at Law, of the NC Bar." This lawyer did not stand so much as bounce on his tiptoes.

Sam bent in a sweeping gesture. "Well, why didn't you say so to begin with?"

Oliver pranced into the office, holding his leather briefcase like a dancing partner. His muttonchops would have looked perfect atop Confederate dress grays. "You have a prisoner named Zebulon Banks, charged with murder. I would like an audience with him, if you please."

Sam had never heard such an accent. "I didn't catch all that, but you ain't taking him anywhere. You can talk to him, but I ain't letting him out."

"Fine, fine, just so we can talk, that's fine."

"This wouldn't be early if I'd got any sleep. Can't you come back later?"

"The law seeks the truth no matter the hour, sir."

Leatherwood had heard of ambulance chasers but never seen one before. The sheriff rubbed his red eyes. "I'll see if he wants to talk to you."

"Thank you. Please give him my card and tell him I can help him."

Sam walked down the narrow hall, stopping at Zeb's cell. "Fellow here wants to see you. Said to give you this." He poked the card through the bars.

"Might as well."

Sam went back to the office. "I'll leave this door open, so don't try nothing stupid."

"Thank you, Sheriff. As for stupidity, you have nothing to fear. Please remember I am an attorney." Oliver blithely walked down the hall and stood before Zeb's cell.

"Oliver W. Babcock, Mr. Banks." He put his hand through the bar. Zeb's expression was cautious and he did not meet Oliver's hand. "I've come because I am confident I can be of assistance in your case."

"Who told you about it?"

"Word travels fast, Mr. Banks. When I heard of the unfortunate accident that befell your father, I knew you would need legal assistance. We must make certain that truth emerges in the full light of day. Only then can your good name be cleared, restoring you to the bosom of your loving family, where you justly belong." He pulled his hand back and dusted his lapels.

Zeb had never heard such an accent. "Where you from?"

"Down east, sir. A smaller town than this, on the coast. Moyock."

What Zeb heard was "muck." "You don't have to run it down like that. What's it called?"

"I told you. Moyock."

"You making fun of me?"

"Assuredly not, Mr. Banks. Just answering your question. Moyock is the name of the town I hail from. It was a fine place in which to grow up, but, as they say, now I'm moving on."

"What brought you to Haywood?"

"I'm here on business for the State of North Carolina, in conjunction with the park commission. But sir, I am totally at your service this morning. May we talk?"

"Suit yourself. I ain't going nowhere."

Oliver walked back to the office. "Sheriff, would you be so kind as to let me in so we can confer about his case?"

Sam turned from the stove. "Keep your shirt on, son. He ain't going to bolt on us." Just then a piece of rich pine caught flame, and pungent black smoke boiled into the room. Sam closed the stove, walked to the cell, and opened the door.

Oliver swung in, right hand extended. Oliver's soft skin told Zeb the lawyer had done no hard work in years, yet there was appreciable grip to his handshake. Zeb sat on the cot and motioned Oliver to the other end.

Oliver took notes about Zeb's account of the altercation, and when he asked about Zeb's relationship with his father and brothers got a brief earful. He asked about questioning Mattie, which made Zeb clam up, so the attorney rattled about justice and circumstantial evidence and the heat of passion. Zeb nodded. The dandy, he thought, loved to hear himself talk, but with that brogue a jury might die laughing at him.

Finally Oliver, pacing the floor, came to the point. "Mr. Banks, I am prepared to offer legal counsel in this matter. I am convinced a jury of your peers would never convict you of murder. It is an open-and-shut case of self-defense." He drew himself up on tiptoes. "Would you like me to represent you?"

"How much would it cost?"

"Fees are never a consideration at a time like this, Mr. Banks."

"My daddy might've been mean, but he wasn't a fool. He taught me never jump into anything without knowing what it cost."

"Mr. Banks, let us put it this way: my fee, should we win your well-deserved freedom, will be exactly what you think it is worth. No more, no less."

They shook hands. "Together we will prevail. Now I am going to see the judge about bail."

When Sam opened the door, Oliver shook Zeb's hand, thanked the sheriff, and darted down the hall.

"Mr. Babcock," Sam shouted, emphasis on the second syllable. "You forgot something."

Oliver returned, brushed by Leatherwood, and stowed his papers in his briefcase. "Sorry, gentlemen, it was the heat of the moment. I shall see you in a little while."

Sam whistled. "That's one mouthpiece couldn't get his ass out of his britches without a wrote-out set of directions. I wouldn't hold my breath if I was you."

Judge Pinkney Sutton, a large, jowly man, prided himself on knowing exactly what was in the voluminous piles of paper on his huge desk. He believed in touching each document at least every three months, and Thursday morning he hoped to get close to the third layer of papers and maybe to discard a few that had become redundant or otherwise been taken care of by the simple passage of time. But almost immediately after he got his coffee there came a rap at his door. "Come in," Sutton yelled, and Oliver produced his card and immediately started talking in his outlandish accent. After a moment the judge stood and put up his hand. He seemed cut from the same wood as his desk. "Hold on, Mr. Badcock. Mr. Banks will stay there until trial. Then, if he's lucky, he can go home. If not, justice will be served."

"It's Babcock, Your Honor. And, sir, I must say, my client has no criminal history, nor does he show any sign of flight to avoid prosecution."

"Damn your hide, the taxpayers can feed his sorry ass until Monday. Now go back to wherever you came from."

Oliver opened his mouth again but, having noticed Judge Sutton's menacing brow and clenched fists, thought better of pressing Zeb's case. "Yes, Your Honor," he said, and left the office. In the hall his chest tightened. If everyone connected with the state were that unfriendly, he might, as his daddy used to say, be heading upcreek at low tide with a spoon for a paddle.

Zeb had not expected bail so was not disappointed in Oliver's news. "Take heart, Mr. Banks, it's only a temporary setback," Oliver said anyway. "Meanwhile, tell me names of folks who would testify to your good character—and, by the way, aren't related to you, at least not closely."

Zeb thought a minute, then offered Polly Rogers, his grandfather Will's third or fourth cousin, and Cassius Davis, who as far as he knew was no relation at all, but for years had been trusted enough to judge shooting matches.

Oliver then left the jail and walked up to Main Street at the courthouse, a redbrick Edwardian structure sporting a clock tower, all four faces of which said four-thirty. It had cost the county a small fortune when it was built in the 1880s but they had sunk not a nickel into it since. The state had condemned its two upper floors, and the county so far had refused to part with money to build a new one. The commissioners rented space from the bank across the street, and the state courts met in the bank's boardroom.

Oliver looked up and down the street, as if for a sign of how to proceed. He had little time in which to prepare Zeb's defense. In the next few days he needed to find the solicitor and get his disclosure, find his two witnesses and hope they would agree to come to court, and talk to Jake Carter, who could be a witness for prosecution or defense. And he needed a haircut.

A barber pole announced Baldwin's Barber Shop past Maney's Furniture on Main Street. Four chairs sat before seven wood-framed mirrors spaced so each barber's reflection registered at least twice. The farthest barber had no customer and was reading the newspaper in his chair. He was short with horn-rimmed glasses and devoid of hair except on the sides, which he combed to a point behind his head. "Bringing Up Father" and "Mutt & Jeff" seemed his only anchors in an otherwise skewed universe. Oliver hung his jacket and hat on the coatrack and walked up to his chair.

"Excuse me, sir, I wonder if I might get a trim and a shave." The barber kept reading. Oliver cleared his throat and asked again, which caused the other three men to stop snipping and shaving. The reading barber, George Fennel by the sign behind the chair, slowly looked up. When his eyes hit Oliver's, he stood smartly and dusted the chair with a striped chair cloth. The barber wrapped Oliver's neck and tied the apron. He lowered the back of the chair so Oliver was almost supine. "How you like your burnsides?"

"Straighten them, don't shorten them, if you please."

"You're the doctor." He stropped a razor, ran hot water into a mug, and whipped it full of lather. He wet Oliver's face with a hot towel.

"You ain't from around here." The barber spoke in a near whisper.

"No, sir. I'm here on business. I'm an attorney."

As George shaved him he spoke in a rasping whisper next to Oliver's left ear. "What you lawyering about, if it's any of my business?"

"I've been working in the park with some land matters."

"When you say park are you talking about Catalooch?"

"Yes, sir."

"You think you're going to get those rascals to move out just by waving money at them?"

"I think most, offered fair market value, will be happy with it."

"Likely they'll be happy to fill your ass full of lead shot." He toweled Oliver off, then raised the chair upright.

Oliver looked at him. "Sir, the ones I have dealt with have been the salt of the earth. Good Christian people."

"I know some of them good Christian people. One comes in here every year for a shave and a haircut. Silas Wright, you know him?"

"I've heard of him."

"Well, he's one of them good Christian salt-of-the-earth men. But I hear he's as muley-hawed a man as ever walked the earth. You start messing with his property, I wouldn't guarantee your safety at all." He started cutting Oliver's hair. "Lots of people over there like him. Be careful, or you could end up like that Banks fellow."

"What do you know about him?"

"The dead one or the one that killed him?"

"Allegedly, sir. Remember, one is innocent till proven guilty. I'll take information about either."

George parted Oliver's hair down the middle, raked the front parts toward his forehead, trimmed an inch, and put them back. "Well, I never met the dead one but I heard plenty about him. Folks was surprised he lived long as he did without somebody plugging him. His boy Zeb used to carry him to town to get bonded whiskey every fall back when you could get it easy. I cut the younger one's hair some. He's a quiet one."

"I'm defending him this week. You need to make me look good for a jury."

"Hear that, boys?" The other barbers stopped. "You think this lawyer looks good enough to defend that Banks boy?"

"I wondered what kind of critter you was," chuckled the near barber, Sam McCrory, a large red-haired man with freckled arms. "You might be bright enough, but you sure don't sound right, and folks put a right smart of stock in that."

Oliver reached from under the apron and scratched his left ear. "In my experience, it's evidence that wins or loses trials, gentlemen. And a jury likes to be taken for the collection of intelligent citizens it is."

"Hold your horses, George." McCrory strode a couple of feet toward Oliver. "That jury you think is so dad-gum intelligent is just Haywood County clodhoppers that don't want to be in that courtroom no more'n Banks does. But if they got to sit there, they want something worth listening at. They don't even mind getting lied to if it's a good story." He and his customer chuckled.

George zeroed in on Oliver again, finishing the sides and starting on the back. "Well," he whispered in Oliver's right ear, "I wish you luck. If you get enough people to say how sorry the old man was, there ain't a jury would convict your boy no matter how outlandish you sound. They fought a lot, them two. They were arguing at the church the night before the old man got *allegedly* shot." He cut silently for a couple of minutes, then rubbed tonic into Oliver's hair and combed it. Removing the clip and neckcloth, he brushed Oliver's neck and made more lather.

Oliver put chin to his chest and closed his eyes. He felt the brief wet heat, listened to the strop, then heard the razor scrape a straight line across his neck. "Know something else?" whispered George. "I hear Sam Leatherwood ain't found that rifle gun." He wiped Oliver's neck with a hot towel and rubbed a few drops of Fitch's into his hands. Oliver flinched as the styptic found a place George had nicked.

"Is that true?"

"Mister, this is a barbershop. We'd have heard it if he had. Why, just a few minutes ago we heard Ted Maney's going to bury the dead Banks tomorrow." George swiveled the chair and held a hand mirror for Oliver to see the back of his neck. Oliver nodded approval, and George turned him forward. He took off the chair cloth, careful to cradle the cut hair in it. "As for that gun, you better hope Leatherwood don't find it."

Oliver fished a quarter from his pants and smiled. He fetched another, grinned at both, and gave them to George.

"Much obliged. Good luck to ye."

"Thank you, sir. I might need it." Oliver donned jacket and hat and brushed at his sleeves. "Good day, gentlemen," he said. As he stepped on the plank sidewalk he heard laughter inside.

Solicitor Martin Osborne was a tall, thin man with a nose people called hawkish or Roman when they were polite. Staff called him Old Horn Beak behind his back when he stuck his nose into their business, which was frequent.

He didn't look up when he heard the knock. "Yes," he said, and the door opened. "Mr. Osborne, a Mr. Oliver Babcock is here to see you." His secretary walked to Osborne's desk, unadorned oak like the rest in the courthouse but a foot wider and deeper, and placed Oliver's card on it. Osborne eyed it like it was a scorpion.

"Who is he?"

"He says he represents Mr. Banks, sir."

"If he wants more than two minutes, tell him to make an appointment like everyone else."

"Yes, sir." She left, shutting the door behind her. A moment later, through the pebbled glass panel, Osborne saw her shadow returning, followed by a dark figure. She ushered Oliver in and quickly disappeared.

Osborne fixed Oliver with a basilisk stare. "Make it snappy." A chair faced the desk but Osborne did not invite Oliver to sit.

"Sir, I represent Mr. Zebulon Banks of Cataloochee Township. I would like to speak with you about the state's case, if you please."

On Osborne's desk sat one open file folder, Oliver's card, and a telephone. Osborne stood and closed the file. "Do you have the coroner's jury report?"

Oliver nodded.

"Then you have everything you need. Good day."

"Sir, I thought you might disclose your evidence so I can prepare properly."

"Damn you, you know good and well what I have—the pistol, the hammer—hellfire, I don't have time to pass with the likes of you."

"I'm sorry to have disturbed you. I just thought in the interest of justice—"

Osborne slapped the flat of his hand on the desktop, dinging the phone bell and flipping Oliver's card onto the floor. "I'll tell you about justice. Justice is for your client to die for killing his father in cold blood. The fact is, they are so confounded backward over there I am surprised he used a gun instead of a club. Now get out of here before I lose my temper."

33

DEEP SUBJECT

At the Ola post office that afternoon Oliver scattered four dirty white Plymouth Rock hens searching for something edible at the road's edge. The cuffs of his black driving gloves covered his forearms halfway to his elbows. He removed them and laid them on the front seat. Two bare-footed boys sniggered at him from the doorway.

Oliver walked into the small store and post office to find no one. He was about to leave when the back door was opened by a fresh-faced woman in her early twenties, wearing a calico frock and a man's denim jacket, bearing an armload of stove wood. She said, "Howdy," and turned to dump the wood in a box by the cast iron heater. A rifle hung over the back door. She wore no rings.

"You're the second automobile up here today. First was Uncle Hub bringing the mail." She brushed wood crumbs from the jacket, hung it on a peg, and stepped toward him. "You're Babcock, that lawyer fellow, ain't you?"

"Yes. I stopped to ask where Mr. Cassius Davis and Mrs. Pauline Rogers can be found. I need to talk to them."

"They're at home, likely." She told him how to get there. "You *are* talking about Cash Davis, ain't you? He's my great-uncle on my mama's side. And it's Miss Rogers. She never married."

"Of course. You're very helpful, thanks. What's your name?"

"I'm Velda. Velda Parham. My daddy, Ernest, used to run this store till he got killed bear hunting three years ago. Me and Mama keep the store now."

Oliver smiled. "Pleased to make your acquaintance, Miss Parham. I have to talk to these folks this afternoon or I'd stay awhile. That is, if you wouldn't care."

"I wouldn't mind company, Mr. Babcock. Come back any old time."

"I'll make a point to call again." He shook her hand. "By the way, has that rifle been over that door a long time?"

"Since I was a little girl. Why?"

"Just asking. Don't know of anyone up here with a new rifle, do you?"

She pursed her lips. "No, sir. Folks don't generally carry guns to the store."

"No, I suppose not."

"I hope you get Zeb Banks off, Mr. Babcock. He's a nice man. I just wanted you to know that."

"I appreciate it. Good day."

Velda went to the window and watched him put his driving gloves back on. "Law me, you can tell he thinks he's stylish, but looks to me like they'd just get in your way."

A half mile up the road a jay hole cut into the bank for cars to turn in led into a path winding up the hollow. Oliver parked the car and trudged up the lane to the cabin, built on the only flat place on the left-hand side of Wright Branch. A stocky woman, wearing a bonnet against the sunshine, sat in a straight chair. Four fieldstones dug into the bank served as steps into the front yard.

"Howdy, there." The voice within the bonnet spoke of tobacco. "I'm Polly Rogers. Come set a spell." Two slender columns on each corner kept the roof from falling, and next to a center post sat a vacant straight chair. Oliver took off his hat and came up to the porch.

"Good afternoon, Miss Rogers. My name is Oliver Babcock. I am an attorney."

She put his card in her apron pocket without looking at it. "Set down, young man. Watching you stand there makes me tired." That last word rhymed with "charred." She looked him up and down. "So this here's what an attorney looks like. Never seed one before."

"Yes, ma'am, at least this is what I look like. We come in all shapes and sizes."

"That a fact?" She could have been fifty or eighty. Her broad nose and blue eyes had once been handsome.

"Care for a drink of water or a little bit of pie?"

"No, ma'am, thanks."

"Tell me, sonny. What's a town lawyer doing up here?"

"Miss Rogers, I am defending Zeb Banks next week. I need you for a character witness because you have known him for some time and you aren't related to him. Would you consider doing that for a neighbor?"

She looked out across the hollow. "Would I have to go to town?"

"Yes, ma'am. Monday. Maybe Tuesday and Wednesday, too."

"I ain't been to town in ages. I bet it's getting all built up."

"Yes, I suppose it is."

"What would I have to say?"

"I'd just ask you some questions. Let's try it. How long have you known Zeb Banks?"

"Oh, ever since he was a baby." She laughed. "One time I come to see Hannah, she'd just had little Zeb. He might've been a month old. I was holding him and he throwed up just like one of them Old Faithfuls out West."

"That's good. Now, have you ever known Zeb to be dishonest?"

"Law, no. Zeb Banks is as good a man as there is in Cataloochee. When he was a boy he used to stack my firewood or set with me like you're doing now. Course that was to get away from his daddy. His daddy used to whip them boys something fierce, but Zeb especially. Many's the time, though, Zeb brought me something Hannah'd made, a cake or something, when he could have been doing something more boylike than keeping company with an old woman. He was always a boy to do what his mother said. I never heared anybody say a word against Zeb. Now his brother, George, that's another story. George's the spitting image of Ezra Banks." She lowered her voice. "You know what? George got his brother into this fix. George waited till his daddy was drinking, then told him Zeb had foxed him out of some land payments. Ezra got so riled he run over there and got hisself killed."

"Where did you hear this?"

"Let's say a little bird told me."

"Did you ever see Ezra when he was drinking?"

"Lord, yes. Many a time. But once it pretty near scared me to death."

"Can you tell me about it?"

"One time I went up there and kind of crept to the back and pecked on the door. It was up in the afternoon, like this, and the sun was on the winder lights so I couldn't see nothing. I couldn't hear nothing inside, either. I pecked again, and that door opened quick as a cat. There he stood, pistol in one hand and a square bottle in the other. He put that old owlhead pistol up to his mouth, like this, to shush me. Hannah was laying on the floor. I just knowed she was dead and he'd kill me, too." A jaybird screamed.

"What did you do, Miss Rogers?"

"What could I do? I come in and kneeled down by Hannah, thanking God she was breathing. I got water and a washrag and wiped her forehead. She come to directly. Ezra had set down at the table with that liquor bottle and he had that pistol in both hands, staring at it. I helped Hannah up to a chair. 'Polly, you go now,' she says. I looked at Ezra and his eyes glowed like fire coals. I hightailed it home."

"Would you be afraid to tell that story in court?"

"Nothing to be affeared of now, sonny. By the way, have you heard when they're going to bury Ezra?"

"Tomorrow, they said at the barbershop." Oliver stood. "Miss Rogers, you have been most informative. I thank you. I will be in touch about the trial."

She shook his hand like a man. "Sonny boy, I ain't got clothes fit to wear to town. You reckon I might could get me a store-bought frock? I ain't never had one."

Oliver smiled. "I'll see what I can do, Miss Rogers."

Cassius Davis, a rail of a man three inches better than six feet, reminded some folks of Ichabod Crane. He kept to his farm except on Saturdays, when he liked, as he put it, to "loafer" at the post office. Cash was in the back rattling stove lids on the kitchen range when he heard Oliver knock.

"Latchstring's outside!" Oliver didn't know what that meant, but the tone was friendly. He entered the front room, where a straight chair, a leather-cushioned rocker, and a small maple table sat in the chimney corner. The other side of the room contained a long table piled with newspapers, a few books, tools, and a ten-gallon crock with a cracked lid. A picture of women gleaning straw hung on the back wall near a calendar with a picture of Grand Canyon National Park.

"Mr. Davis? Hello."

"Come on back. I'm trying to start a dad-jim fire." The word rhymed with "car."

In the back room Oliver found Cash Davis lighting a piece of newspaper under a teepee of pine kindling. He closed the firebox door and angled himself upright, hat crown nearly brushing the ceiling. "Welcome, stranger. In a minute we'll have fire and then we can have coffee." He put out a mottled hand. "Pleased to know you, whoever you be."

Oliver returned the handshake. "Mr. Davis, my name is Oliver Babcock. I'm an attorney. I represent Zeb Banks."

"Well, if that don't beat all. Ain't never had an attorney in my house. Had a undertaker once but he was my wife's brother so I couldn't keep him out. You figuring to get Zeb off?"

"Yes, sir, that's the idea."

"I hope you do, son, I hope you do. Ezra give me more heartache than any neighbor I ever had. And one time I lived next to a preacher. Meanest man I ever knowed."

"The preacher?"

"Banks. But that preacher was low-down, too. They run him off after they caught him getting a bit more than fried chicken from a deacon's wife. Set down, take a load off."

Oliver sat at the table, which was coated with dust. Hundreds of cigarette ducks fouled a huge ashtray hollowed from a poplar round. Beside it sat a saltcellar with no lid. Oliver was glad he didn't salt his coffee.

Davis put the coffeepot on the stove and turned to Oliver, who figured him for eighty years old. Davis's right eye looked straight but the left looked somewhere to Oliver's side. He fished a Chesterfield from his overalls and lit it. "You fancy a coffin nail, son?"

"No, thank you. I never took them up."

"That's good. Wish I hadn't myself, but it's too late now."

As it heated, the coffeepot rumbled and growled. "I'd like to ask if you would testify at Zeb's trial next week," Oliver started.

"Son, can't you wait for our coffee before we talk business? Let's be sociable." He got two saucers and cups and brushed the table with his shirtsleeve. Fishing spoons from a wooden tray, he sat beside Oliver and gave them both a cup. "Now, then. Where're you from? I've heard that brogue but can't hardly place it."

"I'm from down east. Currituck County."

"That's up toward Virginia Beach, ain't it?"

Oliver brightened. "Yes, sir. Have you been there?"

"Mr. Babcock, don't be so surprised that some of us has been over Cataloochee Mountain. No, I ain't been there but I know where it's at because I had a spell of wandering. Eighteen seventy-five, in my twenties, I took a hankering to see the ocean. Headed east on a mule and down about Morganton I run into some boys vagabonding, heading toward the coast. One of them's name was Balance or Ballast or something quare, one I can't remember now was downright foreign-sounding, said they hailed from Currituck. You sound like him."

"Was he from Kilmarlic?"

"I couldn't say. He told about a boatload of Scotsmen running aground and losing a whole raft of Scotch whiskey kegs. Said they cried for years."

"That's Kilmarlic. Finest spot in the county."

"It ain't bad if you like skeeters big enough to diddle a turkey." The pot perked noisily on the stovetop and Cash put a tin cup of sugar on the table. "I'll be right back, Mr. Babcock. I like a little coffee in my cream." He put out his cigarette, headed to the springhouse, and returned with a pint jar of cream.

"So, Mr. Davis, did you ever see the ocean?"

"Lord, son, that's a whole tale in itself. But yes, I did. Me and them boys split up in Warshington. The one on the Pamlico."

"Little Washington's pretty far from the ocean if you're on a mule, Mr. Davis. How long did it take?"

Cash poured coffee from his cup into his saucer and raised it to his lips. "That mule I started out on got traded down about Raleigh." He blew his coffee, slurped, and put it back on the table. "She wasn't much account to start with, but I got enough trading her to buy a train ticket to New Bern, and then bummed my way to Morehead City. That's when I first seed the ocean. Trip took two years, and I learned more than you likely did getting that lawyer degree. Least you don't look like a twenty-dollar lawyer. You *did* get a diploma in Chapel Hill?"

"Yes, sir. What made you come back here?"

Cash finished what was in the saucer, then drank from the cup. He looked straight at Oliver with his right eye. "I seed plumb near everything them two years. I seed a man get killed over a hand of poker. I seed pretty women and poor folks and more black niggers'n you could shake a stick at. Some of them were mighty good to me when I didn't have nothing to eat, let me tell you. I seed what was down there and I liked it, but after a while I couldn't stand getting up in the morning to look at land flat as a table and just pineywoods off in the distance. A man born around here needs to see mountains around him." He drained his coffee. "How about another cup?"

"No, thank you, sir." Oliver was just now adjusting to his first. "Do you think you might testify for Zeb Banks next week?"

"Do I get to stay in a ho-tel?"

"I'm sorry?"

"A ho-tel. You know, like the Bon-Air? They's good times goes on in ho-tels." He winked with his wandering eye.

"I'll see what I can do, Mr. Davis."

"Well, I'll tell that judge we don't need no trial, because Zeb done us a favor."

"That's not exactly what he needs to hear, sir. You need to talk about Zeb's character."

"I can do that right enough. Zeb done many a kindness for me. And his daddy was mean. You know, years ago Ezra beat that boy something awful at church. I mind it because the boy's leg had blood all over it. Turned out it was a splinter drew the blood but I knew that very day Ezra wasn't right." He poured another cup. "Want something stronger to go in that?"

"No, thank you, this is fine. You know of any missing rifles?"

"Son, what makes you ask that?"

"The sheriff thinks there was another weapon besides Ezra's pistol. Tried to find it, but I don't think he did."

"You best ask Jake Carter about that."

Something in Davis's tone reminded Oliver of a clam shutting up. "Mr. Davis, the trial starts Monday. We will make our case Tuesday or Wednesday. Can we can count on you?"

"If it'll help my neighbor I'll be there. Even if I don't get to stay in a ho-tel."

Oliver started the Ford and headed toward Jake's place. The grade there was mild, only one switchback up to the Banks properties. He stopped in Zeb's lane, almost exactly one Ford wide. Past there the road became considerably steeper and very narrow. The sun had set behind the mountain, leaving a golden halo above Davidson Gap.

He heard slow clops and saw Jake approaching on Lilly. Jake dismounted and tied her to the taillight bracket.

"You must be Babcock. I'm Jake Carter." He shook Oliver's gloved hand, removed his glasses, and wiped them with a handkerchief. "You squirrel hunting up here?"

"No, Mr. Carter, I've been talking to Miss Rogers and Mr. Davis, and I was trying to see if my auto would make it to your house."

"My friends call me Jake. Tell you what, Mr. Babcock. It'd make it but I wouldn't trust you to get it there. You want to talk, leave it here and ride up with me and Lilly." He picked a chicory stem from under the running board, then shined the fender with his shirtsleeve. "Wouldn't want this pretty automobile to get scratched."

"I was thinking to ask to stay with you tonight, if it wouldn't be too much trouble. I don't want to have to go back to Waynesville after dark."

"Fine idea. Let's say howdy to Mattie, then head home."

"You certain I'm not imposing?"

"We'd be insulted if you didn't eat supper and stay the night. Matter of fact, Hannah gave me Zeb's suit for you to take to town, don't let me forget it. Rachel's fixing chicken and dumplings. Take some advice. Stow them fancy gloves."

They left gloves and Ford in Lilly's care and walked up the lane to talk to Mattie. They found her there with Hannah, and right away both women asked about Zeb's chances.

"I think they're pretty good. Miss Rogers and Mr. Davis have agreed to be character witnesses. I think both will be believable, although it's going to cost two hotel rooms and a new dress."

Mattie went to the can shed and came out with a bag of the little tomatoes Zeb called tommy-toes. "Give these to Zeb and tell him I miss him something fierce."

Hannah pulled a cloth pouch from her apron pocket. "Mr. Babcock, here's something for Zeb, too. Tell him I made it for good luck."

"I'll do that," said Oliver, and took her hand. "Next week it will be all over. Pray that it goes well."

"I do that every minute. Without ceasing, as the good book says. My mama knew it lid to lid, and she always said pray without ceasing. Don't you want to look at it? I think it's right pretty."

Oliver nodded and opened the parcel. "My stars, this is beautiful." They all admired a blue silk necktie with a pattern of small white flowers with pink centers.

"Sis, where in the world did you get that?" asked Jake.

"Made it. You likely don't remember, but years ago Ernest Parham down at the store, you know he'd buy anything from a peddler, he bought some silk from a real slick talker. Wasn't long before he found out nobody in Cataloochee would buy such a thing as silk, so he decided to cut it into one-yard pieces and give it to the womenfolks. I thought this was real pretty, so I kept it back. When they arrested Zeb, I figured he'd need his suit, you know, to look good at his trial. He never had no tie but a four-in-hand like his daddy, Ezra always said anything fancier would be putting on airs. So I sewed this up on my old Burdick. I'd never made a necktie, but as many things as I've sewed with that old sewing machine it wasn't no trouble."

"Mama Banks, that's the same blue as Zeb's shirts."

"Well, we need him to look good, plus all the luck we can get. By the way, Mr. Babcock, there's another thing. I don't know what your lawyering will cost—or that hotel and frock, for that matter—but Ezra had some money hoarded—I reckon I'll find more and more as I look for it—and I can't think of nothing I'd rather do with it than get Zeb back home. I've lost a husband, sorry as he'd gotten to be. I sure don't want to lose my best son."

"Don't worry, Mrs. Banks," said Oliver. "We can talk about that next week. Meanwhile, I'll put this with Zeb's suit. He'll be proud of it."

Back at the car Jake untied Lilly.

"Oliver, you got your choice. Ride behind me or I'll walk her up and you can walk beside. What'll it be?"

"How far is it?"

"As the crow flies, maybe two hundred yards." Jake pointed. "See that smoke? That's Rachel's cookfire."

"I'll ride if you think I can make it."

"All you do is get up and hold tight. Course, Lilly ain't never let no lawyer ride her, so I can't say for sure she won't try to scrape you off on a tree."

From the porch Rachel saw Lilly trotting with her double burden, Oliver and his bag bouncing to and fro like a ball on a wire.

They pulled up in front of the porch. "Get off the way you got on," said Jake. "Slide off her backside, she'll kick you clean to the gap."

Oliver dismounted and Jake handed him his bag. "This is Rachel. Honey, this here's Zeb's lawyer, Oliver Babcock. He'll stay the night."

Rachel beamed at Oliver. "Proud to meet you, Mr. Oliver Babcock." Her high cheekbones, black eyes, and dark hair with red highlights made Oliver blush like a schoolboy, even though she was twenty years his senior. She wore a ruddy calico dress covered with a white apron, on the pocket of which a tall heron was embroidered in blue thread.

"Pleased to make your acquaintance."

"You want to catch your breath out here or inside?"

"Here is fine." Two locust rockers sat near a couple of slat-bottomed chairs. Rachel dusted out one of the rockers for Oliver.

"Let me take your bag inside. Can I bring you something to drink? We got the best springwater around, and we got stronger if you care for it."

"Water, please, Mrs. Carter."

"That's Rachel, young man. We're all first names around here." She went inside, screen door banging behind her, while Oliver sat and looked off the porch. A hawk slowly circled on an updraft. Black spruce outlined the ridgetop, while sourwoods sported flaming colors.

While Jake flopped in the other rocker, Rachel brought a wooden tray holding three cups and a stoneware pitcher. She poured water, gave it to the men, and raised her cup. "Here's to Mr. Babcock. May he be successful."

"Rachel, you are right," said Oliver. "This is the sweetest water I have ever drunk."

Jake smiled. "Makes good whiskey, too. We might sample that after supper. You a drinking man?"

"I've been known to be from time to time."

"You'd do well," said Rachel, "to leave it alone. My daddy died early from it. And you know what it did to Ezra Banks."

"I just meant a little sup," said Jake. "A toast to Ezra. You know we bury him in the morning."

"That would be proper enough," said Oliver. "I know drinking had a lot to do with his untimely demise, but still, it's the nectar of the gods, eh?"

"Whatever you say, Mr. Babcock."

"Jake, you do have a nice place. How many acres do you have?"

"Well, there's about seventy-five, mostly in hay and apples. It's a good place. Never had children. It's just us and the critters. The house is tight. I fish and hunt all I want to. I'd sure hate to have to leave it because of that park."

Oliver nodded. "Let's not mention that today. I need to talk to you about the trial."

"How's that coming?" asked Rachel.

"Well, the judge bounced me out of his office when I asked for bail, then the solicitor threw me out this morning, so I'll have to guess what he will do with his evidence."

Jake rocked thoughtfully. "What's he got? A dead man with a stove-up owlhead under him. A hammer, a couple of hats. A coroner's report. No witnesses except maybe Mattie. Shoot, maybe he means to convince them Ezra shot hisself four or five times with that old pistol, which means he's trying the wrong Banks. What else?"

"The big question is exactly how those bullets got into Ezra. And you, Jake, first noticed Zeb's rifle was missing, if I heard correctly."

Rachel smiled at Oliver. "The Lord works in mysterious ways. I'm going to get supper on the table. You *can* eat chicken and dumplings, can't you?"

"Yes indeed." She went inside. "Jake, what did she mean?"

"Well, Oliver, let's just say it ain't a problem."

"Jake, I must know. Does Osborne have it?"

"He can't show evidence he don't have, can he? And if I was to tell you, you might get the notion you need to bring it to the trial. And I'd like Mattie to get her husband back. Don't worry about the fool thing."

"So you *did* find it. That's wonderful news. But I'm confused. People said you wanted the truth of this matter. Now you tell me—and be assured this is in strictest confidence—you have concealed evidence from the state. I don't understand."

"Oliver, I haven't said nothing like that, and the only truth in this mess is that Ezra Banks is dead. Once you know that one fact, how he got that way don't matter. When Leatherwood didn't find the rifle, I figured I needed to. Where it is ain't nobody's nevermind."

"Where *was* it?"

"Smack under Leatherwood's nose. I was down there this morning and Mattie and I got to talking. You know what she did?"

Rachel stuck her head outside. "Wash up. It'll be on the table in a minute."

"Thanks, honey." Jake turned back to Oliver. "I asked her if she knew where the rifle was and she didn't say a thing. I said, 'Well?' and she said, 'Deep subject.' After a minute I realized she was telling me where it was."

"I thought Leatherwood searched the well."

"Guess he didn't look deep enough. All he brought out with his magnet was an old grappling hook that he hung on the lip of the well. I fished the rifle out with that very same hook. Now nobody's going to get it. Not you, not Leatherwood. You hear?"

Rachel hollered from inside. "I'm going to throw this to the hogs if you all don't get in here."

Jake stood. "She means it, Oliver. Come on."

34

GOOD AND DEAD

Ted Maney's father, Clarence, started the family furniture and funeral business in Frog Level, down by the Waynesville depot, in 1904. They outgrew that and moved into their new two-story building on Main Street in 1920. Kitchen cabinets, Victrolas, Round Oak ranges, and metal beds displayed in narrow aisles on the main floor were the mainstay of business. Upstairs they showed coffins in the front and embalmed in the back. Ted was in his early thirties, a slender man with black hair. Now that his father was retired—which meant he stayed in the office, feet up, reading the paper—Ted worked the sales floor instead of delivering and collecting. He usually wore a white shirt and a black suit with a silk handkerchief in the front pocket. His father always said customers, whether living or dead, kept your business going, and it never hurt to dress up for them.

The funeral business he mostly left to his brother, John, a loner, but a man gifted at consoling the bereaved. He was especially kind to mothers who had lost babies to influenza or diphtheria. He enjoyed the mortician's role, and joked that, unlike in the furniture store, complaints from his customers were infrequent and fairly low-key. They rarely dealt with Cataloochee folks, who normally buried their own.

Deputy Shuford had brought Ezra's body to the store on Tuesday. After Doc Bennett finished his postmortem, John straightened Ezra's twisted limbs, cleaned, shaved, and embalmed him. No family had come with the body and none had called. They dressed Ezra in a suit of dull brown cheviot and a collarless white shirt, buttoned at the neck. When John came downstairs Thursday morning, Ted asked if he had heard what to do with Ezra's body.

"We likely can keep it." John's carefully oiled hair fell slightly on his forehead. He pushed it in place with an index finger. "His son, they say, killed him, and nobody but the sheriff and the solicitor seems too upset about it."

"John, we got to get him in the ground. Let me find out who's responsible."

"Suit yourself. I got to look after that family of Robersons. Their brother got mangled when that skidder turned over on him in Sunburst. God knows it wasn't easy getting him presentable."

Waynesville had had phones since the turn of the century but the closest telephone to Cataloochee was at Miller's store, twelve miles away in Cove Creek. Ted called there and asked them to have Hub Carter call him. Hub, Levi Marion's brother, brought rural free delivery mail from Waynesville into both Cataloochees. Besides that, Hub carried news and gossip from one Cataloochee to the other, and sometimes people gave him a dime or a sack of potatoes in exchange for a ride.

The phone rang about one, and Ted's wife told him he had a collect call from Cove Creek. "Put me through." The line crackled. "This is Ted Maney with Maney Funeral Home in Waynesville. To whom am I speaking?"

"This is Hub Carter, Mr. Maney. You all right today?" said a wavery voice, sounding like it rose from the bottom of a cistern.

"Yes, I'm tiptop. I am calling about Mr. Banks. We need to know what to do with his body."

"Well, sir, I ain't kin to him. Let's see, his wife Hannah's my daddy's second cousin, something like that. It's her you need to talk to."

"Mr. Carter, can you get a message to her? It's very important."

"Sure. I'll bring the mail over the mountain this evening. I usually don't get to Little Catalooch till in the morning, but I can go this evening if my headlights hold out."

"Good, good," said Ted. "No one gave us instructions about services or burial."

"I know nobody ain't talking about a funeral. But I did hear she traded for a burial plot at the Baptist church. I ain't heard that from her, just folks talking, you know. If somebody wanted to put him in the Carter cemetery, there'd be conniption fits or worse."

"Well. I'd appreciate it if you'd get word to her, Mr. Carter."

"Glad to. Somebody said they didn't reckon we could raise enough folks around here for pallbarriers so we might as well let you folks bury him."

"Doesn't she even want to see him?"

"I'd think she'd seen enough of him in nigh unto fifty years."

John poked his head into the office and threw a penny postcard on Ted's desk. Ted paused. "Mr. Carter, may I ask you to hang on a second?"

"It's your nickel, Mr. Maney."

The postcard was covered with a shaky scrawl: *Please bring Ezra Banks to Ola Baptist Friday if it ain't too much trouble.* It was signed "Hannah Carter Banks." Ted muffled the phone and looked up at John. "Is this the widow?" John nodded. "Mr. Carter, I have a postcard that says Hannah Carter Banks wants me to bring Mr. Banks to the Baptist church tomorrow. Would you tell her I will be there at noon?"

"Sure. Leave it to me. Matter of fact, I'll get my oldest boy to carry Friday's mail. I'd love to see old Ezra, maybe touch him, too."

"Oh," said Ted. "Why might that be?"

"To make sure he's good and dead, Mr. Maney."

Ted cleared his throat. "Well, thank you for carrying the message. Perhaps I shall see you in the morning, sir."

"You bet, Mr. Maney. Come see us, you hear?"

The line went dead and Ted put the phone back. He stood at the window. "Brother, that was the strangest conversation I ever had about a burial. I'll take Banks over myself in the morning. I wouldn't miss this for the world."

Friday morning Ted Maney drove toward Ola, fording the creek slowly not to disturb his burden. He eased the hearse out of the creek and started past the store and post office, where there was no sign of human activity. The road bent left just past Cash Davis's farm, then jogged right and up the steep hill. He stopped the hearse on the level and double-clutched into low gear. Not wanting to lose his burden on the upgrade, he looked in his mirror to make sure the tailgate was secure.

The transmission whined as the black vehicle climbed the hill, rear tires spitting rocks. The church was nestled in a notch at the crest of a hill halfway between the settlement and Ezra's farm. When Ted neared the gap he discovered the hilltop filled with wagons and a couple of automobiles, parked at sygoggling angles. When he pulled even at the top, a throng of men, women, and children stared at him like he was bringing the main attraction to the county fair.

Ted pulled up to the hemlock at the corner of the churchyard, then backed the hearse and cut the wheels hard left, pointing the back end toward the cemetery, down the hill from the door of the clapboard church. He braked it, cut the motor, got out, and looked toward a sky the color of a bad bruise the day it begins to heal. He wedged chocks from the running board compartment behind the rear wheels.

The crowd began to inch toward the hearse, but when it saw the family emerge from the church, parted for them. Jake eased Hannah down the front steps, holding her elbow as if she were a china doll. Behind them came Mattie and Rachel shepherding Ezra's freshly scrubbed grandchildren.

Hannah wore a long gray coat. A black hat with a veil were her only weeds except a black brooch on her lapel.

Jake offered his hand to Ted. "Jake Carter, sir. This is my sister Hannah Banks. We're much obliged to you."

"Ted Maney, sir, at your service." He shook Jake's hand, then tipped his hat to Hannah, who nodded toward the hearse. "Let me look at him," she said, her voice steady and untroubled.

"Of course, madam." Ted opened the door and pulled the pine casket on the hearse's rollers. He had secured the lid in only two places, so he easily unscrewed it and laid it aside.

John had done a good job masking the wound on Ezra's lip. His skin, ruddy as a bleached-out football, looked like paper. Deep circles under his eyes made him appear worn-out tired, and the undertaker's art could not disguise Ezra's angry expression. Ted smoothed the hair with a comb and turned to Hannah, who lifted her veil. She touched her husband's forehead gently. "It's him, all right," she said, and looked at Jake. "He never thought he'd lay in something common as a pine box. And he sure never wore no brown suit."

"Mrs. Banks, absent any instructions, we didn't know what to do. I could substitute a better coffin if you'd rather. And perhaps you have a suit we could dress him in."

"Son, I don't fault you none. I meant he thought he'd cheat God out of a death. Even *I* wondered sometimes if he hadn't got too dern mean to die. Jake, you remember him before he got mean. He was a handsome devil and always provided good for me and the boys. It's a dern shame the way he got."

She took a rawhide string with three keys, two skeletons for the house and one for Ezra's desk, from her coat pocket and slipped them into Ezra's jacket. "There now. He won't ever get locked out again. Young man, the coffin's fine. Never mind about the suit, either. I seen enough. I got to worry about my Zeb now." She gave her elbow to Jake, who walked her back to the church steps.

Mattie, wearing a brown ankle-length coat with hat to match, walked steadily to the right of her son, William, fourteen, taller by half a head. Slightly behind them walked Rachel, herding Mattie's daughters. Doris and Lizzie, twelve and ten, suffered Rachel to guide them in front of the coffin. Alice, eight and black-headed as a crow, shied from the coffin and looked back and forth from Mattie to Rachel.

Mattie squeezed William's hand. "They say he was your age, son, when he left home to go to war. Maybe that made him what he was, I don't know. Be glad you don't have a war to go to."

William put his arm around his mother and patted her shoulder. "He never was mean to me, Mama."

"You're lucky. He beat your daddy something awful. Go on, girls, say good-bye." She reached for her daughters and lined them up beside the coffin.

Doris and Lizzie were silent and watchful, like Ezra might suddenly jump at them. Alice reached for her grandfather's hair and smoothed it against his forehead. When Hannah put her hand on Alice's shoulder, the girl sobbed once, turned, and buried her face in her mother's coat.

Mattie nodded to Ted Maney. "We thank you, sir. You did a good job." She hugged Alice and motioned her children toward the church steps, where they lined up like infantry to watch.

One towheaded child had climbed high in a wild cherry, reminding Ted of Zacchaeus. Ted looked the crowd over for a preacher, but none stepped forward. A pointed stare at Oliver, the only man in a suit, only provoked a shrug.

Men and women filed by the back of the hearse, hats in their weathered hands. Some women held up lap babies to look in the coffin, whispering to them to remember old Ezra Banks. Some touched the box as they peered at their dead neighbor, others kept their arms crossed. Hub Carter touched Ezra's shoulder, then his waxen forehead. A few men pointed to the body and told their teenaged sons to let this be an example for them.

Jake assembled Zeb's brothers and Hub around the coffin, then Ted slid it out to them. They held it as he tightened the lid with six brass screws that squeaked as they bit into the wood, then lifted the coffin to their shoulders for the walk downhill toward the grave. Jake's expression was bland as oatmeal. Hub looked slightly amused, but George and Crate and Rufus appeared choleric enough to throw their father at Zeb had he been there. George stumbled once on the way down but the others held fast. At the grave Ted slid two leather straps under the coffin with which to lower Ezra into the ground. Ted felt a drop of rain hit his hat.

Just then Mattie broke from the family and made her way down the hill. She stood by Jake and pulled from her coat pocket a half-full square whiskey bottle. Before Jake could say anything she poured the liquor in the grave, then heaved the bottle at the coffin. It bounced off the lid with a hollow report. Jake nodded at the gravediggers, who began to fill the hole.

Jake and Ted met at the back of the hearse. "How much do we owe you?" asked Jake, pulling an aged black leather pouch from his pocket.

"Well, there's embalming, that's twenty, and the coffin, suit, and transportation. Sixty dollars ought to do it."

"Mr. Maney, we best cover that hole real good before I give you this pouch. If Ezra knew his wife had given me this he'd jump out of that ground faster'n Lazarus. He carried it off when he left home in sixty-four. They said it was his daddy's. Right now I don't know of a better thing to do with what's in it than get Ezra in the ground."

Ted untied the string and looked in the pouch at two double-eagle gold pieces, which looked, to Ted, ancient as Roman coins. "Thank you, sir. I'll mark a bill paid in full."

Jake and Mattie, expecting the heavens to open any minute, walked back to the church. Mattie pointed at a lone black buzzard circling the top of the mountain to their north. At the grave, men tamped dirt with the backs of shovels.

Ted gathered his straps and got the hearse ready to return. As he started down the hill, he thought, I've never seen anything like that. You couldn't call it a funeral nor even a proper committal. No preacher. No Bible. Nobody said any words. Only one little girl cried. And that insane woman with a whiskey bottle. Wait till I tell John about this.

35

PARRICIDE

The morning of the trial Zeb woke from a nightmare in which his father rode to his house on an outsized gray horse and shot him repeatedly with a pistol that grew each time it was fired. Instead of killing Zeb the shots cut all the buttons off his coat. At the end of the dream his father slid off the end of Zeb's porch into a pit filled with sulfur-colored boiling lava and Mattie threw a rifle in after him. Zeb woke frightened, then realized where he was and almost cried.

He found he had slept through a hard thunderstorm. Looking out the window, Zeb thought he would be fortunate to get to court without drowning. Water gushed down the alleyway. He half expected a dead cat or a bushel of parsnips to wash down the slope.

Footsteps in the narrow hall were too heavy to be Rafe's. Zeb turned and saw Sam Leatherwood, wearing a necktie for a change, carrying a plate wrapped in oilcloth. Water stood in the depression on top.

"Morning, Banks. Here's you some breakfast."

Zeb took the plate and sat on the cot. Under one corner of the cloth he saw half a cathead biscuit smothered in gravy. "Thanks. But why?"

"The missus said a man going on trial needs something that'll stick to his ribs. I told her not to bother, but . . ."

Zeb removed the cloth, careful not to let water slide into the food. Instead it soaked his left knee. Beside the biscuit and gravy lay ham, stewed apples with cinnamon, and a piece of yellow pound cake. Leatherwood gave Zeb a spoon. "Eat, dern you. I'll get you some coffee." Zeb started in on the biscuit and gravy, made with an appreciable amount of black pepper. He tore a bite of ham and chewed steadily. Leatherwood handed coffee through the bars. "I'll bring that lawyer when he gets here."

Zeb nodded, mouth full. He knew he ought not eat so much ham, unless assured there would be water in the courtroom. But the salty meat tasted better than anything he had eaten in a week, and it brought out the taste of the three little tomatoes left from the bagful Mattie had sent.

At seven Rafe came in, disparaging the weather. Zeb heard wind and rain, and the lawmen rattling the stove, their wet feet shuffling on the dirty office floor. He looked out again. Leaves and sticks rushed by, hostages to cascading water. He swished the rest of his coffee in his mouth and cleaned his teeth with his finger.

About eight Oliver delivered Zeb's Sunday suit covered in an oilcloth sack. "Zeb, how are you, my friend?" He shook his client's hand. "Did you keep that hand in an icebox?"

"It ain't hot in here. And I'm a tad nervous. When do we go?"

"Court starts at nine. Get dressed and we'll review some things. Here's a comb. And you have a surprise in your jacket pocket."

Zeb took the new necktie and whistled. "Where in the world did this come from?"

"Your mother made it. It's for luck."

"Those are apple blooms. I ain't never seen such a pretty thing."

"Wear it with confidence, my friend."

Zeb pulled on his trousers, which needed an inch and a half of pleat to stay on his bony haunches. "Sheriff Leatherwood," shouted Oliver, "if my client doesn't get his belt his trousers will fall off."

Leatherwood shuffled down the hall with Zeb's belt. "Son, promise you won't hang your fool self. I've got to deliver the solicitor a live body."

Zeb poked the belt through the loops in his trousers. "I promise. I just don't want my britches to fall down."

"Sure would liven up a trial."

"We don't need it that lively," said Oliver. "Does Judge Sutton usually start on time?"

"You bet your ass he does. If Banks is late, judge's liable to try him, convict him, and ship his ass off to Raleigh before he even gets there."

"Relax, Zeb," said his attorney. "Nobody here's going to Raleigh unless it's to run for governor. I want you looking confident—not cocky, just calm and collected. Look the jury in the eye. Don't smile but don't look like a wounded hound either. If Solicitor Osborne says something you don't like—and he will, you can be sure—don't react. It's his job to paint you lower than a snake's belly. It's my job to tell them you're a paragon of virtue. Understand?"

Zeb admired his necktie. "I'll trust the Lord put you here to get me home. And to show me how to tie this thing."

Oliver tied it around his own neck, then put it on Zeb like a medal. "That's the way to think. See you in a half hour, my friend. And I do believe that's the best-looking cravat in Haywood County."

Oliver left the jail, turned south, and walked quickly up the steep alley to Main Street. It had stopped raining, but water still sluiced, and halfway up the alley the backs of his legs felt wet. At Main Street he turned toward the First National Bank, a three-story building with a chamfered north corner. The sandstone front was nearly obscured by three Golgothan Haywood Electric Power poles. In front, what seemed like half of Cataloochee waited on the sidewalk and in the street. Automobile horns, hoofbeats, muted commotion rang in Oliver's ears. Lige Howell greeted him with a hearty handshake. "Son, that courtroom is fuller'n a tick on a pot-likker hound."

"Lige, how many folks came over the mountain?"

"I don't know, but I brung ten in the truck. Even Aunt Mary's here. Like to have drownded in this pourdown. You remember my nephew Rass? He's twelve year old, laid out of school for this."

Oliver shook Rass's hand. "Young man, I hope it's worth the trip. . . . Lige, have you seen Jake Carter, or Polly Rogers, or Cash Davis?"

"A man couldn't help but see Polly Rogers in that red frock, but I ain't seed Jake, and I ain't sure about Cash. Everybody's pulling for you and Zeb."

"Thank you, Lige. I'll do my best." Oliver shouldered his way to the steps, where a burly man eyed him wearily. "Good morning, sir. I'm counsel for the defense. I need to be upstairs."

"I wondered what you was." Clem Mashburn worked for the bank, and on trial days directed traffic. "Come on in, if you can get in."

Frayed velvet ropes on stanchions created two lines, one to the right where the teller cages were, the other to the upstairs courtroom. When Oliver finally reached the stairs, dozens of folks stood between him and the courtroom, where a short, wide expanse of red announced Miss Rogers. He said, "Coming through, please," and, passing Polly, he whispered, "Why didn't you get a red dress while you were at it?"

Gray light spilled from Main Street onto a platform elevating the bench and the witness stand. The North Carolina flag hung from a pole to the right, and on the left, the national standard. Trays on either end of a long table held water pitchers and glasses. At the table sat Solicitor Osborne, staring straight at the platform. Behind, in forty straight chairs, sat the early birds. The rest lined the walls and perched in windowsills.

To Oliver's relief, Cash Davis stood at the back wearing a gray suit with thin lapels. Mattie sat on one side of Jake, Hannah on the other. As Oliver nodded at her he realized where Zeb got his cleft chin. The lawyer removed his hat, went to the long table, put his briefcase down, and glanced at Solicitor Osborne, who paid him no attention. He extracted a file of papers, a foolscap tablet, and a fat fountain pen.

A commotion on the stairs announced Sam Leatherwood and his deputies with a handcuffed Zeb. Leatherwood unlocked the handcuffs and Zeb rubbed his wrists.

Judge Sutton filled the door frame and the bailiff shouted, "Oyes oyes oyes, this honorable court for the County of Haywood is now open and sitting for the dispatch of its business. God save the state and this honorable court." Everyone stood in unison as Judge Sutton knocked his way past folks hugging the walls. He mounted the platform and stood behind the bench. Nearly half as wide as he was tall, he peered at the audience with deep-set beady eyes.

The bailiff read from a sheaf of papers: "The People versus Zebulon Baird Banks." Judge Sutton looked at the solicitor. "Are the people ready?"

Osborne stood and crossed his arms. "Your Honor, we are. The people, however, request to amend the charge."

The audience rumbled and Judge Sutton whacked his gavel five times. "There will be order in this court, if I have to throw every last one of you clodhoppers out. Mr. Osborne, explain yourself."

"Your Honor, the state does not have a first-degree case against Mr. Banks. However, we will prove Mr. Banks guilty of murder in the second degree and wish to proceed to select a jury, with the court's approval."

Judge Sutton looked at the court reporter. "Let the record show the change in the charge against the defendant. Mr. Banks, please stand." Oliver stood and led Zeb to his feet. The defendant stood unsteadily but, after Oliver's prodding elbow, stood ramrod straight like his father had taught him when he was a little boy. "How do you plead to the new charge?"

"Not guilty, Your Honor." Zeb's voice scratched like a Victrola needle.

"Let the record show the defendant pleads not guilty. Proceed, Mr. Osborne." Zeb fiddled with his coat lapel and stared at the water pitcher. Oliver poured Zeb a glass, leaned over, and whispered, "Remember, when we get a jury, look them in the eye. In fact, as they are called, if you don't like how any of them regard you, nudge me and we'll take a peremptory."

Zeb gulped his water. "What's that?"

"We get to refuse a few jurors just because we want to. So if you don't like somebody's looks, let me know."

Osborne challenged four jurors, two peremptory and two because they were related to Zeb. Meanwhile, Zeb kept nudging Oliver's knee, so Oliver used his peremptories quickly. He figured Zeb knew these folks better than he, and some of these men appeared never to have been curried above the knees. Then one fellow, soaked to the bone, came up and Osborne approved but Oliver objected. "Mr. Badcock, may I remind you, you have used your peremptory challenges?"

"Your Honor, this one's for cause."

"What cause might that be?"

"Your Honor, I don't want a man judging my client if he doesn't have sense enough to come in out of the rain."

The crowd laughed and Sutton banged on the dais. "Counselor, you have a point. Juror dismissed."

With the jury selected a bit after ten-thirty, Osborne stood. "If it please the court," he said, hitching his lapels with his thumbs, "the people will prove that Zebulon Baird Banks did willfully and deliberately murder his father, Ezra Banks, late farmer of Cataloochee Township. This is not only murder but also parricide, a heinous crime that the Bible is particularly explicit about, for it not only says in Exodus the twentieth chapter, the thirteenth verse, 'Thou shalt not kill,' " and here he faced the jury, "but also in the twenty-first chapter, the fifteenth verse, 'he that smiteth his father, or his mother, shall surely be put to death.' The very peace of our county, the stability of our state, the fabric of our nation, is the family. A house divided cannot stand. And yet here is a house so divided the son kills the father—gentlemen, can you even imagine such a crime?—and says afterward he doesn't remember a thing about it." He paused and gave Zeb a scornful glance. "I really think this man considered himself above the law. We have seen others from Cataloochee who thought they were above the law because they live in isolation from refined civilization. But I intend to convince Mr. Banks, and his fellow Cataloochans, that the law applies equally to them. I urge you to view the evidence and listen to the testimony objectively, and if you do, you will convict this man of second-degree murder."

"Mr. Badcock?"

"Your Honor, and gentlemen of the jury," Oliver said, as he rose and buttoned his jacket, "my client, as I will show, is a man of peace and a well-respected member of his community. He is no murderer. I will bring stories of his helpfulness, his uprightness before the law, his good name. In his home, love reigned supreme until it was murderously intruded upon by his father, in the cruel grasp of drink, wielding a pistol and threatening my client, his firstborn son. His own father shot at him with said pistol. There was a struggle. A firearm went off. My client rose and his father did not. I will prove to you, gentlemen of the jury, that this is a plain case of self-defense, and that my client, who has languished in jail since this unfortunate event, deserves to be restored to the bosom of his loving family by you honest, God-fearing men. Listen with open minds and hearts, and you will acquit my client in the name of justice. I thank you, gentlemen." Oliver sat as some jurors, astonished at his brogue, looked at him like an ostrich had wandered in off the street.

Osborne began by calling the coroner, Dr. Bennett, who testified that one bullet entered the right cheek and knocked out a tooth, exiting the body beneath the nose. There was powder residue on this wound. Another bullet entered Ezra's right bicep and passed through the chest between the third and fourth ribs on the right side, went through the pericardium and the upper lobe of the left lung, and passed out the third rib on the left side. In the doctor's opinion this was the cause of death. A third bullet entered from the chest three inches to the right of the spinal column and lodged in the spine. A fourth entered the left side about three inches from the spinal column, passed over the spine, and through the upper lobe of both lungs. None of these wounds exhibited powder residue. Bennett noted a triangular wound on the right side of the head three inches above the right ear, consistent with a hammer blow.

Osborne introduced Zeb's hammer as evidence, along with Ezra's bloodstained felt hat. He showed that the blood and material on the hammer head matched that of the hat. "Could this hammer have been the cause of death?"

"Absolutely not," said Bennett. "It might have stupefied Mr. Banks, but I doubt it would have rendered him unconscious."

"So, in your opinion, sir, death came from a bullet that passed through the chest?"

"Yes, sir."

Oliver saw no reason to cross-examine the doctor. "In that event," said Judge Sutton, "we will recess until twelve-thirty." He banged his gavel, and everyone stood until he was out of the room. Folks pulled out ham and biscuits and corn bread for dinner.

Oliver turned to Zeb. "We're off to a good start. They testified the only weapon they've got so far didn't kill him."

Rather than listening to Oliver, Zeb at the moment was torn between his thirst and seeing Mattie. Mattie asked Leatherwood if she could talk to Zeb, and he nodded. Husband and wife hugged like vines, then Mattie handed a grease-stained paper bag to Zeb. In it were two fried apple pies. Oliver motioned them to sit at the table during recess and poured them glasses of water. He moved back to stand beside Jake and Hannah.

"Oliver," said Jake, "Hannah's here to keep an eye on you." She put out her hand, and Oliver for a second didn't know whether to kiss or shake it. It felt like worn denim.

"Charmed. I didn't know if you'd be here, Mrs. Banks."

"I thought at first to stay home with my grandchildren. But then I decided I better see you do your job proper."

"I promise you I shall do my best. Jake, what do you think so far?"

"You're doing pretty good, not to have said nothing yet. That solicitor scored a run for the home team when he got Doc to say Zeb didn't kill him with the hammer. I worry about a couple of them jurymen, though. They look at Zeb like he's trash."

"Do they strike you as mean?"

"No worse than anybody rurint by this city life, I reckon."

Promptly at twelve-thirty Judge Sutton lumbered through the door and the bailiff reconvened court. Solicitor Osborne called Sam Leatherwood, who read Zeb's statement that his father had ridden up and threatened to kill him, then shot at him and knocked off his hat.

"What did the defendant say then?"

"He said he must have lunged at his father and there was a struggle."

"Where was the pistol during this struggle?"

"Defendant said he didn't exactly know, but the weapon went off."

"Is this the weapon?" Osborne held up Ezra's owlhead.

"Yes, sir, it is." Osborne admitted it into evidence.

"In your opinion, Sheriff Leatherwood, did this weapon cause each and every wound to the deceased?" The courtroom got so quiet Oliver heard his pulse.

"No, sir."

"Why is that?"

"Only the wound to the face had powder burns. I think the pistol caused that one, and the angle of entry and exit is possibly consistent with Mr. Banks's story."

"What do you think about the others?"

Leatherwood twisted in his oak chair. "Sir, I think there was another weapon." Oliver unscrewed his fountain pen. "Not simply because there are no other powder burns, but because the body was shot at from different angles. You know, the first thing Mr. Banks told Deputy Shuford was that he thought his daddy might have shot himself."

"And you are not of that opinion?"

"Well, sir, you'd have to be mighty bent on suicide to shoot yourself four times from different directions." The crowd guffawed and Judge Sutton banged his gavel and glowered.

"Did Mr. Banks stick with that story?"

"No, sir. His written statement is he didn't know what happened."

"His own father is dead in his yard and he doesn't know what happened?"

"That's what he says."

"Do you find that a bit, well, odd?"

"I've known murderers to give that line before. Especially when there's family involved. Ever damn one of them knows, they just ain't telling. At least in my experience."

Oliver jumped to his feet. "Your Honor, I object. The witness—"

"Objection sustained. Mr. Osborne, advise your witness to leave personal experience out of this until we prove something about Mr. Banks."

"Yes, Your Honor. Sheriff, can you tell the court about this other weapon?"

"It was a thirty-two-caliber Remington that used to belong to the deceased. I think that man there or his wife killed him with it, then hid or destroyed it." A sharp intake of breath ran through the courtroom.

"Please tell the court how you know of this weapon," said the solicitor.

"The defendant said he used to own a thirty-two-caliber Remington. Kept it over the kitchen door. He says some time ago he looked up and it was gone."

"When exactly did he notice it missing?"

"He didn't know—maybe two weeks before the murder."

Oliver's hand flew in the air. "Objection, Your Honor."

"Sustained. Mr. Badcock, do you need to go to the bathroom?"

"No, Your Honor."

"Then get that damned hand down. You look like a second grader needing to pee." Sutton hit the bench with his gavel. "Mr. Osborne, I remind you this isn't murder until it's proven. All we have is a dead man and an accused—and I emphasize 'accused'—slayer."

"Yes, Your Honor. Sheriff Leatherwood, did you search for this weapon?"

"Yes, sir. We searched the house and the surrounding property. We didn't find it. I did find a box of shells."

"Were they thirty-two caliber?

"Yes, sir."

"Is this it?" He held up a Winchester box and when Leatherwood nodded, introduced it into evidence. "Was there anything strange about this box of ammunition?"

"No, sir. It didn't look like it had been opened. No fingerprints that we could raise. In fact, there weren't fingerprints on anything except the claw hammer."

"Whose were those?"

"The defendant's."

"No prints on the pistol?"

"No, sir. Either it was wiped clean or it got so dirty we couldn't find nothing."

"Which was it in this case?"

"Could have been both. The pistol was stove up in damp ground. It's hard to get a good print off something's been laying in the dirt several hours."

"So there was a weapon you were unable to find. Did you inquire about it?"

"Sure I did. But ain't nobody over there going to tell me nothing."

"Are you saying the people of Cataloochee are uncooperative with the law?"

"Sir, if they're protecting their own, you might as well talk to a tree."

"So you think most of the people in this room are accessories to murder?"

Oliver rushed to his feet but Sutton beat him to it. "Mr. Osborne, these people are not on trial. And if you call this 'murder' again before there's proof, I'll find you in contempt."

"Yes, Your Honor. I have no further questions." Osborne sat, scowling.

Oliver stood. "Sheriff Leatherwood, have you ever forgotten anything?"

"What do you mean?"

"Exactly what I said, sir. Have you ever forgotten anything?"

"Sure. Ever body has."

Oliver fingered his fountain pen. "You implied that my client has rather conveniently forgotten the details of the afternoon his father came riding over. But put yourself in his shoes. If your father, who by all indications was, at best, difficult, and, at worst, a man with a hair-trigger temper, told you he wanted to kill you, and proceeded to shoot your hat off your head, would you not perhaps want to forget that? In the heat of the moment, something happens. And when it's over, you don't know how. Is that so strange, Sheriff?"

"I think it's pretty damn quare when a father is dead in his son's yard and that son has a missing rifle that nobody remembers exactly when it walked off."

"Have you ever had anything stolen from you, Sheriff?"

"Not to amount to nothing."

"I have, Mr. Leatherwood, and I must tell you that the sense of violation is deep and abiding. You are almost ashamed to tell about it. It's like your—"

"Objection." Osborne's face was red as a pickled beet.

"Sustained. Keep to the subject, young man."

"Yes, Your Honor." Oliver turned to the sheriff. "Sir, my question simply meant to open the possibility my client really *doesn't* know what happened to his rifle. Would you not concede it is *possible* he has no idea where it is?"

Leatherwood clenched his fists "You know, you damn lawyers are all alike. You land a client who's going to come into some money and property if you get him off, and you think he might be telling the truth. I'm here to tell you, Mr. Flatland Lawyer, that man is lying through his teeth. He knows good and well where that rifle they killed his papa with is at."

Judge Sutton banged his gavel, but before he could say anything Leatherwood blurted, "Sorry, Your Honor, it just up and come out." Oliver waited for a contempt citation but it was not forthcoming. He turned back to the sheriff.

"So, Mr. Leatherwood, you testified you did not find the rifle. True?" He faced the jury and arched an eyebrow. Leatherwood seemed on the verge of apoplexy, almost rising from the chair. He opened his mouth, but nothing came out. He suddenly relaxed, like someone had let air out of him with a needle. "True."

"No further questions, Your Honor." Oliver looked at the jury as if to ask how voters elect such a person to office.

Osborne called Rafe Shuford, plowing the ground he had already worked with the sheriff. Osborne finished and sat with hands flat on the table. Oliver had no questions.

Judge Sutton looked at the prosecution. "Mr. Osborne, call your next witness."

Osborne stood and buttoned his jacket. "Your Honor, the state calls John Jacob Carter."

"Can they do that?" Zeb whispered to Oliver.

"They can call Jiggs and Maggie if they like."

Osborne paced in front of the jury box, then turned to Jake. "Mr. Carter, where do you live?"

"Up the road from Zeb. My land joins his on one side and his daddy's on another."

"Are you related to Mr. Banks?"

"Not by blood, sir. My sister's Hannah Banks, the widow."

"So you are an uncle to the defendant?"

"Yes, sir."

"Can you tell the court what you witnessed the afternoon Mr. Banks was killed?" The courtroom had buzzed when Jake took the stand, but now all to be heard was the ticking of a clock.

"I was about to patch a piece of roof. I was on my ladder when I heard a shot."

"Can you describe exactly what you heard?"

"It come from Zeb's or Ezra's. It was a pistol with some size to it or a rifle, I couldn't tell which. I stood on the ladder and listened, 'cause I didn't think nobody ought to be shooting at four in the afternoon."

"Then what happened?"

"Well, sir, like I said, I stood there and waited. There was another shot. Then it was a few minutes, 'cause I remember my feet hurting.

Then four shots. Took maybe a half a minute for them all. I couldn't tell if it was the same gun the first shots come from, but them last four came from the same one."

"So you heard six shots, first one, then after a time another, then four in fairly rapid succession? What then?"

"It got quiet. I nailed down that piece of metal I'd got on the ladder to fix in the first place, then me and Lilly went to Zeb's place."

"Who's Lilly?"

"My mule." The crowd tittered and Judge Sutton gaveled.

"What did you see when you got there?"

"First thing was Old Huldy. That's Ezra's mule. She was in Zeb's front yard, not tied or nothing. I got off Lilly, and Zeb met me at the corner of the front porch."

"Did he say anything?"

Jake paused, took off his glasses, then returned them to his head. "Yes, sir. He told me I better look in the backyard. Said his papa was dead."

"Were those his exact words?"

"Best I remember."

"Then what happened?"

"Well, I went to the backyard and I saw Ezra laying dead as four o'clock."

"Have you heard the testimony from Sheriff Leatherwood and Deputy Shuford regarding the position of the body and the evidence in the yard?"

"Yes, sir."

"Did you see anything to add or subtract from their testimony?"

"They told it about like I saw it."

"Mr. Carter, you testified the defendant told you his father was dead. Did he tell you he killed him?" Osborne turned toward the jury and looked down his substantial nose at them. "Remember, sir, you are under oath."

"I remember, Mr. Osborne. Took it a few minutes ago . . . Zeb said when Ezra shot it scared the wits out of him. Ezra was a crack shot, you know. When Zeb grabbed that hammer it was root hog or die, so he run at Ezra and knocked him in the head. Said they struggled and the pistol went off he didn't remember how many times and when it was over he was alive and Ezra wasn't."

"Mr. Carter, I ask you again: Did Mr. Banks tell you he killed his father?"

"He said he might have."

A murmur went through the crowd like a mouse looking for a place to hide.

"Mr. Carter, what do you mean by that?"

"What I said, sir. He said he didn't know. He didn't remember much except when it was over, his daddy was dead."

"Did you see Mrs. Banks at any point?

"Yes, sir. She was looking out the kitchen window."

"Did she say anything about who killed Mr. Banks?"

"She said she didn't see nothing."

Osborne stopped in midstride and turned. "Really."

"Yes, sir. She said when Ezra rode up Zeb made her get in the house. Said she shut her eyes and when it was over she looked out and Zeb was alive and Ezra wasn't."

"Let the record show this witness is testifying about his nephew's wife."

"Duly noted," said Judge Sutton.

"Are you saying I might be lying?"

"Folks have done it before."

"Now, see here, Mr. Osborne."

"Mr. Carter, settle down," said Judge Sutton. "The man is right. Mr. Badcock, do you plan to cross-examine?"

"No, sir."

"Very well. Mr. Osborne, are you through with this witness?"

"Yes, Your Honor."

"Then this court stands in recess until nine in the morning." Sutton rapped his gavel and all rose as he left in a sea of black fabric.

"What do you reckon that means?" Zeb shifted from foot to foot.

"It means they're scared they don't have a case. We'll see who they call in the morning. But we have a good case for self-defense. With any luck, you only have one more night in jail."

Rafe Shuford took Zeb by the arm. "We got to go back." Zeb held out his hands and Rafe cuffed him and led him down the stairs to the street. Meanwhile, Jake approached Oliver, extending his hand. "Son, you got in some right good objections today."

"Thanks. Did you know he was going to call you?"

"Said he might."

"Did he say anything about the rifle?"

"Nope. I wouldn't have told him nothing, anyhow."

"You also got to tell the truth," said Oliver, a slight grin on his face.

"What *is* truth? Didn't Pontius Pilate ask that one time?"

"My God, Jake. I remember that line from Francis Bacon. How do you know it?"

"Bacon? Never heard of her. Any kin to that bunch of Hoglans up toward Sal's Gap?"

36

THE PEOPLE REST

Martin Osborne woke Tuesday morning with a bad taste in his mouth.
Last night's mug of Postum notwithstanding, he had lain awake most of
the night worrying about whether to call Mattie Banks.

He was afraid without her he had no case. He was also disheartened
by Judge Sutton consistently sustaining Oliver's objections. Whatever
happened to native Haywood County men standing by one another? It
might be worth a try to call Mattie, hoping something would slip from
her testimony that would help his case.

Once he had prosecuted a thief on purely circumstantial evidence.
He had gotten lucky with jury selection. One juror had not disclosed a
feud with the accused's family, and the other eleven, a pretty mean lot,

chose him foreman. The defendant went to Raleigh for fifteen years. So maybe calling Mattie would crack something.

He got up, put on his robe and slippers, and padded to the bathroom. He brushed his teeth with baking soda and went to the kitchen for a cup of coffee. His wife kissed him atop his head.

"Sleep well, dear?"

He grunted. After toast and another cup, he went to the bathroom, shaved, and dressed. Tying his necktie, he resolved to call Mattie. Putting on his vest, he thought better of it. When the jacket went on he didn't know. Maybe he would wait for the spirit to move him. Then something entirely other caused him to remove his jacket and head for the bathroom. When he came out he still didn't know.

He walked up the courtroom stairs at eight-fifty, elbowing his way past spectators, covering his nose with a handkerchief against their various odors. He set his briefcase beside the table and turned to see if Mattie was in the room. Jake leaned and spoke to Mattie, who stared at Osborne. If he had been a little bird and she had been a shotgun, he would have been a feathery mist.

When Oliver came up the stairs, he saw the dark look on Osborne's face, nodded to him, put his briefcase next to the table leg, and took out his tablet.

Leatherwood and Shuford led Zeb to the table. As they unlocked the handcuffs, Mattie winked at Zeb, who managed to smile and wave the end of his necktie at her. Judge Sutton entered and the bailiff yelled the crowd to order. "Mr. Osborne, please continue."

Osborne stood and cleared his throat. "Your Honor," he said, straightening his necktie, "the people recall John Jacob Carter."

As Jake took the stand the judge reminded him he had been sworn.

Osborne looked at the backs of his hands, then at Jake. "Mr. Carter, do you have firsthand knowledge of enmity between the deceased and the defendant?"

"Sir, what exactly do you mean by that?"

"Ill will, sir, bad blood, whatever you folks call it over there. Did they, in your experience, have bad blood between them?"

Jake scratched his chin, cleaned his glasses, and put them back on. "You might say that, sir."

"Don't be coy with me, Mr. Carter. Did you ever hear these men threaten each other?"

"Ever body in Little Catalooch heard Ezra threaten Zeb at one time or the other. In fact, Ezra threatened lots of folks."

"What about the defendant? Did you ever hear him threaten his father?"

"No, sir, not to his face, anyhow."

"Can you be more specific?"

"Well, we was working up at Ezra's on that barn he didn't need, and Ezra told me and Zeb to go home and he'd let us know if he ever wanted to see us again. Zeb got kind of hot about that but not in front of his daddy. He said if he'd had a gun he didn't know what he'd have done that morning. I told him that was his own father he was talking about."

Osborne fingered his lapel and smiled. "Mr. Carter, did the defendant keep talking in that vein?"

"Naw, we just went on home. It was easy to say suchlike about Ezra. He was a man that would make you mad enough to kill him, especially when he was drinking. I didn't think no more about it."

" 'If he'd had a gun,' Mr. Carter. That's what you said the defendant said."

"Yes, sir, but that don't prove nothing in my book."

"What book is that, Mr. Carter?"

"I don't know, Mr. Osborne. I ain't read as many of them as you likely have. I just know that it's legal, last time I looked, for a man to talk about anything he wants to, long as he don't outright do it. And if you ever knew Ezra Banks for more than a day or two, you'd likely have said it yourself."

The crowd buzzed and Judge Sutton smacked his gavel. "Mr. Carter, that is all," said Osborne, straightening his tie. "I thank you for your testimony. Your witness, Mr. Babcock."

"I have no questions at this time, Your Honor."

Judge Sutton looked at Osborne. "Mr. Solicitor, please continue."

Osborne turned once more toward Mattie, whose stare held no more promise of comfort than before. He sighed. "Your Honor, the people rest."

Judge Sutton nearly broke his gavel trying to quiet the crowd. "I will have order in this court. If we have to put a tent on the courthouse lawn and guard it around the clock, I'll charge every one of you with contempt. Now then, Mr. Solicitor. Did I hear you correctly, that the state is finished?"

"Yes, Your Honor."

"Then you may sit down, sir. Mr. Badcock, it is your turn."

Oliver stood and took a deep breath. "Your Honor, the defense makes a motion of nonsuit." He quickly looked at the jurors and then at Judge Sutton's beetling eyebrows.

"Let me understand you. You think the state has not presented a case worthy to put before a jury, is that correct?"

"Yes, Your Honor. I cite the Murphy case as precedent, tried here in 1925."

"I'm quite aware of that case. I presided at that trial, Mr. Badcock."

"May I approach the bench?" Martin Osborne asked.

Judge Sutton motioned him forward. Through the windows, sun illuminated a squirrel on a utility pole.

"Speak, Mr. Osborne."

"Your Honor, this motion should be stricken from the record."

"Maybe wonder boy here is right. Best I remember you have only two weapons, a hammer and a pistol, and the coroner's testimony said neither killed him."

Osborne fingered the knot in his tie. "Your Honor, Ezra Banks was killed in cold blood. We have proved Zeb Banks was present. We have proved that the younger Banks struggled with and hit his father viciously with a hammer. We have proved that shots were fired and that his father died. We have proved there was enmity between father and son, and a recent threat on the part of the son to kill the father. I think that is adequate to convict him of either second-degree murder or manslaughter. The people would take either verdict. With all due respect, this needs to be decided by twelve honest men."

Judge Sutton surveyed the courtroom. Mouse claws on the heart-pine floor would have been deafening. He rapped his gavel. "Recess for ten minutes. Gentlemen, meet me in chambers."

In an anteroom overlooking the street Sutton leaned against a table, the lawyers before him. "Mr. Osborne, the state has not produced a credible weapon nor testimony to put that weapon in the hands of Mr. Banks. I assume Mr. Badcock, if allowed to continue, will tout Mr. Banks as a community pillar, a man who attends three churches, cuts firewood for widow ladies, and makes crutches for cripples in his spare time. Right, Mr. Badcock?"

Oliver choked back a grin. "Yes, Your Honor."

"And I would assume further that Mr. Badcock will plead self-defense?"

"That is correct, Your Honor."

"Martin, I hate to say it, but this flatland boy's got you by the short hairs unless you have something else."

Osborne rubbed his eyes wearily. "Your Honor, I toyed with calling Mrs. Banks. I am cognizant I can't make her testify against her husband. It would be a crapshoot, I admit. But when I saw her look at me this morning I figured I had maybe seen who pulled that second trigger and I knew it wouldn't do a bit of good."

"So you have nothing else for the jury?"

"No, Your Honor."

"Then let's finish this damned medicine show." He removed himself from the table and the two attorneys made way. Back in the courtroom Oliver put his arm around Zeb. "You're going to like this," he whispered.

Judge Sutton banged the gavel three sharp raps and the crowd grew intensely quiet. "If I can have order in the court, I have something to say. Defendant and counselors, please rise."

Zeb slowly unfolded from his chair, and Oliver poked him to straighten up. Osborne stood like a man defying a firing squad. "There is a motion from the defense for non-suit. For those unfamiliar with legal language, that means the defense wants the court to dismiss this case because the state hasn't offered evidence to connect Mr. Banks with the crime of murder in the second degree." Judge Sutton picked up the gavel and looked at it, handle first, then turned it around to look at the head.

"I'll be danged if I've ever seen anything like this," he continued. "Here is a good homegrown Haywood County solicitor and his likewise homegrown sheriff and between them they can't say for sure who killed Ezra Banks. You got a slick-haired flatland dandy who looks like he walked out of law school a week ago, and talks funny to boot, and he's filing a motion for non-suit like he does it every week." Sutton wrinkled his lips. "Son, I am going to grant your motion."

Hannah swooned sideways into Jake's lap, where he fanned her with his hat. Zeb turned to look at Mattie, and neither could help his or her tears. Everywhere people talked and slapped each other on the back. Judge Sutton about broke his gavel.

"I will have order in this court," he bellowed, and when the racket had subsided, he spoke again. "Zebulon Baird Banks, in granting this motion the court declares the charges are dismissed. You are free to go. But if you show up in my courtroom again even remotely associated with another dead man, I'm going to see that you rot in jail until somebody comes up with a weapon. As for you, Martin Osborne, I hope not to see such a waste of the court's time again. Good men of the jury, the court apologizes and thanks you for your service. This court is adjourned." He rapped the gavel once and the bailiff stood. "Oyes oyes oyes. This honorable court stands adjourned sine die. God save the state and this honorable court." Sutton vanished, a wide black shadow descending the stairs.

Oliver turned to shake Zeb's hand but his client was already making for Mattie. Knocking over chairs, they embraced like they hadn't seen each other in twenty years. Mattie produced a handkerchief and dabbed at her husband's eyes. Zeb tried to dry her tears but both started crying again.

Hannah revived enough to sit up in her chair. "Somebody get her some water," Jake said. Cash Davis pulled a batwing from his front pocket and handed it to Jake. Jake unstoppered it and smelled it. "Used to be water, anyhow." He put it under Hannah's nose and she shuddered slightly.

Shortly she sat up, color creeping back into her face. "Much obliged, Jake," she said.

Cash smiled. "Made it myself."

Jake looked to the front of the room and quickly back at Cash. "Don't say that out loud. That Osborne fellow looks like he still wants to try somebody for something."

"You want me to walk Miz Banks outside for some fresh air?"

"Fine idea, Cash. That all right with you, Sis?"

Hannah nodded and stood as Cash took her elbow. Mattie still hadn't let go of Zeb so he put out his hand and squeezed his mother's with it. Something red passed Jake and he turned. "Well, Cousin Polly, look at you. Got you a red dress and you didn't even have to talk for it." She beamed at him and headed outside with her birch-twig toothbrush and snuff.

Meanwhile, Jake came up to Mattie and Zeb. "Folks, I hate to break this love feast up, but we got to get back over the mountain sometime this week. I still haven't cleaned them leaves off my roof."

Jake put his hand out and Zeb pumped it and smiled. "I don't know how I'm going to repay you for this."

"Shucks, Zeb, I just did what any self-respecting citizen would have done."

"Well, you done it fine is all I got to say."

On the street Lige cornered Oliver. "Son, this nephew of mine's about to bust his buttons he's so proud of you. Rass, tell Mr. Babcock how you want to make a lawyer your own self."

Rass shook Oliver's hand. "Sir, that was fine. After this I want to go to law school, too."

"Rass, I'll be glad to recommend you to any law school in the land." Oliver looked the departing crowd over. "I'm grateful this family's troubles are behind them."

Rass swept his cowlick back. "Mr. Babcock, may I ask a question?"

"Certainly, son."

"You work for the park commission, did I hear that right?"

"Yes, I have to get back to that job tomorrow. Why?"

"I'm afraid my family's troubles are just starting. Papa's worried sick about the park. And it's not so much the money, or any of that. Leaving our land behind would be the hardest part for him. I think it might kill him."

"Rass, if I can make your transition any smoother, I will try. Buck up, son. They might find an even better place, who knows? Here's my card. Be in touch."

Jake had quietly joined the group. "Boys, there's going to be a big old celebration at our house. Oliver, you'll be the guest of honor. Rass, you come, too. I'll smooth things over with your papa if need be. Right now we got a family back together and we're going to be happy with them for a day. Then we'll worry about that park mess. Ever thing's got its season."

37

IT'S IN THE BOOK

The Baptist church in Little Cataloochee had seen Reverend Grady Noland preach once a month since 1888. He was their "new preacher"—which most folks had quit calling him around the turn of the century. In those forty years he preached from a head full of Bible and a heart primed by conviction. To write out a sermon would not have occurred to him, nor would notes have been welcome before him. He liked the Spirit to urge him first one way, then another, so his sermons bounded through both testaments like bunches of jumped jackrabbits. A casual listener would think Moses, Jesus, and Paul knew one another. If pressed, Noland would say of course they did, at least after Jesus yanked Moses out of hell and together they led the blinded Paul down the Damascus road.

Tall, with an outsized Adam's apple, he had been redheaded but in his sixth decade one could divine it only when light showed at certain angles through tufts of ear hair. His nose turned up like he'd run facefirst into a boulder when he was young. He'd been licensed in his teens, when he used to preach in overalls, but after ordination he wore black broadcloth. Even at the end of the 1920s he refused to own, drive, or even ride in an automobile, saying such machinery was Satan's invention. He always rode horseback into Little Cataloochee, black suit covered by road dust.

Sunday morning, October 14, 1928, a half hour before Cash Davis showed up to build a fire in the potbellied heater, Noland sat in a back pew staring out the window. His mind tumbled like water in a rocky creekbed. He had tried for a week to latch on to this morning's texts, in fact had corraled a dozen, then pruned them to two or three—a passage in Genesis where blood cries from the ground, the part in Ecclesiastes where everything has its season—and Luke's story about the fool and his barns.

"Lord," he prayed, "while it's quiet speak to your servant. Let me hear what to say this morning. I suspect you need me to give this bunch something to placate their woes.

"Lord, it's a burden to handle two big troubles in a month, at least for me. I'm a little dog, I can't chew on but one bone at a time. But this church has had two knocks on the head, the national park, and old Ezra's killing, enough to set a body to reeling.

"As for the first trouble, who'd ever thought we'd see the end of Cataloochee? Oh, I know you will come, like the spiritual says, no more water but fire next time, and the earth also and the works therein shall be burned up, amen. That's the way a great God ends things. It's in the Book. But this park business is different. It's the government ending it, which ain't the same a-tall.

"I heard Brother Smith over in Big Cataloochee preached about this land being Eden. I hope you see fit to forgive him, even if he *is* a Methodist. Because, Lord, this is pretty country right enough, but mankind tamed this forest and grubbed out these pastures, and that don't make it

Paradise. You made Eden oncet and that's it. You'd think preacher school would have taught him that. We're still suffering from that first sin, penetrated upon Adam by Eve, which got them drove out of the Garden and then them and us both having to work by the sweat of our faces and return to the dust from which you took us, amen. It's in the Book.

"Only thing is, Cataloochee, you could say, is a tad like Eden because getting drove out of the Garden first set brother against brother, and in Cataloochee we got father against son, enough so Zebulon Baird Banks stood accused of parrotcide. Lord, forgive him for what guilt he might have, and Mattie, too, Lord, and bless that family, amen. I still got half a mind to use that passage about blood crying from the ground. That's right after Cain slew Abel his brother. Lord, you know I've always had questions, never figured you'd mind a man asking. F'rinstance, I've wondered how Adam knew to bury Abel instead of leaving him for hyenas and buzzards, except I reckon it was from you saying, Dust thou art and unto dust shalt thou return, amen. It's in the Book.

"But I'm sorry, Lord, we ain't here to answer such as that. What will I take for a text, that is the question. I ask it in your Son's name."

Preacher Noland opened his eyes as boots scraped the threshold. Cash Davis came in and hung his hat on a peg. From his coat pocket he pulled a wad of tinder peeled from the underside of a piece of dry locust bark. It reminded Noland of a mouse nest. Cash opened the heater door, laid the tinder, teepeed kindling over it, and lit a fire. Preacher Noland stretched, then walked toward the back door.

"Morning, Brother Davis."

"Morning, Preacher. Hope I ain't disturbing you none."

"No, I'm about to go to the graveyard a minute."

Before Cash could begin telling a story, Noland was out the door, walking downhill toward Ezra's fresh grave. He strolled between plots marking children both named and unnamed, some remembered with fieldstones and others with store-bought tomb rocks with carved lambs. There were graves of women prematurely dead from childbirth or worse. Two tall store-bought monuments with heaven's gates carved atop them marked Will and Kate Carter's graves. Noland leaned against the south fence.

"Lord," the preacher prayed, "here's that second trouble, Ezra Banks laying here dead, a man we feared would outlive us all by dint of pure cussedness, dead by his oldest son's hand—or maybe not, they never did finish judicating that. Lord, only you and Zeb and Mattie know for sure. Lots of folks said Banks had it coming, and he *was* snurly as a piece of sickymore, and I even heard somebody say he likely busted hell wide open when he died. That ain't for me to say. I just pray your forgiveness on them. And on me, too, sweet Jesus, while you're at it. We're all sinners standing in the need of prayer, amen.

"Lord, Ezra was drinking when he got killed. Here's another one of them questions. Why'd you let Noah plant a vineyard when he came out of the Ark? The Book says he got drunk from it and man's been at it ever since. Lord, some folks say your Son turned water into wine at that wedding in Cana John's gospel tells about but I know better, it was water wine, Jesus wouldn't have got nobody drunk. Wine is a mocker, strong drink is raging, amen, it's in the Book.

"Anyhow, Lord, here's that second trouble, and—hallelujah, Lord, you just now let me look at it right, that Scripture about blood crying out wouldn't help the living none a-tall. And that story about the rich fool that tore down his barns and built new ones, well, it never helped Ezra alive, so it sure won't do no good now. So this must mean you want me to preach from Ecclesiastes.

"Lord, here's another question. I've read that preacher book many a time, and in places it don't sound written by a Christian. Was it? But even so I got to say that third chapter's a very present help in trouble, amen, as the Book says, to ever thing there is a season, and a time to ever purpose under heaven, and that word will help them that'll have to leave here.

"I been riding this circuit forty year, and I know, Lord, this park's going to kill these old folks. Oh, not outright, but when they'll get drove out from where they were born and their kinfolks is buried they'll die pre-naturely, dust to dust, amen. So you might as well say the park will kill them. It'll sure uproot many a man and woman. Sometimes a body can transplant a sarvis tree out of the forest and it'll grow and sometimes the moving kills it. I'll preach from that season passage and pray your blessing on these good folks in their journey from this woods to wherever they'll be transplanted. For their days yet to come, give them good soil and water, not planted in the wilderness, in a dry and thirsty ground, amen. They've had a time to plant and a time to pluck up what's been planted, amen, and they've had a time to kill, now it's a time to heal, now it's time to weep, but we'll pray it'll soon be time to dance. It's in the Book. Hallelujah. Thank you Lord for showing me the way."

Racket in a tree revealed a squirrel turning a walnut like a prayer wheel, crashing it between his teeth after each revolution. When Noland looked up three women headed toward the church, early, like Easter women. Mattie Banks on the left, Rachel Carter on the right, in the middle Ezra's widow, Hannah. As he turned toward them, the women paused in tableau, watching their preacher stand beside the fresh grave of their father-in-law, husband, uncle by marriage. As the women started into the church he hitched up his britches and hastened up the hill, still praying.

"Lord, use me this morning. Let the words of my mouth, and the meditation of my heart be acceptable in thy sight. Forgive all us poor children. And bestow upon me your voice so you can give them strength for their next year's journey, wherever it might lead, amen."

ACKNOWLEDGMENTS

Thanks to all who encouraged me while I licked this cub into shape.

Writers need storytellers. Mine have been neighbors and family, particularly my late aunt, Ruth Caldwell Novotny. Cousin Raymond Caldwell filled my head with tales while we hiked Cataloochee trails. Of many books, two deserve mention: Hattie Caldwell Davis, *Cataloochee Valley: Vanished Settlements of the Smoky Mountains* (1997); and Elizabeth Powers with Mark Hannah, *Cataloochee: Lost Settlement of the Smokies* (1982). Sarah Long, my mother-in-law, gave me the former; Steven and Mary Bruce Woody lent me the latter.

Writers require careful readers. Jake Mills, Lee Smith, and Charles Frazier read various versions and gave thoughtful advice and heartfelt encouragement. And, always, my wife, Mary, is both best reader and best friend.

Writers depend on skillful editors. Ileene Smith taught me bushels about the craft; Stephanie Higgs gave insightful final suggestions, and shepherded this "little booke" surpassingly well; Dan Menaker is simply the best in the business.

And a writer treasures a fine agent. Leigh Feldman examined a bloated typescript years ago with a mixture of admiration and horror, and said no thanks. After the 2003 Sewanee Writer's Conference I cut ruthlessly, and she was kind enough to take a second look. Boy, am I glad.

ABOUT THE AUTHOR

WAYNE CALDWELL was born in Asheville, North Carolina, and was educated at the University of North Carolina at Chapel Hill, Appalachian State University, and Duke University. He began writing fiction in the late 1990s. He has published four short stories and a poem, and won two short story prizes. Caldwell lives near Asheville with his wife, Mary. *Cataloochee* is his first novel.

ABOUT THE TYPE

This book was set in Bembo, a typeface based on an old-style Roman face that was used for Cardinal Bembo's tract *De Aetna* in 1495. Bembo was cut by Francisco Griffo in the early sixteenth century. The Lanston Monotype Company of Philadelphia brought the well-proportioned letterforms of Bembo to the United States in the 1930s.